LIGHT IN AUGUST

MODERN LIBRARY COLLEGE EDITIONS

William Faulkner

LIGHT

IN

AUGUST

Introduction by Cleanth Brooks
Gray Professor of Rhetoric, Yale University

THE MODERN LIBRARY · *New York*

PUBLISHER'S NOTE

The text of this edition of *Light in August* has been reproduced photographically from, and is therefore identical with, a copy of the first printing, which was published October 6, 1932.

THE MODERN LIBRARY

is published by RANDOM HOUSE, INC.

Manufactured in the United States of America

Introduction
by Cleanth Brooks

Light in August is by common consent one of Faulkner's finest novels, but it is not one of his easiest. The reader coming to it for the first time should be warned to discard some of his stereotyped notions of Faulknerian "material." Elsewhere, Faulkner has written magnificently about the Negro, and in *Light in August* there are some brilliant vignettes of Negro life. But none of the prominent characters is a Negro. Negro characters occur in only very minor roles and quite incidentally. (The "Negro" Joe Christmas is, as we shall see, a special case.) Nor do any of Faulkner's "aristocratic" characters appear. There are one or two references to people of the old planter stock like Colonel Sartoris, but the only such character who has a large role is the Rev. Mr. Hightower, who, having disgraced himself in the eyes of the town, has become declassed, and lives as a recluse. Finally, *Light in August* is in a very important sense a book about the race problem but its characters are largely yeoman whites, poor whites, sharecroppers and millhands, and, in several instances, white trash.

Light in August tells the story, not of one person but of half a dozen, and it adds, for good measure, brilliant short sketches of a half-dozen others. For many a reader, herein lies its difficulty. If Faulkner had been content to tell the story of Joe Christmas, the reader would find it easy to grasp the essential unity of the novel. But what about the dozen pieces of the novel that are left over after he has traced Joe's career? What is he to make of incidents and anecdotes which, though they may be highly interesting in themselves, seem to have only the merest relation to Joe — or perhaps no relation at all? Such a reader may be forgiven for concluding that *Light in August* is not a novel to be read and enjoyed but a puzzle to be solved, and in view of the number of curious bits and pieces to be fitted into some hypothetical general pattern, a frustratingly complicated puzzle at that.

It would be a pity to come to any novel in this spirit. When *Light in August* is approached in this way, it suffers more than most other novels, for it is filled with the direct evocation of particular scenes, with actions that are positive and sometimes violent, and with the talk of people who are speaking, not the involved language of a Henry James, but an utterance that is simple and direct and filled with the idiom of a folk culture. This novel is, to be sure, greater than the sum of its parts, but the parts themselves are concretely and vividly rendered, and the reader must feel their impact as particular scenes and incidents if he is to get the massive experience of the novel as a whole.

In spite of the difficulties in Faulkner's manner of narration, there is method in what he is doing, there is order in the apparent confusion, and the irrelevant and discordant elements do finally resolve into a larger harmony. But the reader must be willing to trust the author and his method; he must give himself up to the story that is being told; most of all, he must lay aside those preconceptions and stereotyped expectancies that are almost the standard equipment of a reasonably well-educated American of our day.

Faulkner's tale is about racial violence and the present-day South, but he presents the situation in his own way and on a level even deeper than that of a 1932 anticipation of the "Negro Revolution." Faulkner's special concerns come out in the story of Joe himself, for Joe does not conform to the stereotype of the Negro, either the Northern or the Southern version, and as we shall see, not really even to the stereotyped victim of prejudice.

Faulkner questions whether Joe Christmas is a "Negro" at all; one may well ask whether Joe has any Negro blood. He obviously does not know who his parents were. The only evidence he has to go on is the taunting of the other orphanage children and the baleful scrutiny of the crazed and fanatical old Doc Hines, an attention which, although clearly hostile, can suggest to him no more than that he is somehow "different." As a man, he "passes" for white without question and when Joanna Burden asks him how he knows that he is "part nigger," Joe, after pondering a moment, replies: "I dont know it." Faulkner could hardly have stressed more emphatically that Joe's status as "nigger" is a state of mind rather than a consequence of his possessing some Negro genes, nor could he have shown more persuasively that for Joe the notion that he is a Negro is part of his general alienation from the community. From time to time Joe suggests to other persons that he may be a Negro, sometimes as a means of testing friendship, sometimes as a weapon with which to attack society, and sometimes as a way of exploring his own identity. For example, when he confides to Bobby Allen, his first love, that he is a Negro, he does so presumably to test her love for him; but his motive in announcing to a white prostitute that he is a Negro is to shock, and to express his contempt for her. (He is in turn shocked and deeply disturbed when he finds that the news makes no impression on her.) Sometimes Joe's telling a person that he has Negro blood seems a compulsive act, a picking at the scab of his own distrust and uncertainty. How else can one account for his having told his bootlegging partner, the worthless Lucas Burch, that he is part Negro?

Whatever Joe's motive in confiding in Burch, Burch's motive in abusing Joe's confidence is clear enough; the knowledge becomes his means of bolstering his shaky position with the sheriff when Burch (who has assumed the alias Brown) must explain why he had not acted earlier to prevent Joe's murder of Miss Burden. Indeed, all sorts of people are perfectly willing to accept the notion that Joe has Negro blood as a convenient explanation for his subsequent actions and Faulkner shows that the Negro stereotype is a handle that fits many purposes, even some of Joe's own purposes. But again, whether or not Joe actually had any Negro genes is quite irrelevant to what happens to him. Moreover, Joe's alienation from the Jefferson community and from even the human community springs from deeper causes still. Though his doubt as to whether he is white or Negro provides a powerful means for dramatizing this deeper alienation, it does not in fact account for it. This is why the reader, if he is to understand Joe and the novel, must avoid being trapped by his own stereotyped reactions to the racial conflict. For example, it is often said that Joe Christmas is "lynched" and in some very generally symbolic sense this may be so, for Percy Grimm, by snatching up a butcher knife and emasculating the dying man, reveals his sadistic hatred of the Negro. Yet we risk oversimplifying matters if we make Joe's death simply a "lynching."

The truth is a good deal more subtle and more significant. In the first place, Grimm's act is his own, an act for which he must take sole responsibility. (The other men who have been chasing Joe come up either too late to aid Grimm or to intervene, and the response of one of them to what he sees is not approval but a sudden vomiting in sick horror.) We witness in this terrible scene not a lynching bee — the action of a group of men who have taken the law into their hands — but something quite different. As an authorized deputy pursuing an escaped prisoner, Grimm might have justified his right to fire at a desperate man armed with a gun and barricaded behind a kitchen table; but Grimm's butchery is gratuitous. His act of mayhem is the explosion of bottled up impulses of which he may well have been unconscious and which were evidently not premeditated. Faulkner has in fact been careful to show his reader that Percy Grimm was quite sincere in his desire to protect the good name of the town, that his purpose in getting himself deputized and in training a group of special deputies was to make sure that there should be no jail delivery and that Joe should be allowed his day in court.

If the reader takes full account of Faulkner's spiritual portrait of Percy Grimm, he will discover that Grimm is another alienated man, unsure of himself, who tries by abstract acts to attach himself to a community in which he feels he has no real place. Christmas and Grimm are thus related to each other by antithesis. Joe Christmas, who sullenly or violently attacks the community, and Percy Grimm, who insists on defending the community values even when they are not under attack, are spiritual brothers — indeed, identical twins, duplicate but reversed versions of each other, one left-handed where the other is right-handed. Small wonder that in the vision in which Hightower sees the faces of his friends and acquaintances, some long dead, some still alive, Percy Grimm and Joe Christmas merge into a composite face — "two faces which seem to strive . . . in turn to free themselves one from the other, then fade and blend again." Faulkner's insight is dramatically right; his way of presenting it brilliantly effective.

What has been implied here about the depth of the racial conflict may well be more terrifying than that implied by a simpler story in which a "good" victim is done to death by an inhuman and unbelievable monster. For we are not to suppose that Faulkner, in letting us know how Percy Grimm came to be what he was — in allowing us to see deep within the stormtrooper the young boy anxious to find a place for himself in the world, a boy who "had no one to tell [his suffering to], to open his heart to" — was trying to be easy on Percy Grimm. (Faulkner was later to remark that in Percy Grimm he had created a Nazi before he had ever seen the word in the newspapers.) Nor, for that matter, did Faulkner mean, by providing the elaborate and persuasive account of how Joe Christmas came to be the man he was, to extenuate Joe's murder of Joanna Burden. The issue for Faulkner, as an artist, was obviously not whether to be hard on or easy on either of the murderers or the race issue itself: the matter of consequence was to realize the full truth about the individual and about the society that formed him and within which he now lived. The truth is never easily come by, reality rarely simple. Faulkner seeks to make us understand, but he does not assume that if we know all we will forgive in a realization that the actions of every character are compelled by his environment. Rather, Faulkner asks his reader to avoid the simple judgments and easy stereotypes which prevent one from understanding the complexities of the human situation.

It should be said that Faulkner's world is not only complex but mysterious; yet it is not an "absurd" world. Although Faulkner attracted quite early the attention of the French Existentialists, and drew forth from Jean-Paul Sartre a sympathetic essay, the acts of Faulkner's characters are never quite *actes gratuits*. The world has meaning, and Faulkner's stance more closely resembles that of a nineteenth-century stoic than that of a twentieth-century existentialist. In spite of the novel's topicality, Faulkner is an old-fashioned novelist and he writes out of an old-fashioned culture. To his account of Joe and the other characters he has brought something from his own country and region.

For example, Faulkner makes a sharp criticism of the Protestant ethic, which he tends to label "Calvinism," by showing its effects on his characters. In violent anger, Joe Christmas brains his Puritanical foster-father with a chair, yet Joe himself partakes of the "Calvinistic" ethic. He is cut off from nature even more radically than are McEachern or "Doc" Hines or Joanna Burden, and far more so than is Byron Bunch. Joe suffers from more than a lesion; one discerns a straining away from nature — a desperate effort to hold himself up above nature.

This straining away from nature reflects an aggressively masculine culture, yet in its destructive effects bears hardest on the male. Faulkner obviously thinks of it as to some degree inevitable, an integral part of the male ethos. In its best and healthiest form, this pressure against nature is the disciplined striving celebrated by a seventeenth-century poet: "How poor a thing is man / Unless above himself / Erect himself he can." At its worst, it becomes a vicious hypertrophy of the will and turns man into a grotesque.

There is, of course, a paradox here: the willful denial of nature when carried far enough seems not an assertion of will at all but resembles instead a kind of automatism, as if the characters were responding to an outside force. When obsessed characters like Joe Christmas and Percy Grimm are wrought up to their greatest stress, their actions seem merely instinctive, and Faulkner occasionally describes them toward the end of the novel as if they were not creatures of flesh and blood at all but rather, pawns moved by a mysterious Player. Yet in spite of occasional references to this omnipotent fatalistic power and in spite of his flourishing of the term "Calvinism" with its implications of determinism, Faulkner evidently believes that man does possess freedom of will; in fact, man's responsibility and willingness to make decisions are bound up with his very manhood.

Nevertheless, Faulkner's male characters cannot be pliant and yielding, cannot drift with the tides of nature, cannot let themselves go. Byron Bunch, the methodical bachelor, lives on the fringes of the world of action. Hightower has withdrawn from it completely and asks no more than to be left alone. Joe Christmas, who seems to differ so much from both Bunch or Hightower, is even more deeply hostile to the world of nature and even more sharply repelled by the feminine in all its forms. He cannot abide hearing the "fecundmellow voices of Negro women." Their murmuring recalls "the lightless hot wet primogenitive Female," so much so that he runs, his teeth glaring, to seek "the cold hard air of white people." On the night before he goes into Miss Burden's house for the last time, razor in hand, he finds that he cannot sleep and goes out to the stable. And he thinks aloud, "Why in hell do I want to smell horses?" Then, he reflects, "It's because they are not women. Even a mare horse is a kind of man."

Joe was attracted to Miss Burden because she immediately impressed him as manlike. When he seized her, her struggling betrayed "no feminine vacillation, no coyness of obvious desire and intention to succumb at last. It was as if he struggled physically with another man for an object of no actual value to either, and for which they struggled on principle alone."

Joe is *indeed* more than a victim of racism, as was discussed earlier. His doubt as to whether he is a white man or a Negro leaves him not merely suspended between white and black communities; Joe feels actively repelled by both communities. In addition, Faulkner's account of his childhood and adolescence indicates a latent homosexuality; he fears the female principle. All of Faulkner's "Calvinists" distrust nature and fear the female principle; in this fear and distrust Joe is as "Calvinist" as any of them — including his dour Presbyterian foster-father. Joe's latent homosexuality puts an additional strain on his already tenuous hold on the community.

Faulkner is not attempting a kind of morality play, the preachment of which is that the wages of "Calvinism" are despair and death. He shows us the admirable side of Joe's intransigence, his refusal to take the easy way out. He will not attend the Negro college to which Miss Burden would send him in preparation for a comfortable future. Nor will he accept status in the white community, as he surely could do, since he is a white man in appearance. Joe instead repudiates both communities, but as Faulkner has made plain, is thereby twisted away from the life-giving and nourishing aspects of nature itself. As other critics have observed, Joe resents Miss Burden's attempt to make him accept a place in the Negro world. But what he muttered to himself on the night before he killed her was, "She ought not to started praying over me," for her insistence that he kneel beside her and pray recalls his experiences with his foster-mother. Joe's foster-father's iron discipline and harsh justice, including the beatings dictated by that justice, he had been able to accept. But what he could not endure was Mrs. McEachern's timid attempt to mother him and to protect him from her husband's strap. "It was the woman: that soft kindness which he believed himself doomed to be forever victim of and which he hated worse than he did the hard and ruthless justice of men."

Joe pays a fearful price for his intransigent defiance of nature. If he is, as he has been called, a terrifying example of "institutional man," and if he is a forerunner of the "stranger" in Camus' novel, he is also very clearly related to the South of Faulkner's experience, including its special brand of Protestantism. Perhaps Faulkner's genius lies in his ability here, as in his other novels, to use the particulars of his own culture to point up the important issues of contemporary society everywhere.

But though the dangers in resisting nature are great, to refrain from the struggle makes one less than a man. The worthless Brown, Lena Grove's lover and the father of her child, experiences no internal struggle. He is a coward and a braggart, without honor, or, to use the idiom of Faulkner's countryside, he is "no count." The other workers at the mill despise this shallow and pusillanimous man.

Faulkner, of course, has his own way of putting these

matters. See, for example, his brilliant characterization of Joe Christmas at work in the sawmill:

> ... there was something definitely rootless about him, as though no town nor city was his, no street, no walls, no square of earth his home. ... he carried his knowledge with him always as though it were a banner, with a quality ruthless, lonely, and almost proud.

His manner of using his tools accords with his appearance. Christmas at work is described as "jabbing his shovel into the sawdust slowly and steadily and hard, as though he were chopping up a buried snake"; by contrast, Brown "merely contrived to look scattered and emptily swaggering where ... [Christmas] had looked sullen and quiet and fatal as a snake."

A worker at the mill states the case in a countryman's idiom:

> [Brown] puts me in mind of a horse. Not a mean horse. Just a worthless horse. Looks fine in the pasture, but it's always down in the spring bottom when anybody comes to the gate with a bridle. Runs fast, all right, but it's always got a sore hoof when hitching-up time comes.

To which his companion answers: "I don't reckon he'd do even a mare any permanent harm." Doubtless Brown doesn't do Lena any permanent harm either; it is evident at the end of the novel that Byron Bunch will marry her, child and all.

If one sees the parallels among the male characters — that the Rev. Mr. Hightower in his own way is as much an outcast from the community as is Joe Christmas; that Joe and Percy Grimm are spiritual brothers; that Byron Bunch, before meeting Lena Grove, was also cut off from the tides of life — then one can begin to grasp the novel's basic pattern. The reader will then appreciate that the meeting between Christmas and Hightower, though fleeting, is highly meaningful. The two men share an isolation. Hightower's attempt to save Christmas at the end of the novel, though futile, is a brotherly gesture that has significance at least for himself and may have helped Hightower to understand the truth about his own wasted life.

One might observe here that Joanna Burden, though a woman, shares the men's alienation. She too is a pariah, outlawed from the community from birth. She too is a "masculine" figure, and she attracts Joe Christmas partly because of his latent homosexuality. Hightower views Joanna's plight with sympathetic pity, but his comment as he passes the charred planks and beams of her burned house is justified: "Poor, barren woman. To have not lived only a week longer until luck returned to this place. Until luck and life [with the birth of Lena's child] returned to these barren and ruined acres."

But most of Faulkner's women are closer to nature than are his men, and one or two of his rustic heroines become almost an embodiment of nature. Such a character is Lena Grove, who not only does not "strive" but hardly needs to make any effort at all, and yet all the members of the community are attracted to her and protect and foster her. Countrymen on the road offer her rides in their mule-drawn wagons; even Mrs. Armstid, a "good woman" who disapproves of Lena's obviously unmarried pregnancy, nevertheless breaks her china bank to give Lena the egg-money that she has saved.

In her female role, Lena Grove is as specialized and as

extreme an instance as Joe Christmas is in his male role. Whether we regard Lena as a kind of nature goddess or as merely a complacent animal of bovine instinctiveness, she is close to nature and therefore does not have to struggle against it, or consequently, herself, as do the male characters. She does not agonize over decisions; she is born with a kind of feminine wisdom.

This is why she is, for most members of the community, an attractive force, and why on the other hand she troubles and dismays Hightower and why — had he ever met her — she would have repelled Joe.

The plight of the principal characters is thus clarified when we see them set over against Lena's vitality and essential innocence. The other characters are obsessed: Joe, with his need to establish his identity; Hightower, with the heroic past; Joanna Burden, with a special kind of do-good-ism in which the Negro becomes an albatross hanging about her neck; Percy Grimm, with preventing a lynching that nobody is interested in bringing about, really because it will give him an excuse to put on a uniform and defend the community's honor.

In the light of such considerations, the place of Lena and the world she represents becomes apparent. Faulkner has embedded Joe's story in a matrix, the life of a little Southern community, one which, whatever its limitations, faults, and cruelties, is a true community. Jefferson is not an impersonal, indifferent society in which everyone tends to be like a detached atom and where alienation is therefore the usual situation. The little town is old-fashioned and backward-looking. It is suspicious of any outsiders who would disturb its life, and when it cannot expel the alien, it tries to wall him off in a kind of cultural cyst as bees enclose within waxen walls a beetle or wasp that has got inside the hive. Hightower and Joanna Burden live in such cysts, physically within the community though not a part of it.

Joe's plight is typically modern, the sort that usually is found in an industrialized urban society, but by placing Joe's story in a rural setting, the issues are sharpened; the depths of his alienation are set over against the lives and deaths of people living in an old-fashioned community, people who have no problem of identity, who know who they are and where they belong. For example, Lena Grove, though technically a stranger to the Jefferson community, finds her place in it almost without seeking. But Joe cannot relax, cannot cease his desperate search for an identity long enough to achieve it.

Yet what has Joe's dilemma to do with nature and the slow rhythms of life that buoy up Lena and carry her imperceptibly toward her goal? Is it likely that even under the most auspicious circumstances Joe would have felt any need of establishing a rapport with nature or felt its attraction? The answer is yes and Faulkner has taken the matter quite specifically into account. On the evening before Joe kills Miss Burden, he says to himself that all he wanted was peace. Some days after the murder, hiding in the woods, he actually finds himself attending to nature and seeing it, really, for the first time. Before, "the slow constellations wheeled, the stars of which [Christmas] had been aware for thirty years and not one of which had any name to him or meant anything at all by shape or brightness or position." But now as Joe moves about in the woods, he becomes aware of the physical world around him. Though he had always lacked any conscious concern for the countryside, "his physical shape and his thought had been molded by its compulsions without his learning anything about its actual shape and feel." Now, for a week, hiding from the sheriff, "he has lurked and crept among its secret places, yet he remained a foreigner to the very immutable laws which earth must obey." A strange peace descends upon him and Joe thinks that it is "the looking and seeing" that has given such peace to him and such "unhaste and quiet." But he quickly finds that it is not so: "suddenly the true answer comes to him."

Faulkner has not spelled out the true answer for us, though he clearly implies it in Joe's decision to return and show himself boldly in the town, a decision which he must know will mean his capture and return to trial for murder. Joe's discovery of the attraction of nature lends significant emphasis to his further discovery that he cannot after all find repose in it — cannot sink back into it — cannot, as he puts the matter elsewhere, simply relax and "stop running."

Suddenly, he sees that for thirty years past he has been running, though running in a circle, and in all of his running, he tells himself, "I have never got outside that circle. I have never broken out of the ring of what I have already done and cannot ever undo." Now, having made his decision, he runs — perhaps for the first time since boyhood — with a kind of purpose, "his direction [as] straight as a surveyor's line, disregarding hill and valley and bog." He moves now, not in a circle, but in a straight line, though the straight line will take him, as he must know, to his death.

It has often been argued that Joe, whether or not he has any Negro blood, nevertheless does in the end elect to die as a Negro, and that he returns himself to Jefferson in order to be martyred. But this interpretation will scarcely stand up in the light of what we are told in the novel itself. One of the countrymen who has come in to Mottstown for Saturday shopping describes the manner of the capture. He tells us that a man named Halliday

> . . . saw him and ran up and grabbed him and said, "Ain't your name Christmas?" and the nigger said that it was. He never denied it. He never did anything. He never acted like either a nigger or a white man. That was it. That was what made the folks so mad. For him to be a murderer and all dressed up and walking the town like he dared them to touch him, when he ought to have been skulking and hiding in the woods, muddy and dirty and running. It was like he never even knew he was a murderer, let alone a nigger too.

This semiliterate eyewitness account has the ring of truth. Joe refuses to skulk in the woods or to run away any longer from the sheriff's posse. But he continues his defiance of both the black and the white community, he does not act "like either a nigger or a white man." His conduct does suggest that "he never even knew he was a murderer. . . ." Joe's action here is of a piece with the rest of his life. He asserts to the end his own individuality: he is the outlaw, the stranger, who represents only himself, neither the Negro community nor the white.

Joe's course is, from the beginning, doomed. One cannot kick the earth out from under one's feet. Joe is literally a desperate man; but there is a heroic intensity in his search to find himself and his unwillingness to compromise or make terms with any outside force. Like every truly tragic action, his *agon* is finally a struggle with himself, and Joe is allowed his heroism.

Lena, in contrast, is not heroic — pastoral, rather, even pastoral-comic. But she possesses a dignity and she realizes her nature quite as fully as Joe realizes his. Her presence serves to place Joe's heroic struggle in the full context of human experience. In contrast to Joe's violent effort, Lena represents the inertia of nature. She undergoes no struggle with time: her life is immemorial and will repeat itself in the lives of her daughters. Hightower has a vision of "the good stock peopling . . . the good earth," from Lena's "hearty loins without hurry or haste descending mother and daughter. . . ."

So much for the general structure of this novel, a matter worth discussing since, to many readers, it is not immediately evident. But we do not read novels for the sake of what can be summarized. We read them for the massive experience that they contain, the experience which is humanly compelling, no empty pattern. In the massiveness of such an experience lie the vitality and ultimate significance of the novel.

Light in August abounds in powerfully conceived scenes, incidents, dialogues, and in authentic renderings of character in speech and in action. Consider, for example, the scene in which Joe Christmas lies in the ditch near a spring at dawn, killing time until darkness falls and he can go to confront Joanna Burden. We watch him take from his pocket "the razor, the brush, the soap. Kneeling beside the spring he shaved, using the water's surface for glass, stropping the long bright razor on his shoe." It is the razor with which he will commit the murder. Then he eats breakfast, and while he eats he reads the cheap magazine that he has brought with him. In it

> he had previously read but one story; he began now
> upon the second one, reading the magazine straight
> through as though it were a novel. Now and then he
> would look up from the page, chewing, into the sunshot
> leaves which arched the ditch. "Maybe I have already
> done it," he thought. "Maybe it is no longer now wait-
> ing to be done." It seemed to him that he could see the
> yellow day opening peacefully on before him, like a
> corridor, an arras, into a still chiaroscuro without ur-
> gency. It seemed to him that as he sat there the yellow
> day contemplated him drowsily, like a prone and som-
> nolent yellow cat. . . .

The scene as rendered by Faulkner vibrates with Joe's
obsession and his compulsion.

The incident in which the sheriff dismisses the useless
bloodhounds that have been trailing Joe shows another
mood, indelible in its presentation. Now that Joe has ex-
changed shoes with a Negro sharecropper, the dogs are baying excitedly at the sharecropper's cabin. The sheriff "returned to his men, to the leashed and eager dogs. He looked
down at the dogs while the men asked questions and then
ceased, watching him. They watched him put the pistol back
into his pocket and then turn and kick the dogs, once each,
heavily. 'Get them durn eggsuckers on back to town,'
he said."

In very different mood again is the poignant brief scene
in which twelve-year-old Alice bids the child Joe Christmas
farewell as she leaves the orphanage for the home into
which she has been adopted:

[Joe] had liked her, enough to let her mother him a little; perhaps because of it. And to him she was as mature, almost as large in size, as the adult women who ordered his eating and washing and sleeping, with the difference that she was not and never would be his enemy. One night she waked him. She was telling him goodbye but he did not know it. He was sleepy and a little annoyed, never fully awake, suffering her because she had always tried to be good to him. He didn't know that she was crying because he did not know that grown people cried, and by the time he learned that, memory had forgotten her. He went back into sleep while still suffering her, and the next morning she was gone.

The incident speaks volumes of what the child at the orphanage had lacked, the lack that was to warp him away from womankind.

Faulkner's ability to tell a life story in a few pages should be mentioned: see, for example, his vivid account of Joanna's grandfather, or of Hightower's. Both men were utterly unlike their progeny, full-bodied, lusty, neither of them trapped in the past, though they constitute in their grandchildren's imaginations a past so much more alive than the present that Hightower, for instance, is held back from living his own life.

With its abundance of such scenes, characters, and anecdotes, *Light in August* is "written" up to the hilt. It has what the Elizabethans called *copia*—an abundance and fullness of life; it bursts at the seams with life. But it is also *written*—not simply assembled or thrown together—since the presentation of events has been thoroughly and brilliantly organized. In no other novel has Faulkner managed with greater effectiveness the use of cut-backs and shifts in the time scheme.

Chapter one, for example, closes with Lena's coming to what she hopes will be the end of her journey, Jefferson. The driver of the wagon in which she sits, seeing smoke in the distance, says, "That's a house burning." Chapter two begins with allusions to events that go back some three years and introduces several new characters, but it too ends with a reference to the house that is burning on this Saturday afternoon as Lena talks with Byron Bunch at the Jefferson sawmill. Chapter three takes us even further back in time in recounting the life of Byron's eccentric friend, the Rev. Gail Hightower, but this chapter also, as it concludes, veers back to the story of Lena. For Hightower, on this Sunday evening, is surprised to see Byron Bunch coming up the steps: something unusual must have happened to cause Byron to break his invariable custom of spending the weekend out of town. In Chapter four, we are told what the unusual occurrence was: about the burning house, and about the murder of Miss Burden, and how Lena's fortunes are involved in what has happened. Thus, around one focal point, characters and events are marshaled. We have moved in time from Saturday afternoon to Sunday evening, but the plot has been developed into full complication: a murder has been committed and the father of Lena's unborn child may be implicated in it.

The last chapter, though at first glance suggesting that Faulkner has been careless if not downright capricious in his choice of a narrator, proves on consideration to be beautifully accommodated to the rest of the novel. The preceding chapter has brought us very close up to Joe Christmas during the last two weeks of his life. But as the novel ends, these violently passionate and bloody events are pushed back into the distance. We are made to view them in a much broader context and with a much greater degree of aesthetic distance. Lena and the inertia of nature, the immemorial forces from which Joe has been alienated, reassert themselves in our consciousness. The reason for a change in perspective is not that Lena's story is finally more interesting than Joe's or that Faulkner is looking for a kind of "happy ending" for his novel. Rather, in order to see Joe and his violent and doomed effort in fullest perspective, we need to view him in the widest context. Faulkner's solution to this problem is simple, but brilliantly ingenious, and makes no further manipulation of the element of time. After various dislocations of the time sequence throughout the novel, we observe the final actions of the story unrolling in their normal sequence. In order to transform the atmosphere and to move us toward the pastoral-comic, Faulkner sees to it that our last glimpse of Byron and Lena is through the eyes of someone who knows nothing about either of them—someone who has simply picked them up on the road and, with the detachment of the casual and chance acquaintance, though with amusement and a good deal of human sympathy, now observes Byron's awkward courtship and Lena's maidenly-matronly coyness. But the shift to this previously unknown narrator will seem like a trick only to the reader who has failed to sense the total meaning of the work.

LIGHT IN AUGUST

. 1 .

SITTING beside the road, watching the wagon mount the hill toward her, Lena thinks, 'I have come from Alabama: a fur piece. All the way from Alabama a-walking. A fur piece.' Thinking *although I have not been quite a month on the road I am already in Mississippi, further from home than I have ever been before. I am now further from Doane's Mill than I have been since I was twelve years old*

She had never even been to Doane's Mill until after her father and mother died, though six or eight times a year she went to town on Saturday, in the wagon, in a mail-order dress and her bare feet flat in the wagon bed and her shoes wrapped in a piece of paper beside her on the seat. She would put on the shoes just before the wagon reached town. After she got to be a big girl she would ask her father to stop the wagon at the edge of town and she would get down and walk. She would not tell her father why she wanted to walk in instead of riding. He thought that it was because of the smooth streets, the sidewalks. But it was because she believed that the people who saw her and whom she passed on foot would believe that she lived in the town too.

When she was twelve years old her father and mother died in the same summer, in a log house of three rooms and a hall, without screens, in a room lighted by a bug-swirled kerosene lamp, the naked floor worn smooth as old silver by naked feet. She was the youngest living child. Her mother died first. She said, "Take care of paw." Lena did so. Then one day her father said, "You go to Doane's Mill with McKinley. You get ready to go, be ready when he comes." Then he died. McKinley, the brother, arrived in a wagon. They buried the father in a grove behind a country church one afternoon, with a pine headstone. The next morning she departed forever, though it is possible that she did not know this at the time, in the wagon with McKinley, for Doane's Mill. The wagon was borrowed and the brother had promised to return it by nightfall.

The brother worked in the mill. All the men in the village worked in the mill or for it. It was cutting pine. It had been there seven years and in seven years more it would destroy all the timber within its reach. Then some of the machinery and most of the men who ran it and existed because of and for it would be loaded onto freight cars and moved away. But some of the machinery would be left, since new pieces could always be bought on the installment plan—gaunt, staring, motionless wheels rising from mounds of brick rubble and ragged weeds with a quality profoundly astonishing, and gutted boilers lifting their rusting and un-smoking stacks with an air stubborn, baffled and bemused upon a stumppocked scene of profound and peaceful deso-lation, unplowed, untilled, gutting slowly into red and choked ravines beneath the long quiet rains of autumn and the galloping fury of vernal equinoxes. Then the hamlet which at its best day had borne no name listed on Postoffice Department annals would not now even be remembered by the hookwormridden heirs-at-large who pulled the buildings down and burned them in cookstoves and winter grates.

There were perhaps five families there when Lena arrived. There was a track and a station, and once a day a mixed train fled shrieking through it. The train could be stopped with a red flag, but by ordinary it appeared out of the devastated hills with apparitionlike suddenness and wailing like a banshee, athwart and past that little less-than-village like a forgotten bead from a broken string. The brother was twenty years her senior. She hardly remembered him at all when she came to live with him. He lived in a four room and unpainted house with his labor- and childridden wife. For almost half of every year the sister-in-law was either lying in or recovering. During this time Lena did all the housework and took care of the other children. Later she told herself, 'I reckon that's why I got one so quick myself.'

She slept in a leanto room at the back of the house. It had a window which she learned to open and close again in the dark without making a sound, even though there also slept in the leanto room at first her oldest nephew and then the two oldest and then the three. She had lived there eight years before she opened the window for the first time. She had not opened it a dozen times hardly before she discovered that she should not have opened it at all. She said to herself, 'That's just my luck.'

The sister-in-law told the brother. Then he remarked her changing shape, which he should have noticed some time before. He was a hard man. Softness and gentleness and youth (he was just forty) and almost everything else except a kind of stubborn and despairing fortitude and the bleak heritage of his bloodpride had been sweated out of him. He called her whore. He accused the right man (young bachelors, or sawdust Casanovas anyway, were even fewer in number than families) but she would not admit it, though the man had departed six months ago. She just repeated stubbornly, "He's going to send for me. He said he would send for me"; unshakable, sheeplike, having drawn upon that reserve of patient and steadfast fidelity upon which the Lucas Burches depend and trust, even though they do not intend to be present when the need for it arises. Two weeks later she climbed again through the window. It was a little difficult, this time. 'If it had been this hard to do before, I reckon I would not be doing it now,' she thought. She could have departed by the door, by daylight. Nobody would have stopped her. Perhaps she knew that. But she chose to go by night, and through the window. She carried a palm leaf fan and a small bundle tied neatly in a bandanna handkerchief. It contained among other things thirty-five cents in nickels and dimes. Her shoes were a pair of his own which her brother had given to her. They were but slightly worn, since in the summer neither of them wore shoes at all. When she felt the dust of the road beneath her feet she removed the shoes and carried them in her hand.

She had been doing that now for almost four weeks. Behind her the four weeks, the evocation of *far,* is a peaceful corridor paved with unflagging and tranquil faith and peopled with kind and nameless faces and voices: *Lucas Burch? I dont know. I dont know of anybody by that name*

· 4 ·

around here. This road? It goes to Pocahontas. He might be there. It's possible. Here's a wagon that's going a piece of the way. It will take you that far; backrolling now behind her a long monotonous succession of peaceful and undeviating changes from day to dark and dark to day again, through which she advanced in identical and anonymous and deliberate wagons as though through a succession of creakwheeled and limpeared avatars, like something moving forever and without progress across an urn.

The wagon mounts the hill toward her. She passed it about a mile back down the road. It was standing beside the road, the mules asleep in the traces and their heads pointed in the direction in which she walked. She saw it and she saw the two men squatting beside a barn beyond the fence. She looked at the wagon and the men once: a single glance all-embracing, swift, innocent and profound. She did not stop; very likely the men beyond the fence had not seen her even look at the wagon or at them. Neither did she look back. She went on out of sight, walking slowly, the shoes unlaced about her ankles, until she reached the top of the hill a mile beyond. Then she sat down on the ditchbank, with her feet in the shallow ditch, and removed the shoes. After a while she began to hear the wagon. She heard it for some time. Then it came into sight, mounting the hill.

The sharp and brittle crack and clatter of its weathered and ungreased wood and metal is slow and terrific: a series of dry sluggish reports carrying for a half mile across the hot still pinewiney silence of the August afternoon. Though the mules plod in a steady and unflagging hypnosis, the vehicle does not seem to progress. It seems to hang suspended in the middle distance forever and forever, so infinitesimal is its progress, like a shabby bead upon the mild red string of road. So much is this so that in the watching of it the eye loses it as sight and sense drowsily merge and blend, like the road itself, with all the peaceful and monotonous changes between darkness and day, like already measured thread being rewound onto a spool. So that at last, as though out of some trivial and unimportant region beyond even distance, the sound of it seems to come slow and terrific and without meaning, as though it were a ghost travelling a half mile ahead of its own shape. 'That far within my hearing before my seeing,' Lena thinks. She thinks of herself as already moving, riding again, thinking *then it will be as if I were riding for a half mile before I even got into the wagon, before the wagon even got to where I was waiting, and that when the wagon is empty of me again it will go on for a half mile with me still in it* She waits, not even watching the wagon now, while thinking goes idle and swift and smooth, filled with nameless kind faces and voices: *Lucas Burch? You say you tried in Pocahontas? This road? It goes to Springvale. You wait here. There will be a wagon passing soon that will take you as far as it goes* Thinking, 'And if he is going all the way to Jefferson, I will be riding within the hearing of Lucas Burch before his seeing. He will hear the wagon, but he wont know. So there will be one within his hearing before his seeing. And then he will see me and he will be excited. And so there will be two within his seeing before his remembering.'

While Armstid and Winterbottom were squatting against the shady wall of Winterbottom's stable, they saw her pass in the road. They saw at once that she was young, pregnant, and a stranger. "I wonder where she got that belly," Winterbottom said.

"I wonder how far she has brought it afoot," Armstid said.

"Visiting somebody back down the road, I reckon," Winterbottom said.

"I reckon not. Or I would have heard. And it aint nobody up my way, neither. I would have heard that, too."

"I reckon she knows where she is going," Winterbottom said. "She walks like it."

"She'll have company, before she goes much further," Armstid said. The woman had now gone on, slowly, with her swelling and unmistakable burden. Neither of them had seen her so much as glance at them when she passed in a shapeless garment of faded blue, carrying a palm leaf fan and a small cloth bundle. "She aint come from nowhere close," Armstid said. "She's hitting that lick like she's been at it for a right smart while and had a right smart piece to go yet."

"She must be visiting around here somewhere," Winterbottom said.

"I reckon I would have heard about it," Armstid said. The woman went on. She had not looked back. She went out of sight up the road: swollen, slow, deliberate, unhurried and tireless as augmenting afternoon itself. She walked out of their talking too; perhaps out of their minds too. Because after a while Armstid said what he had come to say. He had already made two previous trips, coming in his wagon five miles and squatting and spitting for three hours beneath the shady wall of Winterbottom's barn with the timeless unhaste and indirection of his kind, in order to say it. It was to make Winterbottom an offer for a cultivator which Winterbottom wanted to sell. At last Armstid looked at the sun and offered the price which he had decided to offer while lying in bed three nights ago. "I know of one in Jefferson I can buy at that figure," he said.

"I reckon you better buy it," Winterbottom said. "It sounds like a bargain."

"Sho," Armstid said. He spat. He looked again at the sun, and rose. "Well, I reckon I better get on toward home."

He got into his wagon and waked the mules. That is, he put them into motion, since only a negro can tell when a mule is asleep or awake. Winterbottom followed him to the fence, leaning his arms on the top rail. "Yes, sir," he said. "I'd sho buy that cultivator at that figure. If you dont take it, I be dog if I aint a good mind to buy it, myself, at that price. I reckon the fellow that owns it aint got a span of mules to sell for about five dollars, has he?"

"Sho," Armstid said. He drove on, the wagon beginning to fall into its slow and mileconsuming clatter. Neither does he look back. Apparently he is not looking ahead either, because he does not see the woman sitting in the ditch beside the road until the wagon has almost reached the top of the hill. In the instant in which he recognises the blue dress he cannot tell if she has ever seen the wagon at all. And no one could have known that he had ever looked at her either as, without any semblance of progress in either of them, they draw slowly together as the wagon crawls terrifically toward her in its slow palpable aura of somnolence and red dust in which the steady feet of the mules move dreamlike and punctuate by the sparse jingle of harness and the limber bobbing of jackrabbit ears, the mules still neither asleep nor awake as he halts them.

From beneath a sunbonnet of faded blue, weathered now by other than formal soap and water, she looks up at him quietly and pleasantly: young, pleasantfaced, candid, friendly, and alert. She does not move yet. Beneath the faded garment of that same weathered blue her body is shapeless and immobile. The fan and the bundle lie on her lap. She wears no stockings. Her bare feet rest side by side in the shallow ditch. The pair of dusty, heavy, manlooking shoes beside them are not more inert. In the halted wagon Armstid sits, humped, bleacheyed. He sees that the rim of the fan is bound neatly in the same faded blue as the sunbonnet and the dress.

"How far you going?" he says.

"I was trying to get up the road a pieceways before dark," she says. She rises and takes up the shoes. She climbs slowly and deliberately into the road, approaching the wagon. Armstid does not descend to help her. He merely holds the team still while she climbs heavily over the wheel and sets the shoes beneath the seat. Then the wagon moves on. "I thank you," she says. "It was right tiring afoot."

Apparently Armstid has never once looked full at her. Yet he has already seen that she wears no wedding ring. He does not look at her now. Again the wagon settles into its slow clatter. "How far you come from?" he says.

She expels her breath. It is not a sigh so much as a peaceful expiration, as though of peaceful astonishment. "A right good piece, it seems now. I come from Alabama."

"Alabama? In your shape? Where's your folks?"

She does not look at him, either. "I'm looking to meet him up this way. You might know him. His name is Lucas Burch. They told me back yonder a ways that he is in Jefferson, working for the planing mill."

"Lucas Burch." Armstid's tone is almost identical with hers. They sit side by side on the sagging and broken-springed seat. He can see her hands upon her lap and her profile beneath the sunbonnet; from the corner of his eye he sees it. She seems to be watching the road as it unrolls between the limber ears of the mules. "And you come all the way here, afoot, by yourself, hunting for him?"

She does not answer for a moment. Then she says: "Folks have been kind. They have been right kind."

"Womenfolks too?" From the corner of his eye he watches her profile, thinking *I dont know what Martha's going to say* thinking, 'I reckon I do know what Martha's going to say. I reckon womenfolks are likely to be good without being very kind. Men, now, might. But it's only a bad woman herself that is likely to be very kind to another woman that needs the kindness' thinking *Yes I do. I know exactly what Martha is going to say.*

She sits a little forward, quite still, her profile quite still, her cheek. "It's a strange thing," she says.

"How folks can look at a strange young gal walking the road in your shape and know that her husband has left her?" She does not move. The wagon now has a kind of rhythm, its ungreased and outraged wood one with the slow afternoon, the road, the heat. "And you aim to find him up here."

She does not move, apparently watching the slow road between the ears of the mules, the distance perhaps road-carved and definite. "I reckon I'll find him. It won't be hard. He'll be where the most folks are gathered together, and the laughing and joking is. He always was a hand for that."

Armstid grunts, a sound savage, brusque. "Get up,

mules," he says; he says to himself, between thinking and saying aloud: 'I reckon she will. I reckon that fellow is fixing to find that he made a bad mistake when he stopped this side of Arkansas, or even Texas.'

The sun is slanting, an hour above the horizon now, above the swift coming of the summer night. The lane turns from the road, quieter even than the road. "Here we are," Armstid says.

The woman moves at once. She reaches down and finds the shoes; apparently she is not even going to delay the wagon long enough to put them on. "I thank you kindly," she says. "It was a help."

The wagon is halted again. The woman is preparing to descend. "Even if you get to Varner's store before sundown, you'll still be twelve miles from Jefferson," Armstid says.

She holds the shoes, the bundle, the fan awkwardly in one hand, the other free to help her down. "I reckon I better get on," she says.

Armstid does not touch her. "You come on and stay the night at my house," he says; "where womenfolks—where a woman can . . . if you— You come on, now. I'll take you on to Varner's first thing in the morning, and you can get a ride into town. There will be somebody going, on a Saturday. He aint going to get away on you overnight. If he is in Jefferson at all, he will still be there tomorrow."

She sits quite still, her possessions gathered into her hand for dismounting. She is looking ahead, to where the road curves on and away, crossslanted with shadows. "I reckon I got a few days left."

"Sho. You got plenty of time yet. Only you are liable to have some company at any time now that can't walk. You come on home with me." He puts the mules into motion without waiting for a reply. The wagon enters the lane, the dim road. The woman sits back, though she still holds the fan, the bundle, the shoes.

"I wouldn't be beholden," she says. "I wouldn't trouble."

"Sho," Armstid says. "You come on with me." For the first time the mules move swiftly of their own accord. "Smelling corn," Armstid says, thinking, 'But that's the woman of it. Her own self one of the first ones to cut the ground from under a sister woman, she'll walk the public country herself without shame because she knows that folks, menfolks, will take care of her. She don't care nothing about womenfolks. It wasn't any woman that got her into what she don't even call trouble. Yes, sir. You just let one of them get married or get into trouble without being married, and right then and there is where she secedes from the woman race and species and spends the balance of her life trying to get joined up with the man race. That's why they dip snuff and smoke and want to vote.'

When the wagon passes the house and goes on toward the barnlot, his wife is watching it from the front door. He does not look in that direction; he does not need to look to know that she will be there, is there. 'Yes,' he thinks with sardonic ruefulness, turning the mules into the open gate, 'I know exactly what she is going to say. I reckon I know exactly.' He halts the wagon, he does not need to look to know that his wife is now in the kitchen, not watching now; just waiting. He halts the wagon. "You go on to the house," he says; he has already descended and the woman is now climbing slowly down, with that inward listening deliberation. "When you meet somebody, it will be Martha. I'll be in when I feed the stock." He does not watch her cross the lot and go on toward the kitchen. He does not need to. Step by step with her he enters the kitchen door also and comes upon the woman who now watches the kitchen door exactly as she had watched the wagon pass from the front one. 'I reckon I know exactly what she will say,' he thinks.

He takes the team out and waters and stalls and feeds them, and lets the cows in from the pasture. Then he goes to the kitchen. She is still there, the gray woman with a cold, harsh, irascible face, who bore five children in six years and raised them to man- and woman-hood. She is not idle. He does not look at her. He goes to the sink and fills a pan from the pail and turns his sleeves back. "Her name is Burch," he says. "At least that's what she says the fellow's name is that she is hunting for. Lucas Burch. Somebody told her back down the road a ways that he is in Jefferson now." He begins to wash, his back to her. "She come all the way from Alabama, alone and afoot, she says."

Mrs Armstid does not look around. She is busy at the table. "She's going to quit being alone a good while before she sees Alabama again," she says.

"Or that fellow Burch either, I reckon." He is quite busy at the sink, with the soap and water. And he can feel her looking at him, at the back of his head, his shoulders in the shirt of sweatfaded blue. "She says that somebody down at Samson's told her there is a fellow named Burch or something working at the planing mill in Jefferson."

"And she expects to find him there. Waiting. With the house all furnished and all."

He cannot tell from her voice if she is watching him or not now. He towels himself with a split floursack. "Maybe she will. If it's running away from her he's after, I reckon he's going to find out he made a bad mistake when he

stopped before he put the Mississippi River between them."
And now he knows that she is watching him: the gray
woman not plump and not thin, manhard, workhard, in a
serviceable gray garment worn savage and brusque, her
hands on her hips, her face like those of generals who have
been defeated in battle.

"You men," she says.

"What do you want to do about it? Turn her out? Let
her sleep in the barn maybe?"

"You men," she says. "You durn men."

They enter the kitchen together, though Mrs Armstid is
in front. She goes straight to the stove. Lena stands just
within the door. Her head is uncovered now, her hair
combed smooth. Even the blue garment looks freshened
and rested. She looks on while Mrs Armstid at the stove
clashes the metal lids and handles the sticks of wood with
the abrupt savageness of a man. "I would like to help,"
Lena says.

Mrs Armstid does not look around. She clashes the stove
savagely. "You stay where you are. You keep off your feet
now, and you'll keep off your back a while longer maybe."

"It would be a beholden kindness to let me help."

"You stay where you are. I been doing this three times a
day for thirty years now. The time when I needed help
with it is done passed." She is busy at the stove, not backlooking. "Armstid says your name is Burch."

"Yes," the other says. Her voice is quite grave now,
quite quiet. She sits quite still, her hands motionless upon
her lap. And Mrs Armstid does not look around either.
She is still busy at the stove. It appears to require an
amount of attention out of all proportion to the savage

· 14 ·

finality with which she built the fire. It appears to engage as much of her attention as if it were an expensive watch.

"Is your name Burch yet?" Mrs Armstid says.

The young woman does not answer at once. Mrs Armstid does not rattle the stove now, though her back is still toward the younger woman. Then she turns. They look at one another, suddenly naked, watching one another: the young woman in the chair, with her neat hair and her inert hands upon her lap, and the older one beside the stove, turning, motionless too, with a savage screw of gray hair at the base of her skull and a face that might have been carved in sandstone. Then the younger one speaks.

"I told you false. My name is not Burch yet. It's Lena Grove."

They look at one another. Mrs Armstid's voice is neither cold nor warm. It is not anything at all. "And so you want to catch up with him so your name will be Burch in time. Is that it?"

Lena is looking down now, as though watching her hands upon her lap. Her voice is quiet, dogged. Yet it is serene. "I dont reckon I need any promise from Lucas. It just happened unfortunate so, that he had to go away. His plans just never worked out right for him to come back for me like he aimed to. I reckon me and him didn't need to make word promises. When he found out that night that he would have to go, he—"

"Found out what night? The night you told him about that chap?"

The other does not answer for a moment. Her face is calm as stone, but not hard. Its doggedness has a soft quality, an inwardlighted quality of tranquil and calm unreason and detachment. Mrs Armstid watches her. Lena is not looking at the other woman while she speaks. "He had done got the word about how he might have to leave a long time before that. He just never told me sooner because he didn't want to worry me with it. When he first heard about how he might have to leave, he knowed then it would be best to go, that he could get along faster somewhere where the foreman wouldn't be down on him. But he kept on putting it off. But when this here happened, we couldn't put it off no longer then. The foreman was down on Lucas because he didn't like him because Lucas was young and full of life all the time and the foreman wanted Lucas' job to give it to a cousin of his. But he hadn't aimed to tell me because it would just worry me. But when this here happened, we couldn't wait any longer. I was the one that said for him to go. He said he would stay if I said so, whether the foreman treated him right or not. But I said for him to go. He never wanted to go, even then. But I said for him to. To just send me word when he was ready for me to come. And then his plans just never worked out for him to send for me in time, like he aimed. Going away among strangers like that, a young fellow needs time to get settled down. He never knowed that when he left, that he would need more time to get settled down in than he figured on. Especially a young fellow full of life like Lucas, that likes folks and jollifying, and liked by folks in turn. He didn't know it would take longer than he planned, being young, and folks always after him because he is a hand for laughing and joking, interfering with his work unbeknownst to him because he never wanted to hurt folks' feelings. And I wanted him to have his last enjoyment, because marriage is different with a young fellow, a lively young fellow, and a woman. It lasts so long with a lively young fellow. Don't you think so?"

Mrs. Armstid does not answer. She looks at the other sitting in the chair with her smooth hair and her still hands lying upon her lap and her soft and musing face. "Like as not, he already sent me the word and it got lost on the way. It's a right far piece from here to Alabama even, and I ain't to Jefferson yet. I told him I would not expect him to write, being as he ain't any hand for letters. 'You just send me your mouthword when you are ready for me,' I told him. 'I'll be waiting.' It worried me a little at first, after he left, because my name wasn't Burch yet and my brother and his folks not knowing Lucas as well as I knew him. How could they?" Into her face there comes slowly an expression of soft and bright surprise, as if she had just thought of something which she had not even been aware that she did not know. "How could they be expected to, you see. But he had to get settled down first; it was him would have all the trouble of being among strangers, and me with nothing to bother about except to just wait while he had all the bother and trouble. But after a while I reckon I just got too busy getting this chap up to his time to worry about what my name was or what folks thought. But me and Lucas dont need no word promises between us. It was something unexpected come up, or he even sent the word and it got lost. So one day I just decided to up and not wait any longer."

"How did you know which way to go when you started?"

Lena is watching her hands. They are moving now, plaiting with rapt bemusement a fold of her skirt. It is not diffidence, shyness. It is apparently some musing reflex of the hand alone. "I just kept asking. With Lucas a lively young fellow that got to know folks easy and quick, I knew that wherever he had been, folks would remember him. So I kept asking. And folks was right kind. And sure enough, I heard two days back on the road that he is in Jefferson, working for the planing mill."

Mrs Armstid watches the lowered face. Her hands are on her hips and she watches the younger woman with an expression of cold and impersonal contempt. "And you believe that he will be there when you get there. Granted that he ever was there at all. That he will hear you are in the same town with him, and still be there when the sun sets."

Lena's lowered face is grave, quiet. Her hand has ceased now. It lies quite still on her lap, as if it had died there. Her voice is quiet, tranquil, stubborn. "I reckon a family ought to all be together when a chap comes. Specially the first one. I reckon the Lord will see to that."

"And I reckon He will have to," Mrs Armstid says, savagely, harshly. Armstid is in bed, his head propped up a little, watching her across the footboard as, still dressed, she stoops into the light of the lamp upon the dresser, hunting violently in a drawer. She produces a metal box and unlocks it with a key suspended about her neck and takes out a cloth sack which she opens and produces a small china effigy of a rooster with a slot in its back. It jingles with coins as she moves it and upends it and shakes it violently above the top of the dresser, shaking from the slot coins in a meagre dribbling. Armstid in the bed watches her.

"What are you fixing to do with your eggmoney this time of night?" he says.

"I reckon it's mine to do with what I like." She stoops into the lamp, her face harsh, bitter. "God knows it was me sweated over them and nursed them. You never lifted no hand."

"Sho," he says. "I reckon it ain't any human in this country is going to dispute them hens with you, lessen it's the possums and the snakes. That rooster bank, neither," he says. Because, stooping suddenly, she jerks off one shoe and strikes the china bank a single shattering blow. From the bed, reclining, Armstid watches her gather the remaining coins from among the china fragments and drop them with the others into the sack and knot it and reknot it three or four times with savage finality.

"You give that to her," she says. "And come sunup you hitch up the team and take her away from here. Take her all the way to Jefferson, if you want."

"I reckon she can get a ride in from Varner's store," he says.

Mrs Armstid rose before day and cooked breakfast. It was on the table when Armstid came in from milking. "Go tell her to come and eat," Mrs Armstid said. When he and Lena returned to the kitchen, Mrs Armstid was not there. Lena looked about the room once, pausing at the door with less than a pause, her face already fixed in an expression immanent with smiling, with speech, prepared speech, Armstid knew. But she said nothing; the pause was less than a pause.

"Let's eat and get on," Armstid said. "You still got a right good piece to go." He watched her eat, again with the tranquil and hearty decorum of last night's supper, though there was now corrupting it a quality of polite and almost finicking restraint. Then he gave her the knotted cloth sack. She took it, her face pleased, warm, though not very much surprised.

"Why, it's right kind of her," she said. "But I won't need it. I'm so nigh there now."

"I reckon you better keep it. I reckon you done noticed how Martha ain't much on being crossed in what she aims to do."

"It's right kind," Lena said. She tied the money up in the bandanna bundle and put on the sunbonnet. The wagon was waiting. When they drove down the lane, past the house, she looked back at it. "It was right kind of you all," she said.

"She done it," Armstid said. "I reckon I can't claim no credit."

"It was right kind, anyway. You'll have to say good-bye to her for me. I had hopened to see her myself, but . . ."

"Sho," Armstid said. "I reckon she was busy or something. I'll tell her."

They drove up to the store in the early sunlight, with the squatting men already spitting across the heelgnawed porch, watching her descend slowly and carefully from the wagon seat, carrying the bundle and the fan. Again Armstid did not move to assist her. He said from the seat: "This here is Miz Burch. She wants to go to Jefferson. If anybody is going in today, she will take it kind to ride with them."

She reached the earth, in the heavy, dusty shoes. She looked up at him, serene, peaceful. "It's been right kind," she said.

"Sho," Armstid said. "I reckon you can get to town now." He looked down at her. Then it seemed an interminable while that he watched his tongue seek words, thinking quiet and swift, thought fleeing *A man. All men. He will pass up a hundred chances to do good for one chance to meddle where meddling is not wanted. He will overlook and fail to see chances, opportunities, for riches and fame and welldoing, and even sometimes for evil. But he won't fail to see a chance to meddle* Then his tongue found words, he listening, perhaps with the same astonishment that she did: "Only I wouldn't set too much store by . . . store in . . ." thinking *She is not listening. If she could hear words like that she would not be getting down from this wagon, with that belly and that fan and that little bundle, alone, bound for a place she never saw before and hunting for a man she ain't going to ever see again and that she has already seen one time too many as it is* "—any time you are passing back this way, tomorrow or even tonight . . ."

"I reckon I'll be all right now," she said. "They told me he is there."

He turned the wagon and drove back home, sitting hunched, bleacheyed, on the sagging seat, thinking, 'It wouldn't have done any good. She would not have believed the telling and hearing it any more than she will believe the thinking that's been going on all around her for . . . It's four weeks now, she said. No more than she will feel it and believe it now. Setting there on that top step, with her hands in her lap and them fellows squatting there and spitting past her into the road. And not even waiting for them to ask her about it before she begins to tell. Telling them of her own accord about that durn fellow like she never had nothing particular to either hide or tell, even when Jody Varner or some of them will tell her that that fellow in Jefferson at the planing mill is named Bunch and not Burch; and that not worrying her either. I reckon she knows more than even Martha does, like when she told Martha last night about how the Lord will see that what is right will get done.'

It required only one or two questions. Then, sitting on the top step, the fan and the bundle upon her lap, Lena tells her story again, with that patient and transparent recapitulation of a lying child, the squatting overalled men listening quietly.

"That fellow's name is Bunch," Varner says. "He's been working there at the mill about seven years. How do you know that Burch is there too?"

She is looking away up the road, in the direction of Jefferson. Her face is calm, waiting, a little detached without being bemused. "I reckon he'll be there. At that planing mill and all. Lucas always did like excitement. He never did like to live quiet. That's why it never suited him back at Doane's Mill. Why he—we decided to make a change: for money and excitement."

"For money and excitement," Varner says. "Lucas aint the first young buck that's throwed over what he was bred to do and them that depended on him doing it, for money and excitement."

But she is not listening apparently. She sits quietly on the top step, watching the road where it curves away, empty and mounting, toward Jefferson. The squatting men along the wall look at her still and placid face and they think as Armstid thought and as Varner thinks: that she is thinking of a scoundrel who deserted her in trouble and who they believe that she will never see again, save his coattails perhaps already boardflat with running. 'Or maybe it's about that Sloane's or Bone's Mill she is thinking,' Varner thinks. 'I reckon that even a fool gal don't have to come as far as Mississippi to find out that whatever place she run from ain't going to be a whole lot different or worse than the place she is at. Even if it has got a brother in it that objects to his sister's nightprowling,' thinking *I would have done the same as the brother; the father would have done the same. She has no mother because fatherblood hates with love and pride, but motherblood with hate loves and cohabits*

She is not thinking about this at all. She is thinking about the coins knotted in the bundle beneath her hands. She is remembering breakfast, thinking how she can enter the store this moment and buy cheese and crackers and even sardines if she likes. At Armstid's she had had but a cup of coffee and a piece of cornbread: nothing more, though Armstid pressed her. 'I et polite,' she thinks, her hands lying upon the bundle, knowing the hidden coins, remembering the single cup of coffee, the decorous morsel of strange bread; thinking with a sort of serene pride: 'Like a lady I et. Like a lady travelling. But now I can buy sardines too if I should so wish.'

So she seems to muse upon the mounting road while the slowspitting and squatting men watch her covertly, believing that she is thinking about the man and the approaching crisis, when in reality she is waging a mild battle with that providential caution of the old earth of and with and by which she lives. This time she conquers. She rises and walking a little awkwardly, a little carefully, she traverses the ranked battery of maneyes and enters the store, the clerk following. 'I'm a-going to do it,' she thinks, even while ordering the cheese and crackers; 'I'm a-going to do it,' saying aloud: "And a box of sardines." She calls them *sour-deens*. "A nickel box."

"We ain't got no nickel sardines," the clerk says. "Sardines is fifteen cents." He also calls them *sour-deens*.

She muses. "What have you got in a can for a nickel?"

"Aint got nothing except shoeblacking. I dont reckon you want that. Not to eat, noway."

"I reckon I'll take the fifteen cent ones, then." She unties the bundle and the knotted sack. It requires some time to solve the knots. But she unties them patiently, one by one, and pays and knots the sack and the bundle again and takes up her purchase. When she emerges onto the porch there is a wagon standing at the steps. A man is on the seat.

"Here's a wagon going to town," they tell her. "He will take you in."

Her face wakes, serene, slow, warm. "Why, you're right kind," she says.

The wagon moves slowly, steadily, as if here within the sunny loneliness of the enormous land it were outside of, beyond all time and all haste. From Varner's store to Jefferson it is twelve miles. "Will we get there before dinner time?" she says.

The driver spits. "We mought," he says.

Apparently he has never looked at her, not even when she got into the wagon. Apparently she has never looked at him, either. She does not do so now. "I reckon you go to Jefferson a right smart."

He says, "Some." The wagon creaks on. Fields and woods seem to hang in some inescapable middle distance, at once static and fluid, quick, like mirages. Yet the wagon passes them.

"I reckon you don't know anybody in Jefferson named Lucas Burch."

"Burch?"

"I'm looking to meet him there. He works at the planing mill."

"No," the driver says. "I don't know that I know him. But likely there is a right smart of folks in Jefferson I don't know. Likely he is there."

"I'll declare, I hope so. Travelling is getting right bothersome."

The driver does not look at her. "How far have you come, looking for him?"

"From Alabama. It's a right far piece."

He does not look at her. His voice is quite casual. "How did your folks come to let you start out, in your shape?"

"My folks are dead. I live with my brother. I just decided to come on."

"I see. He sent you word to come to Jefferson."

She does not answer. He can see beneath the sunbonnet her calm profile. The wagon goes on, slow, timeless. The red and unhurried miles unroll beneath the steady feet of the mules, beneath the creaking and clanking wheels. The sun stands now high overhead; the shadow of the sunbonnet now falls across her lap. She looks up at the sun. "I reckon it's time to eat," she says. He watches from the corner of his eye as she opens the cheese and crackers and the sardines and offers them.

"I wouldn't care for none," he says.

"I'd take it kind for you to share."

"I wouldn't care to. You go ahead and eat."

She begins to eat. She eats slowly, steadily, sucking the rich sardine oil from her fingers with slow and complete relish. Then she stops, not abruptly, yet with utter completeness, her jaw stilled in midchewing, a bitten cracker in her hand and her face lowered a little and her eyes blank, as if she were listening to something very far away or so near as to be inside her. Her face has drained of color, of its full, hearty blood, and she sits quite still, hearing and feeling the implacable and immemorial earth, but without fear or alarm. 'It's twins at least,' she says to herself, without lip movement, without sound. Then the spasm passes. She eats again. The wagon has not stopped; time has not stopped. The wagon crests the final hill and they see smoke.

"Jefferson," the driver says.

"Well, I'll declare," she says. "We are almost there, aint we?"

It is the man now who does not hear. He is looking ahead, across the valley toward the town on the opposite ridge. Following his pointing whip, she sees two columns of smoke: the one the heavy density of burning coal above a tall stack, the other a tall yellow column standing apparently from among a clump of trees some distance beyond the town. "That's a house burning," the driver says. "See?"

But she in turn again does not seem to be listening, to hear. "My, my," she says; "here I aint been on the road but four weeks, and now I am in Jefferson already. My, my. A body does get around."

. 2 .

BYRON BUNCH knows this: It was one Friday morning three years ago. And the group of men at work in the planer shed looked up, and saw the stranger standing there, watching them. They did not know how long he had been there. He looked like a tramp, yet not like a tramp either. His shoes were dusty and his trousers were soiled too. But they were of decent serge, sharply creased, and his shirt was soiled but it was a white shirt, and he wore a tie and a stiffbrim straw hat that was quite new, cocked at an angle arrogant and baleful above his still face. He did not look like a professional hobo in his professional rags, but there was something definitely rootless about him, as though no town nor city was his, no street, no walls, no square of earth his home. And that he carried his knowledge with him always as though it were a banner, with a quality ruthless, lonely, and almost proud. "As if," as the men said later, "he was just down on his luck for a time, and that he didn't intend to stay down on it and didn't give a damn much how he rose up." He was young. And Byron watched him standing there and looking at the men in sweatstained overalls, with a cigarette in one side of his mouth and his face darkly and contemptuously still, drawn down a little on one side because of the smoke. After a while he spat the cigarette without touching his hand to it and turned and went on to the mill office while the men in faded and worksoiled overalls looked at his back with a sort of baffled outrage. "We ought to run him through the planer," the foreman said. "Maybe that will take that look off his face."

They did not know who he was. None of them had ever seen him before. "Except that's a pretty risky look for a man to wear on his face in public," one said: "He might forget and use it somewhere where somebody wont like it." Then they dismissed him, from the talk, anyway. They went back to their work among the whirring and grating belts and shafts. But it was not ten minutes before the mill superintendent entered, with the stranger behind him.

"Put this man on," the superintendent said to the foreman. "He says he can handle a scoop, anyhow. You can put him on the sawdust pile."

The others had not stopped work, yet there was not a man in the shed who was not again watching the stranger in his soiled city clothes, with his dark, insufferable face and his whole air of cold and quiet contempt. The foreman looked at him, briefly, his gaze as cold as the other's. "Is he going to do it in them clothes?"

"That's his business," the superintendent said. "I'm not hiring his clothes."

"Well, whatever he wears suits me if it suits you and him," the foreman said. "All right, mister," he said. "Go down yonder and get a scoop and help them fellows move that sawdust."

The newcomer turned without a word. The others watched him go down to the sawdust pile and vanish and reappear with a shovel and go to work. The foreman and the superintendent were talking at the door. They parted and the foreman returned. "His name is Christmas," he said.

"His name is what?" one said.

"Christmas."

"Is he a foreigner?"

"Did you ever hear of a white man named Christmas?" the foreman said.

"I never heard of nobody a-tall named it," the other said.

And that was the first time Byron remembered that he had ever thought how a man's name, which is supposed to be just the sound for who he is, can be somehow an augur of what he will do, if other men can only read the meaning in time. It seemed to him that none of them had looked especially at the stranger until they heard his name. But as soon as they heard it, it was as though there was something in the sound of it that was trying to tell them what to expect; that he carried with him his own inescapable warning, like a flower its scent or a rattlesnake its rattle. Only none of them had sense enough to recognise it. They just thought that he was a foreigner, and as they watched him for the rest of that Friday, working in that tie and the straw hat and the creased trousers, they said among themselves that that was the way men in his country worked; though there were others who said, "He'll change clothes tonight. He wont have on them Sunday clothes when he comes to work in the morning."

Saturday morning came. As the late arrivals came up just before the whistle blew, they were already saying, "Did he— Where—" The others pointed. The new man was standing alone down at the sawdust pile. His shovel was beside him, and he stood in the same garments of yesterday, with the arrogant hat, smoking a cigarette. "He was there when we come," the first ones said. "Just standing there, like that. Like he hadn't never been to bed, even."

He did not talk to any of them at all. And none of them tried to talk to him. But they were all conscious of him, of the steady back (he worked well enough, with a kind of baleful and restrained steadiness) and arms. Noon came. With the exception of Byron, they had brought no lunch with them today, and they began to gather up their belongings preparatory to quitting until Monday. Byron went alone with his lunch pail to the pump house where they usually ate, and sat down. Then something caused him to look up. A short distance away the stranger was leaning against a post, smoking. Byron knew that he had been there when he entered, and would not even bother to go away. Or worse: that he had come there deliberately, ignoring Byron as if he were another post. "Aint you going to knock off?" Byron said.

The other expelled smoke. Then he looked at Byron. His face was gaunt, the flesh a level dead parchment color. Not the skin: the flesh itself, as though the skull had been molded in a still and deadly regularity and then baked in a fierce oven. "How much do they pay for overtime?" he said. And then Byron knew. He knew then why the other worked in the Sunday clothes, and why he had had no lunch with him either yesterday or today, and why he had not quit with the others at noon. He knew as well as if the man had told him that he did not have a nickel in his pockets and that in all likelihood he had lived on cigarettes for two or three days now. Almost with the thought Byron was offering his own pail, the action as reflex as the thought. Because before the act was completed the man, without changing his indolent and contemptuous attitude, turned his face and looked once at the proffered pail through the drooping smoke of the cigarette. "I ain't hungry. Keep your muck."

Monday morning came and Byron proved himself right. The man came to work in new overalls, and with a paper bag of food. But he did not squat with them in the pump house to eat at noon, and the look was still on his face. "Let it stay there," the foreman said. "Simms ain't hiring his face anymore than his clothes."

Simms hadn't hired the stranger's tongue, either, Byron thought. At least, Christmas didn't seem to think so, to act so. He still had nothing to say to anyone, even after six months. No one knew what he did between mill hours. Now and then one of his fellow workers would pass him on the square down town after supper, and it would be as though Christmas had never seen the other before. He would be wearing then the new hat and the ironed trousers and the cigarette in one side of his mouth and the smoke sneering across his face. No one knew where he lived, slept at night, save that now and then someone would see him following a path that came up through the woods on the edge of town, as if he might live out that way somewhere.

This is not what Byron knows now. This is just what he knew then, what he heard and watched as it came to his knowledge. None of them knew then where Christmas lived and what he was actually doing behind the veil, the screen, of his negro's job at the mill. Possibly no one would ever have known if it had not been for the other stranger,

Brown. But as soon as Brown told, there were a dozen men who admitted having bought whiskey from Christmas for over two years, meeting him at night and alone in the woods behind an old colonial plantation house two miles from town, in which a middleaged spinster named Burden lived alone. But even the ones who bought the whiskey did not know that Christmas was actually living in a tumble down negro cabin on Miss Burden's place, and that he had been living in it for more than two years.

Then one day about six months ago another stranger appeared at the mill as Christmas had done, seeking work. He was young too, tall, already in overalls which looked as though he had been in them constantly for some time, and he looked as though he had been travelling light also. He had an alert, weakly handsome face with a small white scar beside the mouth that looked as if it had been contemplated a great deal in the mirror, and a way of jerking his head quickly and glancing over his shoulder like a mule does in front of an automobile in the road, Byron thought. But it was not alone backwatching, alarm; it seemed also to Byron to possess a quality of assurance, brass, as though the man were reiterating and insisting all the while that he was afraid of nothing that might or could approach him from behind. And when Mooney, the foreman, saw the new hand, Byron believed that he and Mooney had the same thought. Mooney said: "Well, Simms is safe from hiring anything at all when he put that fellow on. He never even hired a whole pair of pants."

"That's so," Byron said. "He puts me in mind of one of these cars running along the street with a radio in it. You can't make out what it is saying and the car ain't going anywhere in particular and when you look at it close you see that there ain't even anybody in it."

"Yes," Mooney said. "He puts me in mind of a horse. Not a mean horse. Just a worthless horse. Looks fine in the pasture, but it's always down in the spring bottom when anybody comes to the gate with a bridle. Runs fast, all right, but it's always got a sore hoof when hitching-up time comes."

"But I reckon maybe the mares like him," Byron said.

"Sho," Mooney said. "I don't reckon he'd do even a mare any permanent harm."

The new hand went to work down in the sawdust pile with Christmas. With a lot of motion to it, telling everybody who he was and where he had been, in a tone and manner that was the essence of the man himself, that carried within itself its own confounding and mendacity. So that a man put no more belief in what he said that he had done than in what he said his name was, Byron thought. There was no reason why his name should not have been Brown. It was that, looking at him, a man would know that at some time in his life he would reach some crisis in his own foolishness when he would change his name, and that he would think of Brown to change it to with a kind of gleeful exultation, as though the name had never been invented. The thing was, there was no reason why he should have had or have needed any name at all. Nobody cared, just as Byron believed that no one (wearing pants, anyway) cared where he came from nor where he went nor how long he stayed. Because wherever he came from and wherever he had been, a man knew that he was just living on the country, like a locust. It was as though he had been doing it for so long now that all of him had become scattered and diffused and now there was nothing left but the transparent and weightless shell blown oblivious and without destination upon whatever wind.

He worked some, though, after a fashion. Byron believed that there was not even enough left of him to do a good, shrewd job of shirking. To desire to shirk, even, since a man must be better than common to do a good job of malingering, the same as a good job at anything else: of stealing and murdering even. He must be aiming at some specific and definite goal, working toward it. And he believed that Brown was not. They heard how he went and lost his entire first week's pay in a crap game on the first Saturday night. Byron said to Mooney: "I am surprised at that. I would have thought that maybe shooting dice would be the one thing he could do."

"Him?" Mooney said. "What makes you think that he could be good at any kind of devilment when he ain't any good at anything as easy as shovelling sawdust? that he could fool anybody with anything as hard to handle as a pair of dice, when he can't with anything as easy to handle as a scoop?" Then he said, "Well, I reckon there ain't any man so sorry he can't beat somebody doing something. Because he can at least beat that Christmas doing nothing at all."

"Sho," Byron said, "I reckon that being good is about the easiest thing in the world for a lazy man."

"I reckon he'd be bad fast enough," Mooney said, "if he just had somebody to show him how."

"Well, he'll find that fellow somewhere, sooner or later," Byron said. They both turned and looked down at the sawdust pile, where Brown and Christmas labored, the one with that brooding and savage steadiness, the other with a higharmed and erratic motion which could not have been fooling even itself.

"I reckon so," Mooney said. "But if I aimed to be bad, I'd sho hate to have him for my partner."

Like Christmas, Brown came to work in the same clothes which he wore on the street. But unlike Christmas, he made no change in his costume for some time. "He'll win just enough in that crap game some Saturday night to buy a new suit and still have fifty cents in nickels to rattle in his pocket," Mooney said. "And on the next Monday morning we aint going to see him again." Meanwhile Brown continued to come to work in the same overalls and shirt in which he had arrived in Jefferson, losing his week's pay in the Saturday night dice game or perhaps winning a little, greeting either the one or the other with the same shouts of imbecile laughter, joking and chaffing with the very men who in all likelihood were periodically robbing him. Then one day they heard that he had won sixty dollars. "Well, that's the last we'll see of him," one said.

"I dont know," Mooney said. "Sixty dollars is the wrong figure. If it had been either ten dollars or five hundred, I reckon you'd be right. But not just sixty. He'll just feel now that he is settled down good here, drawing at last somewhere about what he is worth a week." And on Monday he did return to work, in the overalls; they saw them, Brown and Christmas, down at the sawdust pile. They had been watching the two of them down there from the day when Brown went to work: Christmas jabbing his shovel into the sawdust slowly and steadily and hard, as though he were chopping up a buried snake ("or a man," Mooney said) and Brown leaning on his shovel while he apparently told Christmas a story, an anecdote. Because presently he

· 35 ·

would laugh, shout with laughter, his head backflung, while beside him the other man worked with silent and unflagging savageness. Then Brown would fall to again, working for a time once again as fast as Christmas, but picking up less and less in the scoop until at last the shovel would not even touch the sawdust in its flagging arc. Then he would lean upon it again and apparently finish whatever it was that he was telling Christmas, telling to the man who did not even seem to hear his voice. As if the other were a mile away, or spoke a different language from the one he knew, Byron thought. And they would be seen together down town on Saturday evening sometimes: Christmas in his neat, soberly austere serge-and-white and the straw hat, and Brown in his new suit (it was tan, with a red criss-cross, and he had a colored shirt and a hat like Christmas' but with a colored band) talking and laughing, his voice heard clear across the square and back again in echo, some-what as a meaningless sound in a church seems to come from everywhere at once. Like he aimed for everybody to see how he and Christmas were buddies, Byron thought. And then Christmas would turn and with that still, sullen face of his walk out of whatever small gathering the sheer empty sound of Brown's voice had surrounded them with, with Brown following, still laughing and talking. And each time the other workmen would say, "Well, he wont be back on the job Monday morning." But each Monday he was back. It was Christmas who quit first.

He quit one Saturday night, without warning, after al-most three years. It was Brown who informed them that Christmas had quit. Some of the other workers were family men and some were bachelors and they were of different ages and they led a catholic variety of lives, yet on Monday morning they all came to work with a kind of gravity, almost decorum. Some of them were young, and they drank and gambled on Saturday night, and even went to Memphis now and then. Yet on Monday morning they came quietly and soberly to work, in clean overalls and clean shirts, waiting quietly until the whistle blew and then going quietly to work, as though there were still something of Sabbath in the overlingering air which established a tenet that, no matter what a man had done with his Sabbath, to come quiet and clean to work on Monday morning was no more than seemly and right to do.

That is what they had always remarked about Brown. On Monday morning as likely as not he would appear in the same soiled clothes of last week, and with a black stubble that had known no razor. And he would be more noisy than ever, shouting and playing the pranks of a child of ten. To the sober others it did not look right. To them it was as though he had arrived naked, or drunk. Hence it was Brown who on this Monday morning notified them that Christmas had quit. He arrived late, but that was not it. He hadn't shaved, either; but that was not it. He was quiet. For a time they did not know that he was even present, who by that time should have had half the men there cursing him, and some in good earnest. He appeared just as the whistle blew and went straight to the sawdust pile and went to work without a word to anyone, even when one man spoke to him. And then they saw that he was down there alone, that Christmas, his partner, was not there. When the foreman came in, one said: "Well, I see you have lost one of your apprentice firemen."

Mooney looked down to where Brown was spading into the sawdust pile as though it were eggs. He spat briefly.

"Yes. He got rich too fast. This little old job couldn't hold him."

"Got rich?" another said.

"One of them did," Mooney said, still watching Brown. "I saw them yesterday riding in a new car. He"—he jerked his head toward Brown—"was driving it. I wasn't surprised at that. I am just surprised that even one of them come to work today."

"Well, I don't reckon Simms will have any trouble finding a man to fill his shoes in these times," the other said.

"He wouldn't have any trouble doing that at any time," Mooney said.

"It looked to me like he was doing pretty well."

"Oh," Mooney said. "I see. You are talking about Chrismas."

"Who were you talking about? Has Brown said he is quitting too?"

"You reckon he's going to stay down there, working, with the other one riding around town all day in that new car?"

"Oh." The other looked at Brown too. "I wonder where they got that car."

"I don't," Mooney said. "What I wonder is, if Brown is going to quit at noon or work on until six o'clock."

"Well," Byron said, "if I could get rich enough out here to buy a new automobile, I'd quit too."

One or two of the others looked at Byron. They smiled a little. "They never got that rich out here," one said. Byron looked at him. "I reckon Byron stays out of meanness too much himself to keep up with other folks'," the other said. They looked at Byron. "Brown is what you might call a public servant. Christmas used to make them come way out to them woods back of Miss Burden's place, at night; now Brown brings it right into town for them. I hear tell how if you just know the pass word, you can buy a pint of whiskey out of his shirt front in any alley on a Saturday night."

"What's the pass word?" another said. "Six bits?"

Byron looked from face to face. "Is that a fact? Is that what they are doing?"

"That's what Brown is doing. I don't know about Christmas. I wouldn't swear to it. But Brown aint going to be far away from where Christmas is at. Like to like, as the old folks say."

"That's a fact," another said. "Whether Christmas is in it or not, I reckon we aint going to know. He aint going to walk around in public with his pants down, like Brown does."

"He aint going to need to," Mooney said, looking at Brown.

And Mooney was right. They watched Brown until noon, down there at the sawdust pile by himself. Then the whistle blew and they got their lunch pails and squatted in the pump shed and began to eat. Brown came in, glum, his face at once sullen and injured looking, like a child's, and squatted among them, his hands dangling between his knees. He had no lunch with him today.

"Aint you going to eat any dinner?" one said.

"Cold muck out of a dirty lard bucket?" Brown said. "Starting in at daylight and slaving all day like a durn nigger, with a hour off at noon to eat cold muck out of a tin bucket."

"Well, maybe some folks work like the niggers work where they come from," Mooney said. "But a nigger wouldn't last till the noon whistle, working on this job like some white folks work on it."

But Brown did not seem to hear, to be listening, squatting with his sullen face and his dangling hands. It was as though he were not listening to any save himself, listening to himself: "A fool. A man is a fool that will do it."

"You are not chained to that scoop," Mooney said.

"You durn right I aint," Brown said.

Then the whistle blew. They went back to work. They watched Brown down at the sawdust pile. He would dig for a while, then he would begin to slow, moving slower and slower until at last he would be clutching the shovel as though it were a riding whip, and they could see that he was talking to himself. "Because there aint nobody else down there for him to tell it to," one said.

"It's not that," Mooney said. "He hasn't quite convinced himself yet. He aint quite sold yet."

"Sold on what?"

"On the idea that he's a bigger fool than even I think he is," Mooney said.

The next morning he did not appear. "His address from now on will be the barbershop," one said.

"Or that alley just behind it," another said.

"I reckon we'll see him once more," Mooney said. "He'll be out here once more to draw his time for yesterday."

Which he did. About eleven o'clock he came up. He wore now the new suit and the straw hat, and he stopped at the shed and stood there looking at the working men as Christmas had done on that day three years ago, as if somehow the very attitudes of the master's dead life motivated, unawares to him, the willing muscles of the disciple who had learned too quick and too well. But Brown merely contrived to look scattered and emptily swaggering where the master had looked sullen and quiet and fatal as a snake. "Lay into it, you slaving bastards!" Brown said, in a merry, loud voice cropped with teeth.

Mooney looked at Brown. Then Brown's teeth didn't show. "You aint calling me that," Mooney said, "are you?"

Brown's mobile face performed one of those instantaneous changes which they knew. Like it was so scattered and so lightly built that it wasn't any trouble for even him to change it, Byron thought. "I wasn't talking to you," Brown said.

"Oh, I see." Mooney's tone was quite pleasant, easy. "It was these other fellows you were calling a bastard."

Immediately a second one said: "Were you calling that at me?"

"I was just talking to myself," Brown said.

"Well, you have told God's truth for once in your life," Mooney said. "The half of it, that is. Do you want me to come up there and whisper the other half in your ear?"

And that was the last they saw of him at the mill, though Byron knows and remembers now the new car (with presently a crumpled fender or two) about the town, idle, destinationless, and constant, with Brown lolling behind the wheel and not making a very good job of being dissolute and enviable and idle. Now and then Christmas would be with him, but not often. And it is now no secret what they were doing. It is a byword among young men and even boys that whiskey can be bought from Brown almost on sight, and the town is just waiting for him to get caught, to produce from his raincoat and offer to sell it to an undercover man. They still do not know for certain if Christmas is connected with it, save that no one believes that Brown alone has sense enough to make a profit even from bootlegging, and some of them know that Christmas and Brown both live in a cabin on the Burden place. But even these do not know if Miss Burden knows it or not, and if they did, they would not tell her. She lives in the big house alone, a woman of middleage. She has lived in the house since she was born, yet she is still a stranger, a foreigner whose people moved in from the North during Reconstruction. A Yankee, a lover of negroes, about whom in the town there is still talk of queer relations with negroes in the town and out of it, despite the fact that it is now sixty years since her grandfather and her brother were killed on the square by an exslaveowner over a question of negro votes in a state election. But it still lingers about her and about the place: something dark and outlandish and threatful, even though she is but a woman and but the descendant of them whom the ancestors of the town had reason (or thought that they had) to hate and dread. But it is there: the descendants of both in their relationship to one another ghosts, with between them the phantom of the old spilled blood and the old horror and anger and fear.

If there had been love once, man or woman would have said that Byron Bunch had forgotten her. Or she (meaning love) him, more like—that small man who will not see thirty again, who has spent six days of every week for seven years at the planing mill, feeding boards into the machinery. Saturday afternoons too he spends there, alone now, with the other workmen all down town in their Sunday clothes and neckties, in that terrific and aimless and restive idleness of men who labor.

On these Saturday afternoons he loads the finished boards

into freight cars, since he cannot operate the planer alone, keeping his own time to the final second of an imaginary whistle. The other workmen, the town itself or that part of it which remembers or thinks about him, believe that he does it for the overtime which he receives. Perhaps this is the reason. Man knows so little about his fellows. In his eyes all men or women act upon what he believes would motivate him if he were mad enough to do what that other man or woman is doing. In fact, there is but one man in the town who could speak with any certainty about Bunch, and with this man the town does not know that Bunch has any intercourse, since they meet and talk only at night. This man's name is Hightower. Twenty-five years ago he was minister of one of the principal churches, perhaps the principal church. This man alone knows where Bunch goes each Saturday evening when the imaginary whistle blows (or when Bunch's huge silver watch says that it has blown). Mrs. Beard, at whose boarding house Bunch lives, knows only that shortly after six o'clock each Saturday Bunch enters, bathes and changes to a suit of cheap serge which is not new, eats his supper and saddles the mule which he stables in a shed behind the house which Bunch himself patched up and roofed, and departs on the mule. She does not know where he goes. It is the minister Hightower alone who knows that Bunch rides thirty miles into the country and spends Sunday leading the choir in a country church—a service which lasts all day long. Then some time around midnight he saddles the mule again and rides back to Jefferson at a steady, allnight jog. And on Monday morning, in his clean overalls and shirt he will be on hand at the mill when the whistle blows. Mrs. Beard knows only that from Saturday's supper to Monday's breakfast each week his room and the mule's homemade stable will be vacant. Hightower alone knows where he goes and what he does there, because two or three nights a week Bunch visits Hightower in the small house where the ex-minister lives alone, in what the town calls his disgrace—the house unpainted, small, obscure, poorly lighted, man-smelling, manstale. Here the two of them sit in the minister's study, talking quietly: the slight, nondescript man who is utterly unaware that he is a man of mystery among his fellow workers, and the fifty-year-old outcast who has been denied by his church.

Then Byron fell in love. He fell in love contrary to all the tradition of his austere and jealous country raising which demands in the object physical inviolability. It happens on a Saturday afternoon while he is alone at the mill. Two miles away the house is still burning, the yellow smoke standing straight as a monument on the horizon. They saw it before noon, when the smoke first rose above the trees, before the whistle blew and the others departed. "I reckon Byron'll quit too, today," they said. "With a free fire to watch."

"It's a big fire," another said. "What can it be? I dont remember anything out that way big enough to make all that smoke except that Burden house."

"Maybe that's what it is," another said. "My pappy says he can remember how fifty years ago folks said it ought to be burned, and with a little human fat meat to start it good."

"Maybe your pappy slipped out there and set it afire," a third said. They laughed. Then they went back to work, waiting for the whistle, pausing now and then to look at the smoke. After a while a truck loaded with logs drove in.

They asked the truck driver, who had come through town.

"Burden," the driver said. "Yes. That's the name. Somebody in town said that the sheriff had gone out there too."

"Well, I reckon Watt Kennedy likes to watch a fire, even if he does have to take that badge with him," one said.

"From the way the square looks," the driver said, "he wont have much trouble finding anybody he wants out there to arrest."

The noon whistle blew. The others departed. Byron ate his lunch, the silver watch open beside him. When it said one o'clock, he went back to work. He was alone in the loading shed, making his steady and interminable journeys between the shed and the car, with a piece of folded tow sack upon his shoulder for a pad and bearing upon the pad stacked burdens of staves which another would have said he could not raise nor carry, when Lena Grove walked into the door behind him, her face already shaped with serene anticipatory smiling, her mouth already shaped upon a name. He hears her and turns and sees her face fade like the dying agitation of a dropped pebble in a spring.

"You aint him," she says behind her fading smile, with the grave astonishment of a child.

"No, ma'am," Byron says. He pauses, half turning with the balanced staves. "I dont reckon I am. Who is it I aint?"

"Lucas Burch. They told me—"

"Lucas Burch?"

"They told me I would find him out here." She speaks with a kind of serene suspicion, watching him without blinking, as if she believes that he is trying to trick her. "When I got close to town they kept a-calling it Bunch instead of Burch. But I just thought they was saying it wrong. Or maybe I just heard it wrong."

"Yes, ma'am," he says. "That's what it is: Bunch. Byron Bunch." With the staves still balanced on his shoulder he looks at her, at her swollen body, her heavy loins, at the red dust upon the man's heavy shoes upon her feet. "Are you Miz Burch?"

She does not answer at once. She stands there just inside the door, watching him intently but without alarm, with that untroubled, faintly baffled, faintly suspicious gaze. Her eyes are quite blue. But in them is that shadow of the belief that he is trying to deceive her. "They told me away back on the road that Lucas is working at the planing mill in Jefferson. Lots of them told me. And I got to Jefferson and they told me where the planing mill was, and I asked in town about Lucas Burch and they said, 'Maybe you mean Bunch'; and so I thought they had just got the name wrong and so it wouldn't make any difference. Even when they told me the man they meant wasn't dark complected. You aint telling me you dont know Lucas Burch out here."

Byron puts down the load of staves, in a neat stack, ready to be taken up again. "No, ma'am. Not out here. Not no Lucas Burch out here. And I know all the folks that work here. He may work somewhere in town. Or at another mill."

"Is there another planing mill?"

"No, ma'am. There's some sawmills, a right smart of them, though."

She watches him. "They told me back down the road that he worked for the planing mill."

"I dont know of any here by that name," Byron says. "I dont recall none named Burch except me, and my name is Bunch."

She continues to watch him with that expression not so

. 46 .

much concerned for the future as suspicious of the now. Then she breathes. It is not a sigh: she just breathes deeply and quietly once. "Well," she says. She half turns and glances about, at the sawn boards, the stacked staves. "I reckon I'll set down a while. It's right tiring, walking over them hard streets from town. It seems like walking out here from town tired me more than all that way from Alabama did." She is moving toward a low stack of planks.

"Wait," Byron says. He almost springs forward, slipping the sack pad from his shoulder. The woman arrests herself in the act of sitting and Byron spreads the sack on the planks. "You'll set easier."

"Why, you're right kind." She sits down.

"I reckon it'll set a little easier," Byron says. He takes from his pocket the silver watch and looks at it; then he too sits, at the other end of the stack of lumber. "I reckon five minutes will be about right."

"Five minutes to rest?" she says.

"Five minutes from when you come in. It looks like I done already started resting. I keep my own time on Saturday evenings," he says.

"And every time you stop for a minute, you keep a count of it? How will they know you stopped? A few minutes wouldn't make no difference, would it?"

"I reckon I aint paid for setting down," he says. "So you come from Alabama."

She tells him, in his turn, sitting on the towsack pad, heavybodied, her face quiet and tranquil, and he watching her as quietly; telling him more than she knows that she is telling, as she has been doing now to the strange faces among whom she has travelled for four weeks with the untroubled unhaste of a change of season. And Byron in his turn gets the picture of a young woman betrayed and deserted and not even aware that she has been deserted, and whose name is not yet Burch.

"No, I dont reckon I know him," he says at last. "There aint anybody but me out here this evening, anyway. The rest of them are all out yonder at that fire, more than like." He shows her the yellow pillar of smoke standing tall and windless above the trees.

"We could see it from the wagon before we got to town," she says. "It's a right big fire."

"It's a right big old house. It's been there a long time. Dont nobody live in it but one lady, by herself. I reckon there are folks in this town will call it a judgment on her, even now. She is a Yankee. Her folks come down here in the Reconstruction, to stir up the niggers. Two of them got killed doing it. They say she is still mixed up with niggers. Visits them when they are sick, like they was white. Wont have a cook because it would have to be a nigger cook. Folks say she claims that niggers are the same as white folks. That's why folks dont never go out there. Except one." She is watching him, listening. Now he does not look at her, looking a little aside. "Or maybe two, from what I hear. I hope they was out there in time to help her move her furniture out. Maybe they was."

"Maybe who was?"

"Two fellows named Joe that live out that way somewhere. Joe Christmas and Joe Brown."

"Joe Christmas? That's a funny name."

"He's a funny fellow." Again he looks a little aside from her interested face. "His partner's a sight, too. Brown. He used to work here too. But they done quit now, both of them. Which aint nobody's loss, I reckon."

· 48 ·

The woman sits on the towsack pad, interested, tranquil. The two of them might be sitting in their Sunday clothes, in splint chairs on the patinasmooth earth before a country cabin on a sabbath afternoon. "Is his partner named Joe too?"

"Yes, ma'am. Joe Brown. But I reckon that may be his right name. Because when you think of a fellow named Joe Brown, you think of a bigmouthed fellow that's always laughing and talking loud. And so I reckon that is his right name, even if Joe Brown does seem a little kind of too quick and too easy for a natural name, somehow. But I reckon it is his, all right. Because if he drew time on his mouth, he would be owning this here mill right this minute. Folks seem to like him, though. Him and Christmas get along, anyway."

She is watching him. Her face is still serene, but now it is quite grave, her eyes quite grave and quite intent. "What do him and the other one do?"

"Nothing they hadn't ought to, I reckon. At least, they aint been caught at it yet. Brown used to work here, some; what time he had off from laughing and playing jokes on folks. But Christmas has retired. They live out yonder together, out there somewhere where that house is burning. And I have heard what they do to make a living. But that aint none of my business in the first place. And in the second place, most of what folks tells on other folks aint true to begin with. And so I reckon I aint no better than nobody else."

She is watching him. She is not even blinking. "And he says his name is Brown." It might have been a question, but she does not wait for an answer. "What kind of tales have you heard about what they do?"

"I would injure no man," Byron says. "I reckon I ought not to talked so much. For a fact, it looks like a fellow is bound to get into mischief soon as he quits working."

"What kind of tales?" she says. She has not moved. Her tone is quiet, but Byron is already in love, though he does not yet know it. He does not look at her, feeling her grave, intent gaze upon his face, his mouth.

"Some claim they are selling whiskey. Keeping it hid out there where that house is burning. And there is some tale about Brown was drunk down town one Saturday night and he pretty near told something that ought not to been told, about him and Christmas in Memphis one night, or on a dark road close to Memphis, that had a pistol in it. Maybe two pistols. Because Christmas come in quick and shut Brown up and took him away. Something that Christmas didn't want told, anyway, and that even Brown would have had better sense than to told if he hadn't been drunk. That's what I heard. I wasn't there, myself." When he raises his face now he finds that he has looked down again before he even met her eyes. He seems to have already a foreknowledge of something now irrevocable, not to be recalled, who had believed that out here at the mill alone on Saturday afternoon he would be where the chance to do hurt or harm could not have found him.

"What does he look like?" she says.

"Christmas? Why—"

"I don't mean Christmas."

"Oh. Brown. Yes. Tall, young. Dark complected; women-folks calls him handsome, a right smart do, I hear tell. A big hand for laughing and frolicking and playing jokes on folks. But I . . ." His voice ceases. He cannot look at her, feeling her steady, sober gaze upon his face.

"Joe Brown," she says. "Has he got a little white scar right here by his mouth?"

And he cannot look at her, and he sits there on the stacked lumber when it is too late, and he could have bitten his tongue in two.

. 3 .

FROM his study window he can see the street. It is not far away, since the lawn is not deep. It is a small lawn, containing a half dozen lowgrowing maples. The house, the brown, unpainted and unobtrusive bungalow is small too and by bushing crape myrtle and syringa and Althea almost hidden save for that gap through which from the study window he watches the street. So hidden it is that the light from the corner street lamp scarcely touches it.

From the window he can also see the sign, which he calls his monument. It is planted in the corner of the yard, low, facing the street. It is three feet long and eighteen inches high—a neat oblong presenting its face to who passes and its back to him. But he does not need to read it because he made the sign with hammer and saw, neatly, and he painted the legend which it bears, neatly too, tediously, when he realised that he would have to begin to have to have money for bread and fire and clothing. When he quitted the seminary he had a small income inherited from his father, which, as soon as he got his church, he forwarded promptly on receipt of the quarterly checks to an institution for delinquent girls in Memphis. Then he lost his church, he lost the Church, and the bitterest thing which he believed that he had ever faced—more bitter even than the bereavement and the shame—was the letter which he wrote them to say that from now on he could send them but half the sum which he had previously sent.

So he continued to send them half of a revenue which in its entirety would little more than have kept him. "Luckily there are things which I can do," he said at the time. Hence the sign, carpentered neatly by himself and by himself lettered, with bits of broken glass contrived cunningly into the paint, so that at night, when the corner street lamp shone upon it, the letters glittered with an effect as of Christmas:

REV. GAIL HIGHTOWER, D.D.

Art Lessons
Handpainted Xmas & Anniversary Cards
Photographs Developed

But that was years ago, and he had had no art pupils and few enough Christmas cards and photograph plates, and the paint and the shattered glass had weathered out of the fading letters. They were still readable, however; though, like Hightower himself, few of the townspeople needed to read them anymore. But now and then a negro nursemaid with her white charges would loiter there and spell them aloud with that vacuous idiocy of her idle and illiterate kind, or a stranger happening along the quiet and remote and unpaved and littleused street would pause and read the sign and then look up at the small, brown, almost concealed house, and pass on; now and then the stranger would mention the sign to some acquaintance in the town.

"Oh, yes," the friend would say. "Hightower. He lives there by himself. He come here as minister of the Presbyterian church, but his wife went bad on him. She would slip off to Memphis now and then and have a good time. About twenty-five years ago, that was, right after he come here. Some folks claimed he knew about it. That he couldn't or wouldn't satisfy her himself and that he knew what she was doing. Then one Saturday night she got killed, in a house or something in Memphis. Papers full of it. He had to resign from the church, but he wouldn't leave Jefferson, for some reason. They tried to get him to, for his own sake as well as the town's, the church's. That was pretty bad on the church, you see. Having strangers come here and hear about it, and him refusing to leave the town. But he wouldn't go away. He has lived out there on what used to be the main street ever since, by himself. At least it aint a principal street anymore. That's something. But then he dont worry anybody anymore, and I reckon most folks have forgot about him. Does his own housework. I dont reckon anybody's even been inside that house in twenty-five years. We dont know why he stays here. But any day you pass along there about dusk or nightfall, you can see him sitting in the window. Just sitting there. The rest of the time folks wont hardly see him around the place at all, except now and then working in his garden."

So the sign which he carpentered and lettered is even less to him than it is to the town; he is no longer conscious of it as a sign, a message. He does not remember it at all until he takes his place in the study window just before dusk. Then it is just a familiar low oblong shape without any significance at all, low at the street end of the shallow lawn; it too might have grown up out of the tragic and inescapable earth along with the low spreading maples and the shrubs, without help or hindrance from him. He no longer even looks at it, as he does not actually see the trees beneath and through which he watches the street, waiting for nightfall, the moment of night. The house, the study, is dark behind him, and he is waiting for that instant when all light has failed out of the sky and it would be night save for that faint light which daygranaried leaf and grass blade reluctant suspire, making still a little light on earth though night itself has come. *Now, soon,* he thinks; *soon, now* He does not say even to himself: "There remains yet something of honor and pride, of life."

When Byron Bunch first came to Jefferson seven years ago and saw that little sign *Gail Hightower D.D. Art Lessons Christmas Cards Photographs Developed* he thought, 'D.D. What is D.D.,' and he asked and they told him it meant Done Damned. Gail Hightower Done Damned in Jefferson anyway, they told him. And how Hightower had come straight to Jefferson from the seminary, refusing to accept any other call; how he had pulled every string he could in order to be sent to Jefferson. And how he arrived with his young wife, descending from the train in a state of excitement already, talking, telling the old men and women who were the pillars of the church how he had set his mind on Jefferson from the first, since he had first decided to become a minister; telling them with a kind of glee of the letters he had written and the worrying he had done and the influence he had used in order to be called here. To the people of the town it sounded like a horse-trader's glee over an advantageous trade. Perhaps that is how it sounded to the elders. Because they listened to him with something cold and astonished and dubious, since he sounded like it was the town he desired to live in and not the church and the people who composed the church, that he wanted to serve. As if he did not care about the people, the living people, about whether they wanted him here or not. And he being young too, and the old men and the old women trying to talk down his gleeful excitement with serious matters of the church and its responsibilities and his own. And they told Byron how the young minister was still excited even after six months, still talking about the Civil War and his grandfather, a cavalryman, who was killed, and about General Grant's stores burning in Jefferson until it did not make sense at all. They told Byron how he seemed to talk that way in the pulpit too, wild too in the pulpit, using religion as though it were a dream. Not a nightmare, but something which went faster than the words in the Book; a sort of cyclone that did not even need to touch the actual earth. And the old men and women did not like that, either.

It was as if he couldn't get religion and that galloping cavalry and his dead grandfather shot from the galloping horse untangled from each other, even in the pulpit. And that he could not untangle them in his private life, at home either, perhaps. Perhaps he did not even try to at home, Byron thought, thinking how that is the sort of thing that men do to the women who belong to them; thinking that that is why women have to be strong and should not be held blameable for what they do with or for or because of men, since God knew that being anybody's wife was a tricky enough business. They told him how the wife was a small, quietlooking girl who at first the town thought just had nothing to say for herself. But the town said that if

Hightower had just been a more dependable kind of man, the kind of man a minister should be instead of being born about thirty years after the only day he seemed to have ever lived in—that day when his grandfather was shot from the galloping horse—she would have been all right too. But he was not, and the neighbors would hear her weeping in the parsonage in the afternoons or late at night, and the neighbors knowing that the husband would not know what to do about it because he did not know what was wrong. And how sometimes she would not even come to the church, where her own husband was preaching, even on Sunday, and they would look at him and wonder if he even knew that she was not there, if he had not even forgot that he ever had a wife, up there in the pulpit with his hands flying around him and the dogma he was supposed to preach all full of galloping cavalry and defeat and glory just as when he tried to tell them on the street about the galloping horses, it in turn would get all mixed up with absolution and choirs of martial seraphim, until it was natural that the old men and women should believe that what he preached in God's own house on God's own day verged on actual sacrilege.

And they told Byron how after about a year in Jefferson, the wife began to wear that frozen look on her face, and when the church ladies would go to call Hightower would meet them alone, in his shirt sleeves and without any collar, in a flurry, and for a time it would seem as though he could not even think what they had come for and what he ought to do. Then he would invite them in and excuse himself and go out. And they would not hear a sound anywhere in the house, sitting there in their Sunday dresses, looking at one another and about the room, listening and not hearing a sound. And then he would come back with his coat and collar on and sit and talk with them about the church and the sick, and they talking back, bright and quiet, still listening and maybe watching the door, maybe wondering if he knew what they believed that they already knew.

The ladies quit going there. Soon they did not even see the minister's wife on the street. And he still acting like there was nothing wrong. And then she would be gone for a day or two; they would see her get on the early train, with her face beginning to get thin and gaunted as though she never ate enough and that frozen look on it as if she were not seeing what she was looking at. And he would tell that she had gone to visit her people downstate somewhere, until one day, during one of her absences, a Jefferson woman shopping in Memphis saw her walking fast into a hotel there. It was one Saturday that the woman returned home and told it. But the next day Hightower was in the pulpit, with religion and the galloping cavalry all mixed up again, and the wife returned Monday and the following Sunday she came to church again, for the first time in six or seven months, sitting by herself at the rear of the church. She came every Sunday after that for a while. Then she was gone again, in the middle of the week this time (it was in July and hot) and Hightower said that she had gone to see her folks again, in the country where it would be cool; and the old men, the elders, and the old women watching him, not knowing if he believed what he was telling or not, and the young people talking behind his back.

But they could not tell whether he himself believed or not what he told them, if he cared or not, with his religion and his grandfather being shot from the galloping horse all mixed up, as though the seed which his grandfather had transmitted to him had been on the horse too that night and had been killed too and time had stopped there and then for the seed and nothing had happened in time since, not even him.

The wife returned before Sunday. It was hot; the old people said that it was the hottest spell which the town had ever known. She came to church that Sunday and took her seat on a bench at the back, alone. In the middle of the sermon she sprang from the bench and began to scream, to shriek something toward the pulpit, shaking her hands toward the pulpit where her husband had ceased talking, leaning forward with his hands raised and stopped. Some people nearby tried to hold her but she fought them, and they told Byron how she stood there, in the aisle now, shrieking and shaking her hands at the pulpit where her husband leaned with his hand still raised and his wild face frozen in the shape of the thundering and allegorical period which he had not completed. They did not know whether she was shaking her hands at him or at God. Then he came down and approached and she stopped fighting then and he led her out, with the heads turning as they passed, until the superintendent told the organist to play. That afternoon the elders held a meeting behind locked doors. The people did not know what went on behind them, save that Hightower returned and entered the vestry room and closed the door behind him too.

But the people did not know what had happened. They only knew that the church made up a sum to send the wife to an institution, a sanatorium, and that Hightower took her there and came back and preached the next Sunday, as usual. The women, the neighbors, some of whom had not entered the parsonage in months, were kind to him, taking him dishes now and then, telling one another and their husbands what a mess the parsonage was in, and how the minister seemed to eat like an animal—just when he got hungry and just whatever he could find. Every two weeks he would go and visit his wife in the sanatorium, but he always returned after a day or so; and on Sunday, in the pulpit again, it was as though the whole thing had never happened. The people would ask about her health, curious and kind, and he would thank them. Then Sunday he would be again in the pulpit, with his wild hands and his wild rapt eager voice in which like phantoms God and salvation and the galloping horses and his dead grandfather thundered, while below him the elders sat, and the congregation, puzzled and outraged. In the fall the wife came home. She looked better. She had put on a little flesh. She had changed more than that, even. Perhaps it was that she seemed chastened now; awake, anyway. Anyhow she was now like the ladies had wanted her to be all the time, as they believed that the minister's wife should be. She attended church and prayer meeting regularly, and the ladies called upon her and she called upon them, sitting quiet and humble, even in her own house, while they told her how to run it and what to wear and what to make her husband eat.

It might even be said that they forgave her. No crime or transgression had been actually named and no penance had been actually set. But the town did not believe that the ladies had forgot those previous mysterious trips, with Memphis as their destination and for that purpose regarding which all had the same conviction, though none ever put it into words, spoke it aloud, since the town believed that good women dont forget things easily, good or bad, lest the taste and savor of forgiveness die from the palate of conscience. Because the town believed that the ladies knew the truth, since it believed that bad women can be fooled by badness, since they have to spend some of their time not being suspicious. But that no good woman can be fooled by it because, by being good herself, she does not need to worry anymore about hers or anybody else's goodness; hence she has plenty of time to smell out sin. That was why, they believed, that good can fool her almost any time into believing that it is evil, but that evil itself can never fool her. So when after four or five months the wife went away again on a visit and the husband said again that she had gone to visit her people, the town believed that this time even he was not fooled. Anyway, she came back and he went on preaching every Sunday like nothing had happened, making his calls on the people and the sick and talking about the church. But the wife did not come to church anymore, and soon the ladies stopped calling on her, going to the parsonage at all. And even the neighbors on either side would no longer see her about the house. And soon it was as though she were not there; as though everyone had agreed that she was not there, that the minister did not even have a wife. And he preaching to them every Sunday, not even telling them now that she had gone to visit her people. Maybe he was glad of that, the town thought. Maybe he was glad to not have to lie anymore.

So nobody saw her when she got on the train that Friday, or maybe it was Saturday, the day itself. It was Sunday morning's paper which they saw, telling how she had jumped or fallen from a hotel window in Memphis Saturday night, and was dead. There had been a man in the room with her. He was arrested. He was drunk. They were registered as man and wife, under a fictitious name. The police found her rightful name where she had written it herself on a piece of paper and then torn it up and thrown it into the waste basket. The papers printed it, with the story: wife of the Reverend Gail Hightower, of Jefferson, Mississippi. And the story told how the paper telephoned to the husband at two A.M. and how the husband said that he had nothing to say. And when they reached the church that Sunday morning the yard was full of Memphis reporters taking pictures of the church and the parsonage. Then Hightower came. The reporters tried to stop him but he walked right through them and into the church and up into the pulpit. The old ladies and some of the old men were already in the church, horrified and outraged, not so much about the Memphis business as about the presence of the reporters. But when Hightower came in and actually went up into the pulpit, they forgot about the reporters even. The ladies got up first and began to leave. Then the men got up too, and then the church was empty save for the minister in the pulpit, leaning a little forward, with the Book open and his hands propped on either side of it and his head not bowed either, and the Memphis reporters (they had followed him into the church) sitting in a line in the rear pew. They said he was not watching his congregation leaving; he was not looking at anything.

They told Byron about it; about how at last the minister closed the Book, carefully, and came down into the empty church and walked up the aisle without once looking at the row of reporters, like the congregation had done, and went out the door. There were some photographers waiting out in front, with the cameras all set up and their heads under the black cloths. The minister had evidently expected this. Because he emerged from the church with an open hymn book held before his face. But the cameramen had evidently expected that too. Because they fooled him. Very likely he was not used to it and so was easily fooled, they told Byron. One of the cameramen had his machine set up to one side, and the minister did not see that one at all, or until too late. He was keeping his face concealed from the one in front, and next day when the picture came out in the paper it had been taken from the side, with the minister in the middle of a step, holding the hymn book before his face. And behind the book his lips were drawn back as though he were smiling. But his teeth were tight together and his face looked like the face of Satan in the old prints. The next day he brought his wife home and buried her. The town came to the ceremony. It was not a funeral. He did not take the body to the church at all. He took it straight to the cemetery and he was preparing to read from the Book himself when another minister came forward and took it from his hand. A lot of the people, the younger ones, remained after he and the others had gone, looking at the grave.

Then even the members of the other churches knew that his own had asked him to resign, and that he refused. The next Sunday a lot of them from the other churches came to his church to see what would happen. He came and entered the church. The congregation as one rose and walked out, leaving the minister and those from the other churches who had come as though to a show. So he preached to them, as he had always preached: with that rapt fury which they had considered sacrilege and which those from the other churches believed to be out and out insanity.

He would not resign. The elders asked the church board to recall him. But after the story, the pictures in the papers and all, no other town would have him either. There was nothing against him personally, they all insisted. He was just unlucky. He was just born unlucky. So the people quit coming to the church at all, even the ones from the other churches who had come out of curiosity for a time: he was no longer even a show now; he was now only an outrage. But he would reach the church at the old hour each Sunday morning and go to the pulpit, and the congregation would rise and leave, and the loafers and such would gather along the street outside and listen to him preaching and praying in the empty church. And the Sunday after that when he arrived the door was locked, and the loafers watched him try the door and then desist and stand there with his face still not bowed, with the street lined with men who never went to church anyway, and little boys who did not know exactly what it was but that it was something, stopping and looking with still round eyes at the man standing quite motionless before the locked door. The next day the town heard how he had gone to the elders and resigned his pulpit for the good of the church.

Then the town was sorry with being glad, as people sometimes are sorry for those whom they have at last forced to do as they wanted them to. They thought of course that he would go away now, and the church made up a collection for him to go away on and settle somewhere else. Then he refused to leave the town. They told Byron of the consternation, the more than outrage, when they learned that he had bought the little house on the back street where he now lives and has lived ever since; and the elders held another meeting because they said that they had given him the money to go away on, and when he spent it for something else he had accepted the money under false pretences. They went to him and told him so. He asked them to excuse him; he returned to the room with the sum which had been given him, to the exact penny and in the exact denominations, and insisted that they take it back. But they refused, and he would not tell where he had got the money to buy the house with. So by the next day, they told Byron, there were some who said that he had insured his wife's life and then paid someone to murder her. But everyone knew that this was not so, including the ones who told and repeated it and the ones who listened when it was told.

But he would not leave the town. Then one day they saw the little sign which he had made and painted himself and set in his front yard, and they knew that he meant to stay. He still kept the cook, a negro woman. He had had her all the time. But they told Byron how as soon as his wife was dead, the people seemed to realise all at once that the negro was a woman, that he had that negro woman in the house alone with him all day. And how the wife was hardly cold in the shameful grave before the whispering began. About how he had made his wife go bad and commit suicide because he was not a natural husband, a natural man, and that the negro woman was the reason. And that's all it took; all that was lacking. Byron listened quietly, thinking to himself how people everywhere are about the same, but that it did seem that in a small town, where evil is harder to accomplish, where opportunities for privacy are scarcer, that people can invent more of it in other people's names. Because that was all it required: that idea, that single idle word blown from mind to mind. One day the cook quit. They heard how one night a party of carelessly masked men went to the minister's house and ordered him to fire her. Then they heard how the next day the woman told that she quit herself because her employer asked her to do something which she said was against God and nature. And it was said that some masked men had scared her into quitting because she was what is known as a high brown and it was known that there were two or three men in the town who would object to her doing whatever it was which she considered contrary to God and nature, since, as some of the younger men said, if a nigger woman considered it against God and nature, it must be pretty bad. Anyway, the minister couldn't—or didn't—get another woman cook. Possibly the men scared all the other negro women in town that same night. So he did his own cooking for a while, until they heard one day that he had a negro man to cook for him. And that finished him, sure enough. Because that evening some men, not masked either, took the negro man out and whipped him. And when Hightower waked the next morning his study window was broken and on the floor lay a brick with a note tied to it, commanding him to get out of town by sunset and signed K.K.K. And he did not go, and on the second morning a man found him in the woods about a mile from town. He had been tied to a tree and beaten unconscious.

He refused to tell who had done it. The town knew that that was wrong, and some of the men came to him and tried again to persuade him to leave Jefferson, for his own good, telling him that next time they might kill him. But he refused to leave. He would not even talk about the beating, even when they offered to prosecute the men who had done it. But he would do neither. He would neither tell, nor depart. Then all of a sudden the whole thing seemed to blow away, like an evil wind. It was as though the town realised at last that he would be a part of its life until he died, and that they might as well become reconciled. As though, Byron thought, the entire affair had been a lot of people performing a play and that now and at last they had all played out the parts which had been allotted them and now they could live quietly with one another. They let the minister alone. They would see him working in the yard or the garden, and on the street and in the stores with a small basket on his arm, and they would speak to him. They knew that he did his own cooking and housework, and after a while the neighbors began to send him dishes again, though they were the sort of dishes which they would have sent to a poor mill family. But it was food, and wellmeant. Because, as Byron thought, people forget a lot in twenty years. 'Why,' he thinks, 'I dont reckon there is anybody in Jefferson that knows that he sits in that window from sundown to full dark every day that comes, except me. Or what the inside of that house looks like. And they dont even know that I know, or likely they'd take us both out and whip us again, since folks dont seem to forget much longer than they remember.' Because there is one other thing, which came into Byron's own knowledge and observation, in his own time since he came to Jefferson to live.

Hightower read a great deal. That is, Byron had examined with a kind of musing and respectful consternation the books which lined the study walls: books of religion and history and science of whose very existence

Byron had never heard. One day about four years ago a negro man came running up to the minister's house from his cabin on the edge of town immediately behind it, and said that his wife was at childbed. Hightower had no telephone and he told the negro to run next door and call a doctor. He watched the negro go to the gate of the next house. But instead of entering, the negro stood there for a time and then went on up the street toward town, walking; Hightower knew that the man would walk all the way to town and then spend probably thirty minutes more getting in touch with a doctor, in his fumbling and timeless negro fashion, instead of asking some white woman to telephone for him. Then he went to his kitchen door and he could hear the woman in the not so distant cabin, wailing. He waited no longer. He ran down to the cabin and found that the woman had got out of bed, for what reason he never learned, and she was now on her hands and knees on the floor, trying to get back into the bed, screaming and wailing. He got her back into the bed and told her to lie still, frightened her into obeying him, and ran back to his house and took one of the books from the study shelf and got his razor and some cord and ran back to the cabin and delivered the child. But it was already dead; the doctor when arrived said that she had doubtless injured it when she left the bed where Hightower found her. He also approved of Hightower's work, and the husband was satisfied too.

'But it was just too close to that other business,' Byron thought, 'even despite the fifteen years between them.' Because within two days there were those who said that the child was Hightower's and that he had let it die deliberately. But Byron believed that even the ones who said this did not believe it. He believed that the town had had the habit of saying things about the disgraced minister which they did not believe themselves for too long a time to break themselves of it. 'Because always,' he thinks, 'when anything gets to be a habit, it also manages to get a right good distance away from truth and fact.' And he remembers one evening when he and Hightower were talking together and Hightower said: "They are good people. They must believe what they must believe, especially as it was I who was at one time both master and servant of their believing. And so it is not for me to outrage their believing nor for Byron Bunch to say that they are wrong. Because all that any man can hope for is to be permitted to live quietly among his fellows." That was soon after Byron had heard the story, shortly after the evening visits to Hightower's study began and Byron still wondered why the other remained in Jefferson, almost within sight of, and within hearing of, the church which had disowned and expelled him. One evening Byron asked him.

"Why do you spend your Saturday afternoons working at the mill while other men are taking pleasure down town?" Hightower said.

"I dont know," Byron said. "I reckon that's just my life."

"And I reckon this is just my life, too," the other said. 'But I know now why it is,' Byron thinks. 'It is because a fellow is more afraid of the trouble he might have than he ever is of the trouble he's already got. He'll cling to trouble he's used to before he'll risk a change. Yes. A man will talk about how he'd like to escape from living folks. But it's the dead folks that do him the damage. It's the dead ones that lay quiet in one place and dont try to hold him, that he cant escape from.'

They have thundered past now and crashed silently on into the dusk; night has fully come. Yet he still sits at the study window, the room still dark behind him. The street lamp at the corner flickers and glares, so that the bitten shadows of the unwinded maples seem to toss faintly upon the August darkness. From a distance, quite faint though quite clear, he can hear the sonorous waves of massed voices from the church: a sound at once austere and rich, abject and proud, swelling and falling in the quiet summer darkness like a harmonic tide.

Then he sees a man approaching along the street. On a week night he would have recognised the figure, the shape, the carriage and gait. But on Sunday evening, and with the echo of the phantom hooves still crashing soundlessly in the duskfilled study, he watches quietly the puny, unhorsed figure moving with that precarious and meretricious cleverness of animals balanced on their hinder legs; that cleverness of which the man animal is so fatuously proud and which constantly betrays him by means of natural laws like gravity and ice, and by the very extraneous objects which he has himself invented, like motor cars and furniture in the dark, and the very refuse of his own eating left upon floor or pavement; and he thinks quietly how right the ancients were in making the horse an attribute and symbol of warriors and kings, when he sees the man in the street pass the low sign and turn into his gate and approach the house. He sits forward then, watching the man come up the dark walk toward the dark door; he hears the man stumble heavily at the dark bottom step. "Byron Bunch," he says. "In town on Sunday night. Byron Bunch in town on Sunday."

. 4 .

THEY sit facing one another across the desk. The study is lighted now, by a greenshaded reading lamp sitting upon the desk. Hightower sits behind it, in an ancient swivel chair, Byron in a straight chair opposite. Both their faces are just without the direct downward pool of light from the shaded lamp. Through the open window the sound of singing from the distant church comes. Byron talks in a flat, level voice.

"It was a strange thing. I thought that if there ever was a place where a man would be where the chance to do harm could not have found him, it would have been out there at the mill on a Saturday evening. And with the house burning too, right in my face, you might say. It was like all the time I was eating dinner and I would look up now and then and see that smoke and I would think, 'Well, I wont see a soul out here this evening, anyway. I aint going to be interrupted this evening, at least.' And then I looked up and there she was, with her face all fixed for smiling and with her mouth all fixed to say his name, when she saw that I wasn't him. And I never knowed any better than to blab the whole thing." He grimaces faintly. It is not a smile. His upper lip just lifts momentarily, the movement, even the surface wrinkling, travelling no further and vanishing almost at once. "I never even suspicioned then that what I didn't know was not the worst of it."

"It must have been a strange thing that could keep Byron Bunch in Jefferson over Sunday," Hightower says. "But she was looking for him. And you helped her to find him. Wasn't what you did what she wanted, what she had come all the way from Alabama to find?"

"I reckon I told her, all right. I reckon it aint any question about that. With her watching me, sitting there, swolebellied, watching me with them eyes that a man could not have lied to if he had wanted. And me blabbing on, with that smoke right yonder in plain sight like it was put there to warn me, to make me watch my mouth only I never had the sense to see it."

"Oh," Hightower says. "The house that burned yesterday. But I dont see any connection between— Whose house was it? I saw the smoke, myself, and I asked a passing negro, but he didn't know."

"That old Burden house," Byron says. He looks at the other. They look at one another. Hightower is a tall man, and he was thin once. But he is not thin now. His skin is the color of flour sacking and his upper body in shape is like a loosely filled sack falling from his gaunt shoulders of its own weight, upon his lap. Then Byron says, "You aint heard yet." The other watches him. He says in a musing tone: "That would be for me to do too. To tell on two days to two folks something they aint going to want to hear and that they hadn't ought to have to hear at all."

"What is this that you think I will not want to hear? What is it that I have not heard?"

"Not the fire," Byron says. "They got out of the fire all right."

"They? I understood that Miss Burden lived there alone."

Again Byron looks at the other for a moment. But Hightower's face is merely grave and interested. "Brown and Christmas," Byron says. Still Hightower's face does not change in expression. "You aint heard that, even," Byron says. "They lived out there."

"Lived out there? They boarded in the house?"

"No. In a old nigger cabin in the back. Christmas fixed it up three years ago. He's been living in it ever since, with folks wondering where he slept at night. Then when him and Brown set up together, he took Brown in with him."

"Oh," Hightower said. "But I dont see . . . If they were comfortable, and Miss Burden didn't—"

"I reckon they got along. They were selling whiskey, using that old place for a headquarters, a blind. I dont reckon she knew that, about the whiskey. Leastways, folks dont know if she ever knew or not. They say that Christmas started it by himself three years ago, just selling to a few regular customers that didn't even know one another. But when he took Brown in with him, I reckon Brown wanted to spread out. Selling it by the half a pint out of his shirt bosom in any alley and to anybody. Selling what he never drunk, that is. And I reckon the way they got the whiskey they sold would not have stood much looking into. Because about two weeks after Brown quit out at the mill and taken to riding around in that new car for his steady work, he was down town drunk one Saturday night and bragging to a crowd in the barbershop something about him and Christmas in Memphis one night, or on a road close to Memphis. Something about them and that new car hid in the bushes and Christmas with a pistol, and a lot more about a truck and a hundred gallons of something, until Christmas come in quick and walked up to him and jerked him out of the chair. And Christmas saying in that quiet voice of his, that aint pleasant and aint mad either: 'You ought to be careful about drinking so much of this Jefferson hair tonic. It's gone to your head. First thing you know you'll have a hairlip.' Holding Brown up he was with one hand and slapping his face with the other. They didn't look like hard licks. But the folks could see the red even through Brown's whiskers when Christmas' hand would come away between licks. 'You come out and get some fresh air,' Christmas says. 'You're keeping these folks from working.'" He muses. He speaks again: "And there she was, sitting there on them staves, watching me and me blabbing the whole thing to her, and her watching me. And then she says, 'Did he have a little white scar right here by his mouth?'"

"And Brown is the man," Hightower says. He sits motionless, watching Byron with a sort of quiet astonishment. There is nothing militant in it, nothing of outraged morality. It is as though he were listening to the doings of people of a different race. "Her husband a bootlegger. Well, well, well." Yet Byron can see in the other's face something latent, about to wake, of which Hightower himself is unaware, as if something inside the man were trying to warn or prepare him. But Byron thinks that this is just the reflection of what he himself already knows and is about to tell.

"And so I had already told her before I knew it. And I could have bit my tongue in two, even then, even when I thought that that was all." He is not looking at the other now. Through the window, faint yet clear, the blended organ and voices come from the distant church, across the still evening. *I wonder if he hears it too* Byron thinks *Or maybe he has listened to it so much and so long that he dont even hear it anymore. Dont even need to not listen* "And she set there all the evening while I worked, and the smoke dying away at last, and me trying to think what to tell her and what to do. She wanted to go right on out there, for me to tell her the way. When I told her it was two miles she just kind of smiled, like I was a child or something. 'I done come all the way from Alabama,' she said. 'I reckon I aint going to worry about two miles more.' And then I told her . . ." His voice ceases. He appears to contemplate the floor at his feet. He looks up. "I lied, I reckon. Only in a way it was not a lie. It was because I knowed there would be folks out there watching the fire, and her coming up, trying to find him. I didn't know myself, then, the other. The rest of it. The worst of it. So I told her that he was busy at a job he had, and that the best time to find him would be down town after six o'clock. And that was the truth. Because I reckon he does call it work, carrying all them cold little bottles nekkid against his chest, and if he ever was away from the square it was just because he was a little behind in getting back or had just stepped into a alley for a minute. So I persuaded her to wait and she set there and I went on working, trying to decide what to do. When I think now how worried I was on what little I knowed, now when I know the rest of it, it dont seem like I had anything then to worry me at all. All day I have been thinking how easy it would be if I could just turn back to yesterday and not have any more to worry me than I had then."

"I still cannot see what you have to worry about," Hightower says. "It is not your fault that the man is what he is or she what she is. You did what you could. All that any stranger could be expected to do. Unless . . ." His voice ceases also. Then it dies away on that inflection, as if idle thinking had become speculation and then something like concern. Opposite him Byron sits without moving, his face lowered and grave. And opposite Byron, Hightower does not yet think *love*. He remembers only that Byron is still young and has led a life of celibacy and hard labor, and that by Byron's telling the woman whom he has never seen possesses some disturbing quality at least, even though Byron still believes that it is only pity. So he watches Byron now with a certain narrowness neither cold nor warm, while Byron continues in that flat voice: about how at six o'clock he had still decided on nothing; that when he and Lena reached the square he was still undecided. And now there begins to come into Hightower's puzzled expression a quality of shrinking and foreboding as Byron talks quietly, telling about how he decided after they reached the square to take Lena on to Mrs Beard's. And Byron talking quietly, thinking, remembering: It was like something gone through the air, the evening, making the familiar faces of men appear strange, and he, who had not yet heard, without having to know that something had happened which made of the former dilemma of his innocence a matter for children, so that he knew before he knew what had happened, that Lena must not hear about it. He did not even have to be told in words that he had surely found the lost Lucas Burch; it seemed to him now that only the crassest fatuousness and imbecility should have kept him unaware. It seemed to him that fate, circumstance, had set a warning in the sky all day long in that pillar of yellow smoke, and he too stupid to read it. And so he would not let them tell—the men whom they passed, the air that blew upon them full of it—lest she hear too. Perhaps he knew at the time that she would have to know, hear, it sooner or later; that in a way it was her right to know. It just seemed to him that if he could only get her across the square and into a house his responsibility would be discharged. Not responsibility for the evil to which he held himself for no other reason than that of having spent the afternoon with her while it was happening, having been chosen by circumstance to represent Jefferson to her who had come afoot and without money for thirty days in order to reach there. He did not hope nor intend to avoid that responsibility. It was just to give himself and her time to be shocked and surprised. He tells it quietly, fumbling, his face lowered, in his flat, inflectionless voice, while across the desk Hightower watches him with that expression of shrinking and denial.

They reached the boarding house at last and entered it. It was as though she felt foreboding too, watching him as they stood in the hall, speaking for the first time: "What is it them men were trying to tell you? What is it about that burned house?"

"It wasn't anything," he said, his voice sounding dry and light to him. "Just something about Miss Burden got hurt in the fire."

"How got hurt? How bad hurt?"

"I reckon not bad. Maybe not hurt at all. Just folks talking, like as not. Like they will." He could not look at her, meet her eyes at all. But he could feel her watching him, and he seemed to hear a myriad sounds: voices, the hushed tense voices about the town, about the square through which he had hurried her, where men met among the safe and familiar lights, telling it. The house too seemed filled with familiar sounds, but mostly with inertia, a terrible procrastination as he gazed down the dim hall, thinking *Why dont she come on. Why dont she come on* Then Mrs Beard did come: a comfortable woman, with red arms and untidy grayish hair. "This here is Miz Burch," he said. His expression was almost a glare: importunate, urgent. "She just got to town from Alabama. She is looking to meet her husband here. He aint come yet. So I brought her here, where she can rest some before she gets mixed up in the excitement of town. She aint been in town or talked to anybody yet, and so I thought maybe you could fix her up a place to get rested some before she has to hear talking and . . ." His voice ceased, died, recapitulant, urgent, importunate. Then he believed that she had got his meaning. Later he knew that it was not because of his asking that she refrained from telling what he knew that she had also heard, but because she had already noticed the pregnancy and that she would have kept the matter hidden anyway. She looked at Lena, once, completely, as strange women had been doing for four weeks now.

"How long does she aim to stay?" Mrs Beard said.

"Just a night or two," Byron said. "Maybe just tonight. She's looking to meet her husband here. She just got in, and she aint had time to ask or inquire—" His voice was still recapitulant, meaningful. Mrs Beard watched him now. He thought that she was still trying to get his meaning. But what she was doing was watching him grope, believing (or about to believe) that his fumbling had a different reason and meaning. Then she looked at Lena again. Her eyes were not exactly cold. But they were not warm.

"I reckon she aint got any business trying to go anywhere right now," she said.

"That's what I thought," Byron said, quickly, eagerly. "With all the talk and excitement she might have to listen to, after not hearing no talk and excitement . . . If you are crowded tonight, I thought she might have my room."

"Yes," Mrs Beard said immediately. "You'll be taking out in a few minutes, anyway. You want her to have your room until you get back Monday morning?"

"I aint going tonight," Byron said. He did not look away. "I wont be able to go this time." He looked straight into cold, already disbelieving eyes, watching her in turn trying to read his own, believing that she read what was there instead of what she believed was there. They say that it is the practiced liar who can deceive. But so often the practiced and chronic liar deceives only himself; it is the man who all his life has been selfconvicted of veracity whose lies find quickest credence.

"Oh," Mrs Beard said. She looked at Lena again. "Aint she got any acquaintances in Jefferson?"

"She dont know nobody here," Byron said. "Not this side of Alabama. Likely Mr Burch will show up in the morning."

"Oh," Mrs Beard said. "Where are you going to sleep?" But she did not wait for an answer. "I reckon I can fix her up a cot in my room for tonight. If she wont object to that."

"That'll be fine," Byron said. "It'll be fine."

When the supper bell rang, he was all prepared. He had

· 79 ·

found a chance to speak to Mrs Beard. He had spent more time in inventing that lie than any yet. And then it was not necessary; that which he was trying to shield was its own protection. "Them men will be talking about it at the table," Mrs Beard said. "I reckon a woman in her shape (*and having to find a husband named Burch at the same time* she thought with dry irony) aint got no business listening to any more of man's devilment. You bring her in later, after they have all et." Which Byron did. Lena ate heartily again, with that grave and hearty decorum, almost going to sleep in her plate before she had finished.

"It's right tiring, travelling is," she explained.

"You go set in the parlor and I'll fix your cot," Mrs Beard said.

"I'd like to help," Lena said. But even Byron could see that she would not; that she was dead for sleep.

"You go set in the parlor," Mrs Beard said. "I reckon Mr Bunch wont mind keeping you company for a minute or two."

"I didn't dare leave her alone," Byron says. Beyond the desk Hightower has not moved. "And there we was setting, at the very time when it was all coming out down town at the sheriff's office, at the very time when Brown was telling it all; about him and Christmas and the whiskey and all. Only the whiskey wasn't much news to folks, not since he had took Brown for a partner. I reckon the only thing folks wondered about was why Christmas ever took up with Brown. Maybe it was because like not only finds like; it cant even escape from being found by its like. Even when it's just like in one thing, because even them two with the same like was different. Christmas dared the law to make money, and Brown dared the law because he never even had sense enough to know he was doing it. Like that night in the barbershop and him drunk and talking loud until Christmas kind of run in and dragged him out. And Mr Maxey said, 'What do you reckon that was he pretty near told on himself and that other one?' and Captain McLendon said, 'I dont reckon about it at all,' and Mr Maxey said, 'Do you reckon they was actually holding up somebody else's liquor truck?' and McLendon said, 'Would it surprise you to hear that that fellow Christmas hadn't done no worse than that in his life?'

"That's what Brown was telling last night. But everybody knew about that. They had been saying for a good while that somebody ought to tell Miss Burden. But I reckon there wasn't anybody that wanted to go out there and tell her, because nobody knowed what was going to happen then. I reckon there are folks born here that never even saw her. I dont reckon I'd wanted to go out there to that old house where nobody ever saw her unless maybe it was folks in a passing wagon that would see her now and then standing in the yard in a dress and sunbonnet that some nigger women I know wouldn't have wore ror its shape and how it made her look. Or maybe she already knew it. Being a Yankee and all, maybe she didn't mind. And then couldn't nobody have known what was going to happen.

"And so I didn't dare leave her alone until she was in bed. I aimed to come out and see you last night, right away. But I never dared to leave her. Them other boarders was passing up and down the hall and I didn't know when one of them would take a notion to come in and start talking about it and tell the whole thing; I could already hear them talking about it on the porch, and her still watching me with her face all fixed to ask me again about that fire. And so I didn't dare leave her. And we was setting there in the parlor and she couldn't hardly keep her eyes open then, and me telling her how I would find him for her all right, only I wanted to come and talk to a preacher I knowed that could help her to get in touch with him. And her setting there with her eyes closed while I was telling her, not knowing that I knew that her and that fellow wasn't married yet. She thought she had fooled everybody. And she asked me what kind of a man it was that I aimed to tell about her to and I told her and her setting there with her eyes closed so that at last I said, 'You ain't heard a word I been saying' and she kind of roused up, but without opening her eyes, and said, 'Can he still marry folks?' and I said, 'What? Can he what?' and she said, 'Is he still enough of a preacher to marry folks?'."

Hightower has not moved. He sits erect behind the desk, his forearms parallel upon the armrests of the chair. He wears neither collar nor coat. His face is at once gaunt and flabby; it is as though there were two faces, one imposed upon the other, looking out from beneath the pale, bald skull surrounded by a fringe of gray hair, from behind the twin motionless glares of his spectacles. That part of his torso visible above the desk is shapeless, almost monstrous, with a soft and sedentary obesity. He sits rigid; on his face now that expression of denial and flight has become definite. "Byron," he says; "Byron. What is this you are telling me?"

Byron ceases. He looks quietly at the other, with an expression of commiseration and pity. "I knowed you had not heard yet. I knowed it would be for me to tell you."

They look at one another. "What is it I haven't heard yet?"

"About Christmas. About yesterday and Christmas. Christmas is part nigger. About him and Brown and yesterday."

"Part negro," Hightower says. His voice sounds light, trivial, like a thistle bloom falling into silence without a sound, without any weight. He does not move. For a moment longer he does not move. Then there seems to come over his whole body, as if its parts were mobile like face features, that shrinking and denial, and Byron sees that the still, flaccid, big face is suddenly slick with sweat. But his voice is light and calm. "What about Christmas and Brown and yesterday?" he says.

The sound of music from the distant church has long since ceased. Now there is no sound in the room save the steady shrilling of insects and the monotonous sound of Byron's voice. Beyond the desk Hightower sits erect. Between his parallel and downturned palms and with his lower body concealed by the desk, his attitude is that of an eastern idol.

"It was yesterday morning. There was a countryman coming to town in a wagon with his family. He was the one that found the fire. No: he was the second one to get there, because he told how there was already one fellow there when he broke down the door. He told about how he come into sight of the house and he said to his wife how it was a right smart of smoke coming out of that kitchen, and about how the wagon come on and then his wife said, 'That house is afire.' And I reckon maybe he stopped the wagon and they set there in the wagon for a while, looking at the smoke, and I reckon that after a while he said, 'It looks like it is.' And I reckon it was his wife that made him get down and go and see. 'They dont know it's afire,' she said, I reckon. 'You go up there and tell them.' And he got out of the wagon and went up onto the porch and stood there, hollering 'Hello. Hello' for a while. He told how he could hear the fire then, inside the house, and then he hit the door a lick with his shoulder and went in and then he found the one that had found that fire first. It was Brown. But the countryman didn't know that. He just said it was a drunk man in the hall that looked like he had just finished falling down the stairs, and the countryman said, 'Your house is afire, mister,' before he realised how drunk the man was. And he told how the drunk man kept on saying how there wasn't nobody upstairs and that the upstairs was all afire anyway and there wasn't any use trying to save anything from up there.

"But the countryman knew there couldn't be that much fire upstairs because the fire was all back toward the kitchen. And besides, the man was too drunk to know, anyway. And he told how he suspected there was something wrong from the way the drunk man was trying to keep him from going upstairs. So he started upstairs, and the drunk fellow trying to hold him back, and he shoved the drunk man away and went on up the stairs. He told how the drunk man tried to follow him, still telling him how it wasn't anything upstairs, and he said that when he come back down again and thought about the drunk fellow, he was gone. But I reckon it was some time before he remembered to think about Brown again. Because he went on up the stairs and begun hollering again, opening the doors, and then he opened the right door and he found her."

He ceases. Then there is no sound in the room save the insects. Beyond the open window the steady insects pulse and beat, drowsy and myriad. "Found her," Hightower says. "It was Miss Burden he found." He does not move. Byron does not look at him, he might be contemplating his hands upon his lap while he talks.

"She was lying on the floor. Her head had been cut pretty near off; a lady with the beginning of gray hair. The man said how he stood there and he could hear the fire and there was smoke in the room itself now, like it had done followed him in. And how he was afraid to try to pick her up and carry her out because her head might come clean off. And then he said how he run back down the stairs again and out the front without even noticing that the drunk fellow was gone, and down to the road and told his wife to whip the team on to the nearest telephone and call for the sheriff too. And how he run back around the house to the cistern and he said he was already drawing up a bucket of water before he realised how foolish that was, with the whole back end of the house afire good now. So he run back into the house and up the stairs again and into the room and jerked a cover off the bed and rolled her onto it and caught up the corners and swung it onto his back like a sack of meal and carried it out of the house and laid it down under a tree. And he said that what he was scared of happened. Because the cover fell open and she was lay-ing on her side, facing one way, and her head was turned clean around like she was looking behind her. And he said how if she could just have done that when she was alive, she might not have been doing it now."

Byron ceases and looks, glances once, at the man beyond the desk. Hightower has not moved. His face about the twin blank glares of the spectacles is sweating quietly and steadily. "And the sheriff come out, and the fire department come out too. But there wasn't nothing it could do because there wasn't any water for the hose. And that old house burned all evening and I could see the smoke from the mill and I showed it to her when she come up, because I didn't know then. And they brought Miss Burden to town, and there was a paper at the bank that she had told them would tell what to do with her when she died. It said how she had a nephew in the North where she come from, her folks come from. And they telegraphed the nephew and in two hours they got the answer that the nephew would pay a thousand dollars' reward for who done it.

"And Christmas and Brown were both gone. The sheriff found out how somebody had been living in that cabin, and then right off everybody begun to tell about Christmas and Brown, that had   it a secret long enough for one of them or maybe both of them to murder that lady. But nobody could find either one of them until last night. The countryman didn't know it was Brown that he found drunk in the house. Folks thought that him and Christmas had both run, maybe. And then last night Brown showed up. He was sober then, and he come onto the square about eight o'clock, wild, yelling about how it was Christmas that killed her and making his claim on that thousand dollars. They got the officers and took him to the sheriff's office and they told him the reward would be his all right soon as he caught Christmas and proved he done it. And so Brown told. He told about how Christmas had been living with Miss Burden like man and wife for three years, until Brown and him teamed up. At first, when he moved out to live in the cabin with Christmas, Brown said that Christmas told him he had been sleeping in the cabin all the time. Then he said how one night he hadn't gone to sleep and he told how he heard Christmas get up out of bed and come and stand over Brown's cot for a while, like he was listening, and then he tiptoed to the door and opened it quiet and went out. And Brown said how he got up and followed Christmas and saw him go up to the big house and go in the back door, like either it was left open for him or he had a key to it. Then Brown come on back to the cabin and got into bed. But he said how he couldn't go to sleep for laughing, thinking about how smart Christmas thought he was. And he was laying there when Christmas come back in about a hour. Then he said how he couldn't keep from laughing no longer, and he says to Christmas, 'You old son of a gun.' Then he said how Christmas got right still in the dark, and how he laid there laughing, telling Christmas how he wasn't such a slick one after all and joking Christmas about gray hair and about how if Christmas wanted him to, he would take it week about with him paying the house rent.

"Then he told how he found out that night that sooner or later Christmas was going to kill her or somebody. He said he was laying there, laughing, thinking that Christmas would just maybe get back in bed again, when Christmas struck a match. Then Brown said he quit laughing and he laid there and watched Christmas light the lantern and set it on the box by Brown's cot. Then Brown said how he wasn't laughing and he laid there and Christmas standing there by the cot, looking down at him. 'Now you got a good joke,' Christmas says. 'You can get a good laugh, telling them in the barbershop tomorrow night.' And Brown said he didn't know that Christmas was mad and that he kind of said something back to Christmas, not meaning to make him mad, and Christmas said, in that still way of his: 'You dont get enough sleep. You stay awake too much. Maybe you ought to sleep more,' and Brown said, 'How much more?' and Christmas said, 'Maybe from now on.' And Brown said how he realised then that Christmas was mad and that it wasn't no time to joke him, and he said, 'Aint we buddies? What would I want to tell something that aint none of my business? Cant you trust me?' and Christmas said, 'I dont know. I dont care, neither. But you can trust me.' And he looked at Brown. 'Cant you trust me?' and Brown said he said 'Yes.'

And he told then about how he was afraid that Christmas would kill Miss Burden some night, and the sheriff asked him how come he never reported his fear and Brown said he thought how maybe by not saying nothing he could stay out there and prevent it, without having to bother the officers with it; and the sheriff kind of grunted and said that was thoughtful of Brown and that Miss Burden would sholy appreciate it if she knowed. And then I reckon it begun to dawn on Brown that he had a kind of rat smell too. Because he started in telling about how it was Miss Burden that bought Christmas that auto and how he would try to persuade Christmas to quit selling whiskey before he got them both into trouble; and the officers watching him and him talking faster and faster and more and more; about how he had been awake early Saturday morning and saw Christmas get up about dawn and go out. And Brown knew where Christmas was going, and about seven o'clock Christmas come back into the cabin and stood there, looking at Brown. 'I've done it,' Christmas says. 'Done what?' Brown says. 'Go up to the house and see,' Christmas says.

And Brown said how he was afraid then, but that he never suspected the truth. He just said that at the outside all he expected was that maybe Christmas just beat her some. And he said how Christmas went out again and then he got up and dressed and he was making a fire to cook his breakfast when he happened to look out the door and he said how all the kitchen was afire up at the big house.

"'What time was this?' the sheriff says.

"'About eight o'clock, I reckon,' Brown says. 'When a man would naturally be getting up. Unless he is rich. And God knows I aint that.'

"'And that fire wasn't reported until nigh eleven o'clock,' the sheriff says. 'And that house was still burning at three P.M. You mean to say a old wooden house, even a big one, would need six hours to burn down in?'

"And Brown was setting there, looking this way and that, with them fellows watching him in a circle, hemming him in. 'I'm just telling you the truth,' Brown says. 'That's what you asked for.' He was looking this way and that, jerking his head. Then he kind of hollered: 'How do I know what time it was? Do you expect a man doing the work of a nigger slave at a sawmill to be rich enough to own a watch?'

"'You aint worked at no sawmill nor at anything else in six weeks,' the marshal says. 'And a man that can afford to ride around all day long in a new car can afford to pass the courthouse often enough to see the clock and keep up with the time.'

"'It wasn't none of my car, I tell you!' Brown says. 'It was his. She bought it and give it to him; the woman he murdered give it to him.'

. 89 .

"'That's neither here nor there,' the sheriff says. 'Let him tell the rest of it.'

"And so Brown went on then, talking louder and louder and faster and faster, like he was trying to hide Joe Brown behind what he was telling on Christmas until Brown could get his chance to make a grab at that thousand dollars. It beats all how some folks think that making or getting money is a kind of game where there are not any rules at all. He told about how even when he saw the fire, he never dreamed that she would still be in the house, let alone dead. He said how he never even thought to look into the house at all; that he was just figuring on how to put out the fire.

"'And that was round eight A.M.,' the sheriff says. 'Or so you claim. And Hamp Waller's ˰ ˰ˍˊ ˖ˎˇˍ reported that fire until nigh eleven. It took you a right smart while to find out you couldn't put out that fire with your bare hands.' And Brown sitting there in the middle of them (they had locked the door, but the windows was lined with folks' faces against the glass) with his eyes going this way and that and his lip lifted away from his teeth. 'Hamp says that after he broke in the door, there was already a man inside that house,' the sheriff says. 'And that that man tried to keep him from going up the stairs.' And him setting there in the center of them, with his eyes going and going.

"I reckon he was desperate by then. I reckon he could not only see that thousand dollars getting further and further away from him, but that he could begin to see somebody else getting it. I reckon it was like he could see himself with that thousand dollars right in his hand for somebody else to have the spending of it. Because they said it was like he had been saving what he told them next for just such a time as this. Like he had knowed that if it come to a pinch, this would save him, even if it was almost worse for a white man to admit what he would have to admit than to be accused of the murder itself. 'That's right,' he says. 'Go on. Accuse me. Accuse the white man that's trying to help you with what he knows. Accuse the white man and let the nigger go free. Accuse the white and let the nigger run.'

" 'Nigger?' the sheriff said. 'Nigger?'

"It's like he knew he had them then. Like nothing they could believe he had done would be as bad as what he could tell that somebody else had done. 'You're so smart,' he says. 'The folks in this town is so smart. Fooled for three years. Calling him a foreigner for three years, when soon as I watched him three days I knew he wasn't no more a foreigner than I am. I knew before he even told me himself.' And them watching him now, and looking now and then at one another.

" 'You better be careful what you are saying, if it is a white man you are talking about,' the marshal says. 'I dont care if he is a murderer or not.'

" 'I'm talking about Christmas,' Brown says. 'The man that killed that white woman after he had done lived with her in plain sight of this whole town, and you all letting him get further and further away while you are accusing the one fellow that can find him for you, that knows what he done. He's got nigger blood in him. I knowed it when I first saw him. But you folks, you smart sheriffs and such. One time he even admitted it, told me he was part nigger. Maybe he was drunk when he done it: I dont know. Anyway, the next morning after he told me he come to me and he says (Brown was talking fast now, kind of glaring his

· 91 ·

eyes and his teeth both around at them, from one to another), he said to me, "I made a mistake last night. Dont you make the same one." And I said, "How do you mean a mistake?" and he said, "You think a minute," and I thought about something he done one night when me and him was in Memphis and I knowed my life wouldn't be worth nothing if I ever crossed him and so I said, "I reckon I know what you mean. I aint going to meddle in what aint none of my business. I aint never done that yet, that I know of." And you'd have said that, too,' Brown says, 'way out there, alone in that cabin with him and nobody to hear you if you was to holler. You'd have been scared too, until the folks you was trying to help turned in and accused you of the killing you never done.' And there he sat, with his eyes going and going, and them in the room watching him and the faces pressed against the window from outside.

"'A nigger,' the marshal said. 'I always thought there was something funny about that fellow.'

"Then the sheriff talked to Brown again. 'And that's why you didn't tell what was going on out there until tonight?'

"And Brown setting there in the midst of them, with his lips snarled back and that little scar by his mouth white as a popcorn. 'You just show me the man that would a done different,' he says. 'That's all I ask. Just show me the man that would a lived with him enough to know him like I done, and done different.'

"'Well,' the sheriff says, 'I believe you are telling the truth at last. You go on with Buck, now, and get a good sleep. I'll attend to Christmas.'

"'I reckon that means the jail,' Brown says. 'I reckon you'll lock me up in jail while you get the reward.'

"'You shut your mouth,' the sheriff says, not mad. 'If

that reward is yours, I'll see that you get it. Take him on, Buck.'

"The marshal come over and touched Brown's shoulder and he got up. When they went out the door the ones that had been watching through the window crowded up: 'Have you got him, Buck? Is he the one that done it?'

"'No,' Buck says. 'You boys get on home. Get on to bed, now.'"

Byron's voice ceases. Its flat, inflectionless, country-bred singsong dies into silence. He is now looking at Hightower with that look compassionate and troubled and still, watching across the desk the man who sits there with his eyes closed and the sweat running down his face like tears. Hightower speaks: "Is it certain, proved, that he has negro blood? Think, Byron; what it will mean when the people —if they catch . . . Poor man. Poor mankind."

"That's what Brown says," Byron says, his tone quiet, stubborn, convinced. "And even a liar can be scared into telling the truth, same as a honest man can be tortured into telling a lie."

"Yes," Hightower says. He sits with his eyes closed, erect. "But they have not caught him yet. They have not caught him yet, Byron."

Neither is Byron looking at the other. "Not yet. Not the last I heard. They took some bloodhounds out there today. But they hadn't caught him when I heard last."

"And Brown?"

"Brown," Byron says. "Him. He went with them. He may have helped Christmas do it. But I dont reckon so. I reckon that setting fire to the house was about his limit. And why he done that, if he did, I reckon even he dont know. Unless maybe he thought that if the whole thing was just burned up, it would kind of not ever been at all,

· 93 ·

and then him and Christmas could go on riding around in that new car. I reckon he figured that what Christmas committed was not so much a sin as a mistake." His face is musing, downlooking; again it cracks faintly, with a kind of sardonic weariness. "I reckon he's safe enough. I reckon she can find him now any time she wants, provided him and the sheriff aint out with the dogs. He aint trying to run —not with that thousand dollars hanging over his head, you might say. I reckon he wants to catch Christmas worse than any man of them. He goes with them. They take him out of the jail and he goes along with them, and then they all come back to town and lock Brown up again. It's right queer. Kind of a murderer trying to catch himself to get his own reward. He dont seem to mind though, except to begrudge the time while they aint out on the trail, the time wasted setting down. Yes. I'll tell her tomorrow. I'll just tell her that he is in hock for the time being, him and them two dogs. Maybe I'll take her to town where she can see them, all three of them hitched to the other men, a-straining and yapping."

"You haven't told her yet."

"I aint told her. Nor him. Because he might run again, reward or no reward. And maybe if he can catch Christmas and get that reward, he will marry her in time. But she dont know yet, no more than she knowed yesterday when she got down from that wagon on the square. Swole-bellied, getting down slow from that strange wagon, among them strange faces, telling herself with a kind of quiet astonishment, only I dont reckon it was any astonishment in it, because she had come slow and afoot and telling never bothered her: 'My, my. Here I have come clean from Alabama, and now I am in Jefferson at last, sure enough.'"

. 5 .

IT was after midnight. Though Christmas had been in bed for two hours, he was not yet asleep. He heard Brown before he saw him. He heard Brown approach the door and then blunder into it, in silhouette propping himself erect in the door. Brown was breathing heavily. Standing there between his propped arms, Brown began to sing in a saccharine and nasal tenor. The very longdrawn pitch of his voice seemed to smell of whiskey. "Shut it," Christmas said. He did not move and his voice was not raised. Yet Brown ceased at once. He stood for a moment longer in the door, propping himself upright. Then he let go of the door and Christmas heard him stumble into the room; a moment later he blundered into something. There was an interval filled with hard, labored breathing. Then Brown fell to the floor with a tremendous clatter, striking the cot on which Christmas lay and filling the room with loud and idiot laughter.

Christmas rose from his cot. Invisible beneath him Brown lay on the floor, laughing, making no effort to rise. "Shut it!" Christmas said. Brown still laughed. Christmas stepped across Brown and put his hand out toward where a wooden box that served for table sat, on which the lantern and matches were kept. But he could not find the box, and then he remembered the sound of the breaking lantern when Brown fell. He stooped, astride Brown, and found his collar and hauled him out from beneath the cot and raised Brown's head and began to strike him with his flat hand, short, vicious, and hard, until Brown ceased laughing.

Brown was limp. Christmas held his head up, cursing him in a voice level as whispering. He dragged Brown over to the other cot and flung him onto it, face up. Brown began to laugh again. Christmas put his hand flat upon Brown's mouth and nose, shutting his jaw with his left hand while with the right he struck Brown again with those hard, slow, measured blows, as if he were meting them out by count. Brown had stopped laughing. He struggled. Beneath Christmas's hand he began to make a choked, gurgling noise, struggling. Christmas held him until he ceased and became still. Then Christmas slacked his hand a little. "Will you be quiet now?" he said. "Will you?"

Brown struggled again. "Take your black hand off of me, you damn niggerblooded—" The hand shut down again. Again Christmas struck him with the other hand upon the face. Brown ceased and lay still again. Christmas slacked his hand. After a moment Brown spoke, in a tone cunning, not loud: "You're a nigger, see? You said so yourself. You told me. But I'm white. I'm a wh—" The hand shut down. Again Brown struggled, making a choked whimpering sound beneath the hand, drooling upon the fingers. When he stopped struggling, the hand slacked. Then he lay still, breathing hard.

"Will you now?" Christmas said.

"Yes," Brown said. He breathed noisily. "Let me breathe. I'll be quiet. Let me breathe."

Christmas slacked his hand but he did not remove it. Beneath it Brown breathed easier, his breath came and went easier, with less noise. But Christmas did not remove the hand. He stood in the darkness above the prone body, with Brown's breath alternately hot and cold on his fingers, thinking quietly *Something is going to happen to me. I am going to do something* Without removing his left hand from Brown's face he could reach with his right across to his cot, to his pillow beneath which lay his razor with its five inch blade. But he did not do it. Perhaps thinking had already gone far enough and dark enough to tell him *This is not the right one* Anyway he did not reach for the razor. After a time he removed his hand from Brown's face. But he did not go away. He still stood above the cot, his own breathing so quiet, so calm, as to make no sound even to himself. Invisible too, Brown breathed quieter now, and after a while Christmas returned and sat upon his cot and fumbled a cigarette and a match from his trousers hanging on the wall. In the flare of the match Brown was visible. Before taking the light, Christmas lifted the match and looked at Brown. Brown lay on his back, sprawled, one arm dangling to the floor. His mouth was open. While Christmas watched, he began to snore.

Christmas lit the cigarette and snapped the match toward the open door, watching the flame vanish in midair. Then he was listening for the light, trivial sound which the dead match would make when it struck the floor; and then it seemed to him that he heard it. Then it seemed to him, sitting on the cot in the dark room, that he was hearing a myriad sounds of no greater volume—voices, murmurs, whispers: of trees, darkness, earth; people: his own voice; other voices evocative of names and times and places— which he had been conscious of all his life without knowing it, which were his life, thinking *God perhaps and me not knowing that too* He could see it like a printed sentence, fullborn and already dead *God loves me too* like the faded and weathered letters on a last year's billboard *God loves me too*

He smoked the cigarette down without once touching it with his hand. He snapped it too toward the door. Unlike the match, it did not vanish in midflight. He watched it twinkle end over end through the door. He lay back on the cot, his hands behind his head, as a man lies who does not expect to sleep, thinking *I have been in bed now since ten o'clock and I have not gone to sleep. I do not know what time it is but it is later than m̲i̲d̲night and I have not yet been asleep* "It's because she started praying over me," he said. He spoke aloud, his voice sudden and loud in the dark room, above Brown's drunken snoring. "That's it. Because she started praying over me."

He rose from the cot. His bare feet made no sound. He stood in the darkness, in his underclothes. On the other cot Brown snored. For a moment Christmas stood, his head turned toward the sound. Then he went on toward the door. In his underclothes and barefoot he left the cabin. It was a little lighter outdoors. Overhead the slow constellations wheeled, the stars of which he had been aware for thirty years and not one of which had any name to him or meant anything at all by shape or brightness or position. Ahead, rising from out a close mass of trees, he could see one chimney and one gable of the house. The house itself was invisible and dark. No light shown and no sound came from it when he approached and stood beneath the window of the room where she slept, thinking *If she is asleep too. If she is asleep* The doors were never locked, and it used to be that at whatever hour between dark and dawn that the desire took him, he would enter the house and go to her bedroom and take his sure way through the darkness to her bed. Sometimes she would be awake and waiting and she would speak his name. At others he would waken her with his hard brutal hand and sometimes take her as hard and as brutally before she was good awake.

That was two years ago, two years behind them now, thinking *Perhaps that is where outrage lies. Perhaps I believe that I have been tricked, fooled. That she lied to me about her age, about what happens to women at a certain age* He said, aloud, solitary, in the darkness beneath dark window: "She ought not to started praying over me. She would have been all right if she hadn't started praying over me. It was not her fault that she got too old to be any good any more. But she ought to have had better sense than to pray over me." He began to curse her. He stood beneath the dark window, cursing her with slow and calculated obscenity. He was not looking at the window. In the less than halflight he appeared to be watching his body, seeming to watch it turning slow and lascivious in a whispering of gutter filth like a drowned corpse in a thick still black pool of more than water. He touched himself with his flat hands, hard, drawing his hands hard up his abdomen and chest inside his undergarment. It was held together by a single button at the top. Once he had owned garments with intact buttons. A woman had sewed them on. That was for a time, during a time. Then the time passed. After that he would purloin his own garments from the family wash before she could get to them and replace the missing buttons. When she foiled him he set himself deliberately to learn and remember which buttons were missing and had been restored. With his pocket knife and with the cold and bloodless deliberation of a surgeon he would cut off the buttons which she had just replaced.

His right hand slid fast and smooth as the knife blade had ever done, up the opening in the garment. Edgewise it struck the remaining button a light, swift blow. The dark air breathed upon him, breathed smoothly as the garment slipped down his legs, the cool mouth of darkness, the soft cool tongue. Moving again, he could feel the dark air like water; he could feel the dew under his feet as he had never felt dew before. He passed through the broken gate and stopped beside the road. The August weeds were thightall. Upon the leaves and stalks dust of a month of passing wagons lay. The road ran before him. It was a little paler than the darkness of trees and earth. In one direction town lay. In the other the road rose to a hill. After a time a light began to grow beyond the hill, defining it. Then he could hear the car. He did not move. He stood with his hands on his hips, naked, thighdeep in the dusty weeds, while the car came over the hill and approached, the lights full upon him. He watched his body grow white out of the darkness like a kodak print emerging from the liquid. He looked straight into the headlights as it shot past. From it a woman's shrill voice flew back, shrieking. "White bastards!" he shouted. "That's not the first of your bitches that ever saw . . ." But the car was gone. There was no one to hear, to listen. It was gone, sucking its dust and its light with it and behind it, sucking with it the

shooting one another with pistols. From beneath the pillow on his cot he took his razor and a brush and a stick of shaving soap and put them into his pocket.

When he left the cabin it was quite light. The birds were in full chorus. This time he turned his back on the house. He went on past the stable and entered the pasture beyond it. His shoes and his trouser legs were soon sopping with gray dew. He paused and rolled his trousers gingerly to his knees and went on. At the end of the pasture woods began. The dew was not so heavy here, and he rolled his trousers down again. After a while he came to a small valley in which a spring rose. He put down the magazine and gathered twigs and dried brush and made a fire and sat, his back against a tree and his feet to the blaze. Presently his wet shoes began to steam. Then he could feel the heat moving up his legs, and then all of a sudden he opened his eyes and saw the high sun and that the fire had burned completely out, and he knew that he had been asleep. 'Damned if I haven't,' he thought. 'Damned if I haven't slept again.'

He had slept more than two hours this time, because the sun was shining down upon the spring itself, glinting and glancing upon the ceaseless water. He rose, stretching his cramped and stiffened back, waking his tingling muscles. From his pocket he took the razor, the brush, the soap. Kneeling beside the spring he shaved, using the water's surface for glass, stropping the long bright razor on his shoe.

He concealed the shaving things and the magazine in a clump of bushes and put on the tie again. When he left the spring he bore now well away from the house. When he reached the road he was a half mile beyond the house.

A short distance further on stood a small store with a gasoline pump before it. He entered the store and a woman sold him crackers and a tin of potted meat. He returned to the spring, the dead fire.

He ate his breakfast with his back against the tree, reading the magazine while he ate. He had previously read but one story; he began now upon the second one, reading the magazine straight through as though it were a novel. Now and then he would look up from the page, chewing, into the sunshot leaves which arched the ditch. 'Maybe I have already done it,' he thought. 'Maybe it is no longer now waiting to be done.' It seemed to him that he could see the yellow day opening peacefully on before him, like a corridor, an arras, into a still chiaroscuro without urgency. It seemed to him that as he sat there the yellow day contemplated him drowsily, like a prone and somnolent yellow cat. Then he read again. He turned the pages in steady progression, though now and then he would seem to linger upon one page, one line, perhaps one word. He would not look up then. He would not move, apparently arrested and held immobile by a single word which had perhaps not yet impacted, his whole being suspended by the single trivial combination of letters in quiet and sunny space, so that hanging motionless and without physical weight he seemed to watch the slow flowing of time beneath him, thinking *All I wanted was peace* thinking, 'She ought not to started praying over me.'

When he reached the last story he stopped reading and counted the remaining pages. Then he looked at the sun and read again. He read now like a man walking along a street might count the cracks in the pavement, to the last and final page, the last and final word. Then he rose and struck a match to the magazine and prodded it patiently until it was consumed. With the shaving things in his pocket he went on down the ditch.

After a while it broadened: a smooth, sandblanched floor between steep shelving walls choked, flank and crest, with brier and brush. Over it trees still arched, and in a small cove in one flank a mass of dead brush lay, filling the cove. He began to drag the brush to one side, clearing the cove and exposing a short handled shovel. With the shovel he began to dig in the sand which the brush had concealed, exhuming one by one six metal tins with screw tops. He did not unscrew the caps. He laid the tins on their sides and with the sharp edge of the shovel he pierced them, the sand beneath them darkening as the whiskey spurted and poured, the sunny solitude, the air, becoming redolent with alcohol. He emptied them thoroughly, unhurried, his face completely cold, masklike almost. When they were all empty he tumbled them back into the hole and buried them roughly and dragged the brush back and hid the shovel again. The brush hid the stain but it could not hide the scent, the smell. He looked at the sun again. It was now afternoon.

At seven o'clock that evening he was in town, in a restaurant on a side street, eating his supper, sitting on a backless stool at a frictionsmooth wooden counter, eating.

At nine o'clock he was standing outside the barbershop, looking through the window at the man whom he had taken for a partner. He stood quite still, with his hands in his trousers and cigarette smoke drifting across his still face and the cloth cap worn, like the stiff hat, at that angle at once swaggering and baleful. So cold, so baleful he stood there that Brown inside the shop, among the lights, the air heavy with lotion and hot soap, gesticulant, thickvoiced, in the soiled redbarred trousers and the soiled colored shirt, looked up in midvoice and with his drunken eyes looked into the eyes of the man beyond the glass. So still and baleful that a negro youth shuffling up the street whistling saw Christmas' profile and ceased whistling and edged away and slid past behind him, turning, looking back over his shoulder. But Christmas was moving himself now. It was as if he had just paused there for Brown to look at him.

He went on, not fast, away from the square. The street, a quiet one at all times, was deserted at this hour. It led down through the negro section, Freedman Town, to the station. At seven o'clock he would have passed people, white and black, going toward the square and the picture show; at half past nine they would have been going back home. But the picture show had not turned out yet, and he now had the street to himself. He went on, passing still between the homes of white people, from street lamp to street lamp, the heavy shadows of oak and maple leaves sliding like scraps of black velvet across his white shirt. Nothing can look quite as lonely as a big man going along an empty street. Yet though he was not large, not tall, he contrived somehow to look more lonely than a lone telephone pole in the middle of a desert. In the wide, empty, shadow-brooded street he looked like a phantom, a spirit, strayed out of its own world, and lost.

Then he found himself. Without his being aware the street had begun to slope and before he knew it he was in Freedman Town, surrounded by the summer smell and the summer voices of invisible negroes. They seemed to enclose him like bodiless voices murmuring, talking, laughing, in a language not his. As from the bottom of a thick black pit he saw himself enclosed by cabinshapes, vague, keroselit, so that the street lamps themselves seemed to be further spaced, as if the black life, the black breathing had compounded the substance of breath so that not only voices but moving bodies and light itself must become fluid and accrete slowly from particle to particle, of and with the now ponderable night inseparable and one.

He was standing still now, breathing quite hard, glaring this way and that. About him the cabins were shaped blackly out of blackness by the faint, sultry glow of kerosene lamps. On all sides, even within him, the bodiless fecundmellow voices of negro women murmured. It was as though he and all other manshaped life about him had been returned to the lightless hot wet primogenitive Female. He began to run, glaring, his teeth glaring, his inbreath cold on his dry teeth and lips, toward the next street lamp. Beneath it a narrow and rutted lane turned and mounted to the parallel street, out of the black hollow. He turned into it running and plunged up the sharp ascent, his heart hammering, and into the higher street. He stopped here, panting, glaring, his heart thudding as if it could not or would not yet believe that the air now was the cold hard air of white people.

Then he became cool. The negro smell, the negro voices, were behind and below him now. To his left lay the square, the clustered lights: low bright birds in stillwinged and tremulous suspension. To the right the street lamps marched on, spaced, intermittent with bitten and unstirring branches. He went on, slowly again, his back toward the square, passing again between the houses of white people. There were people on these porches too, and in chairs upon the lawns; but he could walk quiet here. Now and then he could see them: heads in silhouette, a white blurred garmented shape; on a lighted veranda four people sat about a card table, the white faces intent and sharp in the low light, the bare arms of the women glaring smooth and white above the trivial cards. 'That's all I wanted,' he thought. 'That dont seem like a whole lot to ask.'

This street in turn began to slope. But it sloped safely. His steady white shirt and pacing dark legs died among long shadows bulging square and huge against the August stars: a cotton warehouse, a horizontal and cylindrical tank like the torso of a beheaded mastodon, a line of freight cars. He crossed the tracks, the rails coming momentarily into twin green glints from a switch lamp, glinting away again. Beyond the tracks woods began. But he found the path unerringly. It mounted, among the trees, the lights of the town now beginning to come into view again across the valley where the railroad ran. But he did not look back until he reached the crest of the hill. Then he could see the town, the glare, the individual lights where streets radiated from the square. He could see the street down which he had come, and the other street, the one which had almost betrayed him; and further away and at right angles, the far bright rampart of the town itself, and in the angle between the black pit from which he had fled with drumming heart and glaring lips. No light came from it, from here no breath, no odor. It just lay there, black, impenetrable, in its garland of Augusttremulous lights. It might have been the original quarry, abyss itself.

His way was sure, despite the trees, the darkness. He never once lost the path which he could not even see. The woods continued for a mile. He emerged into a road, with dust under his feet. He could see now, the vague spreading world, the horizon. Here and there faint windows glowed. But most of the cabins were dark. Nevertheless his blood began again, talking and talking. He walked fast, in time to it; he seemed to be aware that the group were negroes before he could have seen or heard them at all, before they even came in sight vaguely against the defunctive dust. There were five or six of them, in a straggling body yet vaguely paired; again there reached him, above the noise of his own blood, the rich murmur of womenvoices. He was walking directly toward them, walking fast. They had seen him and they gave to one side of the road, the voices ceasing. He too changed direction, crossing toward them as if he intended to walk them down. In a single movement and as though at a spoken command the women faded back and were going around him, giving him a wide berth. One of the men followed them as if he were driving them before him, looking over his shoulder as he passed. The other two men had halted in the road, facing Christmas. Christmas had stopped also. Neither seemed to be moving, yet they approached, looming, like two shadows drifting up. He could smell negro; he could smell cheap cloth and sweat. The head of the negro, higher than his own, seemed to stoop, out of the sky, against the sky. "It's a white man," he said, without turning his head, quietly. "What you want, whitefolks? You looking for somebody?" The voice was not threatful. Neither was it servile.

"Come on away from there, Jupe," the one who had followed the women said.

"Who you looking for, cap'm?" the negro said.

"Jupe," one of the women said, her voice a little high. "You come on, now."

For a moment longer the two heads, the light and the

dark, seemed to hang suspended in the darkness, breathing upon one another. Then the negro's head seemed to float away; a cool wind blew from somewhere. Christmas, turning slowly, watching them dissolve and fade again into the pale road, found that he had the razor in his hand. It was not open. It was not from fear. "Bitches!" he said, quite loud. "Sons of bitches!"

The wind blew dark and cool; the dust even through his shoes was cool. 'What in hell is the matter with me?' he thought. He put the razor back into his pocket and stopped and lit a cigarette. He had to moisten his lips several times to hold the cigarette. In the light of the match he could watch his own hands shake. 'All this trouble,' he thought. "All this damn trouble," he said aloud, walking again. He looked up at the stars, the sky. 'It must be near ten now,' he thought; and then almost with the thought he heard the clock on the courthouse two miles away. Slow, measured, clear the ten strokes came. He counted them, stopped again in the lonely and empty road. 'Ten o'clock,' he thought. 'I heard ten strike last night too. And eleven. And twelve. But I didn't hear one. Maybe the wind had changed.'

When he heard eleven strike tonight he was sitting with his back against a tree inside the broken gate, while behind him again the house was dark and hidden in its shaggy grove. He was not thinking *Maybe she is not asleep either* tonight. He was not thinking at all now; thinking had not begun now; the voices had not begun now either. He just sat there, not moving, until after a while he heard the clock two miles away strike twelve. Then he rose and moved toward the house. He didn't go fast. He didn't think even then *Something is going to happen. Something is going to happen to me*

6

MEMORY believes before knowing remembers. Believes longer than recollects, longer than knowing even wonders. Knows remembers believes a corridor in a big long garbled cold echoing building of dark red brick sootbleakened by more chimneys than its own, set in a grassless cinderstrewnpacked compound surrounded by smoking factory purlieus and enclosed by a ten foot steel-and-wire fence like a penitentiary or a zoo, where in random erratic surges, with sparrowlike childtrebling, orphans in identical and uniform blue denim in and out of remembering but in knowing constant as the bleak walls, the bleak windows where in rain soot from the yearly adjacenting chimneys streaked like black tears.

In the quiet and empty corridor, during the quiet hour of early afternoon, he was like a shadow, small even for five years, sober and quiet as a shadow. Another in the corridor could not have said just when and where he vanished, into what door, what room. But there was no one else in the corridor at this hour. He knew that. He had been doing this for almost a year, ever since the day when he discovered by accident the toothpaste which the dietitian used.

Once in the room, he went directly on his bare and silent feet to the washstand and found the tube. He was watching the pink worm coil smooth and cool and slow onto his parchmentcolored finger when he heard footsteps in the corridor and then voices just beyond the door. Perhaps he recognised the dietitian's voice. Anyway, he did not wait to see if they were going to pass the door or not. With the tube in his hand and still silent as a shadow on his bare feet he crossed the room and slipped beneath a cloth curtain which screened off one corner of the room. Here he squatted, among delicate shoes and suspended soft woman-garments. Crouching, he heard the dietitian and her companion enter the room.

The dietitian was nothing to him yet, save a mechanical adjunct to eating, to the diningroom, the ceremony of eating at the wooden forms, coming now and then into his vision without impacting at all except as something of pleasing association and pleasing in herself to look at— young, a little fullbodied, smooth, pink-and-white, making his mind think of the diningroom, making his mouth think of something sweet and sticky to eat, and also pinkcolored and surreptitious. On that first day when he discovered the toothpaste in her room he had gone directly there, who had never heard of toothpaste either, as if he already knew that she would possess something of that nature and he would find it. He knew the voice of her companion also. It was that of a young interne from the county hospital who was assistant to the parochial doctor, he too a familiar figure about the house and also not yet an enemy.

He was safe now, behind the curtain. When they went

away, he would replace the toothpaste and also leave. So he squatted behind the curtain, hearing without listening to it the woman's tense whispering voice: "No! No! Not here. Not now. They'll catch us. Somebody will— No, Charley! Please!" The man's words he could not understand at all. The voice was lowered too. It had a ruthless sound, as the voices of all men did to him yet, since he was too young yet to escape from the world of women for that brief respite before he escaped back into it to remain until the hour of his death. He heard other sounds which he did know: a scuffing as of feet, the turn of the key in the door. "No, Charley! Charley, please! Please, Charley!" the woman's whisper said. He heard other sounds, rustlings, whisperings, not voices. He was not listening; he was just waiting, thinking without particular interest or attention that it was a strange hour to be going to bed. Again the woman's fainting whisper came through the thin curtain: "I'm scared! Hurry! Hurry!"

He squatted among the soft womansmelling garments and the shoes. He saw by feel alone now the ruined, once cylindrical tube. By taste and not seeing he contemplated the cool invisible worm as it coiled onto his finger and smeared sharp, automatonlike and sweet, into his mouth. By ordinary he would have taken a single mouthful and then replaced the tube and left the room. Even at five, he knew that he must not take more than that. Perhaps it was the animal warning him that more would make him sick; perhaps the human being warning him that if he took more than that, she would miss it. This was the first time he had taken more. By now, hiding and waiting, he had taken a good deal more. By feel he could see the diminishing tube. He began to sweat. Then he found that he had been sweating for some time, that for some time now he had been doing nothing else but sweating. He was not hearing anything at all now. Very likely he would not have heard a gunshot beyond the curtain. He seemed to be turned in upon himself, watching himself sweating, watching himself smear another worm of paste into his mouth which his stomach did not want. Sure enough, it refused to go down. Motionless now, utterly contemplative, he seemed to stoop above himself like a chemist in his laboratory, waiting. He didn't have to wait long. At once the paste which he had already swallowed lifted inside him, trying to get back out, into the air where it was cool. It was no longer sweet. In the rife, pinkwomansmelling obscurity behind the curtain he squatted, pinkfoamed, listening to his insides, waiting with astonished fatalism for what was about to happen to him. Then it happened. He said to himself with complete and passive surrender: 'Well, here I am.'

When the curtain fled back he did not look up. When hands dragged him violently out of his vomit he did not resist. He hung from the hands, limp, looking with slack-jawed and glassy idiocy into a face no longer smooth pink-and-white, surrounded now by wild and dishevelled hair whose smooth bands once made him think of candy. "You little rat!" the thin, furious voice hissed; "you little rat! Spying on me! You little nigger bastard!"

The dietitian was twentyseven—old enough to have to take a few amorous risks but still young enough to attach a great deal of importance not so much to love, but to being caught at it. She was also stupid enough to believe that a child of five not only could deduce the truth from what he had heard, but that he would want to tell it as an adult would. So when during the following two days she could seem to look nowhere and be nowhere without finding the child watching her with the profound and intent interrogation of an animal, she foisted upon him more of the attributes of an adult: she believed that he not only intended to tell, but that he deferred doing it deliberately in order to make her suffer more. It never occurred to her that he believed that he was the one who had been taken in sin and was being tortured with punishment deferred and that he was putting himself in her way in order to get it over with, get his whipping and strike the balance and write it off.

By the second day she was well nigh desperate. She did not sleep at night. She lay most of the night now tense, teeth and hands clenched, panting with fury and terror and worst of all, regret: that blind fury to turn back time just for an hour, a second. This was to the exclusion of even love during the time. The young doctor was now even less than the child, merely an instrument of her disaster and not even that of her salvation. She could not have said which she hated most. She could not even say when she was asleep and when she was awake. Because always against her eyelids or upon her retinæ was that still, grave, inescapable, parchmentcolored face watching her.

On the third day she came out of the coma state, the waking sleep through which during the hours of light and faces she carried her own face like an aching mask in a fixed grimace of dissimulation that dared not flag. On the third day she acted. She had no trouble finding him. It was in the corridor, the empty corridor during the quiet hour after dinner. He was there, doing nothing at all. Perhaps he had followed her. No one else could have said if he were waiting there or not. But she found him without surprise and he heard and turned and saw her without surprise: the two faces, the one no longer smooth pink-and-white, the other grave, sobereyed, perfectly empty of everything except waiting. 'Now I'll get it over with,' he thought.

"Listen," she said. Then she stopped, looking at him. It was as though she could not think what to say next. The child waited, still, motionless. Slowly and gradually the muscles of his backside were becoming flat and rigid and tense as boards. "Are you going to tell?" she said.

He didn't answer. He believed that anyone should have known that the last thing in the world he would do would be to tell about the toothpaste, the vomit. He was not looking at her face. He was watching her hands, waiting. One of them was clenched inside her skirt pocket. Through the cloth he could see that it was clenched hard. He had never been struck with a fist. Yet neither had he ever waited three days to be punished. When he saw the hand emerge from the pocket he believed that she was about to strike him. But she did not; the hand just opened beneath his eyes. Upon it lay a silver dollar. Her voice was thin, urgent, whispering, though the corridor was empty about them. "You can buy a lot with this. A whole dollar." He had never seen a dollar before, though he knew what it was. He looked at it. He wanted it as he would have wanted the bright cap from a beer bottle. But he did not believe that she would give it to him, because he would not give it to her if it were his. He didn't know what she wanted him to do. He was waiting to get whipped and then be released. Her voice went on, urgent, tense, fast: "A whole dollar. See? How much you could buy. Some to eat every day for a week. And next month maybe I'll give you another one."

He did not move nor speak. He might have been carven, a large toy: small, still, round headed and round eyed, in overalls. He was still with astonishment, shock, outrage. Looking at the dollar, he seemed to see ranked tubes of toothpaste like corded wood, endless and terrifying; his whole being coiled in a rich and passionate revulsion. "I dont want no more," he said. 'I dont never want no more,' he thought.

Then he didn't dare even look at her face. He could feel her, hear her, her long shuddering breath. *Now it's coming* he thought in a flashing instant. But she didn't even shake him. She just held him, hard, not shaking him, as if her hand too didn't know what it wanted to do next. Her face was so near that he could feel her breath on his cheek. He didn't need to look up to know what her face looked like now. "Tell!" she said. "Tell, then! You little nigger bastard! You nigger bastard!"

That was the third day. On the fourth day she became quite calmly and completely mad. She no longer planned at all. Her subsequent actions followed a kind of divination, as if the days and the unsleeping nights during which she had nursed behind that calm mask her fear and fury had turned her psychic along with her natural female infallibility for the spontaneous comprehension of evil.

She was quite calm now. She had escaped for the moment from even urgency. It was as though now she had time to look about and plan. Looking about the scene her glance, her mind, her thought, went full and straight and instantaneous to the janitor sitting in the door of the furnace room. There was no ratiocination in it, no design. She

. 117 .

just seemed to look outside herself for one moment like a passenger in a car, and saw without any surprise at all that small, dirty man sitting in a splint chair in a sootgrimed doorway, reading through steelrimmed spectacles from a book upon his knees—a figure, almost a fixture, of which she had been aware for five years now without once having actually looked at him. She would not have recognised his face on the street. She would have passed him without knowing him, even though he was a man. Her life now seemed straight and simple as a corridor with him sitting at the end of it. She went to him at once, already in motion upon the dingy path before she was aware that she had started.

He was sitting in his splint chair in the doorway, the open book upon his knees. When she approached she saw that it was the Bible. But she just noticed this, as she might have noticed a fly upon his leg. "You hate him too," she said. "You've been watching him too. I've seen you. Dont say you dont." He looked up at her face, the spectacles propped now above his brows. He was not an old man. In his present occupation he was an incongruity. He was a hard man, in his prime; a man who should have been living a hard and active life, and whom time, circumstance, something, had betrayed, sweeping the hale body and thinking of a man of fortyfive into a backwater suitable for a man of sixty or sixtyfive. "You know," she said. "You knew before the other children started calling him Nigger. You came out here at the same time. You weren't working here a month before that Christmas night when Charley found him on the doorstep yonder. Tell me." The janitor's face was round, a little flabby, quite dirty, with a dirty stubble. His eyes were quite clear, quite gray, quite cold. They were quite mad too. But the woman did not notice that. Or perhaps they did not look mad to her. So they faced one another in the coalgrimed doorway, mad eyes looking into mad eyes, mad voice talking to mad voice as calm and quiet and terse as two conspirators. "I've watched you for five years." She believed that she was telling the truth. "Sitting here in this very chair, watching him. You never sit here except when the children are outdoors. But as soon as they come out, you bring this chair here to the door and sit in it where you can watch them. Watching him and hearing the other children calling him Nigger. That's what you are doing. I know. You came here just to do that, to watch him and hate him. You were here ready when he came. Maybe you brought him and left him on the step yonder yourself. But anyway you know. And I've got to know. When he tells I will be fired. And Charley may— will— Tell me. Tell me, now."

"Ah," the janitor said. "I knowed he would be there to catch you when God's time came. I knowed. I know who set him there, a sign and a damnation for bitchery."

"Yes. He was right behind the curtain. As close as you are. You tell me, now. I've seen your eyes when you look at him. Watched you. For five years."

"I know," he said. "I know evil. Aint I made evil to get up and walk God's world? A walking pollution in God's own face I made it. Out of the mouths of little children He never concealed it. You have heard them. I never told them to say it, to call him in his rightful nature, by the name of his damnation. I never told them. They knowed. They was told, but it wasn't by me. I just waited, on His own good time, when He would see fitten to reveal it to

. 119 .

His living world. And it's come now. This is the sign, wrote again in womansinning and bitchery."

"Yes. But what must I do? Tell me."

"Wait. Like I waited. Five years I waited for the Lord to move and show His will. And He done it. You wait too. When He is ready for it He will show His will to them that have the sayso."

"Yes. The sayso." They glared at one another, still, breathing quietly.

"The madam. When He is ready, He will reveal it to her."

"You mean, if the madam knows, she will send him away? Yes. But I cant wait."

"No more can you hurry the Lord God. Aint I waited five years?"

She began to beat her hands lightly together. "But dont you see? This may be the Lord's way. For you to tell me. Because you know. Maybe it's His way for you to tell me and me to tell the madam." Her mad eyes were quite calm, her mad voice patient and calm: it was only her light unceasing hands.

"You'll wait, the same as I waited," he said. "You have felt the weight of the Lord's remorseful hand for maybe three days. I have lived under it for five years, watching and waiting for His own good time, because my sin is greater than your sin." Though he was looking directly at her face he did not seem to see her at all, his eyes did not. They looked like they were blind, wide open, icecold, fanatical. "To what I done and what I suffered to expiate it, what you done and are womansuffering aint no more than a handful of rotten dirt. I done bore mine five years;

who are you to hurry Almighty God with your little womanfilth?"

She turned, at once. "Well. You dont have to tell me. I know, anyway. I've known it all the time that he's part nigger." She returned to the house. She did not walk fast now and she yawned, terrifically. 'All I have to do is to think of some way to make the madam believe it. He wont tell her, back me up.' She yawned again, tremendously, her face emptied now of everything save yawning and then emptied even of yawning. She had just thought of something else. She had not thought of it before, but she believed that she had, had known it all the while, because it seemed so right: he would not only be removed; he would be punished for having given her terror and worry. 'They'll send him to the nigger orphanage,' she thought. 'Of course. They will have to.'

She did not even go to the matron at once. She had started there, but instead of turning toward the office door she saw herself passing it, going on toward the stairs and mounting. It was as though she followed herself to see where she was going. In the corridor, quiet and empty now, she yawned again, with utter relaxation. She entered her room and locked the door and took off her clothes and got into bed. The shades were drawn and she lay still in the more than halfdark, on her back. Her eyes were closed and her face was empty and smooth. After a while she began to open her legs and close them slowly, feeling the sheets flow cool and smooth over them and then flow warm and smooth again. Thinking seemed to hang suspended between the sleep which she had not had now in three nights and the sleep which she was about to receive, her body open to accept sleep as though sleep were a man. 'All I need do is to make the madam believe,' she thought. And then she thought *He will look just like a pea in a pan full of coffee beans*

That was in the afternoon. At nine that evening she was undressing again when she heard the janitor come up the corridor, toward her door. She did not, could not, know who it was, then somehow she did know, hearing the steady feet and then a knock at the door which already began to open before she could spring to it. She didn't call; she sprang to the door, putting her weight against it, holding it to. "I'm undressing!" she said in a thin, agonised voice, knowing who it was. He didn't answer, his weight firm and steady against the crawling door, beyond the crawling gap. "You cant come in here!" she cried, hardly louder than a whisper. "Dont you know they . . ." Her voice was panting, fainting, and desperate. He did not answer. She tried to halt and hold the slow inward crawling of the door. "Let me get some clothes on, and I'll come out there. Will you do that?" She spoke in that fainting whisper, her tone light, inconsequential, like that of one speaking to an unpredictable child or a maniac: soothing, cajoling: "You wait, now. Do you hear? Will you wait, now?" He did not answer. The slow and irresistible crawling of the door did not cease. Leaning against it, wearing nothing save her undergarment, she was like a puppet in some burlesque of rapine and despair. Leaning, downlooking, immobile, she appeared to be in deepest thought, as if the puppet in the midst of the scene had gone astray within itself. Then she turned, releasing the door, and sprang back to the bed, whipping up without looking at it a garment and whirling to face the door, clutching the garment at her breast, huddling. He had already entered; apparently he had been watching her and waiting during the whole blind interval of fumbling and interminable haste.

He still wore the overalls and he now wore his hat. He did not remove it. Again his cold mad gray eyes did not seem to see her, to look at her at all. "If the Lord Himself come into the room of one of you," he said, "you would believe He come in bitchery." He said, "Have you told her?"

The woman sat on the bed. She seemed to sink slowly back upon it, clutching the garment, watching him, her face blanched. "Told her?"

"What will she do with him?"

"Do?" She watched him: those bright, still eyes that seemed not to look at her so much as to envelop her. Her mouth hung open like the mouth of an idiot.

"Where will they send him to?" She didn't answer. "Dont lie to me, to the Lord God. They'll send him to the one for niggers." Her mouth closed; it was as if she had discovered at last what he was talking about. "Ay, I've thought it out. They'll send him to the one for nigger children." She didn't answer, but she was watching him now, her eyes still a little fearful but secret too, calculating. Now he was looking at her; his eyes seemed to contract upon her shape and being. "Answer me, Jezebel!" he shouted.

"Shhhhhhhhh!" she said. "Yes. They'll have to. When they find . . ."

"Ah," he said. His gaze faded; the eyes released her and enveloped her again. Looking at them, she seemed to see herself as less than nothing in them, trivial as a twig floating upon a pool. Then his eyes became almost human. He began to look about the womanroom as if he had never seen one before: the close room, warm, littered, woman-pinksmelling. "Womanfilth," he said. "Before the face of God." He turned and went out. After a while the woman rose. She stood for a time, clutching the garment, motionless, idiotic, staring at the empty door as if she could not think what to tell herself to do. Then she ran. She sprang to the door, flinging herself upon it, crashing it to and locking it, leaning against it, panting, clutching the turned key in both hands.

At breakfast time the next morning the janitor and the child were missing. No trace of them could be found. The police were notified at once. A side door was found to be unlocked, to which the janitor had a key.

"It's because he knows," the dietitian told the matron. "Knows what?"

"That that child, that Christmas boy, is a nigger."

"A what?" the matron said. Backthrust in her chair, she glared at the younger woman. "A ne— I dont believe it!" she cried. "I dont believe it!"

"You dont have to believe it," the other said. "But he knows it. He stole him away because of it."

The matron was past fifty, flabby faced, with weak, kind, frustrated eyes. "I dont believe it!" she said. But on the third day she sent for the dietitian. She looked as if she had not slept in some time. The dietitian, on the contrary, was quite fresh, quite serene. She was still unshaken when the matron told her the news, that the man and the child had been found. "At Little Rock," the matron said. "He tried to put the child into an orphanage there. They thought he was crazy and held him until the police came." She looked at the younger woman. "You told me . . . The other day you said . . . How did you know about this?"

The dietitian did not look away. "I didn't. I had no idea at all. Of course I knew it didn't mean anything when the other children called him Nigger—"

"Nigger?" the matron said. "The other children?"

"They have been calling him Nigger for years. Sometimes I think that children have a way of knowing things that grown people of your and my age dont see. Children, and old people like him, like that old man. That's why he always sat in the door yonder while they were playing in the yard: watching that child. Maybe he found it out from hearing the other children call him Nigger. But he might have known beforehand. If you remember, they came here about the same time. He hadn't been working here hardly a month before the night—that Christmas, dont you remember—when Ch—they found the baby on the doorstep?" She spoke smoothly, watching the baffled, shrinking eyes of the older woman full upon her own as though she could not remove them. The dietitian's eyes were bland and innocent. "And so the other day we were talking and he was trying to tell me something about the child. It was something he wanted to tell me, tell somebody, and finally he lost his nerve maybe and wouldn't tell it, and so I left him. I wasn't thinking about it at all. It had gone completely out of my mind when—" Her voice ceased. She gazed at the matron while into her face there came an expression of enlightenment, sudden comprehension; none could have said if it were simulated or not. "Why, that's why it . . . Why, I see it all, now. What happened just the day before they were gone, missing. I was in the corridor, going to my room; it was the same day I happened to be talking to him and he refused to tell me whatever it was he started to tell, when all of a sudden he came up and stopped me; I thought then it was funny because I had never before seen him inside the house. And he said—he sounded crazy, he looked crazy. I was scared, too scared to move, with him blocking the corridor—he said, 'Have you told her yet?' and I said, 'Told who? Told who what?' and then I realised he meant you; if I had told you that he had tried to tell me something about the child. But I didn't know what he meant for me to tell you and I wanted to scream and then he said, 'What will she do if she finds it out?' and I didn't know what to say or how to get away from him and then he said, 'You dont have to tell me. I know what she will do. She will send him to the one for niggers.' "

"For negroes?"

"I dont see how we failed to see it as long as we did. You can look at his face now, his eyes and hair. Of course it's terrible. But that's where he will have to go, I suppose."

Behind her glasses the weak, troubled eyes of the matron had a harried, jellied look, as if she were trying to force them to something beyond their physical cohesiveness. "But why did he want to take the child away?"

"Well, if you want to know what I think, I think he is crazy. If you could have seen him in the corridor that ni— day like I did. Of course it's bad for the child to have to go to the nigger home, after this, after growing up with white people. It's not his fault what he is. But it's not our fault, either—" She ceased, watching the matron. Behind the glasses the older woman's eyes were still harried, weak, hopeless; her mouth was trembling as she shaped speech with it. Her words were hopeless too, but they were decisive enough, determined enough.

"We must place him. We must place him at once. What applications have we? If you will hand me the file . . ."

When the child wakened, he was being carried. It was pitchdark and cold; he was being carried down stairs by someone who moved with silent and infinite care. Pressed between him and one of the arms which supported him was a wad which he knew to be his clothes. He made no outcry, no sound. He knew where he was by the smell, the air, of the back stairway which led down to the side door from the room in which his bed had been one among forty others since he could remember. He knew also by smell that the person who carried him was a man. But he made no sound, lying as still and as lax as while he had been asleep, riding high in the invisible arms, moving, descending slowly toward the side door which gave onto the playground.

He didn't know who was carrying him. He didn't bother about it because he believed that he knew where he was going. Or why, that is. He didn't bother about where either, yet. It went back two years, to when he was three years old. One day there was missing from among them a girl of twelve named Alice. He had liked her, enough to let her mother him a little; perhaps because of it. And so to him she was as mature, almost as large in size, as the adult women who ordered his eating and washing and sleeping, with the difference that she was not and never would be his enemy. One night she waked him. She was telling him goodbye but he did not know it. He was sleepy and a little annoyed, never full awake, suffering her because she had always tried to be good to him. He didn't know that she was crying because he did not know that grown people cried, and by the time he learned that, memory had forgotten her. He went back into sleep while still suffering her, and the next morning she was gone. Vanished, no trace of her left, not even a garment, the very bed in which she had slept already occupied by a new boy. He never did know where she went to. That day he listened while a few of the older girls who had helped her prepare to leave in that same hushed, secret sibilance in which a half dozen young girls help prepare the seventh one for marriage told, still batebreathed, about the new dress, the new shoes, the carriage which had fetched her away. He knew then that she had gone for good, had passed beyond the iron gates in the steel fence. He seemed to see her then, grown heroic at the instant of vanishment beyond the clashedto gates, fading without diminution of size into something nameless and splendid, like a sunset. It was more than a year before he knew that she had not been the first and would not be the last. That there had been more than Alice to vanish beyond the clashedto gates, in a new dress or new overalls, with a small neat bundle less large sometimes than a shoebox. He believed that that was what was happening to him now. He believed that he knew now how they had all managed to depart without leaving any trace behind them. He believed that they had been carried out, as he was being, in the dead of night.

Now he could feel the door. It was quite near now; he knew to the exact number how many more invisible steps remained to which in turn the man who carried him would lower himself with that infinite and silent care. Against his cheek he could feel the man's quiet, fast, warm breathing; beneath him he could feel the tense and rigid arms, the wadded lump which he knew was his clothing caught up by feel in the dark. The man stopped. As he stooped the child's feet swung down and touched the floor, his toes curling away from the ironcold planks. The man spoke, for the first time. "Stand up," he said. Then the child knew who he was.

He recognised the man at once, without surprise. The surprise would have been the matron's if she had known how well he did know the man. He did not know the man's name and in the three years since he had been a sentient creature they had not spoken a hundred words. But the man was a more definite person than anyone else in his life, not excepting the girl Alice. Even at three years of age the child knew that there was something between them that did not need to be spoken. He knew that he was never on the playground for instant that the man was not watching him from the chair in the furnace room door, and that the man was watching him with a profound and unflagging attention. If the child had been older he would perhaps have thought *He hates me and fears me. So much so that he cannot let me out of his sight* With more vocabulary but no more age he might have thought *That is why I am different from the others: because he is watching me all the time* He accepted it. So he was not surprised when he found who it was who had taken him, sleeping, from his bed and carried him downstairs; as, standing beside the door in the cold pitch dark while the man helped him put on his clothes, he might have thought *He hates me enough even to try to prevent something that is about to happen to me coming to pass*

He dressed obediently, shivering, as swiftly as he could, the two of them fumbling at the small garments, getting them on him somehow. "Your shoes," the man said, in that dying whisper. "Here." The child sat on the cold floor, putting on the shoes. The man was not touching him now, but the child could hear, feel, that the man was stooped too, engaged in something. 'He's putting on his shoes too,' he thought. The man touched him again, groping, lifting him to his feet. His shoes were not laced. He had not learned to do that by himself yet. He did not tell the man that he had not laced them. He made no sound at all. He just stood there and then a bigger garment enveloped him completely —by its smell he knew that it belonged to the man—and then he was lifted again. The door opened, inyawned. The fresh cold air rushed in, and light from the lamps along the street; he could see the lights and the blank factory walls and the tall unsmoking chimneys against the stars. Against the street light the steel fence was like a parade of starved soldiers. As they crossed the empty playground his dangling feet swung rhythmically to the man's striding, the unlaced shoes flapping about his ankles. They reached the iron gates and passed through.

They did not have to wait long for the streetcar. If he had been older he would have remarked how well the man had timed himself. But he didn't wonder or notice. He just stood on the corner beside the man, in the unlaced shoes, enveloped to the heels in the man's coat, his eyes round and wide, his small face still, awake. The car came up, the row of windows, jarring to a stop and humming while they entered. It was almost empty, since the hour was past two o'clock. Now the man noticed the unlaced shoes and laced them, the child watching, quite still on the seat, his legs thrust straight out before him. The station was a long distance away, and he had ridden on a streetcar before, so when they reached the station he was asleep. When he waked it was daylight and they had been on the train for some time. He had never ridden on a train before, but no one could have told it. He sat quite still, as in the streetcar, completely enveloped in the man's coat save for his out-thrust legs and his head, watching the country—hills and trees and cows and such—that he had never seen before flowing past. When the man saw that he was awake he produced food from a piece of newspaper. It was bread, with ham between. "Here," the man said. He took the food and ate, looking out the window.

He said no word, he had shown no surprise, not even when on the third day the policemen came and got him and the man. The place where they now were was no different from the one which they had left in the night—the same children, with different names; the same grown people, with different smells: he could see no more reason why he should not have stayed there than why he should ever have left the first one. But he was not surprised when they came and told him again to get up and dress, neglecting to tell him why or where he was going now. Perhaps he knew that he was going back; perhaps with his child's clair-voyance he had known all the while what the man had not: that it would not, could not, last. On the train again he saw the same hills, the same trees, the same cows, but from another side, another direction. The policeman gave him food. It was bread, with ham between, though it did not come out of a scrap of newspaper. He noticed that, but he said nothing, perhaps thought nothing.

Then he was home again. Perhaps he expected to be punished upon his return, for what, what crime exactly, he did not expect to know, since he had already learned that, though children can accept adults as adults, adults can never accept children as anything but adults too. He had already forgot the toothpaste affair. He was now avoiding the dietitian just as, a month ago, he had been putting himself in her way. He was so busy avoiding her that he had long since forgot the reason for it; soon he had forgotten the trip too, since he was never to know that there was any connection between them. Now and then he thought of it, hazily and vaguely. But that was only when he would look toward the door to the furnace room and remember the man who used to sit there and watch him and who was now gone, completely, without leaving any trace, not even the splint chair in the doorway, after the fashion of all who departed from there. Where he may have gone to also the child did not even think or even wonder.

One evening they came to the schoolroom and got him. It was two weeks before Christmas. Two of the young women—the dietitian was not one—took him to the bathroom and washed him and combed his damp hair and dressed him in clean overalls and fetched him to the matron's office. In the office sat a man, a stranger. And he looked at the man and he knew before the matron even spoke. Perhaps memory knowing, knowing beginning to remember; perhaps even desire, since five is still too young to have learned enough despair to hope. Perhaps he remembered suddenly the train ride and the food, since even memory did not go much further back than that. "Joseph," the matron said, "how would you like to go and live with some nice people in the country?"

He stood there, his ears and face red and burning with harsh soap and harsh towelling, in the stiff new overalls, listening to the stranger. He had looked once and saw a thickish man with a close brown beard and hair cut close though not recently. Hair and beard both had a hard, vigorous quality, unsilvered, as though the pigmentation were impervious to the forty and more years which the face revealed. The eyes were lightcolored, cold. He wore a suit of hard, decent black. On his knee rested a black hat held in a blunt clean hand shut, even on the soft felt of the hat, into a fist. Across his vest ran a heavy silver watch chain. His thick black shoes were planted side by side; they had been polished by hand. Even the child of five years, looking at him, knew that he did not use tobacco himself and would not tolerate it in others. But he did not look at the man because of his eyes.

He could feel the man looking at him though, with a stare cold and intent and yet not deliberately harsh. It was the same stare with which he might have examined a horse or a second hand plow, convinced beforehand that he would see flaws, convinced beforehand that he would buy. His voice was deliberate infrequent, ponderous; the voice of a man who demand d that he be listened to not so much with attention but i silence. "And you either cannot or will not tell me anything more about his parentage."

The matron did not look at him. Behind her glasses her eyes apparently had jellied, for the time at least. She said immediately, almost a little too immediately: "We make no effort to ascertain their parentage. As I told you before, he was left on the doorstep here on Christmas eve will be five years this two weeks. If the child's parentage is important to you, you had better not adopt one at all."

"I would not mean just that," the stranger said. His tone now was a little placative. He contrived at once to apologise without surrendering one jot of his conviction. "I would have thought to talk with Miss Atkins (this was the dietitian's name) since it was with her I have been in correspondence."

Again the matron's voice was cold and immediate, speaking almost before his had ceased: "I can perhaps give you as much information about this or any other of our children as Miss Atkins can, since her official connection here is only with the diningroom and kitchen. It just happened that in this case she was kind enough to act as secretary in our correspondence with you."

"It's no matter," the stranger said. "It's no matter. I had just thought . . ."

"Just thought what? We force no one to take our children, nor do we force the children to go against their wishes, if their reasons are sound ones. That is a matter for the two parties to settle between themselves. We only advise."

"Ay," the stranger said. "It's no matter, as I just said to you. I've no doubt the tyke will do. He will find a good home with Mrs. McEachern and me. We are not young now, and we like quiet ways. And he'll find no fancy food and no idleness. Nor neither more work than will be good for him. I make no doubt that with us he will grow up to fear God and abhor idleness and vanity despite his origin."

Thus the promissory note which he had signed with a tube of toothpaste on that afternoon two months ago was recalled, the yet oblivious executor of it sitting wrapped in a clean horse blanket, small, shapeless, immobile, on the seat of a light buggy jolting through the December twilight up a frozen and rutted lane. They had driven all that day. At noon the man had fed him, taking from beneath the seat a cardboard box containing country food cooked three days ago. But only now did the man speak to him. He spoke a single word, pointing up the lane with a mittened fist which clutched the whip, toward a single light which shown in the dusk. "Home," he said. The child said nothing. The man looked down at him. The man was bundled too against the cold, squat, big, shapeless, somehow rocklike, indomitable, not so much ungentle as ruthless. "I said, there is your home." Still the child didn't answer. He had never seen a home, so there was nothing for him to say about it. And he was not old enough to talk and say nothing at the same time. "You will find food and shelter and the care of Christian people," the man said. "And the work within your strength that will keep you out of mischief. For I will have you learn soon that the two abominations are sloth and idle thinking, the two virtues are work and the fear of God." Still the child said nothing. He had neither ever worked nor feared God. He knew less about God than about work. He had seen work going on in the person of men with rakes and shovels about the playground six days each week, but God had only occurred on Sunday. And then—save for the concomitant ordeal of cleanliness—it was music that pleased the ear and words that did not trouble the ear at all—on the whole, pleasant, even if a little tiresome. He said nothing at all. The buggy jolted on, the stout, wellkept team eagering, homing, barning.

There was one other thing which he was not to remember until later, when memory no longer accepted his face, accepted the surface of remembering. They were in the matron's office; he standing motionless, not looking at the stranger's eyes which he could feel upon him, waiting for the stranger to say what his eyes were thinking. Then it came: "Christmas. A heathenish name. Sacrilege. I will change that."

"That will be your legal right," the matron said. "We

are not interested in what they are called, but in how they are treated."

But the stranger was not listening to anyone anymore than he was talking to anyone. "From now on his name will be McEachern."

"That will be suitable," the matron said. "To give him your name."

"He will eat my bread and he will observe my religion," the stranger said. "Why should he not bear my name?"

The child was not listening. He was not bothered. He did not especially care, anymore than if the man had said the day was hot when it was not hot. He didn't even bother to say to himself *My name aint McEachern. My name is Christmas* There was no need to bother about that yet. There was plenty of time.

"Why not, indeed?" the matron said.

7

AND memory knows this; twenty years later memory is
still to believe *On this day I became a man*

The clean, spartan room was redolent of Sunday. In the
windows the clean, darned curtains stirred faintly in a
breeze smelling of turned earth and crabapple. Upon the
yellow imitation oak melodeon with its pedals padded with
pieces of frayed and outworn carpet sat a fruit jar filled with
larkspur. The boy sat in a straight chair beside the table on
which was a nickel lamp and an enormous Bible with
brass clasps and hinges and a brass lock. He wore a clean
white shirt without a collar. His trousers were dark, harsh,
and new. His shoes had been polished recently and clumsily,
as a boy of eight would polish them, with small dull patches
here and there, particularly about the heels, where the
polish had failed to overlap. Upon the table, facing him and
open, lay a Presbyterian catechism.

McEachern stood beside the table. He wore a clean,
glazed shirt, and the same black trousers in which the boy
had first seen him. His hair, damp, still unsilvered, was
combed clean and stiff upon his round skull. His beard was

also combed, also still damp. "You have not tried to learn it," he said.

The boy did not look up. He did not move. But the face of the man was not more rocklike. "I did try."

"Then try again. I'll give you another hour." From his pocket McEachern took a thick silver watch and laid it face-up on the table and drew up a second straight, hard chair to the table and sat down, his clean, scrubbed hands on his knees, his heavy polished shoes set squarely. On them were no patches where the polish had failed to overlap. There had been last night at suppertime, though. And later the boy, undressed for bed and in his shirt, had received a whipping and then polished them again. The boy sat at the table. His face was bent, still, expressionless. Into the bleak, clean room the springfilled air blew in fainting gusts.

That was at nine o'clock. They had been there since eight. There were churches nearby, but the Presbyterian church was five miles away; it would take an hour to drive it. At half past nine Mrs McEachern came in. She was dressed, in black, with a bonnet—a small woman, entering timidly, a little hunched, with a beaten face. She looked fifteen years older than the rugged and vigorous husband. She did not quite enter the room. She just came within the door and stood there for a moment, in her bonnet and her dress of rusty yet often brushed black, carrying an umbrella and a palm leaf fan, with something queer about her eyes, as if whatever she saw or heard, she saw or heard through a more immediate manshape or manvoice, as if she were the medium and the vigorous and ruthless husband the control. He may have heard her. But he neither looked up nor spoke. She turned and went away.

Exactly on the dot of the hour McEachern raised his head. "Do you know it now?" he said.

The boy did not move. "No," he said.

McEachern rose, deliberately, without haste. He took up the watch and closed it and returned it to his pocket, looping the chain again through his suspender. "Come," he said. He did not look back. The boy followed, down the hall, toward the rear; he too walked erect and in silence, his head up. There was a very kinship of stubbornness like a transmitted resemblance in their backs. Mrs McEachern was in the kitchen. She still wore the hat, still carried the umbrella and the fan. She was watching the door when they passed it. "Pa," she said. Neither of them so much as looked at her. They might not have heard, she might not have spoken, at all. They went on, in steady single file, the two backs in their rigid abnegation of all compromise more alike than actual blood could have made them. They crossed the back yard and went on toward the stable and entered. McEachern opened the crib door and stood aside. The boy entered the crib. McEachern took from the wall a harness strap. It was neither new nor old, like his shoes. It was clean, like the shoes, and it smelled like the man smelled: an odor of clean hard virile living leather. He looked down at the boy.

"Where is the book?" he said. The boy stood before him, still, his face calm and a little pale beneath the smooth parchment skin. "You did not bring it," McEachern said. "Go back and get it." His voice was not unkind. It was not human, personal, at all. It was just cold, implacable, like written or printed words. The boy turned and went out.

When he reached the house Mrs McEachern was in the hall. "Joe," she said. He did not answer. He didn't even look at her, at her face, at the stiff movement of one half lifted hand in stiff caricature of the softest movement which human hand can make. He walked stiffly past her, rigid-faced, his face rigid with pride perhaps and despair. Or maybe it was vanity, the stupid vanity of a man. He got the catechism from the table and returned to the stable.

McEachern was waiting, holding the strap. "Put it down," he said. The boy laid the book on the floor. "Not there," McEachern said, without heat. "You would believe that a stable floor, the stamping place of beasts, is the proper place for the word of God. But I'll learn you that, too." He took up the book himself and laid it on a ledge. "Take down your pants," he said. "We'll not soil them."

Then the boy stood, his trousers collapsed about his feet, his legs revealed beneath his brief shirt. He stood, slight and erect. When the strap fell he did not flinch, no quiver passed over his face. He was looking straight ahead, with a rapt, calm expression like a monk in a picture. McEachern began to strike methodically, with slow and deliberate force, still without heat or anger. It would have been hard to say which face was the more rapt, more calm, more convinced.

He struck ten times, then he stopped. "Take the book," he said. "Leave your pants be." He handed the boy the catechism. The boy took it. He stood so, erect, his face and the pamphlet lifted, his attitude one of exaltation. Save for surplice he might have been a Catholic choir boy, with for nave the looming and shadowy crib, the rough planked wall beyond which in the ammoniac and dryscented obscurity beasts stirred now and then with snorts and indolent thuds. McEachern lowered himself stiffly to the top of a feed box, spreadkneed, one hand on his knee and the silver watch in the other palm, his clean, bearded face as firm as carved stone, his eyes ruthless, cold, but not unkind.

They remained so for another hour. Before it was up Mrs McEachern came to the back door of the house. But she did not speak. She just stood there, looking at the stable, in the hat, with the umbrella and the fan. Then she went back into the house.

Again on the exact second of the hour McEachern returned the watch to his pocket. "Do you know it now?" he said. The boy didn't answer, rigid, erect, holding the open pamphlet before his face. McEachern took the book from between his hands. Otherwise, the boy did not move at all. "Repeat your catechism," McEachern said. The boy stared straight at the wall before him. His face was now quite white despite the smooth rich pallor of his skin. Carefully and deliberately McEachern laid the book upon the ledge and took up the strap. He struck ten times. When he finished, the boy stood for a moment longer motionless. He had had no breakfast yet; neither of them had eaten breakfast yet. Then the boy staggered and would have fallen if the man had not caught his arm, holding him up. "Come," McEachern said, trying to lead him to the feed box. "Sit down here."

"No," the boy said. His arm began to jerk in the man's grasp. McEachern released him.

"Are you all right? Are you sick?"

"No," the boy said. His voice was faint, his face was quite white.

"Take the book," McEachern said, putting it into the boy's hand. Through the crib window Mrs McEachern came into view, emerging from the house. She now wore a faded Mother Hubbard and a sunbonnet, and she carried a cedar bucket. She crossed the window without looking toward the crib, and vanished. After a time the slow creak of a well pulley reached them, coming with a peaceful, startling quality upon the Sabbath air. Then she appeared again in the window, her body balanced now to the bucket's weight in her hand, and reentered the house without looking toward the stable.

Again on the dot of the hour McEachern looked up from the watch. "Have you learned it?" he said. The boy did not answer, did not move. When McEachern approached he saw that the boy was not looking at the page at all, that his eyes were quite fixed and quite blank. When he put his hand on the book he found that the boy was clinging to it as if it were a rope or a post. When McEachern took the book forcibly from his hands, the boy fell at full length to the floor and did not move again.

When he came to it was late afternoon. He was in his own bed in the attic room with its lowpitched roof. The room was quiet, already filling with twilight. He felt quite well, and he lay for some time, looking peacefully up at the slanted ceiling overhead, before he became aware that there was someone sitting beside the bed. It was McEachern. He now wore his everyday clothes also—not the overalls in which he went to the field, but a faded clean shirt without a collar, and faded, clean khaki trousers. "You are awake," he said. His hand came forth and turned back the cover. "Come," he said.

The boy did not move. "Are you going to whip me again?"

"Come," McEachern said. "Get up." The boy rose from the bed and stood, thin, in clumsy cotton underclothes. McEachern was moving also, thickly, with clumsy, muscle-bound movements, as if at the expenditure of tremendous effort; the boy, watching with the amazeless interest of a child, saw the man kneel slowly and heavily beside the bed. "Kneel down," McEachern said. The boy knelt; the two of them knelt in the close, twilit room: the small figure in cutdown underwear, the ruthless man who had never known either pity or doubt. McEachern began to pray. He prayed for a long time, his voice droning, soporific, monotonous. He asked that he be forgiven for trespass against the Sabbath and for lifting his hand against a child, an orphan, who was dear to God. He asked that the child's stubborn heart be softened and that the sin of disobedience be forgiven him also, through the advocacy of the man whom he had flouted and disobeyed, requesting that Almighty be as magnanimous as himself, and by and through and because of conscious grace.

He finished and rose, heaving to his feet. The boy still knelt. He did not move at all. But his eyes were open (his face had never been hidden or even lowered) and his face was quite calm; calm, peaceful, quite inscrutable. He heard the man fumble at the table on which the lamp sat. A match scraped, spurted; the flame steadied upon the wick, beneath the globe upon which the man's hand appeared now as if it had been dipped in blood. The shadows whirled and steadied. McEarchern lifted something from the table beside the lamp: the catechism. He looked down at the boy: a nose, a cheek jutting, granitelike, bearded to the caverned and spectacled eyesocket. "Take the book," he said.

It had begun that Sunday morning before breakfast. He had had no breakfast; likely neither he nor the man had once thought of that. The man himself had eaten no breakfast, though he had gone to the table and demanded absolution for the food and for the necessity of eating it. At the noon meal he had been asleep, from nervous exhaustion. And at supper time neither of them had thought of food. The boy did not even know what was wrong with him, why he felt weak and peaceful.

That was how he felt as he lay in bed. The lamp was still burning; it was now full dark outside. Some time had elapsed, but it seemed to him that if he turned his head he would still see the two of them, himself and the man, kneeling beside the bed, or anyway, in the rug the indentations of the twin pairs of knees without tangible substance. Even the air seemed still to excrete that monotonous voice as of someone talking in a dream, talking, adjuring, arguing with a Presence who could not even make a phantom indentation in an actual rug.

He was lying so, on his back, his hands crossed on his breast like a tomb effigy, when he heard again feet on the cramped stairs. They were not the man's; he had heard McEachern drive away in the buggy, departing in the twilight to drive three miles and to a church which was not Presbyterian, to serve the expiation which he had set himself for the morning.

Without turning his head the boy heard Mrs McEachern toil slowly up the stairs. He heard her approach across the floor. He did not look, though after a time her shadow came and fell upon the wall where he could see it, and he saw that she was carrying something. It was a tray of food. She set the tray on the bed. He had not once looked at her. He had not moved. "Joe," she said. He didn't move. "Joe," she said. She could see that his eyes were open. She did not touch him.

"I aint hungry," he said.

She didn't move. She stood, her hands folded into her apron. She didn't seem to be looking at him, either. She seemed to be speaking to the wall beyond the bed. "I know what you think. It aint that. He never told me to bring it to you. It was me that thought to do it. He dont know. It aint any food he sent you." He didn't move. His face was calm as a graven face, looking up at the steep pitch of the plank ceiling. "You haven't eaten today. Sit up and eat. It wasn't him that told me to bring it to you. He dont know it. I waited until he was gone and then I fixed it myself."

He sat up then. While she watched him he rose from the bed and took the tray and carried it to the corner and turned it upside down, dumping the dishes and food and all onto the floor. Then he returned to the bed, carrying the empty tray as though it were a monstrance and he the bearer, his surplice the cutdown undergarment which had been bought for a man to wear. She was not watching him now, though she had not moved. Her hands were still rolled into her apron. He got back into bed and lay again on his back, his eyes wide and still upon the ceiling. He could see her motionless shadow, shapeless, a little hunched. Then it went away. He did not look, but he could hear her kneel in the corner, gathering the broken dishes back into the tray. Then she left the room. It was quite still then. The lamp burned steadily above the steady wick; on the wall the flitting shadows of whirling moths were as large as birds. From beyond the window he could smell, feel, darkness, spring, the earth.

He was just eight then. It was years later that memory knew what he was remembering; years after that night when, an hour later, he rose from the bed and went and knelt in the corner as he had not knelt on the rug, and above the outraged food kneeling, with his hands ate, like a savage, like a dog.

It was dusk; already he should have been miles toward home. Although his Saturday afternoons were free, he had never before been this far from home this late. When he reached home he would be whipped. But not for what he might have or might not have done during his absence. When he reached home he would receive the same whipping though he had committed no sin as he would receive if McEachern had seen him commit it.

But perhaps he did not yet know himself that he was not going to commit the sin. The five of them were gathered quietly in the dusk about the sagging doorway of a deserted sawmill shed where, waiting hidden a hundred yards away, they had watched the negro girl enter and look back once and then vanish. One of the older boys had arranged it and he went in first. The others, boys in identical overalls, who lived within a three mile radius, who, like the one whom they knew as Joe McEachern, could at fourteen and fifteen plow and milk and chop wood like grown men, drew straws for turns. Perhaps he did not even think of it as a sin until he thought of the man who would be waiting for him at home, since to fourteen the paramount sin would be to be publicly convicted of virginity.

His turn came. He entered the shed. It was dark. At once he was overcome by a terrible haste. There was something in him trying to get out, like when he had used to think of toothpaste. But he could not move at once, standing there, smelling the woman, smelling the negro all at once;

enclosed by the womanshenegro and the haste, driven, having to wait until she spoke: a guiding sound that was no particular word and completely unaware. Then it seemed to him that he could see her—something, prone, abject; her eyes perhaps. Leaning, he seemed to look down into a black well and at the bottom saw two glints like reflection of dead stars. He was moving, because his foot touched her. Then it touched her again because he kicked her. He kicked her hard, kicking into and through a choked wail of surprise and fear. She began to scream, he jerking her up, clutching her by the arm, hitting at her with wide, wild blows, striking at the voice perhaps, feeling her flesh anyway, enclosed by the womanshenegro and the haste.

Then she fled beneath his fist, and he too fled backward as the others fell upon him, swarming, grappling, fumbling, he striking back, his breath hissing with rage and despair. Then it was male he smelled, they smelled; somewhere beneath it the She scuttling, screaming. They trampled and swayed, striking at whatever hand or body touched, until they all went down in a mass, he underneath. Yet he still struggled, fighting, weeping. There was no She at all now. They just fought; it was as if a wind had blown among them, hard and clean. They held him down now, holding him helpless. "Will you quit now? We got you. Promise to quit now."

"No," he said. He heaved, twisting.

"Quit, Joe! You cant fight all of us. Dont nobody want to fight you, anyway."

"No," he said, panting, struggling. None of them could see, tell who was who. They had completely forgot about the girl, why they had fought, if they had ever known. On the part of the other four it had been purely automatic and reflex: that spontaneous compulsion of the male to fight with or because of or over the partner with which he has recently or is about to copulate. But none of them knew why he had fought. And he could not have told them. They held him to the earth, talking to one another in quiet, strained voices.

"Some of you all back there get away. Then the rest of us will turn him loose at the same time."

"Who's got him? Who is this I've got?"

"Here; turn loose. Now wait: here he is. Me and—" Again the mass of them surged, struggled. They held him again. "We got him here. You all turn loose and get out. Give us room."

Two of them rose and backed away, into the door. Then the other two seemed to explode upward out of the earth, the duskfilled shed, already running. Joe struck at them as soon as he was free, but they were already clear. Lying on his back he watched the four of them run on in the dusk, slowing, turning to look back. He rose and emerged from the shed. He stood in the door, brushing himself off, this too purely automatic, while a short distance away they huddled quietly and looked back at him. He did not look at them. He went on, his overalls duskcolored in the dusk. It was late now. The evening star was rich and heavy as a jasmine bloom. He did not look back once. He went on, fading, phantomlike; the four boys who watched him huddled quietly, their faces small and pale with dusk. From the group a voice spoke suddenly, loud: "Yaaah!" He did not look back. A second voice said quietly, carrying quietly, clear: "See you tomorrow at church, Joe." He didn't answer. He went on. Now and then he brushed at his overalls, mechanically, with his hands.

When he came in sight of home all light had departed from the west. In the pasture behind the barn there was a spring: a clump of willows in the darkness smelt and heard but not seen. When he approached the fluting of young frogs ceased like so many strings cut with simultaneous scissors. He knelt; it was too dark to discern even his silhouetted head. He bathed his face, his swollen eye. He went on, crossing the pasture toward the kitchen light. It seemed to watch him, biding and threatful, like an eye.

When he reached the lot fence he stopped, looking at the light in the kitchen window. He stood there for a while, leaning on the fence. The grass was aloud, alive with crickets. Against the dewgray earth and the dark bands of trees fireflies drifted and faded, erratic and random. A mockingbird sang in a tree beside the house. Behind him, in the woods beyond the spring, two whippoorwills whistled. Beyond them, as though beyond some ultimate horizon of summer, a hound howled. Then he crossed the fence and saw someone sitting quite motionless in the door to the stable in which waited the two cows which he had not yet milked.

He seemed to recognise McEachern without surprise, as if the whole situation were perfectly logical and reasonable and inescapable. Perhaps he was thinking then how he and the man could always count upon one another, depend upon one another; that it was the woman alone who was unpredictable. Perhaps he saw no incongruity at all in the fact that he was about to be punished, who had refrained from what McEachern would consider the cardinal sin which he could commit, exactly the same as if he had committed it. McEachern did not rise. He still sat, stolid and rocklike, his shirt a white blur in the door's black yawn.

"I have milked and fed," he said. Then he rose, deliberately. Perhaps the boy knew that he already held the strap in his hand. It rose and fell, deliberate, numbered, with deliberate, flat reports. The boy's body might have been wood or stone; a post or a tower upon which the sentient part of him mused like a hermit, contemplative and remote with ecstasy and selfcrucifixion.

As they approached the kitchen they walked side by side. When the light from the window fell upon them the man stopped and turned, leaning, peering. "Fighting," he said. "What was it about?"

The boy did not answer. His face was quite still, composed. After a while he answered. His voice was quiet, cold. "Nothing."

They stood there. "You mean, you cant tell or you wont tell?" The boy did not answer. He was not looking down. He was not looking at anything. "Then, if you dont know you are a fool. And if you wont tell you have been a knave. Have you been to a woman?"

"No," the boy said. The man looked at him. When he spoke his tone was musing.

"You have never lied to me. That I know of, that is." He looked at the boy, at the still profile. "Who were you fighting with?"

"There was more than one."

"Ah," the man said. "You left marks on them, I trust?"

"I dont know. I reckon so."

"Ah," the man said. "Go and wash. Supper is ready."

When he went to bed that night his mind was made up to run away. He felt like an eagle: hard, sufficient, potent, remorseless, strong. But that passed, though he did not then know that, like the eagle, his own flesh as well as all space was still a cage.

McEachern did not actually miss the heifer for two days. Then he found the new suit where it was hidden in the barn; on examining it he knew that it had never been worn. He found the suit in the forenoon. But he said nothing about it. That evening he entered the barn where Joe was milking. Sitting on the low stool, his head bent against the cow's flanks, the boy's body was now by height at least the body of a man. But McEachern did not see that. If he saw anything at all, it was the child, the orphan of five years who had sat with the still and alert and unrecking passiveness of an animal on the seat of his buggy on that December evening twelve years ago. "I dont see your heifer," McEachern said. Joe didn't answer. He bent above the bucket, above the steady hissing of milk. McEachern stood behind and above him, looking down at him. "I said, your heifer has not come up."

"I know it," Joe said. "I reckon she is down at the creek. I'll look after her, being as she belongs to me."

"Ah," McEachern said. His voice was not raised. "The creek at night is no place for a fifty dollar cow."

"It'll be my loss, then," Joe said. "It was my cow."

"Was?" McEachern said. "Did you say *was* my cow?"

Joe did not look up. Between his fingers the milk hissed steadily into the pail. Behind him he heard McEachern move. But Joe did not look around until the milk no longer responded. Then he turned. McEachern was sitting on a wooden block in the door. "You had better take the milk on to the house first," he said.

Joe stood, the pail swinging from his hand. His voice was dogged though quiet. "I'll find her in the morning."

"Take the milk on to the house," McEachern said. "I will wait for you here."

For a moment longer Joe stood there. Then he moved. He emerged and went on to the kitchen. Mrs McEachern came in as he was setting the pail onto the table. "Supper is ready," she said. "Has Mr McEachern come to the house yet?"

Joe was turning away, back toward the door. "He'll be in soon," he said. He could feel the woman watching him. She said, in a tone tentative, anxious:

"You'll have just time to wash."

"We'll be in soon." He returned to the barn. Mrs McEachern came to the door and looked after him. It was not yet full dark and she could see her husband standing in the barn door. She did not call. She just stood there and watched the two men meet. She could not hear what they said.

"She will be down at the creek, you say?" McEachern said.

"I said she may be. This is a good-sized pasture."

"Ah," McEachern said. Both their voices were quiet. "Where do you think she will be?"

"I dont know. I aint no cow. I dont know where she might be."

McEachern moved. "We'll go see," he said. They entered the pasture in single file. The creek was a quarter of a mile distant. Against the dark band of trees where it flowed fireflies winked and faded. They reached these trees. The trunks of them were choked with marshy undergrowth, hard to penetrate even by day. "Call her," Mc-

Eachern said. Joe did not answer. He did not move. They faced one another.

"She's my cow," Joe said. "You gave her to me. I raised her from a calf because you gave her to me to be my own."

"Yes," McEachern said. "I gave her to you. To teach you the responsibility of possessing, owning, ownership. The responsibility of the owner to that which he owns under God's sufferance. To teach you foresight and aggrandisement. Call her."

For a while longer they faced one another. Perhaps they were looking at one another. Then Joe turned and went on along the marsh, McEachern following. "Why dont you call her?" he said. Joe did not answer. He did not seem to be watching the marsh, the creek, at all. On the contrary he was watching the single light which marked the house, looking back now and then as if he were gauging his distance from it. They did not go fast, yet in time they came to the boundary fence which marked the end of the pasture. It was now full dark. When he reached the fence Joe turned and stopped. Now he looked at the other. Again they stood face to face. Then McEachern said: "What have you done with that heifer?"

"I sold her," Joe said.

"Ah. You sold her. And what did you get for her, might I ask?"

They could not distinguish one another's face now. They were just shapes, almost of a height, though McEachern was the thicker. Above the white blur of his shirt McEachern's head resembled one of the marble cannonballs on Civil War monuments. "It was my cow," Joe said. "If she wasn't mine, why did you tell me she was? Why did you give her to me?"

"You are quite right. She was your own. I have not yet chidden you for selling her, provided you got a good price. And even if you were beat in the trade, which with a boy of eighteen is more than like to be so, I will not chide you for that. Though you would better have asked the advice of some one older in the ways of the world. But you must learn, as I did. What I ask is, Where have you put the money for safekeeping?" Joe didn't answer. They faced one another. "You gave it to your fostermother to keep for you, belike?"

"Yes," Joe said. His mouth said it, told the lie. He had not intended to answer at all. He heard his mouth say the word with a kind of shocked astonishment. Then it was too late. "I gave it to her to put away," he said.

"Ah," McEachern said. He sighed; it was a sound almost luxurious, of satisfaction and victory. "And you will doubtless say also that it was your fostermother who bought the new suit which I found hid in the loft. You have revealed every other sin of which you are capable: sloth, and ingratitude, and irreverence and blasphemy. And now I have taken you in the remaining two: lying and lechery. What else would you want with a new suit if you were not whoring?" And then he acknowledged that the child whom he had adopted twelve years ago was a man. Facing him, the two of them almost toe to toe, he struck at Joe with his fist.

Joe took the first two blows; perhaps from habit, perhaps from surprise. But he took them, feeling twice the man's hard fist crash into his face. Then he sprang back, crouched, licking blood, panting. They faced one another. "Dont you hit me again," he said.

Later, lying cold and rigid in his bed in the attic, he

heard their voices coming up the cramped stairs from the room beneath.

"I bought it for him!" Mrs McEachern said. "I did! I bought it with my butter money. You said that I could have—could spend— Simon! Simon!"

"You are a clumsier liar than even he," the man said. His voice came, measured, harsh, without heat, up the cramped stair to where Joe lay in bed. He was not listening to it. "Kneel down. Kneel down. KNEEL DOWN, WOMAN. Ask grace and pardon of God; not of me."

She had always tried to be kind to him, from that first December evening twelve years ago. She was waiting on the porch—a patient, beaten creature without sex demarcation at all save the neat screw of graying hair and the skirt —when the buggy drove up. It was as though instead of having been subtly slain and corrupted by the ruthless and bigoted man into something beyond his intending and her knowing, she had been hammered stubbornly thinner and thinner like some passive and dully malleable metal, into an attenuation of dumb hopes and frustrated desires now faint and pale as dead ashes.

When the buggy stopped she came forward as though she had already planned it, practiced it: how she would lift him down from the seat and carry him into the house. He had never been carried by a woman since he was big enough to walk. He squirmed down and entered the house on his own feet, marched in, small, shapeless in his wrappings. She followed, hovering about him. She made him sit down; it was as though she hovered about with a kind of strained alertness, an air baffled and alert, waiting to spring it again and try to make himself and her act as she had planned for them to act. Kneeling before him she was trying to take off his shoes, until he realised what she wanted. He put her hands away and removed the shoes himself, not setting them onto the floor though. He held to them. She stripped off his stockings and then she fetched a basin of hot water, fetched it so immediately that anyone but a child would have known that she must have had it ready and waiting all day probably. He spoke for the first time, then. "I done washed just yesterday," he said.

She didn't answer. She knelt before him while he watched the crown of her head and her hands fumbling a little clumsily about his feet. He didn't try to help her now. He didn't know what she was trying to do, not even when he was sitting with his cold feet in the warm water. He didn't know that that was all, because it felt too good. He was waiting for the rest of it to begin; the part that would not be pleasant, whatever it would be. This had never happened to him before either.

Later she put him to bed. For two years almost he had been dressing and undressing himself, unnoticed and unassisted save by occasional Alices. He was already too tired to go to sleep at once, and now he was puzzled and hence nervous, waiting until she went out so he could sleep. Then she did not go out. Instead she drew a chair up to the bed and sat down. There was no fire in the room; it was cold. She had a shawl now about her shoulders, huddled into the shawl, her breath vaporising as though she were smoking. And he became wide awake now. He was waiting for the part to begin which he would not like, whatever it was, whatever it was that he had done. He didn't know that this was all. This had never happened to him before either.

It began on that night. He believed that it was to go on

for the rest of his life. At seventeen, looking back he could see now the long series of trivial, clumsy, vain efforts born of frustration and fumbling and dumb instinct: the dishes she would prepare for him in secret and then insist on his accepting and eating them in secret, when he did not want them and he knew that McEachern would not care anyway; the times when, like tonight, she would try to get herself between him and the punishment which, deserved or not, just or unjust, was impersonal, both the man and the boy accepting it as a natural and inescapable fact until she, getting in the way, must give it an odor, an attenuation, and aftertaste.

Sometimes he thought that he would tell her alone, have her who in her helplessness could neither alter it nor ignore it, know it and need to hide it from the man whose immediate and predictable reaction to the knowledge would so obliterate it as a factor in their relations that it would never appear again. To say to her in secret, in secret payment for the secret dishes which he had not wanted: "Listen. He says he has nursed a blasphemer and an ingrate. I dare you to tell him what he has nursed. That he has nursed a nigger beneath his own roof, with his own food at his own table."

Because she had always been kind to him. The man, the hard, just, ruthless man, merely depended on him to act in a certain way and to receive the as certain reward or punishment, just as he could depend on the man to react in a certain way to his own certain doings and misdoings. It was the woman who, with a woman's affinity and instinct for secrecy, for casting a faint taint of evil about the most trivial and innocent actions. Behind a loose board in the wall of his attic room she had hidden a small hoard of money in a tin can. The amount was trivial and it was apparently a secret to no one but her husband, and the boy believed that he would not have cared. But it had never been a secret from him. Even while he was still a child she would take him with her when with all the intense and mysterious caution of a playing child she would creep to the attic and add to the hoard meagre and infrequent and terrific nickels and dimes (fruit of what small chicanery and deceptions with none anywhere under the sun to say her nay he did not know), putting into the can beneath his round grave eyes coins whose value he did not even recognise. It was she who trusted him, who insisted on trusting him as she insisted on his eating: by conspiracy, in secret, making a secret of the very fact which the act of trusting was supposed to exemplify.

It was not the hard work which he hated, nor the punishment and injustice. He was used to that before he ever saw either of them. He expected no less, and so he was neither outraged nor surprised. It was the woman: that soft kindness which he believed himself doomed to be forever victim of and which he hated worse than he did the hard and ruthless justice of men. 'She is trying to make me cry,' he thought, lying cold and rigid in his bed, his hands beneath his head and the moonlight falling across his body, hearing the steady murmur of the man's voice as it mounted the stairway on its first heavenward stage; 'She was trying to make me cry. Then she thinks that they would have had me.'

. 8 .

MOVING quietly, he took the rope from its hiding place. One end of it was already prepared for making fast inside the window. Now it took him no time at all to reach the ground and to return; now, with more than a year of practice, he could mount the rope hand over hand, without once touching the wall of the house, with the shadowlike agility of a cat. Leaning from the window he let the free end whisper down. In the moonlight it looked not less frail than a spider skein. Then, with his shoes tied together and strung through his belt behind him, he slid down the rope, passing swift as a shadow across the window where the old people slept. The rope hung directly before the window. He drew it tautly aside, flat against the house, and tied it. Then he went on through the moonlight to the stable and mounted to the loft and took the new suit from its hiding place. It was wrapped in paper, carefully. Before unwrapping it he felt with his hands about the folds of the paper. 'He found it,' he thought. 'He knows.' He said aloud, whispering: "The bastard. The son of a bitch."

He dressed in the dark, swiftly. He was already late, because he had had to give them time to get to sleep after all the uproar about the heifer, the uproar which the woman had caused by meddling after it was all over, settled for the night, anyway. The bundle included a white shirt and a tie. He put the tie into his pocket, but he put on the coat so that the white shirt would not be so visible in the moonlight. He descended and emerged from the stable. The new cloth, after his soft, oftenwashed overalls, felt rich and harsh. The house squatted in the moonlight, dark, profound, a little treacherous. It was as though in the moonlight the house had acquired personality: threatful, deceptive. He passed it and entered the lane. He took from his pocket a dollar watch. He had bought it three days ago, with some of the money. But he had never owned a watch before and so he had forgot to wind it. But he did not need the watch to tell him that he was already late.

The lane went straight beneath the moon, bordered on each side by trees whose shadowed branches lay thick and sharp as black paint upon the mild dust. He walked fast, the house now behind him, himself now not visible from the house. The highroad passed the lane a short distance ahead. He expected at any moment to see the car rush past, since he had told her that if he were not waiting at the mouth of the lane, he would meet her at the schoolhouse where the dance was being held. But no car passed, and when he reached the highroad he could hear nothing. The road, the night, were empty. 'Maybe she has already passed,' he thought. He took out the dead watch again and looked at it. The watch was dead because he had had no chance to wind it. He had been made late by them who had given him no opportunity to wind the watch and so know if he were late or not. Up the dark lane, in the now invisible house, the woman now lay asleep, since she had done all she could to make him late. He looked that way, up the lane; he stopped in the act of looking and thinking; mind and body as if on the same switch, believing that he had seen movement among the shadows in the lane. Then he thought that he had not, that it might perhaps have been something in his mind projected like a shadow on a wall. 'But I hope it is him,' he thought. 'I wish it was him. I wish he would follow me and see me get into the car. I wish he would try to follow us. I wish he would try to stop me.' But he could see nothing in the lane. It was empty, intermittent with treacherous shadows. Then he heard, from far down the road toward town, the sound of the car. Looking, he saw presently the glare of the lights.

She was a waitress in a small, dingy, back street restaurant in town. Even a casual adult glance could tell that she would never see thirty again. But to Joe she probably did not look more than seventeen too, because of her smallness. She was not only not tall, she was slight, almost childlike. But the adult look saw that the smallness was not due to any natural slenderness but to some inner corruption of the spirit itself: a slenderness which had never been young, in not one of whose curves anything youthful had ever lived or lingered. Her hair was dark. Her face was prominently boned, always downlooking, as if her head were set so on her neck, a little out of line. Her eyes were like the button eyes of a toy animal: a quality beyond even hardness, without being hard.

It was because of her smallness that he ever attempted her, as if her smallness should have or might have protected her from the roving and predatory eyes of most men, leaving his chances better. If she had been a big woman he would not have dared. He would have thought, 'It wont be any use. She will already have a fellow, a man.'

It began in the fall when he was seventeen. It was a day in the middle of the week. Usually when they came to town it would be Saturday and they would bring food with them—cold dinner in a basket purchased and kept for that purpose—with the intention of spending the day. This time McEachern came to see a lawyer, with the intention of finishing his business and being home again by dinnertime. But it was almost twelve o'clock when he emerged onto the street where Joe waited for him. He came into sight looking at his watch. Then he looked at a municipal clock in the courthouse tower and then at the sun, with an expression of exasperation and outrage. He looked at Joe also with that expression, the open watch in his hand, his eyes cold, fretted. He seemed to be examining and weighing for the first time the boy whom he had raised from childhood. Then he turned. "Come," he said. "It cant be helped now."

The town was a railroad division point. Even in midweek there were many men about the streets. The whole air of the place was masculine, transient: a population even whose husbands were at home only at intervals and on holiday—a population of men who led esoteric lives whose actual scenes were removed and whose intermittent presence was pandered to like that of patrons in a theatre.

Joe had never before seen the place to which McEachern took him. It was a restaurant on a back street—a narrow dingy doorway between two dingy windows. He did not know that it was a restaurant at first. There was no sign outside and he could neither smell nor hear food cooking. What he saw was a long wooden counter lined with backless stools, and a big, blonde woman behind a cigar case near the front and a clump of men at the far end of the counter, not eating, who all turned as one and looked at him and McEachern when they entered, through the smoke of cigarettes. Nobody said anything at all. They just looked at McEachern and Joe as if breathing had stopped with talking, as if even the cigarette smoke had stopped and now drifted aimlessly of its own weight. The men were not in overalls and they all wore hats, and their faces were all alike: not young and not old; not farmers and not townsmen either. They looked like people who had just got off a train and who would be gone tomorrow and who did not have any address.

Sitting on two of the backless stools at the counter, McEachern and Joe ate. Joe ate fast because McEachern was eating fast. Beside him the man, even in the act of eating, seemed to sit in a kind of stiffbacked outrage. The food which McEachern ordered was simple: quickly prepared and quickly eaten. But Joe knew that parsimony had no part in this. Parsimony might have brought them here in preference to another place, but he knew that it was a desire to depart quickly that had chosen the food. As soon as he laid down his knife and fork, McEachern said, "Come," already getting down from his stool. At the cigar counter McEachern paid the brasshaired woman. There was about her a quality impervious to time: a belligerent and diamondsurfaced respectability. She had not so much as looked at them, even when they entered and even when McEachern gave her money. Still without looking at them she made the change, correctly and swiftly, sliding the coins onto the glass counter almost before McEachern had offered the bill; herself somehow definite behind the false glitter of the careful hair, the careful face, like a carved lioness guarding a portal, presenting respectability like a shield behind which the clotted and idle and equivocal men could slant their hats and their thwartfacecurled cigarettes. McEachern counted his change and they went out, into the street. He was looking at Joe again. He said: "I'll have you remember that place. There are places in this world where a man may go but a boy, a youth of your age, may not. That is one of them. Maybe you should never have gone there. But you must see such so you will know what to avoid and shun. Perhaps it was as well that you saw it with me present to explain and warn you. And the dinner there is cheap."

"What is the matter with it?" Joe said.

"That is the business of the town and not of yours. You will only mark my words: I'll not have you go there again unless I am with you. Which will not be again. We'll bring dinner next time, early or no early."

That was what he saw that day while he was eating swiftly beside the unbending and quietly outraged man, the two of them completely isolated at the center of the long counter with at one end of it the brasshaired woman and at the other the group of men, and the waitress with her demure and downlooking face and her big, too big, hands setting the plates and cups, her head rising from beyond the counter at about the height of a tall child. Then he and McEachern departed. He did not expect ever to return. It was not that McEachern had forbidden him. He just did not believe that his life would ever again chance there. It was as if he said to himself, 'They are not my people. I can see them but I dont know what they are doing nor why. I can hear them but I dont know what they are saying nor why nor to whom. I know that there is something about it beside food, eating. But I dont know what. And I never will know.'

So it passed from the surface of thinking. Now and then during the next six months he returned to town, but he did not again even see or pass the restaurant. He could have. But he didn't think to. Perhaps he did not need to. More often that he knew perhaps thinking would have suddenly flowed into a picture, shaping, shaped: the long, barren, somehow equivocal counter with the still, cold-faced, violenthaired woman at one end as though guarding it, and at the other men with inwardleaning heads, smoking steadily, lighting and throwing away their constant cigarettes, and the waitress, the woman not much larger than a child going back and forth to the kitchen with her arms overladen with dishes, having to pass on each journey within touching distance of the men who leaned with their slanted hats and spoke to her through the cigarette smoke, murmured to her somewhere near mirth or exultation, and her face musing, demure, downcast, as if she had not heard. 'I dont even know what they are saying to her,' he thought, thinking *I dont even know that what they are saying to her is something that men do not say to a passing child* believing *I do not know yet that in the instant of sleep the eyelid closing prisons within the eye's self her face demure, pensive; tragic, sad, and young; waiting, colored with all the vague and formless magic of young desire. That already there is something for love to feed upon: that sleeping I know now why I struck refraining that negro*

girl three years ago and that she must know it too and be
proud too, with waiting and pride

So he did not expect to see her again, since love in the young requires as little of hope as of desire to feed upon. Very likely he was as much surprised by his action and what it inferred and revealed as McEachern would have been. It was on Saturday this time, in the spring now. He had turned eighteen. Again McEachern had to see the lawyer. But he was prepared now. "I'll be there an hour," he said. "You can walk about and see the town." Again he looked at Joe, hard, calculating, again a little fretted, like a just man forced to compromise between justice and judgment. "Here," he said. He opened his purse and took a coin from it. It was a dime. "You might try not to throw it away as soon as you can find someone who will take it. It's a strange thing," he said fretfully, looking at Joe, "but it seems impossible for a man to learn the value of money without first having to learn to waste it. You will be here in one hour."

He took that coin and went straight to the restaurant. He did not even put the coin into his pocket. He did it without plan or design, almost without volition, as if his feet ordered his action and not his head. He carried the dime clutched hot and small in his palm as a child might. He entered the screen door, clumsily, stumbling a little. The blonde woman behind the cigar case (it was as if she had not moved in the six months, not altered one strand of her hard bright brassridged hair or even her dress) watched him. At the far end of the counter the group of men with their tilted hats and their cigarettes and their odor of barbershops, watched him. The proprietor was among them. He noticed, saw, the proprietor for the first time. Like the other men, the proprietor wore a hat and was smoking. He was not a big man, not much bigger than Joe himself, with a cigarette burning in one corner of his mouth as though to be out of the way of talking. From that face squinted and still behind the curling smoke from the cigarette which was not touched once with hand until it burned down and was spat out and ground beneath a heel, Joe was to acquire one of his own mannerisms. But not yet. That was to come later, when life had begun to go so fast that accepting would take the place of knowing and believing. Now he just looked at the man who leaned upon the counter from the inward side, in a dirty apron which he wore as a footpad might assume for the moment a false beard. The accepting was to come later, along with the whole sum of entire outrage to credulity: these two people as husband and wife, the establishment as a business for eating, with the successive imported waitresses clumsy with the cheap dishes of simple food as business justified; and himself accepting, taking, during his brief and violent holiday like a young stallion in a state of unbelieving and ecstatic astonishment in a hidden pasture of tired and professional mares, himself in turn victim of nameless and unnumbered men.

But that was not yet. He went to the counter, clutching the dime. He believed that the men had all stopped talking to watch him, because he could hear nothing now save a vicious frying sound from beyond the kitchen door, thinking *She's back there. That's why I dont see her* He slid onto a stool. He believed that they were all watching him. He believed that the blonde woman behind the cigar case was looking at him, and the proprietor too, across whose face now the smoke of the cigarette would have become quite still in its lazy vaporing. Then the proprietor spoke a single word. Joe knew that he had not moved nor touched the cigarette. "Bobbie," he said.

A man's name. It was not-thinking. It was too fast, too complete: *She's gone. They have got a man in her place. I have wasted the dime, like he said* He believed that he could not leave now; that if he tried to go out, the blonde woman would stop him. He believed that the men at the back knew this and were laughing at him. So he sat quite still on the stool, looking down, the dime clutched in his palm. He did not see the waitress until the two overlarge hands appeared upon the counter opposite him and into sight. He could see the figured pattern of her dress and the bib of an apron and the two bigknuckled hands lying on the edge of the counter as completely immobile as if they were something she had fetched in from the kitchen. "Coffee and pie," he said.

Her voice sounded downcast, quite empty. "Lemon cocoanut chocolate."

In proportion to the height from which her voice came, the hands could not be her hands at all. "Yes," Joe said.

The hands did not move. The voice did not move. "Lemon cocoanut chocolate. Which kind." To the others they must have looked quite strange. Facing one another across the dark, stained, greasecrusted and frictionsmooth counter, they must have looked a little like they were praying: the youth countryfaced, in clean and Spartan clothing, with an awkwardness which invested him with a quality unworldly and innocent; and the woman opposite him, downcast, still, waiting, who because of her smallness partook likewise of that quality of his, of something beyond flesh. Her face was highboned, gaunt. The flesh was taut across her cheekbones, circled darkly about the eyes;

beneath the lowered lids her eyes seemed to be without depth, as if they could not even reflect. Her lower jaw seemed too narrow to contain two rows of teeth.

"Cocoanut," Joe said. His mouth said it, because immediately he wanted to unsay it. He had only the dime. He had been holding it too hard to have realised yet that it was only a dime. His hand sweated about it, upon it. He believed that the men were watching him and laughing again. He could not hear them and he did not look at them. But he believed that they were. The hands had gone away. Then they returned, setting a plate and a cup before him. He looked at her now, at her face. "How much is pie?" he said.

"Pie is ten cents." She was just standing there before him, beyond the counter, with her big hands again lying on the dark wood, with that quality spent and waiting. She had never looked at him. He said, in a faint, desperate voice:

"I reckon I dont want no coffee."

For a while she did not move. Then one of the big hands moved and took up the coffee cup; hand and cup vanished. He sat still, downlooking too, waiting. Then it came. It was not the proprietor. It was the woman behind the cigar case. "What's that?" she said.

"He dont want the coffee," the waitress said. Her voice, speaking, moved on, as if she had not paused at the question. Her voice was flat, quiet. The other woman's voice was quiet too.

"Didn't he order coffee too?" she said.

"No," the waitress said, in that level voice that was still in motion, going away. "I misunderstood."

When he got out, when his spirit wrung with abasement and regret and passionate for hiding scuttled past the cold face of the woman behind the cigar case, he believed that he knew he would and could never see her again. He did not believe that he could bear to see her again, even look at the street, the dingy doorway, even from a distance, again, not thinking yet *It's terrible to be young. It's terrible. Terrible* When Saturdays came he found, invented, reasons to decline to go to town, with McEachern watching him, though not with actual suspicion yet. He passed the days by working hard, too hard; McEachern contemplated the work with suspicion. But there was nothing which the man could know, deduce. Working was permitted him. Then he could get the nights passed, since he would be too tired to lie awake. And in time even the despair and the regret and the shame grew less. He did not cease to remember it, to react it. But now it had become wornout, like a gramophone record: familiar only because of the worn threading which blurred the voices. After a while even McEachern accepted a fact. He said:

"I have been watching you lately. And now there is nothing for it but I must misdoubt my own eyes or else believe that at last you are beginning to accept what the Lord has seen fit to allot you. But I will not have you grow vain because I have spoken well of it. You'll have time and opportunity (and inclination too, I dont doubt) to make me regret that I have spoken. To fall into sloth and idleness again. However, reward was created for man the same as chastisement. Do you see that heifer yonder? From today that calf is your own. See that I do not later regret it."

Joe thanked him. Then he could look at the calf and say, aloud: "That belongs to me." Then he looked at it, and it was again too fast and too complete to be thinking: *That is not a gift. It is not even a promise: it is a threat* thinking, 'I didn't ask for it. He gave it to me. I didn't ask for it,' believing *God knows, I have earned it*

It was a month later. It was Saturday morning. "I thought you did not like town anymore," McEachern said.

"I reckon one more trip wont hurt me," Joe said. He had a half dollar in his pocket. Mrs McEachern had given it to him. He had asked for a nickel. She insisted that he take the half dollar. He took it, holding it on his palm, cold, contemptuously.

"I suppose not," McEachern said. "You have worked hard, too. But town is no good habit for a man who has yet to make his way."

He did not need to escape, though he would have, even by violence perhaps. But McEachern made it easy. He went to the restaurant, fast. He entered without stumbling now. The waitress was not there. Perhaps he saw, noticed that she wasn't. He stopped at the cigar counter, behind which the woman sat, laying the half dollar on the counter. "I owe a nickel. For a cup of coffee. I said pie and coffee, before I knew that pie was a dime. I owe you a nickel." He did not look toward the rear. The men were there, in their slanted hats and with their cigarettes. The proprietor was there; waiting, Joe heard him at last, in the dirty apron, speaking past the cigarette:

"What is it? What does he want?"

"He says he owes Bobbie a nickel," the woman said. "He wants to give Bobbie a nickel." Her voice was quiet. The proprietor's voice was quiet.

"Well for Christ's sake," he said. To Joe the room was full of listening. He heard, not hearing; he saw, not looking. He was now moving toward the door. The half dollar lay on the glass counter. Even from the rear of the room the proprietor could see it, since he said, "What's that for?"

"He says he owes for a cup of coffee," the woman said.

Joe had almost reached the door. "Here, Jack," the man said. Joe did not stop. "Give him his money," the man said, flat-voiced, not yet moving. The cigarette smoke would curl still across his face, unwinded by any movement. "Give it back to him," the man said. "I dont know what his racket is. But he cant work it here. Give it back to him. You better go back to the farm, Hiram. Maybe you can make a girl there with a nickel."

Now he was in the street, sweating the half dollar, the coin sweating his hand, larger than a cartwheel, feeling. He walked in laughter. He had passed through the door upon it, upon the laughing of the men. It swept and carried him along the street; then it began to flow past him, dying away, letting him to earth, pavement. He and the waitress were facing one another. She did not see him at once, walking swiftly, downlooking, in a dark dress and a hat. Again, stopped, she did not even look at him, having already looked at him, allseeing, like when she had set the coffee and the pie on the counter. She said, "Oh. And you come back to give it to me. Before them. And they kidded you. Well, say."

"I thought you might have had to pay for it, yourself. I thought—"

"Well, say. Can you tie that. Can you, now."

They were not looking at one another, standing face to face. To another they must have looked like two monks met during the hour of contemplation in a garden path. "I just thought that I . . ."

"Where do you live?" she said. "In the country? Well, say. What's your name?"

"It's not McEachern," he said. "It's Christmas."

"Christmas? Is that your name? Christmas? Well, say."

On the Saturday afternoons during and after adolescence he and the other four or five boys hunted and fished. He saw girls only at church, on Sunday. They were associated with Sunday and with church. So he could not notice them. To do so would be, even to him, a retraction of his religious hatred. But he and the other boys talked about girls. Perhaps some of them—the one who arranged with the negro girl that afternoon, for instance—knew. "They all want to," he told the others. "But sometimes they cant." The others did not know that. They did not know that all girls wanted to, let alone that there were times when they could not. They thought differently. But to admit that they did not know the latter would be to admit that they had not discovered the former. So they listened while the boy told them. "It's something that happens to them once a month." He described his idea of the physical ceremony. Perhaps he knew. Anyway he was graphic enough, convincing enough. If he had tried to describe it as a mental state, something which he only believed, they would not have listened. But he drew a picture, physical, actual, to be discerned by the sense of smell and even of sight. It moved them: the temporary and abject helplessness of that which tantalised and frustrated desire; the smooth and superior shape in which volition dwelled doomed to be at stated and inescapable intervals victims of periodical filth. That was how the boy told it, with the other five listening quietly, looking at one another, questioning and secret. On the next Saturday Joe did not go hunting with them. McEachern thought that he had already gone, since the gun was missing. But Joe was hidden in the barn. He stayed there all that day. On the Saturday following he did go, but alone, early, before the boys called for him. But he did not hunt. He was not three miles from home when in the late afternoon he shot a sheep. He found the flock in a hidden valley and stalked and killed one with the gun. Then he knelt, his hands in the yet warm blood of the dying beast, trembling, drymouthed, backglaring. Then he got over it, recovered. He did not forget what the boy had told him. He just accepted it. He found that he could live with it, side by side with it. It was as if he said, illogical and desperately calm *All right. It is so, then. But not to me. Not in my life and my love* Then it was three or four years ago and he had forgotten it, in the sense that a fact is forgotten when it once succumbs to the mind's insistence that it be neither true nor false.

He met the waitress on the Monday night following the Saturday on which he had tried to pay for the cup of coffee. He did not have the rope then. He climbed from his window and dropped the ten feet to the earth and walked the five miles into town. He did not think at all about how he would get back into his room.

He reached town and went to the corner where she had told him to wait. It was a quiet corner and he was quite early, thinking *I will have to remember. To let her show me what to do and how to do it and when. To not let her find out that I dont know, that I will have to find out from her*

He had been waiting for over an hour when she appeared. He had been that early. She came up on foot. She came and stood before him, small, with that air steadfast, waiting, downlooking, coming up out of the darkness. "Here you are," she said.

"I got here soon as I could. I had to wait for them to go to sleep. I was afraid I would be late."

"Have you been here long? How long?"

"I dont know. I ran, most of the way. I was afraid I would be late."

"You ran? All them three miles?"

"It's five miles. It's not three."

"Well, say." Then they did not talk. They stood there, two shadows facing one another. More than a year later, remembering that night, he said, suddenly knowing *It was like she was waiting for me to hit her* "Well," she said.

He had begun now to tremble a little. He could smell her, smell the waiting: still, wise, a little weary; thinking *She's waiting for me to start and I dont know how* Even to himself his voice sounded idiotic. "I reckon it's late."

"Late?"

"I thought maybe they would be waiting for you. Waiting up until you . . ."

"Waiting for . . . Waiting for . . . " Her voice died, ceased. She said, not moving; they stood like two shadows: "I live with Mame and Max. You know. The restaurant. You ought to remember them, trying to pay that nickel . . ." She began to laugh. There was no mirth in it, nothing in it. "When I think of that. When I think of you coming in there, with that nickel." Then she stopped laughing. There was no cessation of mirth in that, either. The still, abject, downlooking voice reached him. "I made a mistake tonight. I forgot something." Perhaps she was waiting for him to ask her what it was. But he did not. He just stood there, with a still, downspeaking voice dying somewhere about his ears. He had forgot about the shot sheep. He had lived with the fact which the older boy had told him too long now. With the slain sheep he had bought immunity from it for too long now for it to be alive. So he could not understand at first what she was trying to tell him. They stood at the corner. It was at the edge of town, where the street became a road that ran on beyond the ordered and measured lawns, between small, random houses and barren fields—the small, cheap houses which compose the purlieus of such towns. She said, "Listen. I'm sick tonight." He did not understand. He said nothing. Perhaps he did not need to understand. Perhaps he had already expected some fateful mischance, thinking, 'It was too good to be true, anyway'; thinking too fast for even thought: *In a moment she will vanish. She will not be. And then I will be back home, in bed, not having left it at all* Her voice went on: "I forgot about the day of the month when I told you Monday night. You surprised me, I guess. There on the street Saturday. I forgot what day it was, anyhow. Until after you had gone."

His voice was as quiet as hers. "How sick? Haven't you got some medicine at home that you can take?"

"Haven't I got . . ." Her voice died. She said, "Well, say." She said suddenly: "It's late. And you with four miles to walk."

"I've already walked it now. I'm here now." His voice was quiet, hopeless, calm. "I reckon it's getting late," he said. Then something changed. Not looking at him, she sensed something before she heard it in his hard voice: "What kind of sickness have you got?"

She didn't answer at once. Then she said, still, downlooking: "You haven't ever had a sweetheart, yet. I'll bet you haven't." He didn't answer. "Have you?" He didn't answer. She moved. She touched him for the first time. She came and took his arm, lightly, in both hands. Looking down, he could see the dark shape of the lowered head which appeared to have been set out of line a little on the neck when she was born. She told him, halting, clumsily, using the only words which she knew perhaps. But he had heard it before. He had already fled backward, past the slain sheep, the price paid for immunity, to the afternoon when, sitting on a creek bank, he had been not hurt or astonished so much as outraged. The arm which she held jerked free. She did not believe that he had intended to strike her; she believed otherwise, in fact. But the result was the same. As he faded on down the road, the shape, the shadow, she believed that he was running. She could hear his feet for some time after she could no longer see him. She did not move at once. She stood as he had left her, motionless, downlooking, as though waiting for the blow which she had already received.

He was not running. But he was walking fast, and in a direction that was taking him further yet from home, from the house five miles away which he had left by climbing from a window and which he had not yet planned any way of reentering. He went on down the road fast and turned from it and sprang over a fence, into plowed earth. Something was growing in the furrows. Beyond were woods, trees. He reached the woods and entered, among the hard trunks, the branchshadowed quiet, hardfeeling, hardsmelling, invisible. In the notseeing and the hardknowing as though in a cave he seemed to see a diminishing row of suavely shaped urns in moonlight, blanched. And not one was perfect. Each one was cracked and from each crack there issued something liquid, deathcolored, and foul. He touched a tree, leaning his propped arms against it, seeing the ranked and moonlit urns. He vomited.

On the next Monday night he had the rope. He was waiting at the same corner; he was quite early again. Then he saw her. She came up to where he stood. "I thought maybe you wouldn't be here," she said.

"Did you?" He took her arm, drawing her on down the road.

"Where are we going?" she said. He didn't answer, drawing her on. She had to trot to keep up. She trotted clumsily: an animal impeded by that which distinguished her from animals: her heels, her clothes, her smallness. He drew her from the road, toward the fence which he had crossed a week ago. "Wait," she said, the words jolting from her mouth. "The fence—I cant—" As she stooped to go through, between the strands of wire which he had stepped over, her dress caught. He leaned and jerked it free with a ripping sound.

"I'll buy you another one," he said. She said nothing. She let herself be half carried and half dragged among the growing plants, the furrows, and into the woods, the trees.

He kept the rope, neatly coiled, behind the same loose board in his attic room where Mrs McEachern kept her hoard of nickels and dimes, with the difference that the rope was thrust further back into the hole than Mrs Mc-Eachern could reach. He had got the idea from her. Sometimes, with the old couple snoring in the room beneath, when he lifted out the silent rope he would think of the paradox. Sometimes he thought about telling her; of showing her where he kept hidden the implement of his sin, having got the idea, learned how and where to hide it, from her. But he knew that she would merely want to help him conceal it; that she would want him to sin in order that she could help him hide it; that she would at last make such a todo of meaningful whispers and signals that McEachern would have to suspect something despite himself.

Thus he began to steal, to take money from the hoard. It is very possible that the woman did not suggest it to him, never mentioned money to him. It is possible that he did not even know that he was paying with money for pleasure. It was that he had watched for years Mrs McEachern hide money in a certain place. Then he himself had something which it was necessary to hide. He put it in the safest place which he knew. Each time he hid or retrieved the rope, he saw the tin can containing money.

The first time he took fifty cents. He debated for some time between fifty cents and a quarter. Then he took the fifty cents because that was the exact sum he needed. With it he bought a stale and flyspecked box of candy from a man who had won it for ten cents on a punching board in a store. He gave it to the waitress. It was the first thing which he had ever given her. He gave it to her as if no one had ever thought of giving her anything before. Her expression was a little strange when she took the tawdry, shabby box into her big hands. She was sitting at the time on her bed in her bedroom in the small house where she lived with the man and woman called Max and Mame. One night about a week before the man came into the room. She was undressing, sitting on the bed while she removed her stockings. He came in and leaned against the bureau, smoking.

"A rich farmer," he said. "John Jacob Astor from the cowshed."

She had covered herself, sitting on the bed, still, down-looking. "He pays me."

"With what? Hasn't he used up that nickel yet?" He looked at her. "A setup for hayseeds. That's what I brought you down here from Memphis for. Maybe I'd better start giving away grub too."

"I'm not doing it on your time."

"Sure. I cant stop you. I just hate to see you. A kid, that never saw a whole dollar at one time in his life. With this town full of guys making good jack, that would treat you right."

"Maybe I like him. Maybe you hadn't thought of that."

He looked at her, at the still and lowered crown of her head as she sat on the bed, her hands on her lap. He leaned against the bureau, smoking. He said, "Mame!" After a while he said again, "Mame! Come in here." The walls were thin. After a while the big blonde woman came up the hall, without haste. They could both hear her. She entered. "Get this," the man said. "She says maybe she likes him best. It's Romeo and Juliet. For sweet Jesus!"

The blonde woman looked at the dark crown of the waitress' head. "What about that?"

"Nothing. It's fine. Max Confrey presenting Miss Bobbie Allen, the youth's companion."

"Go out," the woman said.

"Sure. I just brought her change for a nickel." He went out. The waitress had not moved. The blonde woman went to the bureau and leaned against it, looking at the other's lowered head.

"Does he ever pay you?" she said.

The waitress did not move. "Yes. He pays me."

The blonde woman looked at her, leaning against the bureau as Max had done. "Coming all the way down here from Memphis. Bringing it all the way down here to give it away."

The waitress did not move. "I'm not hurting Max."

The blonde woman looked at the other's lowered head. Then she turned and went toward the door. "See that you dont," she said. "This wont last forever. These little towns wont stand for this long. I know. I came from one of them."

Sitting on the bed, holding the cheap, florid candy box in her hands, she sat as she had sat while the blonde woman talked to her. But it was now Joe who leaned against the bureau and looked at her. She began to laugh. She laughed, holding the gaudy box in her bigknuckled hands. Joe watched her. He watched her rise and pass him, her face lowered. She passed through the door and called Max by name. Joe had never seen Max save in the restaurant, in the hat and the dirty apron. When Max entered he was not even smoking. He thrust out his hand. "How are you, Romeo?" he said.

Joe was shaking hands almost before he had recognised the man. "My name's Joe McEachern," he said. The blonde woman had also entered. It was also the first time he had even seen her save in the restaurant. He saw her enter, watching her, watching the waitress open the box. She extended it.

"Joe brought it to me," she said.

The blonde woman looked at the box, once. She did not even move her hand. "Thanks," she said. The man also looked at the box, without moving his hand.

"Well, well, well," he said. "Sometimes Christmas lasts a good while. Hey, Romeo?" Joe had moved a little away from the bureau. He had never been in the house before. He was looking at the man, with on his face an expression a little placative and baffled though not alarmed, watching the man's inscrutable and monklike face. But he said nothing. It was the waitress who said,

"If you dont like it, you dont have to eat it." He watched Max, watching his face, hearing the waitress' voice; the voice downlooking: "Not doing you nor nobody else any harm. . . . Not on his time . . ." He was not watching her nor the blonde woman either. He was watching Max, with that expression puzzled, placative, not afraid. The blonde woman now spoke; it was as though they were speaking of him and in his presence and in a tongue which they knew that he did not know.

"Come on out," the blonde woman said.

"For sweet Jesus," Max said. "I was just going to give Romeo a drink on the house."

"Does he want one?" the blonde woman said. Even when she addressed Joe directly it was as if she still spoke to Max. "Do you want a drink?"

"Dont hold him in suspense because of his past behavior. Tell him it's on the house."

"I dont know," Joe said. "I never tried it."

"Never tried anything on the house," Max said. "For sweet Jesus." He had not looked at Joe once again after he entered the room. Again it was as if they talked at and because of him, in a language which he did not understand.

"Come on," the blonde woman said. "Come on, now." They went out. The blonde woman had never looked at him at all, and the man, without looking at him, had never ceased. Then they were gone. Joe stood beside the bureau. In the middle of the floor the waitress stood, downlooking, with the open box of candy in her hand. The room was close, smelling of stale scent. Joe had never seen it before. He had not believed that he ever would. The shades were drawn. The single bulb burned at the end of a cord, shaded by a magazine page pinned about it and already turned brown from the heat. "It's all right," he said. "It's all right." She didn't answer nor move. He thought of the darkness outside, the night in which they had been alone before. "Let's go," he said.

"Go?" she said. Then he looked at her. "Go where?" she said. "What for?" Still he did not understand her. He watched her come to the bureau and set the box of candy upon it. While he watched, she began to take her clothes off, ripping them off and flinging them down.

He said, "Here? In here?" It was the first time he had ever seen a naked woman, though he had been her lover for a month. But even then he did not even know that he had not known what to expect to see.

That night they talked. They lay in the bed, in the dark, talking. Or he talked, that is. All the time he was thinking, 'Jesus. Jesus. So this is it.' He lay naked too, beside her, touching her with his hand and talking about her. Not about where she had come from and what she had even done, but about her body as if no one had ever done this before, with her or with anyone else. It was as if with speech he were learning about women's bodies, with the curiosity of a child. She told him about the sickness of the first night. It did not shock him now. Like the nakedness and the physical shape, it was like something which had never happened or existed before. So he told her in turn what he knew to tell. He told about the negro girl in the mill shed on that afternoon three years ago. He told her quietly and peacefully, lying beside her, touching her. Perhaps he could not even have said if she listened or not. Then he said, "You noticed my skin, my hair," waiting for her to answer, his hand slow on her body.

She whispered also. "Yes. I thought maybe you were a foreigner. That you never come from around here."

"It's different from that, even. More than just a foreigner. You cant guess."

"What? How more different?"

"Guess."

Their voices were quiet. It was still, quiet; night now known, not to be desired, pined for. "I cant. What are you?"

His hand was slow and quiet on her invisible flank. He did not answer at once. It was not as if he were tantalising her. It was as if he just had not thought to speak on. She asked him again. Then he told her. "I got some nigger blood in me."

Then she lay perfectly still, with a different stillness. But he did not seem to notice it. He lay peacefully too, his hand slow up and down her flank. "You're what?" she said.

"I think I got some nigger blood in me." His eyes were closed, his hand slow and unceasing. "I dont know. I believe I have."

She did not move. She said at once: "You're lying."

"All right," he said, not moving, his hand not ceasing.

. 184 .

"I dont believe it," her voice said in the darkness.

"All right," he said, his hand not ceasing.

The next Saturday he took another half dollar from Mrs McEachern's hiding place and gave it to the waitress. A day or two later he had reason to believe that Mrs McEachern had missed the money and that she suspected him of having taken it. Because she lay in wait for him until he knew that she knew that McEachern would not interrupt them. Then she said, "Joe." He paused and looked at her, knowing that she would not be looking at him. She said, not looking at him, her voice flat, level: "I know how a young man growing up needs money. More than p—Mr McEachern gives you. . . ." He looked at her, until her voice ceased and died away. Apparently he was waiting for it to cease. Then he said,

"Money? What do I want with money?"

On the next Saturday he earned two dollars chopping wood for a neighbor. He lied to McEachern about where he was going and where he had been and what he had done there. He gave the money to the waitress. McEachern found out about the work. Perhaps he believed that Joe had hidden the money. Mrs McEachern may have told him so.

Perhaps two nights a week Joe and the waitress went to her room. He did not know at first that anyone else had ever done that. Perhaps he believed that some peculiar dispensation had been made in his favor, for his sake. Very likely until the last he still believed that Max and Mame had to be placated, not for the actual fact, but because of his presence there. But he did not see them again in the house, though he knew that they were there. But he did not know for certain if they knew that he was there or had ever returned after the night of the candy.

Usually they met outside, went somewhere else or just loitered on the way to where she lived. Perhaps he believed up to the last that he had suggested it. Then one night she did not meet him where he waited. He waited until the clock in the courthouse struck twelve. Then he went on to where she lived. He had never done that before, though even then he could not have said that she had ever forbidden him to come there unless she was with him. But he went there that night, expecting to find the house dark and asleep. The house was dark, but it was not asleep. He knew that, that beyond the dark shades of her room people were not asleep and that she was not there alone. How he knew it he could not have said. Neither would he admit what he knew. 'It's just Max,' he thought. 'It's just Max.' But he knew better. He knew that there was a man in the room with her. He did not see her for two weeks, though he knew that she was waiting for him. Then one night he was at the corner when she appeared. He struck her, without warning, feeling her flesh. He knew then what even yet he had not believed. "Oh," she cried. He struck her again. "Not here!" she whispered. "Not here!" Then he found that she was crying. He had not cried since he could remember. He cried, cursing her, striking her. Then she was holding him. Even the reason for striking her was gone then. "Now, now," she said. "Now, now."

They did not leave the corner even that night. They did not walk on loitering nor leave the road. They sat on a sloping grassbank and talked. She talked this time, telling him. It did not take much telling. He could see now what he discovered that he had known all the time: the idle men in the restaurant, with their cigarettes bobbing as they spoke to her in passing, and she going back and forth, constant, downlooking, and abject. Listening to her voice, he seemed to smell the odorreek of all anonymous men above dirt. Her head was a little lowered as she talked, the big hands still on her lap. He could not see, of course. He did not have to see. "I thought you knew," she said.

"No," he said. "I reckon I didn't."

"I thought you did."

"No," he said. "I dont reckon I did."

Two weeks later he had begun to smoke, squinting his face against the smoke, and he drank too. He would drink at night with Max and Mame and sometimes three or four other men and usually another woman or two, sometimes from the town, but usually strangers who would come in from Memphis and stay a week or a month, as waitresses behind the restaurant counter where the idle men gathered all day. He did not always know their names, but he could cock his hat as they did; during the evenings behind the drawn shades of the diningroom at Max's he cocked it so and spoke of the waitress to the others, even in her presence, in his loud, drunken, despairing young voice, calling her his whore. Now and then in Max's car he took her to dances in the country, always careful that McEachern should not hear about it. "I dont know which he would be madder at," he told her; "at you or at the dancing." Once they had to put him to bed, helpless, in the house where he had not even ever dreamed at one time that he could enter. The next morning the waitress drove him out home before daylight so he could get into the house before he was caught. And during the day McEachern watched him with dour and grudging approval.

"But you have still plenty of time to make me regret that heifer," McEachern said.

. 9 .

McEACHERN lay in bed. The room was dark, but he was not asleep. He lay beside Mrs McEachern, whom he did believe to be sleeping, thinking fast and hard, thinking, 'The suit has been worn. But when. It could not have been during the day, because he is beneath my eyes, except on Saturday afternoons. But on any Saturday afternoon he could go to the barn, remove and hide the fit clothing which I require him to wear, and then don apparel which he would and could need only as some adjunct to sinning.' It was as if he knew then, had been told. That would infer then that the garments were worn in secret, and therefore in all likelihood, at night. And if that were so, he refused to believe that the boy had other than one purpose: lechery. He had never committed lechery himself and he had not once failed to refuse to listen to anyone who talked about it. Yet within about thirty minutes of intensive thinking he knew almost as much of Joe's doings as Joe himself could have told him, with the exception of names and places. Very likely he would not have believed those even from Joe's mouth, since men of his kind usually have just as firmly fixed convictions about the mechanics, the theatring of evil as about those of good. Thus bigotry and clairvoyance were practically one, only the bigotry was a little slow, for as Joe, descending on his rope, slid like a fast shadow across the open and moonfilled window behind which McEachern lay, McEachern did not at once recognise him or perhaps believe what he saw, even though he could see the very rope itself. And when he got to the window Joe had already drawn the rope back and made it fast and was now on his way toward the barn. As McEachern watched him from the window, he felt something of that pure and impersonal outrage which a judge must feel were he to see a man on trial for his life lean and spit on the bailiff's sleeve.

Hidden in the shadows of the lane halfway between the house and the road, he could see Joe at the mouth of the lane. He too heard the car and saw it come up and stop and Joe get into it. Possibly he did not even care who else was in it. Perhaps he already knew, and his purpose had been merely to see in which direction it went. Perhaps he believed that he knew that too, since the car could have gone almost anywhere in a country full of possible destinations with roads that led to them. Because he turned now back toward the house, walking fast, in that same pure and impersonal outrage, as if he believed so that he would be guided by some greater and purer outrage that he would not even need to doubt personal faculties. In carpet slippers, without a hat, his nightshirt thrust into his trousers and his braces dangling, he went straight as an arrow to the stable and saddled his big, old, strong white horse and returned back down the lane and to the road at a heavy gallop, though Mrs McEachern from the kitchen door called his name when he rode out of the lot. He turned into the road at that slow and ponderous gallop, the two of them, man and beast, leaning a little stiffly forward as though in some juggernautish simulation of terrific speed though the actual speed itself was absent, as if in that cold and implacable and undeviating conviction of both omnipotence and clairvoyance of which they both partook known destination and speed were not necessary.

He rode at that same speed straight to the place which he sought and which he had found out of a whole night and almost a whole half of a county, though it was not that far distant. He had gone hardly four miles when he heard music ahead and then he saw beside the road lights in a school house, a oneroom building. He had known where the building was, but he had had neither reason nor manner of knowing that there would be a dance held in it. But he rode straight to it and into the random shadows of parked cars and buggies and saddled horses and mules which filled the grove which surrounded the school, and dismounted almost before the horse had stopped. He did not even tether it. He got down, and in the carpet slippers and the dangling braces and his round head and his short, blunt, outraged beard ran toward the open door and the open windows where the music came and where kerosene-lit shadows passed in a certain orderly uproar.

Perhaps, if he were thinking at all, he believed that he had been guided and were now being propelled by some militant Michael Himself as he entered the room. Apparently his eyes were not even momentarily at fault with the sudden light and the motion as he thrust among bodies with turned heads as, followed by a wake of astonishment and incipient pandemonium, he ran toward the youth whom he had adopted of his own free will and whom he had tried to raise as he was convinced was right. Joe and the waitress were dancing and Joe had not seen him yet. The woman had never seen him but once, but perhaps she remembered him, or perhaps his appearance now was enough. Because she stopped dancing and upon her face came an expression very like horror, which Joe saw and turned. As he turned, McEachern was upon them. Neither had McEachern ever seen the woman but once, and very likely then he had not looked at her, just as he had refused to listen when men spoke of fornication. Yet he went straight to her, ignoring Joe for the moment. "Away, Jezebel!" he said. His voice thundered, into the shocked silence, the shocked surrounding faces beneath the kerosene lamps, into the ceased music, into the peaceful moonlit night of young summer. "Away, harlot!"

Perhaps it did not seem to him that he had been moving fast nor that his voice was loud. Very likely he seemed to himself to be standing just and rocklike and with neither haste nor anger while on all sides the sluttishness of weak human men seethed in a long sigh of terror about the actual representative of the wrathful and retributive Throne. Perhaps they were not even his hands which struck at the face of the youth whom he had nurtured and sheltered and clothed from a child, and perhaps when the face ducked the blow and came up again it was not the face of that child. But he could not have been surprised at that, since it was not that child's face which he was concerned with: it was the face of Satan, which he knew as well. And when, staring at the face, he walked steadily toward it with his hand still raised, very likely he walked toward it in the furious and dreamlike exaltation of a martyr who has already been absolved, into the descending chair which Joe swung at his head, and into nothingness. Perhaps the nothingness astonished him a little, but not much, and not for long.

Then to Joe it all rushed away, roaring, dying, leaving him in the center of the floor, the shattered chair clutched in his hand, looking down at his adopted father. McEachern lay on his back. He looked quite peaceful now. He appeared to sleep: bluntheaded, indomitable even in repose, even the blood on his forehead peaceful and quiet.

Joe was breathing hard. He could hear it, and also something else, thin and shrill and far away. He seemed to listen to it for a long time before he recognised it for a voice, a woman's voice. He looked and saw two men holding her and she writhing and struggling, her hair shaken forward, her white face wrung and ugly beneath the splotches of savage paint, her mouth a small jagged hole filled with shrieking. "Calling me a harlot!" she screamed, wrenching at the men who held her. "That old son of a bitch! Let go! Let go!" Then her voice stopped making words again and just screamed; she writhed and threshed, trying to bite the hands of the men who struggled with her.

Still carrying the shattered chair Joe walked toward her. About the walls, huddling, clotted, the others watched him: the girls in stiff offcolors and mailorder stockings and heels; the men, young men in illcut and boardlike garments also from the mailorder, with hard, ruined hands and eyes already revealing a heritage of patient brooding upon endless furrows and the slow buttocks of mules. Joe began to run, brandishing the chair. "Let her go!" he said. At once she ceased struggling and turned on him the fury, the shrieking, as if she had just seen him, realised that he was also there.

"And you! You brought me here. Goddamn bastard clod-hopper. Bastard you! Son of a bitch you and him too. Putting him at me that never ever saw—" Joe did not appear to be running at anyone in particular, and his face was quite calm beneath the uplifted chair. The others fell back from about the woman, freeing her, though she continued to wrench her arms as if she did not yet realise it.

"Get out of here!" Joe shouted. He whirled, swinging the chair; yet his face was still quite calm. "Back!" he said, though no one had moved toward him at all. They were all as still and as silent as the man on the floor. He swung the chair, backing now toward the door. "Stand back! I said I would kill him some day! I told him so!" He swung the chair about him, calmfaced, backing toward the door. "Dont a one of you move, now," he said, looking steadily and ceaselessly at faces that might have been masks. Then he flung the chair down and whirled and sprang out the door, into soft, dappled moonlight. He overtook the waitress as she was getting into the car in which they had come. He was panting, yet his voice was calm too: a sleeping face merely breathing hard enough to make sounds. "Get on back to town," he said. "I'll be there soon as I . . ." Apparently he was not aware of what he was saying nor of what was happening; when the woman turned suddenly in the door of the car and began to beat him in the face he did not move, his voice did not change: "Yes. That's right. I'll be there soon as I—" Then he turned and ran, while she was still striking at him.

He could not have known where McEachern had left the horse, nor for certain if it was even there. Yet he ran straight to it, with something of his adopted father's complete faith in an infallibility in events. He got onto it and swung it back toward the road. The car had already turned into the road. He saw the taillight diminish and disappear.

The old, strong, farmbred horse returned home at its slow and steady canter. The youth upon its back rode lightly, balanced lightly, leaning well forward, exulting perhaps at that moment as Faustus had, of having put behind now at once and for all the Shalt Not, of being free at last of honor and law. In the motion the sweet sharp sweat of the horse blew, sulphuric; the invisible wind flew past. He cried aloud, "I have done it! I have done it! I told them I would!"

He entered the lane and rode through the moonlight up to the house without slowing. He had thought it would be dark, but it was not. He did not pause; the careful and hidden rope were as much a part of his dead life now as honor and hope, and the old wearying woman who had been one of his enemies for thirteen years and who was now awake, waiting for him. The light was in hers and McEachern's bedroom and she was standing in the door, with a shawl over her nightdress. "Joe?" she said. He came down the hall fast. His face looked as McEachern had seen it as the chair fell. Perhaps she could not yet see it good. "What is it?" she said. "Paw rode away on the horse. I heard . . ." She saw his face then. But she did not even have time to step back. He did not strike her; his hand on her arm was quite gentle. It was just hurried, getting her out of the path, out of the door. He swept her aside as he might have a curtain across the door.

"He's at a dance," he said. "Get away, old woman." She turned, clutching the shawl with one hand, her other against the door face as she fell back, watching him as he crossed the room and began to run up the stairs which mounted to his attic. Without stopping he looked back. Then she could see his teeth shining in the lamp. "At a dance, you hear? He's not dancing, though." He laughed back, into the lamp; he turned his head and his laughing, running on up the stairs, vanishing as he ran, vanishing upward from the head down as if he were running headfirst and laughing into something that was obliterating him like a picture in chalk being erased from a blackboard.

She followed, toiling up the stairs. She began to follow almost as soon as he passed her, as if that implacable urgency which had carried her husband away had returned like a cloak on the shoulders of the boy and had been passed from him in turn to her. She dragged herself up the cramped stair, clutching the rail with one hand and the shawl with the other. She was not speaking, not calling to him. It was as though she were a phantom obeying the command sent back by the absent master. Joe had not lighted his lamp. But the room was filled with refracted moonglow, and even without that very likely she could have told what he was doing. She held herself upright by the wall, fumbling her hand along the wall until she reached the bed and sank onto it, sitting. It had taken her some time, because when she looked toward where the loose plank was, he was already approaching toward the bed, where the moonlight fell directly, and she watched him empty the tin can onto the bed and sweep the small mass of coins and bills into his hand and ram the hand into his pocket. Only then did he look at her as she sat, backfallen a little now, propped on one arm and holding the shawl with the other hand. "I didn't ask you for it," he said. "Remember that. I didn't ask, because I was afraid you would give it to me. I just took it. Dont forget that." He was turning almost before his voice ceased. She watched him turn into the lamplight which fell up the stair, descending. He passed out of sight, but she could still hear him. She heard him in the hall again, fast, and after a while she heard the horse again, galloping; and after a while the sound of the horse ceased.

A clock was striking one somewhere when Joe urged the now spent old horse through the main street of town. The horse had been breathing hard for some time now, but Joe still held it at a stumbling trot with a heavy stick that fell rhythmically across its rump. It was not a switch: it was a section of broom handle which had been driven into Mrs McEachern's flower bed in front of the house for something to grow on. Though the horse was still going through the motion of galloping, it was not moving much faster than a man could walk. The stick too rose and fell with the same spent and terrific slowness, the youth on the horse's back leaning forward as if he did not know that the horse had flagged, or as though to lift forward and onward the failing beast whose slow hooves rang with a measured hollow sound through the empty and moondappled street. It— the horse and the rider—had a strange, dreamy effect, like a moving picture in slow motion as it galloped steady and flagging up the street and toward the old corner where he used to wait, less urgent perhaps but not less eager, and more young.

The horse was not even trotting now, on stiff legs, its breathing deep and labored and rasping, each breath a groan. The stick still fell; as the progress of the horse slowed, the speed of the stick increased in exact ratio. But the horse slowed, sheering into the curb. Joe pulled at its head, beating it, but it slowed into the curb and stopped, shadowdappled, its head down, trembling, its breathing almost like a human voice. Yet still the rider leaned forward in the arrested saddle, in the attitude of terrific speed, beating the horse across the rump with the stick. Save for the rise and fall of the stick and the groaning respirations of the animal, they might have been an equestrian statue strayed from its pedestal and come to rest in an attitude of ultimate exhaustion in a quiet and empty street splotched and dappled by moonshadows.

Joe descended. He went to the horse's head and began to tug it, as if he would drag it into motion by main strength and then spring onto its back. The horse did not move. He desisted; he seemed to be leaning a little toward the horse. Again they were motionless: the spent beast and the youth, facing one another, their heads quite near, as if carved in an attitude of listening or of prayer or of consultation. Then Joe raised the stick and fell to beating the horse about its motionless head. He beat it steadily until the stick broke. He continued to strike it with a fragment not much longer than his hand. But perhaps he realised that he was inflicting no pain, or perhaps his arm grew tired at last, because he threw the stick away and turned, whirled, already in full stride. He did not look back. Diminishing, his white shirt pulsing and fading in the moonshadows, he ran as completely out of the life of the horse as if it had never existed.

He passed the corner where he used to wait. If he noticed, thought, at all, he must have said *My God how long. How long ago that was* The street curved into the gravel road.

He had almost a mile yet to go, so he ran not fast but carefully, steadily, his face lowered a little as if he contemplated the spurned road beneath his feet, his elbows at his sides like a trained runner. The road curved on, moonblanched, bordered at wide intervals by the small, random, new, terrible little houses in which people who came yesterday from nowhere and tomorrow will be gone wherenot, dwell on the edges of towns. They were all dark save the one toward which he ran.

He reached the house and turned from the road, running, his feet measured and loud in the late silence. Perhaps he could see already the waitress, in a dark dress for travelling, with her hat on and her bag packed, waiting. (How they were to go anywhere, by what means depart, likely he had never thought.) And perhaps Max and Mame too, likely undressed—Max coatless or maybe even in his undershirt, and Mame in the light blue kimono—the two of them bustling about in that loud, cheerful, seeing-someone-off way. But actually he was not thinking at all, since he had never told the waitress to get ready to leave at all. Perhaps he believed that he had told her, or that she should know, since his recent doings and his future plans must have seemed to him simple enough for anyone to understand. Perhaps he even believed that he had told her he was going home in order to get money when she got into the car.

He ran onto the porch. Heretofore, even during his heyday in the house, his impulse had been always to glide from the road and into the shadow of the porch and into the house itself where he was expected, as swiftly and inconspicuously as possible. He knocked. There was a light in her room, and another at the end of the hall, as he had expected; and voices from beyond the curtained windows too, several voices which he could discern to be intent rather than cheerful: that he expected too, thinking *Perhaps they think I am not coming. That damn horse. That damn horse* He knocked again, louder, putting his hand on the knob, shaking it, pressing his face against the curtained glass in the front door. The voices ceased. Then there was no sound whatever from within the house. The two lights, the lighted shade to her room and the opaque curtain in the door, burned with a steady and unwavering glare, as if all the people in the house had suddenly died when he touched the knob. He knocked again, with scarce interval between; he was still knocking when the door (no shadow had fallen upon the curtain and no step had approached beyond it) fled suddenly and silently from under his rapping hand. He was already stepping across the threshold as if he were attached to the door, when Max emerged from behind it, blocking it. He was completely dressed, even to the hat. "Well, well, well," he said. His voice was not loud, and it was almost as if he had drawn Joe swiftly into the hall and shut the door and locked it before Joe knew that he was inside. Yet his voice held again that ambiguous quality, that quality hearty and completely empty and completely without pleasure or mirth, like a shell, like something he carried before his face and watched Joe through it, which in the past had caused Joe to look at Max with something between puzzlement and anger. "Here's Romeo at last," he said. "The Beale Street Playboy." Then he spoke a little louder, saying Romeo quite loud. "Come in and meet the folks."

Joe was already moving toward the door which he knew, very nearly running again, if he had ever actually stopped. He was not listening to Max. He had never heard of Beale

Street, that three or four Memphis city blocks in comparison with which Harlem is a movie set. Joe had not looked at anything. Because suddenly he saw the blonde woman standing in the hall at the rear. He had not seen her emerge into the hall at all, yet it was empty when he entered. And then suddenly she was standing there. She was dressed, in a dark skirt, and she held a hat in her hand. And just beyond an open dark door beside him was a pile of luggage, several bags. Perhaps he did not see them. Or perhaps looking saw once, faster than thought *I didn't think she would have that many* Perhaps he thought then for the first time that they had nothing to travel in, thinking *How can I carry all those* But he did not pause, already turning toward the door which he knew. It was only as he put his hand on the door that he became aware of complete silence beyond it, a silence which he at eighteen knew that it would take more than one person to make. But he did not pause; perhaps he was not even aware that the hall was empty again, that the blonde woman had vanished again without his having seen or heard her move.

He opened the door. He was running now; that is, as a man might run far ahead of himself and his knowing in the act of stopping stock still. The waitress sat on the bed as he had seen her sitting so many times. She wore the dark dress and the hat, as he had expected, known. She sat with her face lowered, not even looking at the door when it opened, a cigarette burning in one still hand that looked almost monstrous in its immobility against the dark dress. And in the same instant he saw the second man. He had never seen the man before. But he did not realise this now. It was only later that he remembered that, and remembered the piled luggage in the dark room which he had looked at for an instant while thought went faster than seeing.

The stranger sat on the bed too, also smoking. His hat was tipped forward so that the shadow of the brim fell across his mouth. He was not old, yet he did not look young either. He and Max might have been brothers in the sense that any two white men strayed suddenly into an African village might look like brothers to them who live there. His face, his chin where the light fell upon it, was still. Whether or not the stranger was looking at him, Joe did not know. And that Max was standing just behind him Joe did not know either. And he heard their actual voices without knowing what they said, without even listening: *Ask him*

How would he know Perhaps he heard the words. But likely not. Likely they were as yet no more significant than the rasping of insects beyond the closedrawn window, or the packed bags which he had looked at and had not yet seen. *He cleared out right afterward, Bobbie said*

He might know. Let's find out if we can just what we are running from, at least

Though Joe had not moved since he entered, he was still running. When Max touched his shoulder he turned as if he had been halted in midstride. He had not been aware that Max was even in the room. He looked at Max over his shoulder with a kind of furious annoyance. "Let's have it, kid," Max said. "What about it?"

"What about what?" Joe said.

"The old guy. Do you think you croaked him? Let's have it straight. You dont want to get Bobbie in a jam."

"Bobbie," Joe said, thinking *Bobbie. Bobbie* He turned,

running again; this time Max caught his shoulder, though not hard.

"Come on," Max said. "Aint we all friends here? Did you croak him?"

"Croak him?" Joe said, in that fretted tone of impatience and restraint, as if he were being detained and questioned by a child.

The stranger spoke. "The one you crowned with the chair. Is he dead?"

"Dead?" Joe said. He looked at the stranger. When he did so, he saw the waitress again and he ran again. He actually moved now. He had completely dismissed the two men from his mind. He went to the bed, dragging at his pocket, on his face an expression both exalted and victorious. The waitress did not look at him. She had not looked at him once since he entered, though very likely he had completely forgot that. She had not moved; the cigarette still burned in her hand. Her motionless hand looked as big and dead and pale as a piece of cooking meat. Again someone grasped him by the shoulder. It was the stranger now. The stranger and Max stood shoulder to shoulder, looking at Joe.

"Quit stalling," the stranger said. "If you croaked the guy, say so. It cant be any secret long. They are bound to hear about it by next month at the outside."

"I dont know, I tell you!" Joe said. He looked from one to the other, fretted but not yet glaring. "I hit him. He fell down. I told him I was going to do it someday." He looked from one to the other of the still, almost identical faces. He began to jerk his shoulder under the stranger's hand.

Max spoke. "What did you come here for, then?"

"What did—" Joe said. "What did I . . ." he said, in a

tone of fainting amazement, glaring from face to face with a sort of outraged yet still patient exasperation. "What did I come for? I came to get Bobbie. Do you think that I— when I went all the way home to get the money to get married—" Again he completely forgot, dismissed them. He jerked free and turned to the woman with once more that expression oblivious, exalted, and proud. Very likely at that moment the two men were blown as completely out of his life as two scraps of paper. Very likely he was not even aware when Max went to the door and called and a moment later the blonde woman entered. He was bending above the bed upon which sat the immobile and down-looking waitress, stooping above her, dragging the wadded mass of coins and bills from his pocket, onto her lap and onto the bed beside her. "Here! Look at it. Look. I've got. See?"

Then the wind blew upon him again, like in the school house three hours ago among the gaped faces there of which he had for the time been oblivious. He stood in a quiet, dreamlike state, erect now where the upward spring of the sitting waitress had knocked him, and saw her, on her feet, gather up the wadded and scattered money and fling it; he saw quietly her face strained, the mouth scream-ing, the eyes screaming too. He alone of them all seemed to himself quiet, calm; his voice alone quiet enough to register upon the ear: "You mean you wont?" he said. "You mean, you wont?"

It was very much like it had been in the school house: someone holding her as she struggled and shrieked, her hair wild with the jerking and tossing of her head; her face, even her mouth, in contrast to the hair as still as a dead mouth in a dead face. "Bastard! Son of a bitch! Getting me into a jam, that always treated you like you were a white man. A white man!"

But very likely to him even yet it was just noise, not registering at all: just a part of the long wind. He just stared at her, at the face which he had never seen before, saying quietly (whether aloud or not, he could not have said) in a slow amazement: *Why, I committed murder for her. I even stole for her* as if he had just heard of it, thought of it, been told that he had done it.

Then she too seemed to blow out of his life on the long wind like a third scrap of paper. He began to swing his arm as if the hand still clutched the shattered chair. The blonde woman had been in the room some time. He saw her for the first time, without surprise, having apparently materialised out of thin air, motionless, with that diamond-surfaced tranquillity which invested her with a respectability as implacable and calm as the white lifted glove of a policeman, not a hair out of place. She now wore the pale blue kimono over the dark garment for travelling. She said quietly: "Take him. Let's get out of here. There'll be a cop out here soon. They'll know where to look for him."

Perhaps Joe did not hear her at all, nor the screaming waitress: "He told me himself he was a nigger! The son of a bitch! Me f—ing for nothing a nigger son of a bitch that would get me in a jam with clodhopper police. At a clodhopper dance!" Perhaps he heard only the long wind, as, swinging his hand as though it still clutched the chair, he sprang forward upon the two men. Very likely he did not even know that they were already moving toward him. Because with something of the exaltation of his adopted father he sprang full and of his own accord into the stranger's fist. Perhaps he did not feel either blow, though the stranger struck him twice in the face before he reached the floor, where like the man whom he had struck down, he lay upon his back, quite still. But he was not out because his eyes were still open, looking quietly up at them. There was nothing in his eyes at all, no pain, no surprise. But apparently he could not move; he just lay there with a profoundly contemplative expression, looking quietly up at the two men, and the blonde woman still as immobile and completely finished and surfaced as a cast statue. Perhaps he could not hear the voices either, or perhaps he did and they once more had no more significance than the dry buzzing of the steady insects beyond the window:

Bitching up as sweet a little setup as I could have wanted
He ought to stay away from bitches
He cant help himself. He was born too close to one
Is he really a nigger? He dont look like one
That's what he told Bobbie one night. But I guess she still dont know any more about what he is than he does. These country bastards are liable to be anything

We'll find out. We'll see if his blood is black Lying peaceful and still Joe watched the stranger lean down and lift his head from the floor and strike him again in the face, this time with a short slashing blow. After a moment he licked his lip a little, somewhat as a child might lick a cooking spoon. He watched the stranger's hand go back. But it did not fall.

That's enough. Let's get on to Memphis
Just one more Joe lay quietly and watched the hand. Then Max was beside the stranger, stooping too. *We'll need a little more blood to tell for sure*

Sure. He dont need to worry. This one is on the house too

The hand did not fall. Then the blonde woman was there too. She was holding the stranger's lifted arm by the wrist. *I said that will do*

.10.

KNOWING not grieving remembers a thousand savage and lonely streets. They run from that night when he lay and heard the final footfall and then the final door (they did not even turn the light out) and then lay quietly, on his back, with open eyes while above the suspended globe burned with aching and unwavering glare as though in the house where all the people had died. He did not know how long he lay there. He was not thinking at all, not suffering. Perhaps he was conscious of somewhere within him the two severed wireends of volition and sentience lying, not touching now, waiting to touch, to knit anew so that he could move. While they finished their preparations to depart they stepped now and then across him, like people about to vacate a house forever will across some object which they intend to leave. *Here bobbie here kid heres your comb you forgot it heres romeos chicken feed too jesus he must have tapped the sunday school till on the way out its bobbies now didnt you see him give it to her didnt you see old bighearted thats right pick it up kid you can keep it as an installment or a souvenir or something what dont she want it well say thats too bad now thats tough but we cant leave it lay here on the floor itll rot a hole in the floor its already helped to rot one hole pretty big for its size pretty big for any size hey bobbie hey kid sure ill just keep it for bobbie like hell you will well i mean ill keep half of it for bobbie leave it there you bastards what do you want with it it belongs to him well for sweet jesus what does he want with it he doesnt use money he doesnt need it ask bobbie if he needs money they give it to him that the rest of us have to pay for it leave it there i said like hell this aint mine to leave its bobbies it aint yours neither unless sweet jesus youre going to tell me he owes you jack too that he has been f—ing you too behind my back on credit i said leave it go chase yourself it aint but five or six bucks apiece* Then the blonde woman stood above him and stooping, he watching quietly, she lifted her skirt and took from the top of her stocking a flat folded sheaf of banknotes and removed one and stopped and thrust it into the fob pocket of his trousers. Then she was gone. *get on get out of here you aint ready yet yourself you got to put that kimono in and close your bag and powder your face again bring my bag and hat in here go on now and you take bobbie and them other bags and get in the car and wait for me and max you think im going to leave either one of you here alone to steal that one off of him too go on now get out of here*

Then they were gone: the final feet, the final door. Then he heard the car drown the noise of the insects, riding above, sinking to the level, sinking below the level so that he heard only the insects. He lay there beneath the light. He could not move yet, as he could look without actually seeing, hear without actually knowing; the two wireends not yet knit as he lay peacefully, licking his lips now and then as a child does.

Then the wireends knit and made connection. He did not know the exact instant, save that suddenly he was aware of his ringing head, and he sat up slowly, discovering himself again, getting to his feet. He was dizzy; the room went round him, slowly and smoothly as thinking, so that thinking said *Not yet* But he still felt no pain, not even when, propped before the bureau, he examined in the glass his swollen and bloody face and touched his face. "Sweet Jesus," he said. "They sure beat me up." He was not thinking yet; it had not yet risen that far *I reckon I better get out of here I reckon I better get out of here* He went toward the door, his hands out before him like a blind man or a sleepwalker. He was in the hall without having remembered passing through the door, and he found himself in another bedroom while he still hoped perhaps not believed that he was moving toward the front door. It was small too. Yet it still seemed to be filled with the presence of the blonde woman, its very cramped harsh walls bulged outward with that militant and diamond-surfaced respectability. On the bare bureau sat a pint bottle almost full of whiskey. He drank it, slowly, not feeling the fire at all, holding himself upright by holding to the bureau. The whiskey went down his throat cold as molasses, without taste. He set the empty bottle down and leaned on the bureau, his head lowered, not thinking, waiting perhaps without knowing it, perhaps not even waiting. Then the whiskey began to burn in him and he began to shake his head slowly from side to side, while thinking became one with the slow, hot coiling and recoiling of his entrails: 'I got to get out of here.' He reentered the hall. Now it was his head that was clear and his body that would not behave. He had to coax it along the hall, sliding it along one wall toward the front, thinking, 'Come on, now; pull yourself together. I got to get out.' Thinking *If I can just get it outside, into the air, the cool air, the cool dark* He watched his hands fumbling at the door, trying to help them, to coax and control them. 'Anyway, they didn't lock it on me,' he thought. 'Sweet Jesus, I could not have got out until morning then. It never would have opened a window and climbed through it.' He opened the door at last and passed out and closed the door behind him, arguing again with his body which did not want to bother to close the door, having to be forced to close it upon the empty house where the two lights burned with their dead and unwavering glare, not knowing that the house was empty and not caring, not caring anymore for silence and desolation than they had cared for the cheap and brutal nights of stale oftused glasses and stale oftused beds. His body was acquiescing better, becoming docile. He stepped from the dark porch, into the moonlight, and with his bloody head and his empty stomach hot, savage, and courageous with whiskey, he entered the street which was to run for fifteen years.

The whiskey died away in time and was renewed and died again, but the street ran on. From that night the thousand streets ran as one street, with imperceptible corners and changes of scene, broken by intervals of begged and stolen rides, on trains and trucks, and on country wagons with he at twenty and twentyfive and thirty sitting on the seat with his still, hard face and the clothes (even when soiled and worn) of a city man and the driver of the wagon not knowing who or what the passenger was and not daring to ask. The street ran into Oklahoma and Missouri and as far south as Mexico and then back north to Chicago and Detroit and then back south again and at last to Mississippi. It was fifteen years long: it ran between the savage and spurious board fronts of oil towns where, his inevitable serge clothing and light shoes black with bottomless mud, he ate crude food from tin dishes that cost him ten and fifteen dollars a meal and paid for them with a roll of banknotes the size of a bullfrog and stained too with the rich mud that seemed as bottomless as the gold which it excreted. It ran through yellow wheat fields waving beneath the fierce yellow days of labor and hard sleep in haystacks beneath the cold mad moon of September, and the brittle stars: he was in turn laborer, miner, prospector, gambling tout; he enlisted in the army, served four months and deserted and was never caught. And always, sooner or later, the street ran through cities, through an identical and wellnigh interchangeable section of cities without remembered names, where beneath the dark and equivocal and symbolical archways of midnight he bedded with the women and paid them when he had the money, and when he did not have it he bedded anyway and then told them that he was a negro. For a while it worked; that was while he was still in the south. It was quite simple, quite easy. Usually all he risked was a cursing from the woman and the matron of the house, though now and then he was beaten unconscious by other patrons, to waken later in the street or in the jail.

That was while he was still in the (comparatively speaking) south. Because one night it did not work. He rose from the bed and told the woman that he was a negro. "You are?" she said. "I thought maybe you were just another wop or something." She looked at him, without particular interest; then she evidently saw something in his face: she said, "What about it? You look all right. You ought to seen the shine I turned out just before your turn came." She was looking at him. She was quite still now. "Say, what do you think this dump is, anyhow? The Ritz hotel?" Then she quit talking. She was watching his face and she began to move backward slowly before him, staring at him, her face draining, her mouth open to scream. Then she did scream. It took two policemen to subdue him. At first they thought that the woman was dead.

He was sick after that. He did not know until then that there were white women who would take a man with a black skin. He stayed sick for two years. Sometimes he would remember how he had once tricked or teased white men into calling him a negro in order to fight them, to beat them or be beaten; now he fought the negro who called him white. He was in the north now, in Chicago and then Detroit. He lived with negroes, shunning white people. He ate with them, slept with them, belligerent, unpredictable, uncommunicative. He now lived as man and wife with a woman who resembled an ebony carving. At night he would lie in bed beside her, sleepless, beginning to breathe deep and hard. He would do it deliberately, feeling, even watching, his white chest arch deeper and deeper within his ribcage, trying to breathe into himself the dark odor, the dark and inscrutable thinking and being of negroes, with each suspiration trying to expel from himself the white blood and the white thinking and being. And all the while his nostrils at the odor which he was trying to make his own would whiten and tauten, his whole being writhe and strain with physical outrage and spiritual denial.

He thought that it was loneliness which he was trying to escape and not himself. But the street ran on: catlike, one place was the same as another to him. But in none of them could he be quiet. But the street ran on in its moods and phases, always empty: he might have seen himself as in numberless avatars, in silence, doomed with motion, driven by the courage of flagged and spurred despair; by the despair of courage whose opportunities had to be flagged and spurred. He was thirtythree years old.

One afternoon the street had become a Mississippi country road. He had been put off a southbound freight train near a small town. He did not know the name of the town; he didn't care what word it used for name. He didn't even see it, anyway. He skirted it, following the woods, and came to the road and looked in both directions. It was not a gravelled road, though it looked to be fairly well used. He saw several negro cabins scattered here and there along it; then he saw, about a half mile away, a larger house. It was a big house set in a grove of trees; obviously a place of some pretensions at one time. But now the trees needed pruning and the house had not been painted in years. But he could tell that it was inhabited, and he had not eaten in twentyfour hours. 'That one might do,' he thought.

But he did not approach it at once, though the afternoon was drawing on. Instead he turned his back upon it and went on in the other direction, in his soiled white shirt and worn serge trousers and his cracked, dusty, town-shaped shoes, his cloth cap set at an arrogant angle above a threeday's stubble. Yet even then he did not look like a tramp; at least apparently not to the negro boy whom he met presently coming up the road and swinging a tin bucket. He stopped the boy. "Who lives in the big house back there?" he said.

"That where Miz Burden stay at."

"Mr and Mrs Burden?"

"No, sir. Aint no Mr Burden. Aint nobody live there but her."

"Oh. An old woman, I guess."

"No, sir. Miz Burden aint old. Aint young neither."

"And she lives there by herself. Dont she get scared?"

"Who going to harm her, right here at town? Colored folks around here looks after her."

"Colored folks look after her?"

At once it was as if the boy had closed a door between himself and the man who questioned him. "I reckon aint nobody round here going to do her no harm. She aint harmed nobody."

"I guess not," Christmas said. "How far is it to the next town over this way?"

" 'Bout thirty miles, they say. You aint fixing to walk it, is you?"

"No," Christmas said. He turned then, going on. The boy looked after him. Then he too turned, walking again, the tin bucket swinging against his faded flank. A few steps later he looked back. The man who had questioned him was walking on, steadily though not fast. The boy went on again, in his faded, patched, scant overalls. He was barefoot. Presently he began to shuffle, still moving forward, the red dust rising about his lean, chocolatecolored shanks and the frayed legs of the too short overalls; he began to chant, tuneless, rhythmic, musical, though on a single note:

Say dont didn't.
Didn't dont who.
Want dat yaller gal's
Pudden dont hide.

Lying in a tangle of shrubbery a hundred yards from the house, Christmas heard a far clock strike nine and then ten. Before him the house bulked square and huge from its mass of trees. There was a light in one window upstairs. The shades were not drawn and he could see that the light was a kerosene lamp, and now and then he saw through the window the shadow of a moving person cross the further wall. But he never saw the person at all. After a while the light went out.

The house was now dark; he quit watching it then. He lay in the copse, on his belly on the dark earth. In the copse the darkness was impenetrable; through his shirt and trousers it felt a little chill, close, faintly dank, as if the sun never reached the atmosphere which the copse held. He could feel the neversunned earth strike, slow and receptive, against him through his clothes: groin, hip, belly, breast, forearms. His arms were crossed, his forehead rested upon them, in his nostrils the damp rich odor of the dark and fecund earth.

He did not look once again toward the dark house. He lay perfectly still in the copse for more than an hour before he rose up and emerged. He did not creep. There was nothing skulking nor even especially careful about his approach to the house. He simply went quietly as if that were his natural manner of moving and passed around the now dimensionless bulk of the house, toward the rear, where the kitchen would be. He made no more noise than a cat as he paused and stood for a while beneath the window where the light had shown. In the grass about his feet the crickets, which had ceased as he moved, keeping a little island of silence about him like thin yellow shadow of their small voices, began again, ceasing again when he moved with that tiny and alert suddenness. From the rear of the house a single storey wing projected. 'That will be the kitchen,' he thought. 'Yes. That will be it.' He walked without sound, moving in his tiny island of abruptly ceased insects. He could discern a door in the kitchen wall. He would have found it unlocked if he had tried it. But he did not. He passed it and paused beneath a window. Before he tried it he remembered that he had seen no screen in the lighted window upstairs.

The window was even open, propped open with a stick. 'What do you think about that,' he thought. He stood beside the window, his hands on the sill, breathing quietly, not listening, not hurrying, as if there were no need for haste anywhere under the sun. 'Well. Well. Well. What do you know about that. Well. Well. Well.' Then he climbed into the window; he seemed to flow into the dark kitchen: a shadow returning without a sound and without locomotion to the allmother of obscurity and darkness. Perhaps he thought of that other window which he had used to use and of the rope upon which he had had to rely; perhaps not.

Very likely not, no more than a cat would recall another window; like the cat, he also seemed to see in the darkness as he moved as unerringly toward the food which he wanted as if he knew where it would be; that, or were being manipulated by an agent which did know. He ate something from an invisible dish, with invisible fingers:

invisible food. He did not care what it would be. He did not know that he had even wondered or tasted until his jaw stopped suddenly in midchewing and thinking fled for twentyfive years back down the street, past all the imperceptible corners of bitter defeats and more bitter victories, and five miles even beyond a corner where he used to wait in the terrible early time of love, for someone whose name he had forgot; five miles even beyond that it went *I'll know it in a minute. I have eaten it before, somewhere. In a minute I will* memory clicking knowing *I see I see I more than see hear I hear I see my head bent I hear the monotonous dogmatic voice which I believe will never cease going on and on forever and peeping I see the indomitable bullet head the clean blunt beard they too bent and I thinking How can he be so nothungry and I smelling my mouth and tongue weeping the hot salt of waiting my eyes tasting the hot steam from the dish* "It's peas," he said, aloud. "For sweet Jesus. Field peas cooked with molasses."

More of him than thinking may have been absent; he should have heard the sound before he did, since whoever was creating it was trying no more for silence and caution than he had. Perhaps he did hear it. But he did not move at all as the soft sound of slippered feet approached the kitchen from the house side of it, and when he did at last turn suddenly, his eyes glowing suddenly, he saw already beneath the door which entered the house itself, the faint approaching light. The open window was at his hand: he could have been through it in a single step almost. But he did not move. He didn't even set down the dish. He did not even cease to chew. Thus he was standing in the center of the room, holding the dish and chewing, when the door opened and the woman entered. She wore a faded dressing gown and she carried a candle, holding it high, so that its light fell upon her face: a face quiet, grave, utterly un-alarmed. In the soft light of the candle she looked to be not much past thirty. She stood in the door. They looked at one another for more than a minute, almost in the same attitude: he with the dish, she with the candle. He had stopped chewing now.

"If it is just food you want, you will find that," she said in a voice calm, a little deep, quite cold.

.11.

BY the light of the candle she did not look much more than thirty, in the soft light downfalling upon the softungirdled presence of a woman prepared for sleep. When he saw her by daylight he knew that she was better than thirtyfive. Later she told him that she was forty. 'Which means either fortyone or fortynine, from the way she said it,' he thought. But it was not that first night, nor for many succeeding ones, that she told him that much even.

She told him very little, anyway. They talked very little, and that casually, even after he was the lover of her spinster's bed. Sometimes he could almost believe that they did not talk at all, that he didn't know her at all. It was as though there were two people: the one whom he saw now and then by day and looked at while they spoke to one another with speech that told nothing at all since it didn't try to and didn't intend to; the other with whom he lay at night and didn't even see, speak to, at all.

Even after a year (he was working at the planing mill now) when he saw her by day at all, it would be on Saturday afternoon or Sunday or when he would come to the house for the food which she would prepare for him and leave upon the kitchen table. Now and then she would come to the kitchen, though she would never stay while he ate, and at times she met him at the back porch, where during the first four or five months of his residence in the cabin below the house, they would stand for a while and talk almost like strangers. They always stood: she in one of her apparently endless succession of clean calico house dresses and sometimes a cloth sunbonnet like a country-woman, and he in a clean white shirt now and the serge trousers creased now every week. They never sat down to talk. He had never seen her sitting save one time when he looked through a downstairs window and saw her writing at a desk in the room. And it was a year after he had remarked without curiosity the volume of mail which she received and sent, and that for a certain period of each fore-noon she would sit at the worn, scarred, rolltop desk in one of the scarceused and sparsely furnished downstairs rooms, writing steadily, before he learned that what she received were business and private documents with fifty different postmarks and what she sent were replies—advice, business, financial and religious, to the presidents and faculties and trustees, and advice personal and practical to young girl students and even alumnæ, of a dozen negro schools and colleges through the south. Now and then she would be absent from home three and four days at a time, and though he could now see her at his will on any night, it was a year before he learned that in these absences she visited the schools in person and talked to the teachers and the students. Her business affairs were conducted by a negro lawyer in Memphis, who was a trustee of one of the schools, and in whose safe, along with her will, reposed the written instructions (in her own hand) for the disposal of her body after death. When he learned that, he understood the town's attitude toward her, though he knew that the town did not know as much as he did. He said to himself: 'Then I wont be bothered here.'

One day he realised that she had never invited him inside the house proper. He had never been further than the kitchen, which he had already entered of his own accord, thinking, liplifted, 'She couldn't keep me out of here. I guess she knows that.' And he had never entered the kitchen by day save when he came to get the food which she prepared for him and set out upon the table. And when he entered the house at night it was as he had entered it that first night; he felt like a thief, a robber, even while he mounted to the bedroom where she waited. Even after a year it was as though he entered by stealth to despoil her virginity each time anew. It was as though each turn of dark saw him faced again with the necessity to despoil again that which he had already despoiled—or never had and never would.

Sometimes he thought of it in that way, remembering the hard, untearful and unselfpitying and almost manlike yielding of that surrender. A spiritual privacy so long intact that its own instinct for preservation had immolated it, its physical phase the strength and fortitude of a man. A dual personality: the one the woman at first sight of whom in the lifted candle (or perhaps the very sound of the slippered approaching feet) there had opened before him, instantaneous as a landscape in a lightningflash, a horizon of physical security and adultery if not pleasure; the other the mantrained muscles and the mantrained habit of thinking born of heritage and environment with which he had to fight up to the final instant. There was no feminine vacillation, no coyness of obvious desire and intention to succumb at last. It was as if he struggled physically with another man for an object of no actual value to either, and for which they struggled on principle alone.

When he saw her next, he thought, 'My God. How little I know about women, when I thought I knew so much.' It was on the very next day; looking at her, being spoken to by her, it was as though what memory of less than twelve hours knew to be true could never have happened, thinking *Under her clothes she cant even be made so that it could have happened* He had not started to work at the mill then. Most of that day he spent lying on his back on the cot which she had loaned him, in the cabin which she had given him to live in, smoking, his hands beneath his head. 'My God,' he thought, 'it was like I was the woman and she was the man.' But that was not right, either. Because she had resisted to the very last. But it was not woman resistance, that resistance which, if really meant, cannot be overcome by any man for the reason that the woman observes no rules of physical combat. But she had resisted fair, by the rules that decreed that upon a certain crisis one was defeated, whether the end of resistance had come or not. That night he waited until he saw the light go out in the kitchen and then come on in her room. He went to the house. He did not go in eagerness, but in a quiet rage. "I'll show her," he said aloud. He did not try to be quiet. He entered the house boldly and mounted the stairs; she heard him at once. "Who is it?" she said. But there was no alarm in her tone. He didn't answer. He mounted the stairs and entered the room. She was still dressed, turning, watching the door as he entered. But she did not speak to him. She just watched him as he went to the table and blew out the lamp, thinking, 'Now she'll run.' And so he sprang forward, toward the door to intercept her. But she did not flee. He found her in the dark exactly where the light had lost her, in the same attitude. He began to tear at her clothes. He was talking to her, in a tense, hard, low voice: "I'll show you! I'll show the bitch!" She did not resist at all. It was almost as though she were helping him, with small changes of position of limbs when the ultimate need for help arose. But beneath his hands the body might have been the body of a dead woman not yet stiffened. But he did not desist; though his hands were hard and urgent it was with rage alone. 'At least I have made a woman of her at last,' he thought. 'Now she hates me. I have taught her that, at least.'

The next day he lay again all day long on his cot in the cabin. He ate nothing; he did not even go to the kitchen to see if she had left food for him. He was waiting for sunset, dusk. 'Then I'll blow,' he thought. He did not expect ever to see her again. 'Better blow,' he thought. 'Not give her the chance to turn me out of the cabin too. That much, anyway. No white woman ever did that. Only a nigger woman ever give me the air, turned me out.' So he lay on the cot, smoking, waiting for sunset. Through the open door he watched the sun slant and lengthen and turn copper. Then the copper faded into lilac, into the fading lilac of full dusk. He could hear the frogs then, and fireflies began to drift across the open frame of the door, growing brighter as the dusk faded. Then he rose. He owned nothing but the razor; when he had put that into his pocket, he was ready to travel one mile or a thousand, wherever the street of the imperceptible corners should choose to run again. Yet when he moved, it was toward the house. It was as though, as soon as he found that his feet intended to go there, that he let go, seemed to float, surrendered, thinking *All right All right* floating, riding across the dusk, up to the house and onto the back porch and to the door by which he would enter, that was never locked. But when he put his hand upon it, it would not open. Perhaps for the moment neither hand nor believing would believe; he seemed to stand there, quiet, not yet thinking, watching his hand shaking the door, hearing the sound of the bolt on the inside. He turned away quietly. He was not yet raging. He went to the kitchen door. He expected that to be locked also. But he did not realise until he found that it was open, that he had wanted it to be. When he found that it was not locked it was like an insult. It was as though some enemy upon whom he had wreaked his utmost of violence and contumely stood, unscathed and unscarred, and contemplated him with a musing and insufferable contempt. When he entered the kitchen, he did not approach the door into the house proper, the door in which she had appeared with the candle on the night when he first saw her. He went directly to the table where she set out his food. He did not need to see. His hands saw; the dishes were still a little warm, thinking *Set out for the nigger. For the nigger.*

He seemed to watch his hand as if from a distance. He watched it pick up a dish and swing it up and back and hold it there while he breathed deep and slow, intensely cogitant. He heard his voice say aloud, as if he were playing a game: "Ham," and watched his hand swing and hurl the dish crashing into the wall, the invisible wall, waiting for the crash to subside and silence to flow completely back before taking up another one. He held this dish poised, sniffing. This one required some time. "Beans or greens?" he said. "Beans or spinach? . . . All right. Call it beans." He hurled it, hard, waiting until the crash ceased. He raised the third dish. "Something with onions," he said, thinking *This is fun. Why didn't I think of this before?* "Woman's muck." He hurled it, hard and slow, hearing the crash, waiting. Now he heard something else: feet within the house, approaching the door. 'She'll have the lamp this time,' he thought thinking *If I were to look now, I could see the light under the door* As his hand swung up and back. *Now she has almost reached the door* "Potatoes," he said at last, with judicial finality. He did not look around, even when he heard the bolt in the door and heard the door inyawn and light fell upon him where he stood with the dish poised. "Yes, it's potatoes," he said, in the preoccupied and oblivious tone of a child playing alone. He could both see and hear this crash. Then the light went away; again he heard the door yawn, again he heard the bolt. He had not yet looked around. He took up the next dish. "Beets," he said. "I dont like beets, anyhow."

The next day he went to work at the planing mill. He went to work on Friday. He had eaten nothing now since Wednesday night. He drew no pay until Saturday evening, working overtime Saturday afternoon. He ate Saturday night, in a restaurant downtown, for the first time in three days. He did not return to the house. For a time he would not even look toward it when he left or entered the cabin. At the end of six months he had worn a private path between the cabin and the mill. It ran almost stringstraight, avoiding all houses, entering the woods soon and running straight and with daily increasing definition and precision, to the sawdust pile where he worked. And always, when the whistle blew at five thirty, he returned by it to the cabin, to change into the white shirt and the dark creased trousers before walking the two miles back to town to eat, as if he were ashamed of the overalls. Or perhaps it was not shame, though very likely he could no more have said what it was than he could have said that it was not shame.

He no longer deliberately avoided looking at the house; neither did he deliberately look at it. For a while he believed that she would send for him. 'She'll make the first sign,' he thought. But she did not; after a while he believed that he no longer expected it. Yet on the first time that he deliberately looked again toward the house, he felt a shocking surge and fall of blood; then he knew that he had been afraid all the time that she would be in sight, that she had been watching him all the while with that perspicuous and still contempt; he felt a sensation of sweating, of having surmounted an ordeal. 'That's over,' he thought. 'I have done that now.' So that when one day he did see her, there was no shock. Perhaps he was prepared. Anyway, there was no shocking surge and drop of blood when he looked up, completely by chance, and saw her in the back yard, in a gray dress and the sunbonnet. He could not tell if she had been watching him or had seen him or were watching him now or not. 'You dont bother me and I dont bother you,' he thought, thinking *I dreamed it. It didn't happen. She has nothing under her clothes so that it could have happened*

He went to work in the spring. One evening in September he returned home and entered the cabin and stopped in midstride, in complete astonishment. She was sitting on the cot, looking at him. Her head was bare. He had never seen it bare before, though he had felt in the dark the loose abandon of her hair, not yet wild, on a dark pillow. But he had never seen her hair before and he stood staring at it alone while she watched him; he said suddenly to himself, in the instant of moving again: 'She's trying to. *I had expected it to have gray in it* She's trying to be a woman and she dont know how.' Thinking, knowing *She has come to talk to me* Two hours later she was still talking, they sitting side by side on the cot in the now dark cabin. She told him that she was fortyone years old and that she had been born in the house yonder and had lived there ever since. That she had never been away from Jefferson for a longer period than six months at any time and these only at wide intervals filled with homesickness for the sheer boards and nails, the earth and trees and shrubs, which composed the place which was a foreign land to her and her people; when she spoke even now, after forty years, among the slurred consonants and the flat vowels of the land where her life had been cast, New England talked as plainly as it did in the speech of her kin who had never left New Hampshire and whom she had seen perhaps three times in her life, her forty years. Sitting beside her on the dark cot while the light failed and at last her voice was without source, steady, interminable, pitched almost like the voice of a man, Christmas thought, 'She is like all the rest of them. Whether they are seventeen or fortyseven, when they finally come to surrender completely, it's going to be in words.'

Calvin Burden was the son of a minister named Nathaniel Burrington. The youngest of ten children, he ran away from home at the age of twelve, before he could write his name (or would write it, his father believed) on a ship. He made the voyage around the Horn to California and turned Catholic; he lived for a year in a monastery. Ten years later he reached Missouri from the west. Three weeks after he arrived he was married, to the daughter of a family of Huguenot stock which had emigrated from Carolina by way of Kentucky. On the day after the wedding he said, "I guess I had better settle down." He began that day to settle down. The wedding celebration was still in progress, and his first step was to formally deny allegiance to the Catholic church. He did this in a saloon, insisting that every one present listen to him and state their objections; he was a little insistent on there being objections, though there were none; not, that is, up to the time when he was led away by friends. The next day he said that he meant it, anyhow; that he would not belong to a church full of frogeating slaveholders. That was in Saint Louis. He bought a home there, and a year later he was a father. He said then that he had denied the Catholic church a year ago for the sake of his son's soul; almost as soon as the boy was born, he set about to imbue the child with the religion of his New England forebears. There was no Unitarian meetinghouse available, and Burden could not read the English Bible. But he had learned to read in Spanish from the priests in California, and as soon as the child could walk Burden (he pronounced it Burden now, since he could not spell it at all and the priests had taught him to write it laboriously so with a hand more apt for a rope or a gunbutt or a knife than a pen) began to read to the child in Spanish from the book which he had brought with him from California, interspersing the fine, sonorous flowing of mysticism in a foreign tongue with harsh, extemporised dissertations composed half of the bleak and bloodless logic which he remembered from his father on interminable New England Sundays, and half of immediate hellfire and tangible brimstone of which any country Methodist circuit rider would have been proud. The two of them would be alone in the room: the tall, gaunt, Nordic man, and the small, dark, vivid child who had inherited his mother's build and coloring, like people of two different races. When the boy was about five, Burden killed a man in an argument over slavery and had to take his family and move, leave Saint Louis. He moved westward, "to get away from Democrats," he said.

The settlement to which he moved consisted of a store, a blacksmith shop, a church and two saloons. Here Burden spent much of his time talking politics and in his harsh loud voice cursing slavery and slaveholders. His reputation had come with him and he was known to carry a pistol, and his opinions were received without comment, at least. At times, especially on Saturday nights, he came home, still full of straight whiskey and the sound of his own ranting. Then he would wake his son (the mother was dead now and there were three daughters, all with blue eyes) with his hard hand. "I'll learn you to hate two things," he would say, "or I'll frail the tar out of you. And those things are hell and slaveholders. Do you hear me?"

"Yes," the boy would say. "I cant help but hear you. Get on to bed and let me sleep."

He was no proselyter, missionary. Save for an occasional minor episode with pistols, none of which resulted fatally, he confined himself to his own blood. "Let them all go to their own benighted hell," he said to his children. "But I'll beat the loving God into the four of you as long as I can raise my arm." That would be on Sunday, each Sunday when, washed and clean, the children in calico or denim, the father in his broadcloth frockcoat bulging over the pistol in his hip pocket, and the collarless plaited shirt which the oldest girl laundered each Saturday as well as the dead mother ever had, they gathered in the clean crude parlor while Burden read from the once gilt and blazoned book in that language which none of them understood. He continued to do that up to the time when his son ran away from home.

The son's name was Nathaniel. He ran away at fourteen and did not return for sixteen years, though they heard from him twice in that time by word-of-mouth messenger. The first time was from Colorado, the second time from Old Mexico. He did not say what he was doing in either place. "He was all right when I left him," the messenger said. This was the second messenger; it was in 1863, and the messenger was eating breakfast in the kitchen, bolting his food with decorous celerity. The three girls, the two oldest almost grown now, were serving him, standing with arrested dishes and softly open mouths in their full, coarse, clean dresses, about the crude table, the father sitting opposite the messenger across the table, his head propped on his single hand. The other arm he had lost two years ago while a member of a troop of partisan guerilla horse in the Kansas fighting, and his head and beard were grizzled now. But he was still vigorous, and his frockcoat still bulged behind over the butt of the heavy pistol. "He got into a little trouble," the messenger said. "But he was still all right the last I heard."

"Trouble?" the father said.

"He killed a Mexican that claimed he stole his horse. You know how them Spanish are about white men, even when they dont kill Mexicans." The messenger drank some coffee. "But I reckon they have to be kind of strict, with the country filling up with tenderfeet and all.—Thank you kindly," he said, as the oldest girl slid a fresh stack of corn cakes onto his plate; "yessum, I can reach the sweetening fine.—Folks claim it wasn't the Mexican's horse noways. Claim the Mexican never owned no horse. But I reckon even them Spanish have got to be strict, with these Easterners already giving the West such a bad name."

The father grunted. "I'll be bound. If there was trouble there, I'll be bound he was in it. You tell him," he said violently, "if he lets them yellowbellied priests bamboozle him, I'll shoot him myself quick as I would a Reb."

"You tell him to come on back home," the oldest girl said. "That's what you tell him."

"Yessum," the messenger said. "I'll shore tell him. I'm going east to Indianny for a spell. But I'll see him soon as I get back. I'll shore tell him. Oh, yes; I nigh forgot. He said to tell you the woman and kid was fine."

"Whose woman and kid?" the father said.

"His," the messenger said. "I thank you kindly again. And good-bye all."

They heard from the son a third time before they saw him again. They heard him shouting one day out in front of the house, though still some distance away. It was in 1866. The family had moved again, a hundred miles further west, and it had taken the son two months to find them, riding back and forth across Kansas and Missouri in a buckboard with two leather sacks of gold dust and minted coins and crude jewels thrown under the seat like a pair of old shoes, before he found the sod cabin and drove up to it, shouting. Sitting in a chair before the cabin door was a man. "There's father," Nathaniel said to the woman on the buckboard seat beside him. "See?" Though the father was only in his late fifties, his sight had begun to fail. He did not distinguish his son's face until the buckboard had stopped and the sisters had billowed shrieking through the door. Then Calvin rose; he gave a long, booming shout. "Well," Nathaniel said; "here we are."

Calvin was not speaking sentences at all. He was just yelling, cursing. "I'm going to frail the tar out of you!" he roared. "Girls! Vangie! Beck! Sarah!" The sisters had already emerged. They seemed to boil through the door in their full skirts like balloons on a torrent, with shrill cries, above which the father's voice boomed and roared. His coat—the frockcoat of Sunday or the wealthy or the retired —was open now and he was tugging at something near his waist with the same gesture and attitude with which he might be drawing the pistol. But he was merely dragging from about his waist with his single hand a leather strap, and flourishing it he now thrust and shoved through the shrill and birdlike hovering of the women. "I'll learn you yet!" he roared. "I'll learn you to run away!" The strap fell twice across Nathaniel's shoulders. It fell twice before the two men locked.

It was in play, in a sense: a kind of deadly play and smiling seriousness: the play of two lions that might or might not leave marks. They locked, the strap arrested: face to face and breast to breast they stood: the old man with his gaunt, grizzled face and his pale New England eyes, and the young one who bore no resemblance to him at all, with his beaked nose and his white teeth smiling. "Stop it," Nathaniel said. "Dont you see who's watching yonder in the buckboard?"

They had none of them looked at the buckboard until now. Sitting on the seat was a woman and a boy of about twelve. The father looked once at the woman; he did not even need to see the boy. He just looked at the woman, his jaw slacked as if he had seen a ghost. "Evangeline!" he said. She looked enough like his dead wife to have been her sister. The boy who could hardly remember his mother at all, had taken for wife a woman who looked almost exactly like her.

"That's Juana," he said. "That's Calvin with her. We come home to get married."

After supper that night, with the woman and child in bed, Nathaniel told them. They sat about the lamp: the father, the sisters, the returned son. There were no ministers out there where he had been, he explained; just priests and Catholics. "So when we found that the chico was on the way, she begun to talk about a priest. But I wasn't going to have any Burden born a heathen. So I begun to look around, to humor her. But first one thing and then another come up and I couldn't get away to meet a minister; and then the boy came and so it wasn't any rush anymore. But she kept on worrying, about priests and such, and so in a couple of years I heard how there was to be a white minister in Santa Fe on a certain day. So we packed up and started out and got to Santa Fe just in time to see the dust of the stage that was carrying the minister on away. So we waited there and in a couple more years we had another chance, in Texas. Only this time I got kind of mixed up with helping some Rangers that were cleaning up some kind of a mess where some folks had a deputy treed in a dance hall. So when that was over we just decided to come on home and get married right. And here we are."

The father sat, gaunt, grizzled, and austere, beneath the lamp. He had been listening, but his expression was brooding, with a kind of violently slumbering contemplativeness and bewildered outrage. "Another damn black Burden," he said. "Folks will think I bred to a damn slaver. And now he's got to breed to one, too." The son listened quietly, not even attempting to tell his father that the woman was Spanish and not Rebel. "Damn, lowbuilt black folks: low built because of the weight of the wrath of God, black because of the sin of human bondage staining their blood and flesh." His gaze was vague, fanatical, and convinced. "But we done freed them now, both black and white alike. They'll bleach out now. In a hundred years they will be white folks again. Then maybe we'll let them come back into America." He mused, smoldering, immobile. "By God," he said suddenly, "he's got a man's build, anyway, for all his black look. By God, he's going to be as big a man as his grandpappy; not a runt like his pa. For all his black dam and his black look, he will."

She told Christmas this while they sat on the cot in the darkening cabin. They had not moved for over an hour. He could not see her face at all now; he seemed to swing faintly, as though in a drifting boat, upon the sound of her voice as upon some immeasurable and drowsing peace evocative of nothing of any moment, scarce listening. "His name was Calvin, like grandpa's, and he was as big as grandpa, even if he was dark like father's mother's people and like his mother. She was not my mother: he was just my halfbrother. Grandpa was the last of ten, and father was the last of two, and Calvin was the last of all." He had just turned twenty when he was killed in the town two miles away by an ex-slaveholder and Confederate soldier named Sartoris, over a question of negro voting.

She told Christmas about the graves—the brother's, the grandfather's, the father's and his two wives—on a cedar knoll in the pasture a half mile from the house; listening quietly, Christmas thought. 'Ah. She'll take me to see them. I will have to go.' But she did not. She never mentioned the graves to him again after that night when she told him where they were and that he could go and see them for himself if he wished. "You probably cant find them, anyway," she said. "Because when they brought grandfather and Calvin home that evening, father waited until after dark and buried them and hid the graves, levelled the mounds and put brush and things over them."

"Hid them?" Christmas said.

There was nothing soft, feminine, mournful and retrospective in her voice. "So they would not find them. Dig them up. Maybe butcher them." She went on, her voice a little impatient, explanatory: "They hated us here. We were Yankees. Foreigners. Worse than foreigners: enemies. Carpetbaggers. And it—the War—still too close for even the ones that got whipped to be very sensible. Stirring up the negroes to murder and rape, they called it. Threatening white supremacy. So I suppose that Colonel Sartoris was a town hero because he killed with two shots from the same pistol an old onearmed man and a boy who had never even cast his first vote. Maybe they were right. I dont know."

"Oh," Christmas said. "They might have done that? dug them up after they were already killed, dead? Just when do men that have different blood in them stop hating one another?"

"When do they?" Her voice ceased. She went on: "I dont know. I dont know whether they would have dug them up or not. I wasn't alive then. I was not born until fourteen years after Calvin was killed. I dont know what men might have done then. But father thought they might have. So he hid the graves. And then Calvin's mother died and he buried her there, with Calvin and grandpa. And so it sort of got to be our burying ground before we knew it. Maybe father hadn't planned to bury her there. I remember how my mother (father sent for her up to New Hampshire where some of our kin people still live, soon after Calvin's mother died. He was alone here, you see. I suppose if it hadn't been for Calvin and grandpa buried out yonder, he would have gone away) told me that father started once to move away, when Calvin's mother died. But she died in the summer, and it would have been too hot then to take her back to Mexico, to her people. So he buried her here. Maybe that's why he decided to stay here. Or maybe it was because he was getting old too then, and all the men who had fought in the War were getting old and the negroes hadn't raped or murdered anybody to speak of. Anyway, he buried her here. He had to hide that grave too, because he thought that someone might see it and happen to remember Calvin and grandfather. He couldn't take the risk, even if it was all over and past and done then. And the next year he wrote to our cousin in New Hampshire. He said, 'I am fifty years old. I have all she will ever need. Send me a good woman for a wife. I dont care who she is, just so she

is a good housekeeper and is at least thirtyfive years old.'
He sent the railroad fare in the letter. Two months later
my mother got here and they were married that day. That
was quick marrying, for him. The other time it took him
over twelve years to get married, that time back in Kansas
when he and Calvin and Calvin's mother finally caught up
with grandfather. They got home in the middle of the
week, but they waited until Sunday to have the wedding.
They had it outdoors, down by the creek, with a barbecued
steer and a keg of whiskey and everybody that they could
get word to or that heard about it, came. They began to get
there Saturday morning, and on Saturday night the
preacher came. All that day father's sisters worked, making
Calvin's mother a wedding gown and a veil. They made
the gown out of flour sacks and the veil out of some
mosquito netting that a saloon keeper had nailed over a
picture behind the bar. They borrowed it from him. They
even made some kind of a suit for Calvin to wear. He was
twelve then, and they wanted him to be the ringbearer. He
didn't want to. He found out the night before what they
intended to make him do, and the next day (they had intended to have the wedding about six or seven o'clock the
next morning) after everybody had got up and eaten breakfast, they had to put off the ceremony until they could find
Calvin. At last they found him and made him put on the
suit and they had the wedding, with Calvin's mother in
the homemade gown and the mosquito veil and father with
his hair slicked with bear's grease and the carved Spanish
boots he had brought back from Mexico. Grandfather gave
the bride away. Only he had been going back to the keg
of whiskey every now and then while they were hunting
for Calvin, and so when his time came to give the bride

away he made a speech instead. He got off on Lincoln and slavery and dared any man there to deny that Lincoln and the negro and Moses and the children of Israel were the same, and that the Red Sea was just the blood that had to be spilled in order that the black race might cross into the Promised Land. It took them some time to make him stop so the wedding could go on. After the wedding they stayed about a month. Then one day father and grandfather went east, to Washington, and got a commission from the government to come down here, to help with the freed negroes. They came to Jefferson, all except father's sisters. Two of them got married, and the youngest one went to live with one of the others, and grandfather and father and Calvin and his mother came here and bought the house. And then what they probably knew all the time was going to happen did happen, and father was alone until my mother came from New Hampshire. They had never even seen one another before, not even a picture. They got married the day she got here and two years later I was born and father named me Joanna after Calvin's mother. I dont think he even wanted another son at all. I cant remember him very well. The only time I can remember him as somebody, a person, was when he took me and showed me Calvin's and grandpa's graves. It was a bright day, in the spring. I remember how I didn't want to go, without even knowing where it was that we were going. I didn't want to go into the cedars. I dont know why I didn't want to. I couldn't have known what was in there; I was just four then. And even if I had known, that should not have frightened a child. I think it was something about father, something that came from the cedar grove to me, through him. A something that I felt that he had put on the cedar grove, and that when I went into it, the grove would put on me so that I would never be able to forget it. I dont know. But he made me go in, and the two of us standing there, and he said, 'Remember this. Your grandfather and brother are lying there, murdered not by one white man but by the curse which God put on a whole race before your grandfather or your brother or me or you were even thought of. A race doomed and cursed to be forever and ever a part of the white race's doom and curse for its sins. Remember that. His doom and his curse. Forever and ever. Mine. Your mother's. Yours, even though you are a child. The curse of every white child that ever was born and that ever will be born. None can escape it.' And I said, 'Not even me?' And he said, 'Not even you. Least of all, you.' I had seen and known negroes since I could remember. I just looked at them as I did at rain, or furniture, or food or sleep. But after that I seemed to see them for the first time not as people, but as a thing, a shadow in which I lived, we lived, all white people, all other people. I thought of all the children coming forever and ever into the world, white, with the black shadow already falling upon them before they drew breath. And I seemed to see the black shadow in the shape of a cross. And it seemed like the white babies were struggling, even before they drew breath, to escape from the shadow that was not only upon them but beneath them too, flung out like their arms were flung out, as if they were nailed to the cross. I saw all the little babies that would ever be in the world, the ones not yet even born—a long line of them with their arms spread, on the black crosses. I couldn't tell then whether I saw it or dreamed it. But it was terrible to me. I cried at night. At last I told father, tried to tell him. What I wanted to tell him was that I must escape, get away from under the shadow, or I would die. 'You cannot,' he said. 'You must struggle, rise. But in order to rise, you must raise the shadow with you. But you can never lift it to your level. I see that now, which I did not see until I came down here. But escape it you cannot. The curse of the black race is God's curse. But the curse of the white race is the black man who will be forever God's chosen own because He once cursed Him.'" Her voice ceased. Across the vague oblong of open door fireflies drifted. At last Christmas said:

"There was something I was going to ask you. But I guess I know the answer myself now."

She did not stir. Her voice was quiet. "What?"

"Why your father never killed that fellow—what's his name? Sartoris."

"Oh," she said. Then there was silence again. Across the door the fireflies drifted and drifted. "You would have. Wouldn't you?"

"Yes," he said, at once, immediately. Then he knew that she was looking toward his voice almost as if she could see him. Her voice was almost gentle now, it was so quiet, so still.

"You dont have any idea who your parents were?"

If she could have seen his face she would have found it sullen, brooding. "Except that one of them was part nigger. Like I told you before."

She was still looking at him; her voice told him that. It was quiet, impersonal, interested without being curious. "How do you know that?"

He didn't answer for some time. Then he said: "I dont know it." Again his voice ceased; by its sound she knew that he was looking away, toward the door. His face was sullen, quite still. Then he spoke again, moving; his voice now had an overtone, unmirthful yet quizzical, at once humorless and sardonic: "If I'm not, damned if I haven't wasted a lot of time."

She in turn seemed to muse now, quiet, scarcebreathing, yet still with nothing of selfpity or retrospect: "I had thought of that. Why father didn't shoot Colonel Sartoris. I think that it was because of his French blood."

"French blood?" Christmas said. "Dont even Frenchmen get mad when a man kills his father and his son on the same day? I guess your father must have got religion. Turned preacher, maybe."

She did not answer for a time. The fireflies drifted; somewhere a dog barked, mellow, sad, faraway. "I thought about that," she said. "It was all over then. The killing in uniform and with flags, and the killing without uniforms and flags. And none of it doing or did any good. None of it. And we were foreigners, strangers, that thought differently from the people whose country we had come into without being asked or wanted. And he was French, half of him. Enough French to respect anybody's love for the land where he and his people were born and to understand that a man would have to act as the land where he was born had trained him to act. I think that was it."

. 12 .

IN this way the second phase began. It was as though he had fallen into a sewer. As upon another life he looked back upon that first hard and manlike surrender, that surrender terrific and hard, like the breaking down of a spiritual skeleton the very sound of whose snapping fibers could be heard almost by the physical ear, so that the act of capitulation was anticlimax, as when a defeated general on the day after the last battle, shaved overnight and with his boots cleaned of the mud of combat, surrenders his sword to a committee.

The sewer ran only by night. The days were the same as they had ever been. He went to work at half past six in the morning. He would leave the cabin without looking toward the house at all. At six in the evening he returned, again without even looking toward the house. He washed and changed to the white shirt and the dark creased trousers and went to the kitchen and found his supper waiting on the table and he sat and ate it, still without having seen her at all. But he knew that she was in the house and that the coming of dark within the old walls was breaking down something and leaving it corrupt with waiting. He knew how she had spent the day; that her days also were no different from what they had always been, as if in her case too another person had lived them. All day long he would imagine her, going about her housework, sitting for that unvarying period at the scarred desk, or talking, listening, to the negro women who came to the house from both directions up and down the road, following paths which had been years in the wearing and which radiated from the house like wheelspokes. What they talked about to her he did not know, though he had watched them approaching the house in a manner not exactly secret, yet purposeful, entering usually singly though sometimes in twos and threes, in their aprons and headrags and now and then with a man's coat thrown about their shoulders, emerging again and returning down the radiating paths not fast and yet not loitering. They would be brief in his mind, thinking *Now she is doing this. Now she is doing that* not thinking much about her. He believed that during the day she thought no more about him than he did about her, too. Even when at night, in her dark bedroom, she insisted on telling him in tedious detail the trivial matters of her day and insisted on his telling her of his day in turn, it was in the fashion of lovers: that imperious and insatiable demand that the trivial details of both days be put into words, without any need to listen to the telling. Then he would finish his supper and go to her where she waited. Often he would not hurry. As time went on and the novelty of the second phase began to wear off and become habit, he would stand in the kitchen door and look out across the dusk and see, perhaps with foreboding and premonition, the savage and lonely street which he had chosen of his own will, waiting for him, thinking *This is not my life. I dont belong here*

At first it shocked him: the abject fury of the New England glacier exposed suddenly to the fire of the New England biblical hell. Perhaps he was aware of the abnegation in it: the imperious and fierce urgency that concealed an actual despair at frustrate and irrevocable years, which she appeared to attempt to compensate each night as if she believed that it would be the last night on earth by damning herself forever to the hell of her forefathers, by living not alone in sin but in filth. She had an avidity for the forbidden wordsymbols; an insatiable appetite for the sound of them on his tongue and on her own. She revealed the terrible and impersonal curiosity of a child about forbidden subjects and objects; that rapt and tireless and detached interest of a surgeon in the physical body and its possibilities. And by day he would see the calm, coldfaced, almost manlike, almost middleaged woman who had lived for twenty years alone, without any feminine fears at all, in a lonely house in a neighborhood populated, when at all, by negroes, who spent a certain portion of each day sitting tranquilly at a desk and writing tranquilly for the eyes of both youth and age the practical advice of a combined priest and banker and trained nurse.

During that period (it could not be called a honeymoon) Christmas watched her pass through every avatar of a woman in love. Soon she more than shocked him: she astonished and bewildered him. She surprised and took him unawares with fits of jealous rage. She could have had no such experience at all, and there was neither reason for the scene nor any possible protagonist: he knew that she knew that. It was as if she had invented the whole thing deliberately, for the purpose of playing it out like a play. Yet she did it with such fury, with such convincingness and such conviction, that on the first occasion he thought that she was under a delusion and the third time he thought that she was mad. She revealed an unexpected and infallible instinct for intrigue. She insisted on a place for concealing notes, letters. It was in a hollow fence post below the rotting stable. He never saw her put a note there, yet she insisted on his visiting it daily; when he did so, the letter would be there. When he did not and lied to her, he would find that she had already set traps to catch him in the lie; she cried, wept.

Sometimes the notes would tell him not to come until a certain hour, to that house which no white person save himself had entered in years and in which for twenty years now she had been all night alone; for a whole week she forced him to climb into a window to come to her. He would do so and sometimes he would have to seek her about the dark house until he found her, hidden, in closets, in empty rooms, waiting, panting, her eyes in the dark glowing like the eyes of cats. Now and then she appointed trysts beneath certain shrubs about the grounds, where he would find her naked, or with her clothing half torn to ribbons upon her, in the wild throes of nymphomania, her body gleaming in the slow shifting from one to another of such formally erotic attitudes and gestures as a Beardsley of the time of Petronius might have drawn. She would be wild then, in the close, breathing halfdark without walls, with her wild hair, each strand of which would seem to come alive like octopus tentacles, and her wild hands and her breathing: "Negro! Negro! Negro!"

Within six months she was completely corrupted. It

could not be said that he corrupted her. His own life, for all its anonymous promiscuity, had been conventional enough, as a life of healthy and normal sin usually is. The corruption came from a source even more inexplicable to him than to her. In fact, it was as though with the corruption which she seemed to gather from the air itself, she began to corrupt him. He began to be afraid. He could not have said of what. But he began to see himself as from a distance, like a man being sucked down into a bottomless morass. He had not exactly thought that yet. What he was now seeing was the street lonely, savage, and cool. That was it: cool; he was thinking, saying aloud to himself sometimes, "I better move. I better get away from here."

But something held him, as the fatalist can always be held: by curiosity, pessimism, by sheer inertia. Meanwhile the affair went on, submerging him more and more by the imperious and overriding fury of those nights. Perhaps he realised that he could not escape. Anyway, he stayed, watching the two creatures that struggled in the one body like two moongleamed shapes struggling drowning in alternate throes upon the surface of a black thick pool beneath the last moon. Now it would be that still, cold, contained figure of the first phase who, even though lost and damned, remained somehow impervious and impregnable; then it would be the other, the second one, who in furious denial of that impregnability strove to drown in the black abyss of its own creating that physical purity which had been preserved too long now even to be lost. Now and then they would come to the black surface, locked like sisters; the black waters would drain away. Then the world would rush back: the room, the walls, the peaceful myriad sound of insects from beyond the summer windows where insects had whirred for forty years. She would stare at him then with the wild, despairing face of a stranger; looking at her then he paraphrased himself: "She wants to pray, but she dont know how to do that either."

She had begun to get fat.

The end of this phase was not sharp, not a climax, like the first. It merged into the third phase so gradually that he could not have said where one stopped and the other began. It was summer becoming fall, with already, like shadows before a westering sun, the chill and implacable import of autumn cast ahead upon summer; something of dying summer spurting again like a dying coal, in the fall. This was over a period of two years. He still worked at the planing mill, and in the meantime he had begun to sell a little whiskey, very judiciously, restricting himself to a few discreet customers none of whom knew the others. She did not know this, although he kept his stock hidden on the place and met his clients in the woods beyond the pasture. Very likely she would not have objected. But neither would Mrs McEachern have objected to the hidden rope; perhaps he did not tell her for the same reason that he did not tell Mrs McEachern. Thinking of Mrs McEachern and the rope, and of the waitress whom he had never told where the money came from which he gave to her, and now of his present mistress and the whiskey, he could almost believe that it was not to make money that he sold the whiskey but because he was doomed to conceal always something from the women who surrounded him. Meanwhile he would see her from a distance now and then in the daytime, about the rear premises, where moved articulate beneath the clean, austere garments which she wore that rotten richness ready to flow into putrefaction at a touch, like something growing in a swamp, not once looking toward the cabin or toward him. And when he thought of that other personality that seemed to exist somewhere in physical darkness itself, it seemed to him that what he now saw by daylight was a phantom of someone whom the night sister had murdered and which now moved purposeless about the scenes of old peace, robbed even of the power of lamenting.

Of course the first fury of the second phase could not last. At first it had been a torrent; now it was a tide, with a flow and ebb. During its flood she could almost fool them both. It was as if out of her knowledge that it was just a flow that must presently react was born a wilder fury, a fierce denial that could flag itself and him into physical experimentation that transcended imagining, carried them as though by momentum alone, bearing them without volition or plan. It was as if she knew somehow that time was short, that autumn was almost upon her, without knowing yet the exact significance of autumn. It seemed to be instinct alone: instinct physical and instinctive denial of the wasted years. Then the tide would ebb. Then they would be stranded as behind a dying mistral, upon a spent and satiate beach, looking at one another like strangers, with hopeless and reproachful (on his part with weary: on hers with despairing) eyes.

But the shadow of autumn was upon her. She began to talk about a child, as though instinct had warned her that now was the time when she must either justify or expiate. She talked about it in the ebb periods. At first the beginning of the night was always a flood, as if the hours of light and of separation had damned up enough of the wasting stream to simulate torrent for a moment at least. But after a while the stream became too thin for that: he would go to her now with reluctance, a stranger, already backlooking; a stranger he would leave her after having sat with her in the dark bedroom, talking of still a third stranger. He noticed now how, as though by premeditation, they met always in the bedroom, as though they were married. No more did he have to seek her through the house; the nights when he must seek her, hidden and panting and naked, about the dark house or among the shrubbery of the ruined park were as dead now as the hollow fencepost below the barn.

That was all dead: the scenes, the faultlessly played scenes of secret and monstrous delight and of jealousy. Though if she had but known it now, she had reason for jealousy. He made trips every week or so, on business, he told her. She did not know that the business took him to Memphis, where he betrayed her with other women, women bought for a price. She did not know it. Perhaps in the phase in which she now was she could not have been convinced, would not have listened to proof, would not have cared. Because she had taken to lying sleepless most of the night, making up the sleep in the afternoons. She was not sick; it was not her body. She had never been better; her appetite was enormous and she weighed thirty pounds more than she had ever weighed in her life. It was not that that kept her awake. It was something out of the darkness, the earth, the dying summer itself: something threatful and terrible to her because instinct assured her that it would not harm her; that it would overtake and betray her completely, but she would not be harmed: that on the contrary, she would be saved, that life would go on the same and even better, even less terrible. What was terrible was that she did not want to be saved. "I'm not ready to pray yet," she said aloud, quietly, rigid, soundless, her eyes wide open, while the moon poured and poured into the window, filling the room with something cold and irrevocable and wild with regret. "Dont make me have to pray yet. Dear God, let me be damned a little longer, a little while." She seemed to see her whole past life, the starved years, like a gray tunnel, at the far and irrevocable end of which, as unfading as a reproach, her naked breast of three short years ago ached as though in agony, virgin and crucified; "Not yet, dear God. Not yet, dear God."

So when he now came to her, after the passive and cold and seemly transports of sheer habit she began to speak of a child. She talked about it impersonally at first, discussing children. Perhaps it was sheer and instinctive feminine cunning and indirection, perhaps not. Anyway, it was some time before he discovered with a kind of shock that she was discussing it as a possibility, a practical thought. He said No at once.

"Why not?" she said. She looked at him, speculative. He was thinking fast, thinking *She wants to be married. That's it. She wants a child no more than I do* 'It's just a trick,' he thought. 'I should have known it, expected it. I should have cleared out of here a year ago.' But he was afraid to tell her this, to let the word marriage come between them, come aloud, thinking, 'She may not have thought of it, and I will just put the notion in her head.' She was watching him. "Why not?" she said. And then something in him flashed *Why not? It would mean ease, security, for the rest of your life. You would never have to move again. And you might as well be married to her as this* thinking, 'No. If I give in now, I will deny all the

. 250 .

thirty years that I have lived to make me what I chose to be.' He said:

"If we were going to have one, I guess we would have had one two years ago."

"We didn't want one then."

"We dont want one now, either," he said.

That was in September. Just after Christmas she told him that she was pregnant. Almost before she ceased to speak, he believed that she was lying. He discovered now that he had been expecting her to tell him that for three months. But when he looked at her face, he knew that she was not. He believed that she also knew that she was not. He thought, 'Here it comes. She will say it now: marry. But I can at least get out of the house first.'

But she did not. She was sitting quite still on the bed, her hands on her lap, her still New England face (it was still the face of a spinster: prominently boned, long, a little thin, almost manlike: in contrast to it her plump body was more richly and softly animal than ever) lowered. She said, in a tone musing, detached, impersonal: "A full measure. Even to a bastard negro child. I would like to see father's and Calvin's faces. This will be a good time for you to run, if that's what you want to do." But it was as though she were not listening to her own voice, did not intend for the words to have any actual meaning: that final upflare of stubborn and dying summer upon which autumn, the dawning of halfdeath, had come unawares. 'It's over now,' she thought quietly; 'finished.' Except the waiting, for one month more to pass, to be sure; she had learned that from the negro women, that you could not always tell until after two months. She would have to wait another month, watching the calendar. She made a mark on the calendar to be sure, so there would be no mistake; through the bedroom window she watched that month accomplish. A frost had come, and some of the leaves were beginning to turn. The marked day on the calendar came and passed; she gave herself another week, to be doubly sure. She was not elated, since she was not surprised. "I am with child," she said, quietly, aloud.

'I'll go tomorrow,' he told himself, that same day. 'I'll go Sunday,' he thought. 'I'll wait and get this week's pay, and then I am gone.' He began to look forward to Saturday, planning where he would go. He did not see her all that week. He expected her to send for him. When he entered or left the cabin he would find himself avoiding looking toward the house, as he had during the first week he was there. He did not see her at all. Now and then he would see the negro women, in nondescript garments against the autumn chill, coming or going along the worn paths, entering or leaving the house. But that was all. When Saturday came, he did not go. 'Might as well have all the jack I can get,' he thought. 'If she aint anxious for me to clear out, no reason why I should be. I'll go next Saturday.'

He stayed on. The weather remained cold, bright and cold. When he went to bed now in his cotton blanket, in the draughty cabin, he would think of the bedroom in the house, with its fire, its ample, quilted, lintpadded covers. He was nearer to selfpity than he had ever been. 'She might at least send me another blanket,' he thought. So might he have bought one. But he did not. Neither did she. He waited. He waited what he thought was a long time. Then one evening in February he returned home and found a note from her on his cot. It was brief; it was an order almost, directing him to come to the house that night. He was not surprised. He had never yet known a woman who, without another man available, would not come around in time. And he knew now that tomorrow he would go. 'This must be what I have been waiting for,' he thought; 'I have just been waiting to be vindicated.' When he changed his clothes, he shaved also. He prepared himself like a bridegroom, unaware of it. He found the table set for him in the kitchen, as usual; during all the time that he had not seen her, that had never failed. He ate and went upstairs. He did not hurry. 'We got all night,' he thought. 'It'll be something for her to think about tomorrow night and the next one, when she finds that cabin empty.' She was sitting before the fire. She did not even turn her head when he entered. "Bring that chair up with you," she said.

This was how the third phase began. It puzzled him for a while, even more than the other two. He had expected eagerness, a kind of tacit apology; or lacking that, an acquiescence that wanted only to be wooed. He was prepared to go that length, even. What he found was a stranger who put aside with the calm firmness of a man his hand when at last and in a kind of baffled desperation he went and touched her. "Come on," he said, "if you have something to tell me. We always talk better afterward. It wont hurt the kid, if that's what you have been afraid of."

She stayed him with a single word; for the first time he looked at her face: he looked upon a face cold, remote, and fanatic. "Do you realise," she said, "that you are wasting your life?" And he sat looking at her like a stone, as if he could not believe his own ears.

It took him some time to comprehend what she meant. She did not look at him at all. She sat looking into the fire, her face cold, still, brooding, talking to him as if he were a stranger, while he listened in outraged amazement. She wanted him to take over all her business affairs—the correspondence and the periodical visits—with the negro schools. She had the plan all elaborated. She recited it to him in detail while he listened in mounting rage and amazement. He was to have complete charge, and she would be his secretary, assistant: they would travel to the schools together, visit in the negro homes together; listening, even with his anger, he knew that the plan was mad. And all the while her calm profile in the peaceful firelight was as grave and tranquil as a portrait in a frame. When he left, he remembered that she had not once mentioned the expected child.

He did not yet believe that she was mad. He thought that it was because she was pregnant, as he believed that was why she would not let him touch her. He tried to argue with her. But it was like trying to argue with a tree: she did not even rouse herself to deny, she just listened quietly and then talked again in that level, cold tone as if he had never spoken. When he rose at last and went out he did not even know if she was aware that he had gone.

He saw her but once more within the next two months. He followed his daily routine, save that he did not approach the house at all now, taking his meals downtown again, as when he had first gone to work at the mill. But then, when he first went to work, he would not need to think of her during the day; he hardly ever thought about her. Now he could not help himself. She was in his mind so constantly that it was almost as if he were looking at her, there in the house, patient, waiting, inescapable, crazy. During the first phase it had been as though he were outside a house where snow was on the ground, trying to get into the house; during the second phase he was at the bottom of a pit in the hot wild darkness; now he was in the middle of a plain where there was no house, not even snow, not even wind.

He began now to be afraid, whose feeling up to now had been bewilderment and perhaps foreboding and fatality. He now had a partner in his whiskey business: a stranger named Brown who had appeared at the mill one day early in the spring, seeking work. He knew that the man was a fool, but at first he thought, 'At least he will have sense enough to do what I tell him to do. He wont have to think himself at all'; it was not until later that he said to himself: 'I know now that what makes a fool is an inability to take even his own good advice.' He took Brown because Brown was a stranger and had a certain cheerful and unscrupulous readiness about him, and not overmuch personal courage, knowing that in the hands of a judicious man, a coward within his own limitations can be made fairly useful to anyone except himself.

His fear was that Brown might learn about the woman in the house and do something irrevocable out of his own unpredictable folly. He was afraid that the woman, since he had avoided her, might take it into her head to come to the cabin some night. He had not seen her but once since February. That was when he sought her to tell her that Brown was coming to live with him in the cabin. It was on Sunday. He called her, and she came out to where he stood on the back porch and listened quietly. "You didn't have to do that," she said. He didn't understand then what she meant. It was not until later that thinking again flashed, complete, like a printed sentence: *She thinks that I brought him out here to keep her off. She believes that I think that with him there, she wont dare come down to the cabin; that she will have to let me alone*

Thus he put his belief, his fear of what she might do, into his own mind by believing that he had put it into hers. He believed that, since she had thought that, that Brown's presence would not only not deter her: it would be an incentive for her to come to the cabin. Because of the fact that for over a month now she had done nothing at all, made no move at all, he believed that she might do anything. Now he too lay awake at night. But he was thinking, 'I have got to do something. There is something that I am going to do.'

So he would trick and avoid Brown in order to reach the cabin first. He expected each time to find her waiting. When he would reach the cabin and find it empty, he would think in a kind of impotent rage of the urgency, the lying and the haste, and of her alone and idle in the house all day, with nothing to do save to decide whether to betray him at once or torture him a little longer. By ordinary he would not have minded whether Brown knew about their relations or not. He had nothing in his nature of reticence or of chivalry toward women. It was practical, material. He would have been indifferent if all Jefferson knew he was her lover: it was that he wanted no one to begin to speculate on what his private life out there was because of the hidden whiskey which was netting him thirty or forty dollars a week. That was one reason. Another reason was vanity. He would have died or murdered rather than have anyone, another man, learn what their relations had now become. That not only had she changed her life completely, but that she was trying to change his too and make of him something between a hermit and a missionary to negroes. He believed that if Brown learned the one, he must inevitably learn the other. So he would reach the cabin at last, after the lying and the hurry, and as he put his hand on the door, remembering the haste and thinking that in a moment he would find that it had not been necessary at all and yet to neglect which precaution he dared not, he would hate her with a fierce revulsion of dread and impotent rage. Then one evening he opened the door and found the note on the cot.

He saw it as soon as he entered, lying square and white and profoundly inscrutable against the dark blanket. He did even stop to think that he believed he knew what the message would be, would promise. He felt no eagerness; he felt relief. 'It's over now,' he thought, not yet taking up the folded paper. 'It will be like it was before now. No more talking about niggers and babies. She has come around. She has worn the other out, seen that she was getting nowhere. She sees now that what she wants, needs, is a man. She wants a man by night; what he does by daylight does not matter.' He should have realised then the reason why he had not gone away. He should have seen that he was bound just as tightly by that small square of still undivulging paper as though it were a lock and chain. He did not think of that. He saw only himself once again on the verge of promise and delight. It would be quieter though, now. They would both want it so; besides the whiphand which he would now have. 'All that foolishness,' he thought, holding the yet unopened paper in his hands; 'all that damn foolishness. She is still she and I am still I. And now, after all this damn foolishness'; thinking how they would both laugh over it tonight, later, afterward, when the time for quiet talking and quiet laughing came: at the whole thing, at one another, at themselves.

He did not open the note at all. He put it away and washed and shaved and changed his clothes, whistling while he did so. He had not finished when Brown came in. "Well, well, well," Brown said. Christmas said nothing. He was facing the shard of mirror nailed to the wall, knotting his tie. Brown had stopped in the center of the floor: a tall, lean, young man in dirty overalls, with a dark, weakly handsome face and curious eyes. Beside his mouth there was a narrow scar as white as a thread of spittle. After a while Brown said: "Looks like you are going somewhere."

"Does it?" Christmas said. He did not look around. He whistled monotonously but truely: something in minor, plaintive and negroid.

"I reckon I wont bother to clean up none," Brown said, "seeing as you are almost ready."

Christmas looked back at him. "Ready for what?"

"Aint you going to town?"

"Did I ever say I was?" Christmas said. He turned back to the glass.

"Oh," Brown said. He watched the back of Christmas's head. "Well, I reckon from that that you're going on private business." He watched Christmas. "This here's a cold night to be laying around on the wet ground without nothing under you but a thin gal."

"Aint it, though?" Christmas said, whistling, preoccupied and unhurried. He turned and picked up his coat and put it on, Brown still watching him. He went to the door. "See you in the morning," he said. The door did not close behind him. He knew that Brown was standing in it, looking after him. But he did not attempt to conceal his purpose. He went on toward the house. 'Let him watch,' he thought. 'Let him follow me if he wants to.'

The table was set for him in the kitchen. Before sitting down he took the unopened note from his pocket and laid it beside his plate. It was not enclosed, not sealed; it sprang open of its own accord, as though inviting him, insisting. But he did not look at it. He began to eat. He ate without haste. He had almost finished when he raised his head suddenly, listening. Then he rose and went to the door through which he had entered, with the noiselessness of a cat, and jerked the door open suddenly. Brown stood just outside, his face leaned to the door, or where the door had been. The light fell upon his face and upon it was an expression of intent and infantile interest which became surprise while Christmas looked at it, then it recovered, falling back a little. Brown's voice was gleeful though quiet, cautious, conspiratorial, as if he had already established his alliance and sympathy with Christmas, unasked, and without waiting to know what was going on, out of loyalty to his partner or perhaps to abstract man as opposed to all woman. "Well, well, well," he said. "So this is where you tomcat to every night. Right at our front door, you might say—"

Without saying a word Christmas struck him. The blow did not fall hard, because Brown was already in innocent and gleeful backmotion, in midsnicker as it were. The blow cut his voice short off; moving, springing backward, he vanished from the fall of light, into the darkness, from which his voice came, still not loud, as if even now he would not jeopardise his partner's business, but tense now with alarm, astonishment: "Dont you hit me!" He was the taller of the two: a gangling shape already in a ludicrous diffusion of escape as if he were on the point of clattering to earth in complete disintegration as he stumbled backward before the steady and still silent advance of the other. Again Brown's voice came, high, full of alarm and spurious threat: "Dont you hit me!" This time the blow struck his shoulder as he turned. He was running now. He ran for a hundred yards before he slowed, looking back. Then he stopped and turned. "You durn yellowbellied wop," he said, in a tentative tone, jerking his head immediately, as if his voice had made more noise, sounded louder, than he had intended. There was no sound from the house; the kitchen door was dark again, closed again. He raised his voice a little: "You durn yellowbellied wop! I'll learn you who you are monkeying with." There came no sound anywhere. It was chilly. He turned and went back to the cabin, mumbling to himself.

When Christmas reentered the kitchen he did not even look back at the table on which lay the note which he had not yet read. He went on through the door which led into the house and on to the stairs. He began to mount, not fast. He mounted steadily; he could now see the bedroom door, a crack of light, firelight, beneath it. He went steadily on and put his hand upon the door. Then he opened it and he stopped dead still. She was sitting at a table, beneath the lamp. He saw a figure that he knew, in a severe garment that he knew—a garment that looked as if it had been made for and worn by a careless man. Above it he saw a head with hair just beginning to gray drawn gauntly back to a knot as savage and ugly as a wart on a diseased bough. Then she looked up at him and he saw that she wore steelrimmed spectacles which he had never seen before. He stood in the door, his hand still on the knob, quite motionless. It seemed to him that he could actually hear the words inside him: *You should have read that note. You should have read that note* thinking, 'I am going to do something. Going to do something.'

He was still hearing that while he stood beside the table on which papers were scattered and from which she had not risen, and listened to the calm enormity which her cold, still voice unfolded, his mouth repeating the words after her while he looked down at the scattered and enigmatic papers and documents and thinking fled smooth and idle, wondering what this paper meant and what that paper meant. "To school," his mouth said.

"Yes," she said. "They will take you. Any of them will. On my account. You can choose any one you want among them. We wont even have to pay."

"To school," his mouth said. "A nigger school. Me."

"Yes. Then you can go to Memphis. You can read law in Peebles's office. He will teach you law. Then you can take charge of all the legal business. All this, all that he does, Peebles does."

"And then learn law in the office of a nigger lawyer," his mouth said.

"Yes. Then I will turn over all the business to you, all the money. All of it. So that when you need money for yourself you could . . . you would know how; lawyers know how to do it so that it . . . You would be helping them up out of darkness and none could accuse or blame you even if they found out . . . even if you did not replace . . . but you could replace the money and none would ever know. . . ."

"But a nigger college, a nigger lawyer," his voice said, quiet, not even argumentative; just promptive. They were not looking at one another; she had not looked up since he entered.

"Tell them," she said.

"Tell niggers that I am a nigger too?" She now looked at him. Her face was quite calm. It was the face of an old woman now.

"Yes. You'll have to do that. So they wont charge you anything. On my account."

Then it was as if he said suddenly to his mouth: 'Shut up. Shut up that drivel. Let me talk.' He leaned down. She did not move. Their faces were not a foot apart: the one cold, dead white, fanatical, mad; the other parchment-colored, the lip lifted into the shape of a soundless and rigid snarl. He said quietly: "You're old. I never noticed that before. An old woman. You've got gray in your hair." She struck him, at once, with her flat hand, the rest of her body not moving at all. Her blow made a flat sound; his blow as close upon it as echo. He struck with his fist, then in that long blowing wind he jerked her up from the chair and held her, facing him, motionless, not a flicker upon her still face, while the long wind of knowing rushed down upon him. "You haven't got any baby," he said. "You never had one. There is not anything the matter with you except being old. You just got old and it happened to you and now you are not any good anymore. That's all that's wrong with you." He released her and struck her again. She fell huddled onto the bed, looking up at him, and he struck her in the face again and standing over her he spoke to her the words which she had once loved to hear on his tongue, which she used to say that she could taste there, murmurous, obscene, caressing. "That's all. You're just worn out. You're not any good anymore. That's all."

She lay on the bed, on her side, her head turned and looking up at him across her bleeding mouth. "Maybe it would be better if we both were dead," she said.

He could see the note lying on the blanket as soon as he opened the door. Then he would go and take it up and open it. He would now remember the hollow fencepost as something of which he had heard told, as having taken place in another life from any that he had ever lived. Because the paper, the ink, the form and shape, were the same. They had never been long; they were not long now. But now there was nothing evocative of unspoken promise, of rich and unmentionable delights, in them. They were now briefer than epitaphs and more terse than commands.

His first impulse would be to not go. He believed that he dared not go. Then he knew that he dared not fail to go. He would not change his clothes now. In his sweat-stained overalls he would traverse the late twilight of May and enter the kitchen. The table was never set with food for him now. Sometimes he would look at it as he passed and he would think, 'My God. When have I sat down in peace to eat.' And he could not remember.

He would go on into the house and mount the stairs. Already he would be hearing her voice. It would increase as he mounted and until he reached the door to the bedroom. The door would be shut, locked; from beyond it the monotonous steady voice came. He could not distinguish the words; only the ceaseless monotone. He dared not try to distinguish the words. He did not dare let himself know what she was at. So he would stand there and wait, and after a while the voice would cease and she would open the door and he would enter. As he passed the bed he would look down at the floor beside it and it would seem to him that he could distinguish the prints of knees and he would jerk his eyes away as if it were death that they had looked at.

Likely the lamp would not yet be lighted. They did not sit down. Again they stood to talk, as they used to do two years ago; standing in the dusk while her voice repeated its tale: ". . . not to school, then, if you dont want to go . . . Do without that . . . Your soul. Expiation of . . ." And he waiting, cold, still, until she had finished: ". . . hell . . . forever and ever and ever . . ."

"No," he said. And she would listen as quietly, and he knew that she was not convinced and she knew that he was not. Yet neither surrendered; worse: they would not let one another alone; he would not even go away. And they would stand for a while longer in the quiet dusk peopled, as though from their loins, by a myriad ghosts of dead sins and delights, looking at one another's still and fading face, weary, spent, and indomitable.

Then he would leave. And before the door had shut and the bolt had shot to behind him, he would hear the voice again, monotonous, calm, and despairing, saying what and to what or whom he dared not learn nor suspect. And as he sat in the shadows of the ruined garden on that August night three months later and heard the clock in the court-house two miles away strike ten and then eleven, he believed with calm paradox that he was the volitionless serv-ant of the fatality in which he believed that he did not be-lieve. He was saying to himself *I had to do it* already in the past tense; *I had to do it. She said so herself*

She had said it two nights ago. He found the note and went to her. As he mounted the stairs the monotonous voice grew louder, sounded louder and clearer than usual. When he reached the top of the stairs he saw why. The door was open this time, and she did not rise from where she knelt beside the bed when he entered. She did not stir; her voice did not cease. Her head was not bowed. Her face was lifted, almost with pride, her attitude of formal abjectness a part of the pride, her voice calm and tranquil and abnegant in the twilight. She did not seem to be aware that he had entered until she finished a period. Then she turned her head. "Kneel with me," she said.

"No," he said.

"Kneel," she said. "You wont even need to speak to Him yourself. Just kneel. Just make the first move."

"No," he said. "I'm going."

She didn't move, looking back and up at him. "Joe," she said, "will you stay? Will you do that much?"

"Yes," he said. "I'll stay. But make it fast."

She prayed again. She spoke quietly, with that abjectness of pride. When it was necessary to use the symbolwords which he had taught her, she used them, spoke them forthright and without hesitation, talking to God as if He were a man in the room with two other men. She spoke of herself and of him as of two other people, her voice still, monotonous, sexless. Then she ceased. She rose quietly. They stood in the twilight, facing one another. This time she did not even ask the question; he did not even need to reply. After a time she said quietly:

"Then there's just one other thing to do."

"There's just one other thing to do," he said.

'So now it's all done, all finished,' he thought quietly, sitting in the dense shadow of the shrubbery, hearing the last stroke of the far clock cease and die away. It was a spot where he had overtaken her, found her on one of the wild nights two years ago. But that was in another time, another life. Now it was still, quiet, the fecund earth now coolly suspirant. The dark was filled with the voices, myriad, out of all time that he had known, as though all the past was a flat pattern. And going on: tomorrow night, all the tomorrows, to be a part of the flat pattern, going on. He thought of that with quiet astonishment: going on, myriad, familiar, since all that had ever been was the same as all that was to be, since tomorrow to-be and had-been would be the same. Then it was time.

He rose. He moved from the shadow and went around the house and entered the kitchen. The house was dark. He had not been to the cabin since early morning and he did not know if she had left a note for him or not, expected him or not. Yet he did not try for silence. It was as if he were not thinking of sleep, of whether she would be asleep or not. He mounted the stairs steadily and entered the bedroom. Almost at once she spoke from the bed. "Light the lamp," she said.

"It wont need any light," he said.

"Light the lamp."

"No," he said. He stood over the bed. He held the razor in his hand. But it was not open yet. But she did not speak again and then his body seemed to walk away from him. It went to the table and his hands laid the razor on the table and found the lamp and struck the match. She was sitting up in the bed, her back against the headboard. Over her nightdress she wore a shawl drawn down across her breast. Her arms were folded upon the shawl, her hands hidden from sight. He stood at the table. They looked at one another.

"Will you kneel with me?" she said. "I dont ask it."

"No," he said.

"I dont ask it. It's not I who ask it. Kneel with me."

"No."

They looked at one another. "Joe," she said, "for the last time. I dont ask it. Remember that. Kneel with me."

"No," he said. Then he saw her arms unfold and her right hand come forth from beneath the shawl. It held an old style, single action, cap-and-ball revolver almost as long and heavier than a small rifle. But the shadow of it and of her arm and hand on the wall did not waver at all, the shadow of both monstrous, the cocked hammer monstrous, backhooked and viciously poised like the arched head of a snake; it did not waver at all. And her eyes did not waver at all. They were as still as the round black ring of the pistol muzzle. But there was no heat in them, no fury. They were calm and still as all pity and all despair and all conviction. But he was not watching them. He was watching the shadowed pistol on the wall; he was watching when the cocked shadow of the hammer flicked away.

Standing in the middle of the road, with his right hand lifted full in the glare of the approaching car, he had not actually expected it to stop. Yet it did, with a squealing and sprawling suddenness that was almost ludicrous. It was a small car, battered and old. When he approached it, in the reflected glare of the headlights two young faces seemed to float like two softcolored and aghast balloons, the nearer one, the girl's, backshrunk in a soft, wide horror. But Christmas did not notice this at the time. "How about riding with you, as far as you go?" he said. They said nothing at all, looking at him with that still and curious horror which he did not notice So he opened the door to enter the rear seat.

When he did so, the girl began to make a choked wailing sound which would be much louder in a moment, as fear gained courage as it were. Already the car was in motion; it seemed to leap forward, and the boy, without moving his hands from the wheel or turning his head toward the girl hissed: "Shut up! Hush! It's our only chance! Will you hush now?" Christmas did not hear this either. He was sitting back now, completely unaware that he was riding directly behind desperate terror. He only thought with momentary interest that the small car was travelling at a pretty reckless speed for a narrow country road.

"How far does this road go?" he said.

The boy told him, naming the same town which the negro boy had named to him on that afternoon three years ago, when he had first seen Jefferson. The boy's voice had a dry, light quality. "Do you want to go there, cap'm?"

"All right," Christmas said. "Yes. Yes. That will do. That will suit me. Are you going there?"

"Sure," the boy said, in that light, flat tone. "Wherever you say." Again the girl beside him began that choked, murmurous, small-animallike moaning; again the boy hissed at her, his face still rigidly front, the little car rushing and bouncing onward: "Hush! Shhhhhhhhhh. Hush! Hush!" But again Christmas did not notice. He saw only the two young, rigidly forwardlooking heads against the light glare, into which the ribbon of the road rushed swaying and fleeing. But he remarked both them and the fleeing road without curiosity; he was not even paying attention when he found that the boy had apparently been speaking to him for some time; how far they had come or where they were he did not know. The boy's diction was slow now, recapitulant, each word as though chosen simply and carefully and spoken slowly and clearly for the ear of a foreigner: "Listen, cap'm. When I turn off up here. It's just a short cut. A short cutoff to a better road. I am going to take the cutoff. When I come to the short cut. To the better road. So we can get there quicker. See?"

"All right," Christmas said. The car bounced and rushed on, swaying on the curves and up the hills and fleeing down again as if the earth had dropped from under them. Mail boxes on posts beside the road rushed into the lights and flicked past. Now and then they passed a dark house. Again the boy was speaking:

"Now, this here cutoff I was telling you about. It's right down here. I'm going to turn into it. But it dont mean I am leaving the road. I am just going a little way across to a better road. See?"

"All right," Christmas said. Then for no reason he said: "You must live around here somewhere."

Now it was the girl who spoke. She turned in the seat, whirling, her small face wan with suspense and terror and blind and ratlike desperation: "We do!" she cried. "We both do! Right up yonder! And when my pappy and brothers—" Her voice ceased, cut short off; Christmas saw the boy's hand clapped upon her lower face and her hands tugging at the wrist while beneath the hand itself her smothered voice choked and bubbled. Christmas sat forward.

"Here," he said. "I'll get out here. You can let me out here."

"Now you've done it!" the boy cried, too, thinly, with desperate rage too. "If you'd just kept quiet—"

"Stop the car," Christmas said. "I aint going to hurt either of you. I just want to get out." Again the car stopped with sprawling suddenness. But the engine still raced, and the car leaped forward again before he was clear of the step; he had to leap forward running for a few steps to recover his balance. As he did so, something heavy and hard struck him on the flank. The car rushed on, fading at top speed. From it floated back the girl's shrill wailing. Then it was gone; the darkness, the now impalpable dust, came down again, and the silence beneath the summer stars. The object which had struck him had delivered an appreciable blow; then he discovered that the object was attached to his right hand. Raising the hand, he found that it held the ancient heavy pistol. He did not know that he had it; he did not remember having picked it up at all, nor why. But there it was. 'And I flagged that car with my right hand,' he thought. 'No wonder she . . . they . . .' He drew his right hand back to throw, the pistol balanced upon it. Then he paused, and he struck a match and examined the pistol in the puny dying glare. The match burned down and went out, yet he still seemed to see the ancient thing with its two loaded chambers: the one upon which the hammer had already fallen and which had not exploded, and the other upon which no hammer had yet fallen but upon which a hammer had been planned to fall. 'For her and for me,' he said. His arm came back, and threw. He heard the pistol crash once through undergrowth. Then there was no sound again. 'For her and for me.'

. 13 .

WITHIN five minutes after the countrymen found the fire, the people began to gather. Some of them, also on the way to town in wagons to spend Saturday, also stopped. Some came afoot from the immediate neighborhood. This was a region of negro cabins and gutted and outworn fields out of which a corporal's guard of detectives could not have combed ten people, man, woman or child, yet which now within thirty minutes produced, as though out of thin air, parties and groups ranging from single individuals to entire families. Still others came out from town in racing and blatting cars. Among these came the sheriff of the county—a fat, comfortable man with a hard, canny head and a benevolent aspect—who thrust away those who crowded to look down at the body on the sheet with that static and childlike amaze with which adults contemplate their own inescapable portraits. Among them the casual Yankees and the poor whites and even the southerners who had lived for a while in the north, who believed aloud that it was an anonymous negro crime committed not by a negro but by Negro and who knew, believed, and hoped that she had been ravished too: at least once before her throat was cut and at least once afterward. The sheriff came up and looked himself once and then sent the body away, hiding the poor thing from the eyes.

Then there was nothing for them to look at except the place where the body had lain and the fire. And soon nobody could remember exactly where the sheet had rested, what earth it had covered, and so then there was only the fire to look at. So they looked at the fire, with that same dull and static amaze which they had brought down from the old fetid caves where knowing began, as though, like death, they had never seen fire before. Presently the fire truck came up gallantly, with noise, with whistles and bells. It was new, painted red, with gilt trim and a handpower siren and a bell gold in color and in tone serene, arrogant, and proud. About it hatless men and youths clung with the astonishing disregard of physical laws that flies possess. It had mechanical ladders that sprang to prodigious heights at the touch of a hand, like opera hats; only there was now nothing for them to spring to. It had neat and virgin coils of hose evocative of telephone trust advertisements in the popular magazines; but there was nothing to hook them to and nothing to flow through them. So the hatless men, who had deserted counters and desks, swung down, even including the one who ground the siren. They came too and were shown several different places where the sheet had lain, and some of them with pistols already in their pockets began to canvass about for someone to crucify.

But there wasn't anybody. She had lived such a quiet life, attended so to her own affairs, that she bequeathed to the town in which she had been born and lived and died a foreigner, an outlander, a kind of heritage of astonishment and outrage, for which, even though she had supplied them at last with an emotional barbecue, a Roman holiday almost, they would never forgive her and let her be dead in peace and quiet. Not that. Peace is not that often. So they moiled and clotted, believing that the flames, the blood, the body that had died three years ago and had just now begun to live again, cried out for vengeance, not believing that the rapt infury of the flames and the immobility of the body were both affirmations of an attained bourne beyond the hurt and harm of man. Not that. Because the other made nice believing. Better than the shelves and the counters filled with longfamiliar objects bought, not because the owner desired them or admired them, could take any pleasure in the owning of them, but in order to cajole or trick other men into buying them at a profit; and who must now and then contemplate both the objects which had not yet sold and the men who could buy them but had not yet done so, with anger and maybe outrage and maybe despair too. Better than the musty offices where the lawyers waited lurking among ghosts of old lusts and lies, or where the doctors waited with sharp knives and sharp drugs, telling man, believing that he should believe, without resorting to printed admonishments, that they labored for that end whose ultimate attainment would leave them with nothing whatever to do. And the women came too, the idle ones in bright and sometimes hurried garments, with secret and passionate and glittering looks and with secret frustrated breasts (who have ever loved death better than peace) to print with a myriad small hard heels to the constant murmur *Who did it? Who did it?* periods such as perhaps *Is he still free? Ah. Is he? Is he?*

The sheriff also stared at the flames with exasperation

and astonishment, since there was no scene to investigate. He was not yet thinking of himself as having been frustrated by a human agent. It was the fire. It seemed to him that the fire had been selfborn for that end and purpose. It seemed to him that that by and because of which he had had ancestors long enough to come himself to be, had allied itself with crime. So he continued to walk in a baffled and fretted manner about that heedless monument of the color of both hope and catastrophe until a deputy came up and told how he had discovered in a cabin beyond the house, traces of recent occupation. And immediately the countryman who had discovered the fire (he had not yet got to town; his wagon had not progressed one inch since he descended from it two hours ago, and he now moved among the people, wildhaired, gesticulant, with on his face a dulled, spent, glaring expression and his voice hoarsed almost to a whisper) remembered that he had seen a man in the house when he broke in the door.

"A white man?" the sheriff said.

"Yes, sir. Blumping around in the hall like he had just finished falling down the stairs. Tried to keep me from going upstairs at all. Told me how he had already been up there and it wasn't nobody up there. And when I come back down, he was gone."

The sheriff looked about at them. "Who lived in that cabin?"

"I didn't know anybody did," the deputy said. "Niggers, I reckon. She might have had niggers living in the house with her, from what I have heard. What I am surprised at is that it was this long before one of them done for her."

"Get me a nigger," the sheriff said. The deputy and two

or three others got him a nigger. "Who's been living in that cabin?" the sheriff said.

"I dont know, Mr Watt," the negro said. "I aint never paid it no mind. I aint even knowed anybody lived in it."

"Bring him on down here," the sheriff said.

They were gathering now about the sheriff and the deputy and the negro, with avid eyes upon which the sheer prolongation of empty flames had begun to pall, with faces identical one with another. It was as if all their individual five senses had become one organ of looking, like an apotheosis, the words that flew among them wind- or air-engendered *Is that him? Is that the one that did it? Sheriff's got him. Sheriff has already caught him* The sheriff looked at them. "Go away," he said. "All of you. Go look at the fire. If I need any help, I can send for you. Go on away." He turned and led his party down to the cabin. Behind him the repulsed ones stood in a clump and watched the three white men and the negro enter the cabin and close the door. Behind them in turn the dying fire roared, filling the air though not louder than the voices and much more unsourceless *By God, if that's him, what are we doing, standing around here? Murdering a white woman the black son of a* None of them had ever entered the house. While she was alive they would not have allowed their wives to call on her. When they were younger, children (some of their fathers had done it too) they had called after her on the street, "Nigger lover! Nigger lover!"

In the cabin the sheriff sat down on one of the cots, heavily. He sighed: a tub of a man, with the complete and rocklike inertia of a tub. "Now, I want to know who lives in this cabin," he said.

"I done told you I dont know," the negro said. His voice

was a little sullen, quite alert, covertly alert. He watched the sheriff. The other two white men were behind him, where he could not see them. He did not look back at them, not so much as a glance. He was watching the sheriff's face as a man watches a mirror. Perhaps he saw it, as in a mirror, before it came. Perhaps he did not, since if change, flicker, there was in the sheriff's face it was no more than a flicker. But the negro did not look back; there came only into his face when the strap fell across his back a wince, sudden, sharp, fleet, jerking up the corners of his mouth and exposing his momentary teeth like smiling. Then his face smoothed again, inscrutable.

"I reckon you aint tried hard enough to remember," the sheriff said.

"I cant remember because I cant know," the negro said. "I dont even live nowhere near here. You ought to know where I stay at, white folks."

"Mr Buford says you live right down the road yonder," the sheriff said.

"Lots of folks live down that road. Mr Buford ought to know where I stay at."

"He's lying," the deputy said. His name was Buford. He was the one who wielded the strap, buckle end outward. He held it poised. He was watching the sheriff's face. He looked like a spaniel waiting to be told to spring into the water.

"Maybe so; maybe not," the sheriff said. He mused upon the negro. He was still, huge, inert, sagging the cot springs. "I think he just dont realise yet that I aint playing. Let alone them folks out there that aint got no jail to put him into if anything he wouldn't like should come up. That wouldn't bother to put him into a jail if they had one."

Perhaps there was a sign, a signal, in his eyes again; perhaps not. Perhaps the negro saw it; perhaps not. The strap fell again, the buckle raking across the negro's back. "You remember yet?" the sheriff said.

"It's two white men," the negro said. His voice was cold, not sullen, not anything. "I dont know who they is nor what they does. It aint none of my business. I aint never seed them. I just heard talk about how two white men lived here. I didn't care who they was. And that's all I know. You can whup the blood outen me. But that's all I know."

Again the sheriff sighed. "That'll do. I reckon that's right."

"It's that fellow Christmas, that used to work at the mill, and another fellow named Brown," the third man said. "You could have picked out any man in Jefferson that his breath smelled right and he could have told you that much."

"I reckon that's right, too," the sheriff said.

He returned to town. When the crowd realised that the sheriff was departing, a general exodus began. It was as if there were nothing left to look at now. The body had gone, and now the sheriff was going. It was as though he carried within him, somewhere within that inert and sighing mass of flesh, the secret itself: that which moved and evoked them as with a promise of something beyond the sluttishness of stuffed entrails and monotonous days. So there was nothing left to look at now but the fire; they had now been watching it for three hours. They were now used to it, accustomed to it; now it had become a permanent part of their lives as well as of their experiences, standing beneath its windless column of smoke taller than and impregnable as a monument which could be returned to at any time.

So when the caravan reached town it had something of that arrogant decorum of a procession behind a catafalque, the sheriff's car in the lead, the other cars honking and blatting behind in the sheriff's and their own compounded dust. It was held up momentarily at a street intersection near the square by a country wagon which had stopped to let a passenger descend. Looking out, the sheriff saw a young woman climbing slowly and carefully down from the wagon, with that careful awkwardness of advanced pregnancy. Then the wagon pulled aside; the caravan went on, crossing the square, where already the cashier of the bank had taken from the vault the envelope which the dead woman had deposited with him and which bore the inscription *To be opened at my death. Joanna Burden* The cashier was waiting at the sheriff's office when the sheriff came in, with the envelope and its contents. This was a single sheet of paper on which was written, by the same hand which inscribed the envelope *Notify E. E. Peebles, Attorney, —— Beale St., Memphis, Tenn., and Nathaniel Burrington, —— St. Exeter, N. H.* That was all.

"This Peebles is a nigger lawyer," the cashier said.

"Is that so?" the sheriff said.

"Yes. What do you want me to do?"

"I reckon you better do what the paper says," the sheriff said. "I reckon maybe I better do it myself." He sent two wires. He received the Memphis reply in thirty minutes. The other came two hours later; within ten minutes afterward the word had gone through the town that Miss Burden's nephew in New Hampshire offered a thousand dollars' reward for the capture of her murderer. At nine o'clock that evening the man whom the countryman had found in the burning house when he broke in the front door, appeared. They did not know then that he was the man. He did not tell them so. All they knew was that a man who had resided for a short time in the town and whom they knew as a bootlegger named Brown, and not much of a bootlegger at that, appeared on the square in a state of excitement, seeking the sheriff. Then it began to piece together. The sheriff knew that Brown was associated somehow with another man, another stranger named Christmas about whom, despite the fact that he had lived in Jefferson for three years, even less was known than about Brown; it was only now that the sheriff learned that Christmas had been living in the cabin behind Miss Burden's house for three years. Brown wanted to talk; he insisted on talking, loud, urgent; it appeared at once that what he was doing was claiming the thousand dollars' reward.

"You want to turn state's evidence?" the sheriff asked him.

"I dont want to turn nothing," Brown said, harsh, hoarse, a little wild in the face. "I know who done it and when I get my reward, I'll tell."

"You catch the fellow that done it, and you'll get the reward," the sheriff said. So they took Brown to the jail for safekeeping. "Only I reckon it aint no actual need of that," the sheriff said. "I reckon as long as that thousand dollars is where he can smell it, you couldn't run him away from here." When Brown was taken away, still hoarse, still gesticulant and outraged, the sheriff telephoned to a neighboring town, where there was a pair of bloodhounds. The dogs would arrive on the early morning train.

About the bleak platform, in the sad dawn of that Sunday morning, thirty or forty men were waiting when the train came in, the lighted windows fleeing and jarring to a momentary stop. It was a fast train and it did not always stop at Jefferson. It halted only long enough to disgorge the two dogs: a thousand costly tons of intricate and curious metal glaring and crashing up and into an almost shocking silence filled with the puny sounds of men, to vomit two gaunt and cringing phantoms whose droopeared and mild faces gazed with sad abjectness about at the weary, pale faces of men who had not slept very much since night before last, ringing them about with something terrible and eager and impotent. It was as if the very initial outrage of the murder carried in its wake and made of all subsequent actions something monstrous and paradoxical and wrong, in themselves against both reason and nature.

It was just sunrise when the posse reached the cabin behind the charred and now cold embers of the house. The dogs, either gaining courage from the light and warmth of the sun or catching the strained and tense excitement from the men, began to surge and yap about the cabin. Snuffing loudly and as one beast they took a course, dragging the man who held the leashes. They ran side by side for a hundred yards, where they stopped and began to dig furiously into the earth and exposed a pit where someone had buried recently emptied food tins. They dragged the dogs away by main strength. They dragged them some distance from the cabin and made another cast. For a short time the dogs moiled, whimpering, then they set off again, fulltongued, drooling, and dragged and carried the running and cursing men at top speed back to the cabin, where, feet planted and with backflung heads and backrolled eyeballs, they bayed the empty doorway with the passionate abandon of two baritones singing Italian opera. The men took the dogs back to town, in cars, and fed them. When they crossed the square the church bells were ringing, slow and peaceful, and along the streets the decorous people moved sedately beneath parasols, carrying Bibles and prayerbooks.

That night a youth, a countryboy, and his father came in to see the sheriff. The boy told of having been on the way home in a car late Friday night, and of a man who stopped him a mile or two beyond the scene of the murder, with a pistol. The boy believed that he was about to be robbed and even killed, and he told how he was about to trick the man into permitting him to drive right up into his own front yard, where he intended to stop the car and spring out and shout for help, but that the man suspected something and forced him to stop the car and let him out. The father wanted to know how much of the thousand dollars would become theirs.

"You catch him and we'll see," the sheriff said. So they waked the dogs and put them into another car and the youth showed them where the man had got out, and they cast the dogs, who charged immediately into the woods and with their apparent infallibility for metal in any form, found the old pistol with its two loaded chambers almost at once.

"It's one of them old Civil War, cap-and-ball pistols," the deputy said. "One of the caps has been snapped, but it never went off. What do you reckon he was doing with that?"

"Turn them dogs loose," the sheriff said. "Maybe them leashes worry them." They did so. The dogs were free now; thirty minutes later they were lost. Not the men lost the dogs; the dogs lost the men. They were just across a small creek and a ridge, and the men could hear them plainly.

They were not baying now, with pride and assurance and perhaps pleasure. The sound which they now made was a longdrawn and hopeless wailing, while steadily the men shouted at them. But apparently the animals could not hear either. Both voices were distinguishable, yet the bell-like and abject wailing seemed to come from a single throat, as though the two beasts crouched flank to flank. After a while the men found them so, crouched in a ditch. By that time their voices sounded almost like the voices of children. The men squatted there until it was light enough to find their way back to the cars. Then it was Monday morning.

The temperature began to rise Monday. On Tuesday, the night, the darkness after the hot day, is close, still, oppressive; as soon as Byron enters the house he feels the corners of his nostrils whiten and tauten with the thick smell of the stale, mankept house. And when Hightower approaches, the smell of plump unwashed flesh and unfresh clothing—that odor of unfastidious sedentation, of static overflesh not often enough bathed—is well nigh overpowering. Entering, Byron thinks as he has thought before: 'That is his right. It may not be my way, but it is his way and his right.' And he remembers how once he had seemed to find the answer, as though by inspiration, divination: 'It is the odor of goodness. Of course it would smell bad to us that are bad and sinful.'

They sit again opposite one another in the study, the desk, the lighted lamp, between. Byron sits again on the hard chair, his face lowered, still. His voice is sober, stubborn: the voice of a man saying something which will be not only unpleasing, but will not be believed. "I am going to find another place for her. A place where it will be more private. Where she can . . ."

Hightower watches his lowered face. "Why must she move? When she is comfortable there, with a woman at hand if she should need one?" Byron does not answer. He sits motionless, downlooking; his face is stubborn, still; looking at it, Hightower thinks, 'It is because so much happens. Too much happens. That's it. Man performs, engenders, so much more than he can or should have to bear. That's how he finds that he can bear anything. That's it. That's what is so terrible. That he can bear anything, anything.' He watches Byron. "Is Mrs Beard the only reason why she is going to move?"

Still Byron does not look up, speaking in that still, stubborn voice: "She needs a place where it will be kind of home to her. She aint got a whole lot more time, and in a boarding house, where it's mostly just men . . . A room where it will be quiet when her time comes, and not every durn horsetrader or courtjury that passes through the hallway . . ."

"I see," Hightower says. He watches Byron's face. "And you want me to take her in here." Byron makes to speak, but the other goes on: his tone too is cold, level: "It wont do, Byron. If there were another woman here, living in the house. It's a shame too, with all the room here, the quiet. I'm thinking of her, you see. Not myself. I would not care what was said, thought."

"I am not asking that." Byron does not look up. He can feel the other watching him. He thinks *He knows that is not what I meant, too. He knows. He just said that. I know what he is thinking. I reckon I expected it. I reckon it is not any reason for him to think different from other*

folks, even about me "I reckon you ought to know that."
Perhaps he does know it. But Byron does not look up to see.
He talks on, in that dull, flat voice, downlooking, while beyond the desk Hightower, sitting a little more than erect,
looks at the thin, weatherhardened, laborpurged face of the
man opposite him. "I aint going to get you mixed up in it
when it aint none of your trouble. You haven't even seen
her, and I dont reckon you ever will. I reckon likely you
have never seen him to know it either. It's just that I
thought maybe . . ." His voice ceases. Across the desk the
unbending minister looks at him, waiting, not offering to
help him. "When it's a matter of not-do, I reckon a man
can trust himself for advice. But when it comes to a matter
of doing, I reckon a fellow had better listen to all the advice
he can get. But I aint going to mix you up in it. I dont want
you to worry about that."

"I think I know that," Hightower says. He watches the
other's downlooking face. 'I am not in life anymore,' he
thinks. 'That's why there is no use in even trying to meddle, interfere. He could hear me no more than that man
and that woman (ay, and that child) would hear or heed
me if I tried to come back into life.' "But you told me she
knows that he is here."

"Yes," Byron says, brooding. "Out there where I thought
the chance to harm ere a man or woman or child could not
have found me. And she hadn't hardly got there before I
had to go and blab the whole thing."

"I dont mean that. You didn't know yourself, then. I
mean, the rest of it. About him and the—that . . . It has
been three days. She must know, whether you told her or
not. She must have heard by now."

"Christmas." Byron does not look up. "I never said any

more, after she asked about that little white scar by his mouth. All the time we were coming to town that evening I was afraid she would ask. I would try to think up things to talk to her about so she would not have a chance to ask me any more. And all the time I thought I was keeping her from finding out that he had not only run off and left her in trouble, he had changed his name to keep her from finding him, and that now when she found him at last, what she had found was a bootlegger, she already knew it. Already knew that he was a nogood." He says now, with a kind of musing astonishment: "I never even had any need to keep it from her, to lie it smooth. It was like she knew beforehand what I would say, that I was going to lie to her. Like she had already thought of that herself, and that she already didn't believe it before I even said it, and that was all right too. But the part of her that knew the truth, that I could not have fooled anyway . . ." He fumbles, gropes, the unbending man beyond the desk watching him, not offering to help. "It's like she was in two parts, and one of them knows that he is a scoundrel. But the other part believes that when a man and a woman are going to have a child, that the Lord will see that they are all together when the right time comes. Like it was God that looks after women, to protect them from men. And if the Lord dont see fit to let them two parts meet and kind of compare, then I aint going to do it either."

"Nonsense," Hightower says. He looks across the desk at the other's still, stubborn, ascetic face: the face of a hermit who has lived for a long time in an empty place where sand blows. "The thing, the only thing, for her to do is to go back to Alabama. To her people."

"I reckon not," Byron says. He says it immediately, with

immediate finality, as if he has been waiting all the while for this to be said. "She wont need to do that. I reckon she wont need to do that." But he does not look up. He can feel the other looking at him.

"Does Bu—Brown know that she is in Jefferson?"

For an instant Byron almost smiles. His lip lifts: a thin movement almost a shadow, without mirth. "He's been too busy. After that thousand dollars. It's right funny to watch him. Like a man that cant play a tune, blowing a horn right loud, hoping that in a minute it will begin to make music. Being drug across the square on a handcuff every twelve or fifteen hours, when likely they couldn't run him away if they was to sick them bloodhounds on him. He spent Saturday night in jail, still talking about how they were trying to beat him out of his thousand dollars by trying to make out that he helped Christmas do the killing, until at last Buck Conner went up to his cell and told him he would put a gag in his mouth if he didn't shut up and let the other prisoners sleep. And he shut up, and Sunday night they went out with the dogs and he raised so much racket that they had to take him out of jail and let him go too. But the dogs never got started. And him hollering and cussing the dogs and wanting to beat them because they never struck a trail, telling everybody again how it was him that reported Christmas first and that all he wanted was fair justice, until the sheriff took him aside and talked to him. They didn't know what the sheriff said to him. Maybe he threatened to lock him back up in jail and not let him go with them next time. Anyway, he calmed down some, and they went on. They never got back to town until late Monday night. He was still quiet. Maybe he was wore out. He hadn't slept none in some time, and they said how he was trying to outrun the dogs so that the sheriff finally threatened to handcuff him to a deputy to keep him back so the dogs could smell something beside him. He needed a shave already when they locked him up Saturday night, and he needed one bad by now. I reckon he must have looked more like a murderer than even Christmas. And he was cussing Christmas now, like Christmas had done hid out just for meanness, to spite him and keep him from getting that thousand dollars. And they brought him back to jail and locked him up that night. And this morning they went and took him out again and they all went off with the dogs, on a new scent. Folks said they could hear him hollering and talking until they were clean out of town."

"And she doesn't know that, you say. You say you have kept that from her. You had rather that she knew him to be a scoundrel than a fool: is that it?"

Byron's face is still again, not smiling now; it is quite sober. "I dont know. It was last Sunday night, after I came out to talk to you and went back home. I thought she would be asleep in bed, but she was still sitting up in the parlor, and she said, 'What is it? What has happened here?' And I didn't look at her and I could feel her looking at me. I told her it was a nigger killed a white woman. I didn't lie then. I reckon I was so glad I never had to lie then. Because before I thought, I had done said 'and set the house afire.' And then it was too late. I had pointed out the smoke, and I had told her about the two fellows named Brown and Christmas that lived out there. And I could feel her watching me the same as I can you now, and she said, 'What was the nigger's name?' It's like God sees that they find out what they need to know out of men's lying, without needing to ask. And that they dont find out what they dont need to know, without even knowing they have not found it out. And so I dont know for sure what she knows and what she dont know. Except that I have kept it from her that it was the man she is hunting for that told on the murderer and that he is in jail now except when he is out running with dogs the man that took him up and befriended him. I have kept that from her."

"And what are you going to do now? Where does she want to move?"

"She wants to go out there and wait for him. I told her that he is away on business for the sheriff. So I didn't lie altogether. She had already asked me where he lived and I had already told her. And she said that was the place where she belonged until he came back, because that is his house. She said that's what he would want her to do. And I couldn't tell her different, that that cabin is the last place in the world he would want her to ever see. She wanted to go out there as soon as I got home from the mill this evening. She had her bundle all tied up and her bonnet on, waiting for me to get home. 'I started once to go on by myself,' she said. 'But I wasn't sho I knowed the way.' And I said 'Yes; only it was too late today and we would go out there tomorrow, and she said, 'It's a hour till dark yet. It aint but two miles, is it?' and I said to let's wait because I would have to ask first, and she said, 'Ask who? Aint it Lucas's house?' and I could feel her watching me and she said, 'I thought you said that that was where Lucas lived,' and she was watching me and she said, 'Who is this preacher you keep on going to talk to about me?'"

"And you are going to let her go out there to live?"

"It might be best. She would be private out there, and

she would be away from all the talking until this business is over."

"You mean, she has got her mind set on it, and you wont stop her. You dont want to stop her."

Byron does not look up. "In a way, it is his house. The nighest thing to a home of his own he will ever own, I reckon. And he is her . . ."

"Out there alone, with a child coming. The nearest house a few negro cabins a half mile away." He watches Byron's face.

"I have thought of that. There are ways, things that can be done . . ."

"What things? What can you do to protect her out there?"

Byron does not answer at once; he does not look up. When he speaks his voice is dogged. "There are secret things a man can do without being evil, Reverend. No matter how they might look to folks."

"I dont think that you could do anything that would be very evil, Byron, no matter how it looked to folks. But are you going to undertake to say just how far evil extends into the appearance of evil? just where between doing and appearing evil stops?"

"No," Byron says. Then he moves slightly; he speaks as if he too were waking: "I hope not. I reckon I am trying to do the right thing by my lights."—'And that,' Hightower thinks, 'is the first lie he ever told me. Ever told anyone, man or woman, perhaps including himself.' He looks across the desk at the stubborn, dogged, sober face that has not yet looked at him. 'Or maybe it is not lie yet because he does not know himself that it is so.' He says:

"Well." He speaks now with a kind of spurious brusqueness which, flabbyjowled and darkcaverneyed, his face belies. "That is settled, then. You'll take her out there, to his house, and you'll see that she is comfortable and you'll see that she is not disturbed until this is over. And then you'll tell that man—Bunch, Brown—that she is here."

"And he'll run," Byron says. He does not look up, yet through him there seems to go a wave of exultation, of triumph, before he can curb and hide it, when it is too late to try. For the moment he does not attempt to curb it; backthrust too in his hard chair, looking for the first time at the minister, with a face confident and bold and suffused. The other meets his gaze steadily.

"Is that what you want him to do?" Hightower says. They sit so in the lamplight. Through the open window comes the hot, myriad silence of the breathless night. "Think what you are doing. You are attempting to come between man and wife."

Byron has caught himself. His face is no longer triumphant. But he looks steadily at the older man. Perhaps he tried to catch his voice too. But he cannot yet. "They aint man and wife yet," he says.

"Does she think that? Do you believe that she will say that?" They look at one another. "Ah, Byron, Byron. What are a few mumbled words before God, before the steadfastness of a woman's nature? Before that child?"

"Well, he may not run. If he gets that reward, that money. Like enough he will be drunk enough on a thousand dollars to do anything, even marry."

"Ah, Byron, Byron."

"Then what do you think we—I ought to do? What do you advise?"

"Go away. Leave Jefferson." They look at one another.

"No," Hightower says. "You dont need my help. You are already being helped by someone stronger than I am."

For a moment Byron does not speak. They look at one another, steadily. "Helped by who?"

"By the devil," Hightower says.

'And the devil is looking after *him,* too,' Hightower thinks. He is in midstride, halfway home, his laden small market basket on his arm. 'Him, too. Him, too,' he thinks, walking. It is hot. He is in his shirt sleeves, tall, with thin blackclad legs and spare, gaunt arms and shoulders, and with that flabby and obese stomach like some monstrous pregnancy. The shirt is white, but it is not fresh; his collar is soiled, as is the white lawn cravat carelessly knotted, and he has not shaved for two or three days. His panama hat is soiled, and beneath it, between hat and skull against the heat, the edge and corners of a soiled handkerchief protrude. He has been to town to do his semiweekly marketing, where, gaunt, misshapen, with his gray stubble and his dark spectacleblurred eyes and his blackrimmed hands and the rank manodor of his sedentary and unwashed flesh, he entered the one odorous and cluttered store which he patronised and paid with cash for what he bought.

"Well, they found that nigger's trail at last," the proprietor said.

"Negro?" Hightower said. He became utterly still, in the act of putting into his pocket the change from his purchases.

"That bah—fellow; the murderer. I said all the time that he wasn't right. Wasn't a white man. That there was something funny about him. But you cant tell folks nothing until—"

"Found him?" Hightower said.

"You durn right they did. Why, the fool never even had sense enough to get out of the county. Here the sheriff has been telephoning all over the country for him, and the black son—uh was right here under his durn nose all the time."

"And they have . . ." He leaned forward against the counter, above his laden basket. He could feel the counter edge against his stomach. It felt solid, stable enough; it was more like the earth itself were rocking faintly, preparing to move. Then it seemed to move, like something released slowly and without haste, in an augmenting swoop, and cleverly, since the eye was tricked into believing that the dingy shelves ranked with flyspecked tins, and the merchant himself behind the counter, had not moved; outraging, tricking sense. And he thinking, 'I wont! I wont! I have bought immunity. I have paid. I have paid.'

"They aint caught him yet," the proprietor said. "But they will. The sheriff taken the dogs out to the church before daylight this morning. They aint six hours behind him. To think that the durn fool never had no better sense . . . show he is a nigger, even if nothing else. . . ." Then the proprietor was saying, "Was that all today?"

"What?" Hightower said. "What?"

"Was that all you wanted?"

"Yes. Yes. That was . . ." He began to fumble in his pocket, the proprietor watching him. His hand came forth, still fumbling. It blundered upon the counter, shedding coins. The proprietor stopped two or three of them as they were about to roll off the counter.

"What's this for?" the proprietor said.

"For the . . ." Hightower's hand fumbled at the laden basket. "For—"

"You already paid." The proprietor was watching him, curious. "That's your change here, that I just gave you. For the dollar bill."

"Oh," Hightower said. "Yes. I . . . I just—" The merchant was gathering up the coins. He handed them back. When the customer's hand touched his it felt like ice.

"It's this hot weather," the proprietor said. "It does wear a man out. Do you want to set down a spell before you start home?" But Hightower apparently did not hear him. He was moving now, toward the door, while the merchant watched him. He passed through the door and into the street, the basket on his arm, walking stiffly and carefully, like a man on ice. It was hot; heat quivered up from the asphalt, giving to the familiar buildings about the square a nimbus quality, a quality of living and palpitant chiaroscuro. Someone spoke to him in passing; he did not even know it. He went on, thinking *And him too. And him too* walking fast now, so that when he turned the corner at last and entered that dead and empty little street where his dead and empty small house waited, he was almost panting. 'It's the heat,' the top of his mind was saying to him, reiterant, explanatory. But still, even in the quiet street where scarce anyone ever paused now to look at, remember, the sign, and his house, his sanctuary, already in sight, it goes on beneath the top of his mind that would cozen and soothe him: 'I wont. I wont. I have bought immunity.' It is like words spoken aloud now: reiterative, patient, justificative: 'I paid for it. I didn't quibble about the price. No man can say that. I just wanted peace; I paid them their price without quibbling.' The street shimmers and swims; he has been sweating, but now even the air of noon feels cool upon him. Then sweat, heat, mirage, all, rushes fused into a finality which abrogates all logic and justification and obliterates it like fire would: I *will* not! I *will* not!

When, sitting in the study window in the first dark, he saw Byron pass into and then out of the street lamp, he sat suddenly forward in his chair. It was not that he was surprised to see Byron there, at that hour. At first, when he first recognised the figure, he thought *Ah. I had an idea he would come tonight. It is not in him to support even the semblance of evil* It was while he was thinking that that he started, sat forward: for an instant after recognising the approaching figure in the full glare of the light he believed that he was mistaken, knowing all the while that he could not be, that it could be no one except Byron, since he was already turning into the gate.

Tonight Byron is completely changed. It shows in his walk, his carriage; leaning forward Hightower says to himself *As though he has learned pride, or defiance* Byron's head is erect, he walks fast and erect; suddenly Hightower says, almost aloud: 'He has done something. He has taken a step.' He makes a clicking sound with his tongue, leaning in the dark window, watching the figure pass swiftly from sight beyond the window and in the direction of the porch, the entrance, and where in the next moment Hightower hears his feet and then his knock. 'And he didn't offer to tell me,' he thinks. 'I would have listened, let him think aloud to me.' He is already crossing the room, pausing at the desk to turn on the light. He goes to the front door.

"It's me, Reverend," Byron says.

"I recognised you," Hightower says. "Even though you didn't stumble on the bottom step this time. You have entered this house on Sunday night, but until tonight you have never entered it without stumbling on the bottom step, Byron." This was the note upon which Byron's calls usually opened: this faintly overbearing note of levity and warmth to put the other at his ease, and on the part of the caller that slow and countrybred diffidence which is courtesy. Sometimes it would seem to Hightower that he would actually hale Byron into the house by a judicious application of pure breath, as though Byron wore a sail.

But this time Byron is already entering, before Hightower has finished his sentence. He enters immediately, with that new air born somewhere between assurance and defiance. "And I reckon you are going to find that you hate it worse when I dont stumble than when I do," Byron says.

"Is that a hope, or is it a threat, Byron?"

"Well, I dont mean it to be a threat," Byron says.

"Ah," Hightower says. "In other words, you can offer no hope. Well, I am forewarned, at least. I was forewarned as soon as I saw you in the street light. But at least you are going to tell me about it. What you have already done, even if you didn't see fit to talk about it beforehand." They are moving toward the study door. Byron stops; he looks back and up at the taller face.

"Then you know," he says. "You have already heard." Then, though his head has not moved, he is no longer looking at the other. "Well," he says. He says: "Well, any man has got a free tongue. Woman too. But I would like to know who told you. Not that I am ashamed. Not that I aimed to keep it from you. I come to tell you myself, when I could."

They stand just without the door to the lighted room. Hightower sees now that Byron's arms are laden with bundles, parcels that look like they might contain groceries. "What?" Hightower says. "What have you come to tell me?—But come in. Maybe I do know what it is already. But I want to see your face when you tell me. I forewarn you too, Byron." They enter the lighted room. The bundles are groceries: he has bought and carried too many like them himself not to know. "Sit down," he says.

"No," Byron says. "I aint going to stay that long." He stands, sober, contained, with that air compassionate still, but decisive without being assured, confident without being assertive: that air of a man about to do something which someone dear to him will not understand and approve, yet which he himself knows to be right just as he knows that the friend will never see it so. He says: "You aint going to like it. But there aint anything else to do. I wish you could see it so. But I reckon you cant. And I reckon that's all there is to it."

Across the desk, seated again, Hightower watches him gravely. "What have you done, Byron?"

Byron speaks in that new voice: that voice brief, terse, each word definite of meaning, not fumbling. "I took her out there this evening. I had already fixed up the cabin, cleaned it good. She is settled now. She wanted it so. It was the nearest thing to a home he ever had and ever will have, so I reckon she is entitled to use it, especially as the owner aint using it now. Being detained elsewhere, you might say. I know you aint going to like it. You can name lots of reasons, good ones. You'll say it aint his cabin to give to her. All right. Maybe it aint. But it aint any living man or woman in this country or state to say she cant use it. You'll say that in her shape she ought to have a woman with her. All right. There is a nigger woman, one old enough to be sensible, that dont live over two hundred yards away. She can call to her without getting up from the chair or the bed. You'll say, but that aint a white woman. And I'll ask you what will she be getting from the white women in Jefferson about the time that baby is due, when here she aint been in Jefferson but a week and already she cant talk to a woman ten minutes before that woman knows she aint married yet, and as long as that durn scoundrel stays above ground where she can hear of him now and then, she aint going to be married. How much help will she be getting from the white ladies about that time? They'll see that she has a bed to lay on and walls to hide her from the street all right. I dont mean that. And I reckon a man would be justified in saying she dont deserve no more than that, being as it wasn't behind no walls that she got in the shape she is in. But that baby never done the choosing. And even if it had, I be durn if any poor little tyke, having to face what it will have to face in this world, deserves—deserves more than—better than— But I reckon you know what I mean. I reckon you can even say it." Beyond the desk Hightower watches him while he talks in that level, restrained tone, not once at a loss for words until he came to something still too new and nebulous for him to more than feel. "And for the third reason. A white woman out there alone. You aint going to like that. You will like that least of all."

"Ah, Byron, Byron."

Byron's voice is now dogged. Yet he holds his head up still. "I aint in the house with her. I got a tent. It aint close, neither. Just where I can hear her at need. And I fixed a bolt on the door. Any of them can come out, at any time, and see me in the tent."

"Ah, Byron, Byron."

"I know you aint thinking what most of them think. Are thinking. I know you would know better, even if she wasn't—if it wasn't for—I know you said that because of what you know that the others will think."

Hightower sits again in the attitude of the eastern idol, between his parallel arms on the armrests of the chair. "Go away, Byron. Go away. Now. At once. Leave this place forever, this terrible place, this terrible, terrible place. I can read you. You will tell me that you have just learned love; I will tell you that you have just learned hope. That's all; hope. The object does not matter, not to the hope, not even to you. There is but one end to this, to the road that you are taking: sin or marriage. And you would refuse the sin. That's it, God forgive me. It will, must be, marriage or nothing with you. And you will insist that it be marriage. You will convince her; perhaps you already have, if she but knew it, would admit it: else, why is she content to stay here and yet make no effort to see the man whom she has come to find? I cannot say to you, Choose the sin, because you would not only hate me: you would carry that hatred straight to her. So I say, Go away. Now. At once. Turn your face now, and dont look back. But not this, Byron."

They look at one another. "I knew you would not like it," Byron says. "I reckon I done right not to make myself a guest by sitting down. But I did not expect this. That you too would turn against a woman wronged and betrayed—"

"No woman who has a child is ever betrayed; the husband of a mother, whether he be the father or not, is already a cuckold. Give yourself at least the one chance in ten, Byron. If you must marry, there are single women, girls, virgins. It's not fair that you should sacrifice yourself to a woman who has chosen once and now wishes to renege that choice. It's not right. It's not just. God didn't intend it so when He made marriage. Made it? Women made marriage."

"Sacrifice? Me the sacrifice? It seems to me the sacrifice—"

"Not to her. For the Lena Groves there are always two men in the world and their number is legion: Lucas Burches and Byron Bunches. But no Lena, no woman, deserves more than one of them. No woman. There have been good women who were martyrs to brutes, in their cups and such. But what woman, good or bad, has ever suffered from any brute as men have suffered from good women? Tell me that, Byron."

They speak quietly, without heat, giving pause to weigh one another's words, as two men already impregnable each in his own conviction will. "I reckon you are right," Byron says. "Anyway, it aint for me to say that you are wrong. And I dont reckon it's for you to say that I am wrong, even if I am."

"No," Hightower says.

"Even if I am," Byron says. "So I reckon I'll say good night." He says, quietly: "It's a good long walk out there."

"Yes," Hightower says. "I used to walk it myself, now and then. It must be about three miles."

"Two miles," Byron says. "Well." He turns. Hightower does not move. Byron shifts the parcels which he has not put down. "I'll say good night," he says, moving toward the door. "I reckon I'll see you, sometime soon."

"Yes," Hightower says. "Is there anything I can do? Anything you need? bedclothes and such?"

"I'm obliged. I reckon she has a plenty. There was some already there. I'm obliged."

"And you will let me know? If anything comes up. If the child— Have you arranged for a doctor?"

"I'll get that attended to."

"But have you seen one yet? Have you engaged one?"

"I aim to see to all that. And I'll let you know."

Then he is gone. From the window again Hightower watches him pass and go on up the street, toward the edge of town and his two mile walk, carrying his paper-wrapped packages of food. He passed from sight walking erect and at a good gait; such a gait as an old man already gone to flesh and short wind, an old man who has already spent too much time sitting down, could not have kept up with. And Hightower leans there in the window, in the August heat, oblivious of the odor in which he lives—that smell of people who no longer live in life: that odor of over-plump desiccation and stale linen as though a precursor of the tomb—listening to the feet which he seems to hear still long after he knows that he cannot, thinking, 'God bless him. God help him'; thinking *To be young. To be young. There is nothing else like it: there is nothing else in the world* He is thinking quietly: 'I should not have got out of the habit of prayer.' Then he hears the feet no longer. He hears now only the myriad and interminable insects, leaning in the window, breathing the hot still rich maculate smell of the earth, thinking of how when he was young, a youth, he had loved darkness, of walking or sitting alone among trees at night. Then the ground, the bark of trees, became actual, savage, filled with, evocative of, strange and baleful half delights and half terrors. He was afraid of it. He feared; he loved in being afraid. Then one day while at the seminary he realised that he was no longer afraid. It was as though a door had shut somewhere. He was no longer afraid of darkness. He just hated it; he would flee from it, to walls, to artificial light. 'Yes,' he thinks. 'I should never have let myself get out of the habit of prayer.' He turns from the window. One wall of the study is lined with books. He pauses before them, seeking, until he finds the one which he wants. It is Tennyson. It is dogeared. He has had it ever since the seminary. He sits beneath the lamp and opens it. It does not take long. Soon the fine galloping language, the gutless swooning full of sapless trees and dehydrated lusts begins to swim smooth and swift and peaceful. It is better than praying without having to bother to think aloud. It is like listening in a cathedral to a eunuch chanting in a language which he does not even need to not understand.

. 14 .

"THERE'S somebody out there in that cabin," the deputy told the sheriff. "Not hiding: living in it."

"Go and see," the sheriff said.

The deputy went and returned.

"It's a woman. A young woman. And she's all fixed up to live there a good spell, it looks like. And Byron Bunch is camped in a tent about as far from the cabin as from here to the post-office."

"Byron Bunch?" the sheriff says. "Who is the woman?"

"I dont know. She is a stranger. A young woman. She told me all about it. She begun telling me almost before I got inside the cabin, like it was a speech. Like she had done got used to telling it, done got into the habit. And I reckon she has, coming here from over in Alabama somewhere, looking for her husband. He had done come on ahead of her to find work, it seems like, and after a while she started out after him and folks told her on the road that he was here. And about that time Byron come in and he said he could tell me about it. Said he aimed to tell you."

"Byron Bunch," the sheriff says.

"Yes," the deputy says. He says: "She's fixing to have a kid. It aint going to be long, neither."

"A kid?" the sheriff says. He looks at the deputy. "And from Alabama. From anywhere. You cant tell me that about Byron Bunch."

"No more am I trying to," the deputy says. "I aint saying it's Byron's. Leastways, Byron aint saying it's his. I'm just telling you what he told me."

"Oh," the sheriff says. "I see. Why she is out there. So it's one of them fellows. It's Christmas, is it?"

"No. This is what Byron told me. He took me outside and told me, where she couldn't hear. He said he aimed to come and tell you. It's Brown's. Only his name aint Brown. It's Lucas Burch. Byron told me. About how Brown or Burch left her over in Alabama. Told her he was just coming to find work and fix up a home and then send for her. But her time come nigh and she hadn't heard from him, where he was at or anything, so she just decided to not wait any longer. She started out afoot, asking along the road if anybody knowed a fellow named Lucas Burch, getting a ride here and there, asking everybody she met if they knew him. And so after a while somebody told her how there was a fellow named Burch or Bunch or something working at the planing mill in Jefferson, and she come on here. She got here Saturday, on a wagon, while we were all out at the murder, and she come out to the mill and found it was Bunch instead of Burch. And Byron said he told her that her husband was in Jefferson before he knew it. And then he said she had him pinned down and he had to tell her where Brown lived. But he aint told her that Brown or Burch is mixed up with Christmas in this killing. He just told her that Brown was away on business. And I reckon you can call it business. Work, anyway. I never saw a man want a thousand dollars badder and suffer more to get it, than him. And so she said that Brown's house was bound to be the one that Lucas Burch had promised to get ready for her to live in, and so she moved out to wait until Brown come back from this here business he is away on. Byron said he couldn't stop her because he didn't want to tell her the truth about Brown after he had already lied to her in a way of speaking. He said he aimed to come and tell you about it before now, only you found it out too quick, before he had got her settled down good."

"Lucas Burch?" the sheriff says.

"I was some surprised, myself," the deputy says. "What do you aim to do about it?"

"Nothing," the sheriff says. "I reckon they wont do no harm out there. And it aint none of my house to tell her to get out of it. And like Byron told her, Burch or Brown or whatever his name is, is going to be right busy for a while longer yet."

"Do you aim to tell Brown about her?"

"I reckon not," the sheriff says. "It aint any of my business. I aint interested in the wives he left in Alabama, or anywhere else. What I am interested in is the husband he seems to have had since he come to Jefferson."

The deputy guffaws. "I reckon that's a fact," he says. He sobers, muses. "If he dont get that thousand dollars, I reckon he will just die."

"I reckon he wont," the sheriff says.

At three o'clock Wednesday morning a negro rode into town on a saddleless mule. He went to the sheriff's home and waked him. He had come direct from a negro church twenty miles away, where a revival meeting was in nightly progress. On the evening before, in the middle of a hymn, there had come a tremendous noise from the rear of the church, and turning the congregation saw a man standing in the door. The door had not been locked or even shut yet the man had apparently grasped it by the knob and hurled it back into the wall so that the sound crashed into the blended voices like a pistol shot. Then the man came swiftly up the aisle, where the singing had stopped short off, toward the pulpit where the preacher leaned, his hands still raised, his mouth still open. Then they saw that the man was white. In the thick, cavelike gloom which the two oil lamps but served to increase, they could not tell at once what he was until he was halfway up the aisle. Then they saw that his face was not black, and a woman began to shriek, and people in the rear sprang up and began to run toward the door; and another woman on the mourners' bench, already in a semihysterical state, sprang up and whirled and glared at him for an instant with white rolling eyes and screamed, "It's the devil! It's Satan himself!" Then she ran, quite blind. She ran straight toward him and he knocked her down without stopping and stepped over her and went on, with the faces gaped for screaming falling away before him, straight to the pulpit and put his hand on the minister.

"Wasn't nobody bothering him, even then," the messenger said. "It was all happening so fast, and nobody knowed him, who he was or what he wanted or nothing. And the women hollering and screeching and him done retch into the pulpit and caught Brother Bedenberry by the throat, trying to snatch him outen the pulpit. We could see Brother Bedenberry talking to him, trying to pacify him quiet, and him jerking at Brother Bedenberry and slapping his face with his hand. And the womenfolks screeching and hollering so you couldn't hear what Brother Bedenberry was saying, cep he never tried to hit back nor nothing, and then some of the old men, the deacons, went up to him and tried to talk to him and he let Brother Bedenberry go and he whirled and he knocked seventy year old Pappy Thompson clean down into the mourners' pew and then he retch down and caught up a chair and whirled and made a pass at the others until they give back. And the folks still yelling and screeching and trying to get out. Then he turned and clumb into the pulpit, where Brother Bedenberry had done clumb out the other side, and he stood there—he was all muddy, his pants and his shirt, and his jaw black with whiskers—with his hands raised like a preacher. And he begun to curse, hollering it out, at the folks, and he cursed God louder than the women screeching, and some of the men trying to hold Roz Thompson, Pappy Thompson's daughter's boy, that was six foot tall and had a razor nekkid in his hand, hollering, 'I'll kill him. Lemme go, folks. He hit my grandpappy. I'll kill him. Lemme go. Please lemme go,' and the folks trying to get out, rushing and trompling in the aisle and through the door, and him in the pulpit cursing God and the men dragging Roz Thompson out backwards and Roz still begging them to let him go. But they got Roz out and we went back into the bushes and him still hollering and cursing back there in the pulpit. Then he quit after a while and we seed him come to the door and stand there. And they had to hold Roz again. He must have heard the racket they made holding Roz, because he begun to laugh. He stood there in the door, with the light behind him, laughing loud, and then he begun to curse again and we could see him snatch up a bench leg and swing it back. And we heard the first lamp bust, and it got dim in the church, and then we heard the other lamp bust and then it was dark and we couldn't see him no more. And where they was trying to hold Roz a terrible racket set up, with them hollerwhispering, 'Hold him! Hold him! Ketch him! Ketch him!' Then somebody hollered, 'He's done got loose,' and we could hear Roz running back toward the church and Deacon Vines says to me, 'Roz will kill him. Jump on a mule and ride for the sheriff. Tell him just what you seen.' And wasn't nobody bothering him, captain," the negro said. "We never even knowed him to call his name. Never even seed him before. And we tried to hold Roz back. But Roz a big man, and him done knocked down Roz' seventy year old grandpappy and Roz with that nekkid razor in his hand, not caring much who else he had to cut to carve his path back to the church where that white man was. But 'fore God we tried to hold Roz."

That was what he told, because that was what he knew. He had departed immediately: he did not know that at the time he was telling it, the negro Roz was lying unconscious in a neighboring cabin, with his skull fractured where Christmas, just inside the now dark door, had struck him with the bench leg when Roz plunged into the church. Christmas struck just once, hard, savagely, at the sound of running feet, the thick shape which rushed headlong through the doorway, and heard it without pause plunge on crashing among the overturned benches and become still. Also without pausing Christmas sprang out and to the earth, where he stood lightly poised, still grasping the bench leg, cool, not even breathing hard. He was quite cool, no sweat; the darkness cool upon him. The church-yard was a pallid crescent of trampled and beaten earth, shaped and enclosed by undergrowth and trees. He knew that the undergrowth was full of negroes: he could feel the eyes. 'Looking and looking,' he thought. 'Dont even know they cant see me.' He breathed deeply; he found that he was hefting the bench leg, curiously, as though trying its balance, as if he had never touched it before. 'I'll cut a notch in it tomorrow,' he thought. He leaned the leg care-fully against the wall beside him and took from his shirt a cigarette and a match. As he struck the match he paused, and with the yellow flame spurting punily into life he stood, his head turned a little. It was hooves which he heard. He heard them come alive and grow swift, diminishing. "A mule," he said aloud, not loud. "Bound for town with the good news." He lit the cigarette and flipped the match away and he stood there, smoking, feeling the negro eyes upon the tiny living coal. Though he stood there until the cigarette was smoked down, he was quite alert. He had set his back against the wall and he held the bench leg in his right hand again. He smoked the cigarette completely down, then he flipped it, twinkling, as far as he could toward the undergrowth where he could feel the negroes crouching. "Have a butt, boys," he said, his voice sudden and loud in the silence. In the undergrowth where they crouched they watched the cigarette twinkle toward the earth and glow there for a time. But they could not see him when he departed, nor which way he went.

At eight o'clock the next morning the sheriff arrived, with his posse and the bloodhounds. They made one cap-ture immediately, though the dogs had nothing to do with it. The church was deserted; there was not a negro in sight.

The posse entered the church and looked quietly about at the wreckage. Then they emerged. The dogs had struck something immediately, but before they set out a deputy found, wedged into a split plank on the side of the church, a scrap of paper. It had been obviously put there by the hand of man, and opened, it proved to be an empty cigarette container torn open and spread smooth, and on the white inner side was a pencilled message. It was raggedly written, as though by an unpractised hand or perhaps in the dark, and it was not long. It was addressed to the sheriff by name and it was unprintable—a single phrase—and it was unsigned. "Didn't I tell you?" one of the party said. He was unshaven too and muddy, like the quarry which they had not yet even seen, and his face looked strained and a little mad, with frustration, outrage, and his voice was hoarse, as though he had been doing a good deal of unheeded shouting or talking recently. "I told you all the time! I told you!"

"Told me what?" the sheriff said, in a cold, level voice, bearing upon the other a gaze cold and level, the pencilled message in his hand. "What did you tell me when?" The other looked at the sheriff, outraged, desperate, frayed almost to endurance's limit; looking at him, the deputy thought, 'If he dont get that reward, he will just die.' His mouth was open though voiceless as he glared at the sheriff with a kind of baffled and unbelieving amaze. "And I done told you, too," the sheriff said, in his bleak, quiet voice, "if you dont like the way I am running this, you can wait back in town. There's a good place there for you to wait in. Cool, where you wont stay so heated up like out here in the sun. Aint I told you, now? Talk up."

The other closed his mouth. He looked away, as though

with a tremendous effort; as though with a tremendous effort he said "Yes" in a dry, suffocated voice.

The sheriff turned heavily, crumpling the message. "You try to keep that from slipping your mind again, then," he said. "If you got any mind to even slip on you." They were ringed about with quiet, interested faces in the early sunlight. "About which I got the Lord's own doubts, if you or anybody else wants to know." Some one guffawed, once. "Shet up that noise," the sheriff said. "Let's get going. Get them dogs started, Bufe."

The dogs were cast, still on leash. They struck immediately. The trail was good, easily followed because of the dew. The fugitive had apparently made no effort whatever to hide it. They could even see the prints of his knees and hands where he had knelt to drink from a spring. "I never yet knew a murderer that had more sense than that about the folks that would chase him," the deputy said. "But this durn fool dont even suspect that we might use dogs."

"We been putting dogs on him once a day ever since Sunday," the sheriff said. "And we aint caught him yet."

"Them were cold trails. We aint had a good hot trail until today. But he's made his mistake at last. We'll get him today. Before noon, maybe."

"I'll wait and see, I reckon," the sheriff said.

"You'll see," the deputy said. "This trail is running straight as a railroad. I could follow it, myself almost. Look here. You can even see his footprints. The durn fool aint even got enough sense to get into the road, in the dust, where other folks have walked and where the dogs cant scent him. Them dogs will find the end of them footprints before ten o'clock."

Which the dogs did. Presently the trail bent sharply at

right angles. They followed it and came onto a road, which they followed behind the lowheaded and eager dogs who, after a short distance, swung to the roadside where a path came down from a cotton house in a nearby field. They began to bay, milling, tugging, their voices loud, mellow, ringing; whining and surging with excitement. "Why, the durn fool!" the deputy said. "He set down here and rested: here's his footmarks: them same rubber heels. He aint a mile ahead right now! Come on, boys!" They went on, the leashes taut, the dogs baying, the men moving now at a trot. The sheriff turned to the unshaven man.

"Now's your chance to run ahead and catch him and get that thousand dollars," he said. "Why dont you do it?"

The man did not answer; none of them had much breath for talking, particularly when after about a mile the dogs, still straining and baying, turned from the road and followed a path which went quartering up a hill and into a corn field. Here they stopped baying, but if anything their eagerness seemed to increase; the men were running now. Beyond the headtall corn was a negro cabin. "He's in there," the sheriff said, drawing his pistol. "Watch yourselves now, boys. He'll have a gun now."

It was done with finesse and skill: the house surrounded by concealed men with drawn pistols, and the sheriff, followed by the deputy, getting himself for all his bulk swiftly and smartly flat against the cabin wall, out of range of any window. Still flat to the wall he ran around the corner and kicked open the door and sprang, pistol first, into the cabin. It contained a negro child. The child was stark naked and it sat in the cold ashes on the hearth, eating something. It was apparently alone, though an instant later a woman appeared in an inner door, her mouth open, in the act of dropping an iron skillet. She was wearing a pair of man's shoes, which a member of the posse identified as having belonged to the fugitive. She told them about the white man on the road about daylight and how he had swapped shoes with her, taking in exchange a pair of her husband's brogans which she was wearing at the time. The sheriff listened. "That happened right by a cotton house, didn't it?" he said. She told him Yes. He returned to his men, to the leashed and eager dogs. He looked down at the dogs while the men asked questions and then ceased, watching him. They watched him put the pistol back into his pocket and then turn and kick the dogs, once each, heavily. "Get them durn eggsuckers on back to town," he said.

But the sheriff was a good officer. He knew as well as his men that he would return to the cotton house, where he believed that Christmas had been hidden all the while, though he knew now that Christmas would not be there when they returned. They had some trouble getting the dogs away from the cabin, so that it was in the hot brilliance of ten o'clock that they surrounded the cotton house carefully and skilfully and quietly and surprised it with pistols, quite by the rules and without any particular hope; and found one astonished and terrified field rat. Nevertheless the sheriff had the dogs—they had refused to approach the cotton house at all; they refused to leave the road, leaning and straining against the collars with simultaneous and reverted heads pointed back down the road toward the cabin from which they had been recently dragged away—brought up. It took two men by main strength to fetch them up, where as soon as the leashes were slacked, they sprang as one and rushed around the cotton house and through the very marks which the fugitive's legs had left in the tall and still dewed weeds in the house's shadow, and rushed leaping and straining back toward the road, dragging the two men for fifty yards before they succeeded in passing the leashes about a sapling and snubbing the dogs up. This time the sheriff did not even kick them.

At last the noise and the alarms, the sound and fury of the hunt, dies away, dies out of his hearing. He was not in the cotton house when the man and the dogs passed, as the sheriff believed. He paused there only long enough to lace up the brogans: the black shoes, the black shoes smelling of negro. They looked like they had been chopped out of iron ore with a dull axe. Looking down at the harsh, crude, clumsy shapelessness of them, he said "Hah" through his teeth. It seemed to him that he could see himself being hunted by white men at last into the black abyss which had been waiting, trying, for thirty years to drown him and into which now and at last he had actually entered, bearing now upon his ankles the definite and ineradicable gauge of its upward moving.

It is just dawn, daylight: that gray and lonely suspension filled with the peaceful and tentative waking of birds. The air, inbreathed, is like spring water. He breathes deep and slow, feeling with each breath himself diffuse in the neutral grayness, becoming one with loneliness and quiet that has never known fury or despair. 'That was all I wanted,' he thinks, in a quiet and slow amazement. 'That was all, for thirty years. That didn't seem to be a whole lot to ask in thirty years.'

He has not slept very much since Wednesday, and now Wednesday has come and gone again, though he does not know it. When he thinks about time, it seems to him now that for thirty years he has lived inside an orderly parade of named and numbered days like fence pickets, and that one night he went to sleep and when he waked up he was outside of them. For a time after he fled on that Friday night he tried to keep up with the days, after the old habit. Once, after lying all night in a haystack, he was awake in time to watch the farm house wake. He saw before daylight a lamp come yellowly alive in the kitchen, and then in the gray yetdark he heard the slow, clapping sound of an axe, and movement, manmovement, among the waking cattle sounds in the nearby barn. Then he could smell smoke, and food, the hot fierce food, and he began to say over and over to himself *I have not eaten since I have not eaten since* trying to remember how many days it had been since Friday in Jefferson, in the restaurant where he had eaten his supper, until after a while, in the lying still with waiting until the men should have eaten and gone to the field, the name of the day of the week seemed more important than the food. Because when the men were gone at last and he descended, emerged, into the level, jonquilcolored sun and went to the kitchen door, he didn't ask for food at all. He had intended to. He could feel the harsh words marshaling in his mind, just behind his mouth. And then the gaunt, leatherhard woman come to the door and looked at him and he could see shock and recognition and fear in her eyes and while he was thinking *She knows me. She has got the word too* he heard his mouth saying quietly: "Can you tell me what day this is? I just want to know what day this is."

"What day it is?" Her face was gaunt as his, her body as gaunt and as tireless and as driven. She said: "You get away from here! It's Tuesday! You get away from here! I'll call my man!"

He said, "Thank you," quietly as the door banged. Then he was running. He did not remember starting to run. He thought for a while that he ran because of and toward some destination that the running had suddenly remembered and hence his mind did not need to bother to remember why he was running, since the running was not difficult. It was quite easy, in fact. He felt quite light, weightless. Even in full stride his feet seemed to stray slowly and lightly and at deliberate random across an earth without solidity, until he fell. Nothing tripped him. He just fell full length, believing for a while that he was still on his feet and still running. But he was down, lying on his face in a shallow ditch at the edge of a plowed field. Then he said suddenly, "I reckon I better get up." When he sat up he found that the sun, halfway up the sky, now shone upon him from the opposite direction. At first he believed that he was merely turned around. Then he realised that it was now evening. That it was morning when he fell running and that, though it seemed to him that he had sat up at once, it was now evening. 'I have been asleep,' he thought. 'I have slept more than six hours. I must have gone to sleep running without knowing it. That is what I did.'

He felt no surprise. Time, the spaces of light and dark, had long since lost orderliness. It would be either one now, seemingly at an instant, between two movements of the eyelids, without warning. He could never know when he would pass from one to the other, when he would find that he had been asleep without remembering having lain down, or find himself walking without remembering having waked. Sometimes it would seem to him that a night of sleep, in hay, in a ditch, beneath an abandoned roof, would be followed immediately by another night without interval of day, without light between to see to flee by; that a day would be followed by another day filled with fleeing and urgency, without any night between or any interval for rest, as if the sun had not set but instead had turned in the sky before reaching the horizon and retraced its way. When he went to sleep walking or even kneeling in the act of drinking from a spring, he could never know if his eyes would open next upon sunlight or upon stars.

For a while he had been hungry all the time. He gathered and ate rotting and wormriddled fruit; now and then he crept into fields and dragged down and gnawed ripened ears of corn as hard as potato graters. He thought of eating all the time, imagining dishes, food. He would think of that meal set for him on the kitchen table three years ago and he would live again through the steady and deliberate backswinging of his arm as he hurled the dishes into the wall, with a kind of writhing and excruciating agony of regret and remorse and rage. Then one day he was no longer hungry. It came sudden and peaceful. He felt cool, quiet. Yet he knew that he had to eat. He would make himself eat the rotten fruit, the hard corn, chewing it slowly, tasting nothing. He would eat enormous quantities of it, with resultant crises of bleeding flux. Yet immediately afterward he would be obsessed anew with the need and the urge to eat. It was not with food that he was obsessed now, but with the necessity to eat. He would try to remember when he had eaten last of cooked, of decent food. He could feel, remember, somewhere a house, a cabin. House or cabin, white or black: he could not remember which. Then, as he sat quite still, with on his gaunt, sick, stubbled face an expression of rapt bemusement, he smelled negro. Motionless (he was sitting against a tree beside a spring, his head back, his hands upon his lap, his face worn and peaceful) he smelled and saw negro dishes, negro food. It was in a room. He did not remember how he got there. But the room was filled with flight and abrupt consternation, as though people had fled it recently and suddenly and in fear. He was sitting at a table, waiting, thinking of nothing in an emptiness, a silence filled with flight. Then there was food before him, appearing suddenly between long, limber black hands fleeing too in the act of setting down the dishes. It seemed to him that he could hear without hearing them wails of terror and distress quieter than sighs all about him, with the sound of the chewing and the swallowing. 'It was a cabin that time,' he thought. 'And they were afraid. Of their brother afraid.'

That night a strange thing came into his mind. He lay ready for sleep, without sleeping, without seeming to need the sleep, as he would place his stomach acquiescent for food which it did not seem to desire or need. It was strange in the sense that he could discover neither derivation nor motivation nor explanation for it. He found that he was trying to calculate the day of the week. It was as though now and at last he had an actual and urgent need to strike off the accomplished days toward some purpose, some definite day or act, without either falling short or overshooting. He entered the coma state which sleeping had now become with the need in his mind. When he waked in the dewgray of dawn, it was so crystallised that the need did not seem strange anymore.

It is just dawn, daylight. He rises and descends to the spring and takes from his pocket the razor, the brush, the soap. But it is still too dim to see his face clearly in the water, so he sits beside the spring and waits until he can see better. Then he lathers his face with the hard, cold water, patiently. His hand trembles, despite the urgency he feels a lassitude so that he must drive himself. The razor is dull; he tries to whet it upon the side of one brogan, but the leather is ironhard and wet with dew. He shaves, after a fashion. His hand trembles; it is not a very good job, and he cuts himself three or four times, stanching the blood with the cold water until it stops. He puts the shaving tools away and begins to walk. He follows a straight line, disregarding the easier walking of the ridges. After a short distance he comes out upon a road and sits down beside it. It is a quiet road, appearing and vanishing quietly, the pale dust marked only by narrow and infrequent wheels and by the hooves of horses and mules and now and then by the print of human feet. He sits beside it, coatless, the once white shirt and the once creased trousers muddy and stained, his gaunt face blotched with patches of stubble and with dried blood, shaking slowly with weariness and cold as the sun rises and warms him. After a time two negro children appear around the curve, approaching. They do not see him until he speaks; they halt, dead, looking at him with whiterolling eyes. "What day of the week is it?" he repeats. They say nothing at all, staring at him. He moves his head a little. "Go on," he says. They go on. He does not watch them. He sits, apparently musing upon the place where they had stood, as though to him they had in moving merely walked out of two shells. He does not see that they are running.

Then, sitting there, the sun warming him slowly, he goes to sleep without knowing it, because the next thing of which he is conscious is a terrific clatter of jangling and rattling wood and metal and trotting hooves. He opens his eyes in time to see the wagon whirl slewing around the curve beyond and so out of sight, its occupants looking back at him over their shoulders, the whiphand of the driver rising and falling. 'They recognised me too,' he thinks. 'Them, and that white woman. And the negroes where I ate that day. Any of them could have captured me, if that's what they want. Since that's what they all want: for me to be captured. But they all run first. They all want me to be captured, and then when I come up ready to say Here I am *Yes I would say Here I am I am tired I am tired of running of having to carry my life like it was a basket of eggs* they all run away. Like there is a rule to catch me by, and to capture me that way would not be like the rule says.'

So he moves back into the bushes. This time he is alert and he hears the wagon before it comes into sight. He does not show himself until the wagon is abreast of him. Then he steps forth and says, "Hey." The wagon stops, jerked up. The negro driver's head jerks also; into his face also comes the astonishment, then the recognition and the terror. "What day is this?" Christmas says.

The negro glares at him, slackjawed. "W-what you say?"

"What day of the week is this? Thursday? Friday? What? What day? I am not going to hurt you."

"It's Friday," the negro says. "O Lawd God, it's Friday."

"Friday," Christmas says. Again he jerks his head. "Get on." The whip falls, the mules surge forward. This wagon too whirls from sight at a dead run, the whip rising and falling. But Christmas has already turned and entered the woods again.

Again his direction is straight as a surveyor's line, disregarding hill and valley and bog. Yet he is not hurrying. He is like a man who knows where he is and where he wants to go and how much time to the exact minute he has to get there in. It is as though he desires to see his native earth in all its phases for the first or the last time. He had grown to manhood in the country, where like the unswimming sailor his physical shape and his thought had been molded by its compulsions without his learning anything about its actual shape and feel. For a week now he has lurked and crept among its secret places, yet he remained a foreigner to the very immutable laws which earth must obey. For some time as he walks steadily on, he thinks that this is what it is—the looking and seeing—which gives him peace and unhaste and quiet, until suddenly the true answer comes to him. He feels dry and light. 'I dont have to bother about having to eat anymore,' he thinks. 'That's what it is.'

By noon he has walked eight miles. He comes now to a broad gravelled road, a highway. This time the wagon stops quietly at his raised hand. On the face of the negro youth who drives it there is neither astonishment nor recognition. "Where does this road go?" Christmas says.

"Mottstown. Whar I gwine."

"Mottstown. You going to Jefferson too?"

The youth rubs his head. "Dont know whar that is. I gwine to Mottstown."

"Oh," Christmas says. "I see. You dont live around here, then."

"Naw, sir. I stays two counties back yonder. Been on the road three days. I gwine to Mottstown to get a yellin calf pappy bought. You wanter go to Mottstown?"

"Yes," Christmas says. He mounts to the seat beside the

youth. The wagon moves on. 'Mottstown,' he thinks. Jefferson is only twenty miles away. 'Now I can let go for a while,' he thinks. 'I haven't let go for seven days, so I guess I'll let go for a while.' He thinks that perhaps, sitting, with the wagon's motion to lull him, he will sleep. But he does not sleep. He is not sleepy or hungry or even tired. He is somewhere between and among them, suspended, swaying to the motion of the wagon without thought, without feeling. He has lost account of time and distance; perhaps it is an hour later, perhaps three. The youth says:

"Mottstown. Dar tis."

Looking, he can see the smoke low on the sky, beyond an imperceptible corner; he is entering it again, the street which ran for thirty years. It had been a paved street, where going should be fast. It had made a circle and he is still inside of it. Though during the last seven days he has had no paved street, yet he has travelled further than in all the thirty years before. And yet he is still inside the circle. 'And yet I have been further in these seven days than in all the thirty years,' he thinks. 'But I have never got outside that circle. I have never broken out of the ring of what I have already done and cannot ever undo,' he thinks quietly, sitting on the seat, with planted on the dashboard before him the shoes, the black shoes smelling of negro: that mark on his ankles the gauge definite and ineradicable of the black tide creeping up his legs, moving from his feet upward as death moves.

. 15 .

ON that Friday when Christmas was captured in
Mottstown, there lived in the town an old couple
named Hines. They were quite old. They lived in a small
bungalow in a neighborhood of negroes; how, upon what,
the town in general did not know since they appeared to
live in filthy poverty and complete idleness, Hines, as far
as the town knew, not having done any work, steady work,
in twentyfive years.

They came to Mottstown thirty years ago. One day the
town found the woman established in the small house
where they had lived ever since, though for the next five
years Hines was at home only once a month, over the weekend. Soon it became known that he held some kind of a
position in Memphis. Exactly what, was not known, since
even at that time he was a secret man who could have been
either thirtyfive or fifty, with something in his glance coldly
and violently fanatical and a little crazed, precluding questioning, curiosity. The town looked upon them both as
being a little touched—lonely, gray in color, a little smaller
than most other men and women, as if they belonged to a

different race, species—even though for the next five or six years after the man appeared to have come to Mottstown to settle down for good in the small house where his wife lived, people hired him to do various odd jobs which they considered within his strength. But in time he stopped this, too. The town wondered for a while, how they would live now, then it forgot to speculate about this just as later when the town learned that Hines went on foot about the county, holding revival services in negro churches, and that now and then negro women carrying what were obviously dishes of food would be seen entering from the rear the house where the couple lived, and emerging emptyhanded, it wondered about this for a time and then forgot it. In time the town either forgot or condoned, because Hines was an old man and harmless, that which in a young man it would have crucified. It just said, "They are crazy; crazy on the subject of negroes. Maybe they are Yankees," and let it go at that. Or perhaps what it condoned was not the man's selfdedication to the saving of negro souls, but the public ignoring of the fact of that charity which they received from negro hands, since it is a happy faculty of the mind to slough that which conscience refuses to assimilate.

So for twentyfive years the old couple had had no visible means of support, the town blinding its collective eye to the negro women and the covered dishes and pans, particularly as some of the dishes and pans had in all likelihood been borne intact from white kitchens where the women cooked. Perhaps this was a part of the mind's sloughing. Anyway the town did not look, and for twentyfive years now the couple had lived in the slack backwater of their lonely isolation, as though they had been two muskoxen strayed from the north pole, or two homeless and belated beasts from beyond the glacial period.

The woman was hardly ever seen at all, though the man —he was known as Uncle Doc—was a fixture about the square: a dirty little old man with a face which had once been either courageous or violent—either a visionary or a supreme egoist—collarless, in dirty blue jean clothes and with a heavy piece of handpeeled hickory worn about the grip dark as walnut and smooth as glass. At first, while he held the Memphis position, on his monthly visits he had talked a little about himself, with a selfconfidence not alone of the independent man, but with a further quality, as though at one time in his life he had been better than independent, and that not long ago. There was nothing beaten about him. It was rather that confidence of a man who has had the controlling of lesser men and who had voluntarily and for a reason which he believed that no other man could question or comprehend, changed his life. But what he told about himself and his present occupation did not make sense, for all its apparent coherence. So they believed that he was a little crazy, even then. It was not that he seemed to be trying to conceal one thing by telling another. It was that his words, his telling, just did not synchronise with what his hearers believed would (and must) be the scope of a single individual. Sometimes they decided that he had once been a minister. Then he would talk about Memphis, the city, in a vague and splendid way, as though all his life he had been incumbent there of some important though still nameless municipal office. "Sure," the men in Mottstown said behind his back; "he was railroad superintendent there. Standing in the middle of the street crossing with a red flag every time a train passed," or "He's a big newspaperman. Gathers up the papers from under the park benches." They did not say this to his face, not the boldest among them, not the ones with the most precariously nourished reputations for wit.

Then he lost the Memphis job, or quit it. One weekend he came home, and when Monday came he did not go away. After that he was downtown all day long, about the square, untalkative, dirty, with that furious and preclusive expression about the eyes which the people took for insanity: that quality of outworn violence like a scent, an odor; that fanaticism like a fading and almost extinct ember, of some kind of twofisted evangelism which had been one quarter violent conviction and three quarters physical hardihood. So they were not so surprised when they learned that he was going about the county, usually on foot, preaching in negro churches; not even when a year later they learned what his subject was. That this white man who very nearly depended on the bounty and charity of negroes for sustenance was going singlehanded into remote negro churches and interrupting the service to enter the pulpit and in his harsh, dead voice and at times with violent obscenity, preach to them humility before all skins lighter than theirs, preaching the superiority of the white race, himself his own exhibit A, in fanatic and unconscious paradox. The negroes believed that he was crazy, touched by God, or having once touched Him. They probably did not listen to, could not understand much of, what he said. Perhaps they took him to be God Himself, since God to them was a white man too and His doings also a little inexplicable.

He was downtown that afternoon when Christmas' name first flew up and down the street, and the boys and men—

the merchants, the clerks, the idle and the curious, with countrymen in overalls predominating—began to run. Hines ran too. But he could not run fast and he was not tall enough to see over the clotted shoulders when he did arrive. Nevertheless he tried, as brutal and intent as any there, to force his way into the loud surging group as though in a resurgence of the old violence which had marked his face, clawing at the backs and at last striking at them with the stick until men turned and recognised him and held him, struggling, striking at them with the heavy stick. "Christmas?" he shouted. "Did they say Christmas?"

"Christmas!" one of the men who held him cried back, his face too strained, glaring. "Christmas! That white nigger that did that killing up at Jefferson last week!"

Hines glared at the man, his toothless mouth lightly foamed with spittle. Then he struggled again, violent, cursing: a frail little old man with the light, frail bones of a child, trying to fight free with the stick, trying to club his way into the center where the captive stood bleeding about the face. "Now, Uncle Doc!" they said, holding him; "now, Uncle Doc. They got him. He cant get away. Here, now."

But he struggled and fought, cursing, his voice cracked, thin, his mouth slavering, they who held him struggling too like men trying to hold a small threshing hose in which the pressure is too great for its size. Of the entire group the captive was the only calm one. They held Hines, cursing, his old frail bones and his stringlike muscles for the time inherent with the fluid and supple fury of a weasel. He broke free of them and sprang forward, burrowing, and broke through and came face to face with the captive. Here he paused for an instant, glaring at the captive's face. It was a full pause, but before they could grasp him again he had raised the stick and struck the captive once and he was trying to strike again when they caught him at last and held him impotent and raging, with that light, thin foam about his lips. They had not stopped his mouth. "Kill the bastard!" he cried. "Kill him. Kill him."

Thirty minutes later two men brought him home in a car. One of them drove while the other held Hines up in the back seat. His face was pale now beneath the stubble and the dirt, and his eyes were closed. They lifted him bodily from the car and carried him through the gate and up the walk of rotting bricks and shards of concrete, to the steps. His eyes were open now, but they were quite empty, rolled back into his skull until the dirty, bluish whites alone showed. But he was still quite limp and helpless. Just before they reached the porch the front door opened and his wife came out and closed the door behind her and stood there, watching them. They knew that it was his wife because she came out of the house where he was known to live. One of the men, though a resident of the town, had never seen her before. "What is it?" she said.

"He's all right," the first man said. "We just been having a right smart of excitement downtown a while ago, and with this hot weather and all, it was a little too much for him." She stood before the door as if she were barring them from the house—a dumpy, fat little woman with a round face like dirty and unovened dough, and a tight screw of scant hair. "They just caught that nigger Christmas that killed that lady up at Jefferson last week," the man said. "Uncle Doc just got a little upset over it."

Mrs Hines was already turning back, as though to open the door. As the first man said later to his companion, she halted in the act of turning, as if someone had hit her lightly with a thrown pebble. "Caught who?" she said.

"Christmas," the man said. "That nigger murderer. Christmas."

She stood at the edge of the porch, looking down at them with her gray, still face. "As if she already knew what I would tell her," the man said to his companion as they returned to the car. "Like she wanted all at the same time for me to tell her it was him and it wasn't him."

"What does he look like?" she said.

"I never noticed much," the man said. "They had to bloody him up some, catching him. Young fellow. He dont look no more like a nigger than I do, either." The woman looked at them, down at them. Between the two men Hines stood on his own legs now, muttering a little now as if he were waking from sleep. "What do you want us to do with Uncle Doc?" the man said.

She did not answer that at all. It was as though she had not even recognised her husband, the man told his companion later. "What are they going to do with him?" she said.

"Him?" the man said. "Oh. The nigger. That's for Jefferson to say. He belongs to them up there."

She looked down at them, gray, still, remote. "Are they going to wait on Jefferson?"

"They?" the man said. "Oh," he said. "Well, if Jefferson aint too long about it." He shifted his grip on the old man's arm. "Where do you want us to put him?" The woman moved then. She descended the steps and approached. "We'll tote him into the house for you," the man said.

"I can tote him," she said. She and Hines were about the same height, though she was the heavier. She grasped him beneath the arms. "Eupheus," she said, not loud; "Eupheus." She said to the two men, quietly: "Let go. I got him." They released him. He walked a little now. They watched her help him up the steps and into the door. She did not look back.

"She never even thanked us," the second man said. "Maybe we ought to take him back and put him in jail with the nigger, since he seemed to know him so well."

"Eupheus," the first man said. "Eupheus. I been wondering for fifteen years what his name might be. Eupheus."

"Come on. Let's get on back. We might miss some of it."

The first man looked at the house, at the closed door through which the two people had vanished. "She knowed him too."

"Knowed who?"

"That nigger. Christmas."

"Come on." They returned to the car. "What do you think about that durn fellow, coming right into town here, within twenty miles of where he done it, walking up and down the main street until somebody recognised him. I wish it had been me that recognised him. I could have used that thousand dollars. But I never do have any luck." The car moved on. The first man was still looking back at the blank door through which the two people had disappeared.

In the hall of that little house dark and small and rankly-odored as a cave, the old couple stood. The old man's spent condition was still little better than coma, and when his wife led him to a chair and helped him into it, it seemed a matter of expediency and concern. But there was no need to return and lock the front door, which she did. She came and stood over him for a while. At first it seemed as if she were just watching him, with concern and solicitude. Then a third person would have seen that she was trembling violently and that she had lowered him into the chair either before she dropped him to the floor or in order to hold him prisoner until she could speak. She leaned above him: dumpy, obese, gray in color, with a face like that of a drowned corpse. When she spoke her voice shook and she strove with it, shaking, her hands clenched upon the arms of the chair in which he half lay, her voice shaking, restrained: "Eupheus. You listen to me. You got to listen to me. I aint worried you before. In thirty years I aint worried you. But now I am going to. I am going to know and you got to tell me. What did you do with Milly's baby?"

Through the long afternoon they clotted about the square and before the jail—the clerks, the idle, the countrymen in overalls; the talk. It went here and there about the town, dying and borning again like a wind or a fire until in the lengthening shadows the country people began to depart in wagons and dusty cars and the townspeople began to move supperward. Then the talk flared again, momentarily revived, to wives and families about supper tables in electrically lighted rooms and in remote hill cabins with kerosene lamps. And on the next day, the slow, pleasant country Sunday while they squatted in their clean shirts and decorated suspenders, with peaceful pipes about country churches or about the shady dooryards of houses where the visiting teams and cars were tethered and parked along the fence and the womenfolks were in the kitchen, getting dinner, they told it again: "He dont look any more like a nigger than I do. But it must have been the nigger blood in him. It looked like he had set out to get himself caught like a man might set out to get married. He had got clean away for a whole week. If he had not set fire to the house, they might not have found out about the murder for a month. And they would not have suspected him then if it hadn't been for a fellow named Brown, that the nigger used to sell whiskey while he was pretending to be a white man and tried to lay the whiskey and the killing both on Brown and Brown told the truth.

"Then yesterday morning he come into Mottstown in broad daylight, on a Saturday with the town full of folks. He went into a white barbershop like a white man, and because he looked like a white man they never suspected him. Even when the bootblack saw how he had on a pair of second hand brogans that were too big for him, they never suspected. They shaved him and cut his hair and he payed them and walked out and went right into a store and bought a new shirt and a tie and a straw hat, with some of the very money he stole from the woman he murdered. And then he walked the streets in broad daylight, like he owned the town, walking back and forth with people passing him a dozen times and not knowing it, until Halliday saw him and ran up and grabbed him and said, 'Aint your name Christmas?' and the nigger said that it was. He never denied it. He never did anything. He never acted like either a nigger or a white man. That was it. That was what made the folks so mad. For him to be a murderer and all dressed up and walking the town like he dared them to touch him, when he ought to have been skulking and hiding in the woods, muddy and dirty and running. It was like he never even knew he was a murderer, let alone a nigger too.

"And so Halliday (he was excited, thinking about that thousand dollars, and he had already hit the nigger a couple of times in the face, and the nigger acting like a nigger for the first time and taking it, not saying anything: just bleeding sullen and quiet)—Halliday was hollering and holding him when the old man they call Uncle Doc Hines come up and begun to hit the nigger with his walking stick until at last two men had to hold Uncle Doc quiet and took him home in a car. Nobody knew if he really did know the nigger or not. He just come hobbling up, screeching, 'Is his name Christmas? Did you say Christmas?' and shoved up and took one look at the nigger and then begun to beat him with the walking stick. He acted like he was hypnotised or something. They had to hold him, and his eyes rolling blue into his head and slobbering at the mouth and cutting with that stick at everything that come into reach, until all of a sudden he kind of flopped. Then two fellows carried him home in a car and his wife come out and took him into the house, and the two fellows come on back to town. They didn't know what was wrong with him, to get so excited after the nigger was caught, but anyway they thought that he would be all right now. But here it was not a half an hour before he was back downtown again. He was pure crazy by now, standing on the corner and yelling at whoever would pass, calling them cowards because they wouldn't take the nigger out of jail and hang him right then and there, Jefferson or no Jefferson. He looked crazy in the face, like somebody that had done slipped away from a crazy house and that knew he wouldn't have much time before they come and got him again. Folks say that he used to be a preacher, too.

"He said that he had a right to kill the nigger. He never said why, and he was too worked up and crazy to make sense even when somebody would stop him long enough to ask a question. There was a right good crowd around him by then, and him yelling about how it was his right to say first whether the nigger should live or should die. And folks were beginning to think that maybe the place for him was in the jail with the nigger, when here his wife come up.

"There are folks that have lived in Mottstown for thirty years and haven't ever seen her. They didn't know who she was then until she spoke to him, because the ones that had seen her, she was always around that little house in Niggertown where they live, in a mother hubbard and one of his woreout hats. But she was dressed up now. She had on a purple silk dress and a hat with a plume on it and she was carrying a umbrella and she come up to the crowd where he was hollering and yelling and she said, 'Eupheus.' He stopped yelling then and he looked at her, with that stick still raised in his hand and it kind of shaking, and his jaw dropped slack, slobbering. She took him by the arm. A lot of folks had been scared to come nigh him because of that stick; he looked like he might hit anybody at any minute and not even knowed it or intended it. But she walked right up under the stick and took him by the arm and led him across to where there was a chair in front of a store and she set him down in the chair and she said, 'You stay here till I come back. Dont you move, now. And you quit that yelling.'

"And he did. He sho did. He set right there where she put him, and she never looked back, neither. They all noticed that. Maybe it was because folks never saw her except around home, staying at home. And him being a kind of fierce little old man that a man wouldn't cross without he thought about it first. Anyhow they were surprised. They hadn't even thought of him taking orders from anybody.

· 333 ·

It was like she had got something on him and he had to mind her. Because he sat down when she told him to, in that chair, not hollering and talking big now, but with his head bent down and his hands shaking on that big walking stick and a little slobber still running out of his mouth, onto his shirt.

"She went straight to the jail. There was a big crowd in front of it, because Jefferson had sent word that they were on the way down to get the nigger. She walked right through them and into the jail and she said to Metcalf, 'I want to see that man they caught.'

"'What do you want to see him for?' Metcalf said.

"'I aint going to bother him,' she said. 'I just want to look at him.'

"Metcalf told her there was a right smart of other folks that wanted to do that, and that he knew she didn't aim to help him escape, but that he was just the jailer and he couldn't let anybody in without he had permission from the sheriff. And her standing there, in that purple dress and the plume not even nodding and bending, she was that still. 'Where is the sheriff?' she said.

"'He might be in his office,' Metcalf said. 'You find him and get permission from him. Then you can see the nigger.' Metcalf thought that that would finish it. So he watched her turn and go out and walk through the crowd in front of the jail and go back up the street toward the square. The plume was nodding now. He could see it nodding along above the fence. And then he saw her go across the square and in to the courthouse. The folks didn't know what she was doing, because Metcalf hadn't had time to tell them what happened at the jail. They just watched her go on into the courthouse, and then Russell said how he was in the office and he happened to look up and there that hat was with the plume on it just beyond the window across the counter. He didn't know how long she had been standing there, waiting for him to look up. He said she was just tall enough to see over the counter, so that she didn't look like she had any body at all. It just looked like somebody had sneaked up and set a toy balloon with a face painted on it and a comic hat set on top of it, like the Katzenjammer kids in the funny paper. 'I want to see the sheriff,' she says.

" 'He aint here,' Russell says. 'I'm his deputy. What can I do for you?'

"He said she didn't answer for a while, standing there. Then she said, 'Where can I find him?'

" 'He might be at home,' Russell says. 'He's been right busy, this week. Up at night some, helping those Jefferson officers. He might be home taking a nap. But maybe I can—' But he said that she was already gone. He said he looked out the window and watched her go on across the square and turn the corner toward where the sheriff lived. He said he was still trying to place her, to think who she was.

"She never found the sheriff. But it was too late then, anyway. Because the sheriff was already at the jail, only Metcalf hadn't told her, and besides she hadn't got good away from the jail before the Jefferson officers came up in two cars and went into the jail. They came up quick and went in quick. But the word had already got around that they were there, and there must have been two hundred men and boys and women too in front of the jail when the two sheriffs come out onto the porch and our sheriff made a speech, asking the folks to respect the law and that

· 335 ·

him and the Jefferson sheriff both promised that the nigger would get a quick and fair trial; and then somebody in the crowd says, 'Fair, hell. Did he give that white woman a fair trial?' And they hollered then, crowding up, like they were hollering for one another to the dead woman and not to the sheriffs. But the sheriff kept on talking quiet to them, about how it was his sworn word given to them on the day they elected him that he was trying to keep. 'I have no more sympathy with nigger murderers than any other white man here,' he says. 'But it is my sworn oath, and by God I aim to keep it. I dont want no trouble, but I aint going to dodge it. You better smoke that for a while.' And Halliday was there too, with the sheriffs. He was the foremost one about reason and not making trouble. 'Yaaah,' somebody hollers; 'we reckon you dont want him lynched. But he aint worth any thousand dollars to us. He aint worth a thousand dead matches to us.' And then the sheriff says quick: 'What if Halliday dont want him killed? Dont we all want the same thing? Here it's a local citizen that will get the reward: the money will be spent right here in Mottstown. Just suppose it was a Jefferson man was going to get it. Aint that right, men? Aint that sensible?' His voice sounded little, like a doll's voice, like even a big man's voice will sound when he is talking not against folks' listening but against their already half-made-up minds.

"Anyway, that seemed to convince them, even if folks did know that Mottstown or nowhere else was going to see enough of that thousand dollars to fat a calf, if Halliday was the one that had the spending of it. But that did it. Folks are funny. They cant stick to one way of thinking or doing anything unless they get a new reason for doing it ever so often. And then when they do get a new reason, they are liable to change anyhow. So they didn't give back exactly; it was like when before that the crowd had kind of milled from the inside out, now it begun to mill from the outside in. And the sheriffs knew it, the same as they knew that it might not last very long, because they went back into the jail quick and then came out again, almost before they had time to turn around, with the nigger between them and five or six deputies following. They must have had him ready just inside the jail door all the time, because they come out almost at once, with the nigger between them with his face sulled up and his wrists handcuffed to the Jefferson sheriff; and the crowd kind of says, 'Ahhhhhhhhhhhhh.'

"They made a kind of lane down to the street, where the first Jefferson car was waiting with the engine running and a man behind the wheel, and the sheriffs were coming along without wasting any time, when she come up again, the woman, Mrs Hines. She was shoving up through the crowd. She was so lowbuilt that all the folks could see was that plume kind of bumping along slow, like something that could not have moved very fast even if there wasn't anything in the way, and that couldn't anything stop, like a tractor. She shoved right on through and out into the lane the folks had made, right out in front of the two sheriffs with the nigger between them, so that they had to stop to keep from running over her. Her face looked like a big hunk of putty and her hat had got knocked sideways so the plume hung down in front of her face and she had to push it back to see. But she didn't do anything. She just stopped them dead for a minute while she stood there and looked at the nigger. She never said a word, like that was all she had wanted and had been worrying folks for, like that was the reason she had dressed up and come to town: just to look that nigger in the face once. Because she turned and begun to burrow back into the crowd again, and when the cars drove off with the nigger and the Jefferson law and the folks looked around, she was gone. And they went back to the square then, and Uncle Doc was gone too from the chair where she had set him and told him to wait. But all of the folks didnt go straight back to the square. A lot of them stayed there, looking at the jail like it might have been just the nigger's shadow that had come out.

"They thought that she had taken Uncle Doc home. It was in front of Dollar's store and Dollar told about how he saw her come back up the street ahead of the crowd. He said that Uncle Doc had not moved, that he was still sitting in the chair where she had left him like he was hypnotised, until she come up and touched his shoulder and he got up and they went on together with Dollar watching him. And Dollar said that from the look on Uncle Doc's face, home was where he ought to be.

"Only she never took him home. After a while folks saw that she wasn't having to take him anywhere. It was like they both wanted to do the same thing. The same thing but for different reasons, and each one knew that the other's reason was different and that whichever of them got his way, it would be serious for the other one. Like they both knew it without saying it and that each was watching the other, and that they both knew that she would have the most sense about getting them started.

"They went straight to the garage where Salmon keeps his rent car. She did all the talking. She said they wanted to go to Jefferson. Maybe they never dreamed that Salmon would charge them more than a quarter apiece, because when he said three dollars she asked him again, like maybe she could not believe her ears. 'Three dollars,' Salmon says. 'I couldn't do it for no less.' And them standing there and Uncle Doc not taking any part, like he was waiting, like it wasn't any concern of his, like he knew that he wouldn't need to bother: that she would get them there.

"'I cant pay that,' she says.

"'You wont get it done no cheaper,' Salmon says. 'Unless by the railroad. They'll take you for fiftytwo cents apiece.' But she was already going away, with Uncle Doc following her like a dog would.

"That was about four o'clock. Until six o'clock the folks saw them sitting on a bench in the courthouse yard. They were not talking: it was like each one never even knew the other one was there. They just sat there side by side, with her all dressed up in her Sunday clothes. Maybe she was enjoying herself, all dressed up and downtown all Saturday evening. Maybe it was to her what being in Memphis all day would be to other folks.

"They set there until the clock struck six. Then they got up. Folks that saw it said she never said a word to him; that they just got up at the same time like two birds do from a limb and a man cant tell which one of them give the signal. When they walked, Uncle Doc walked a little behind her. They crossed the square this way and turned into the street toward the depot. And the folks knew that there wasn't any train due for three hours and they wondered if they actually were going somewhere on the train, before they found out that they were going to do something that surprised the folks more than that, even. They went to that little café down by the depot and ate supper, that hadn't even been seen together on the street before, let alone eating in a café, since they come to Jefferson. But that's where she took him; maybe they were afraid they would miss the train if they ate downtown. Because they were there before half past six o'clock, sitting on two of them little stools at the counter, eating what she had ordered without asking Uncle Doc about it at all. She asked the café man about the train to Jefferson and he told her it went at two A.M. 'Lots of excitement in Jefferson tonight,' he says. 'You can get a car downtown and be in Jefferson in fortyfive minutes. You dont need to wait until two o'clock on that train.' He thought they were strangers maybe; he told her which way town was.

"But she didn't say anything and they finished eating and she paid him, a nickel and a dime at a time out of a tied up rag that she took out of the umbrella, with Uncle Doc setting there and waiting with that dazed look on his face like he was walking in his sleep. Then they left, and the café man thought they were going to take his advice and go to town and get that car when he looked out and saw them going on across the switch tracks, toward the depot. Once he started to call, but he didn't. 'I reckon I misunderstood her,' he says he thought. 'Maybe it's the nine o'clock southbound they want.'

"They were sitting on the bench in the waiting room when the folks, the drummers and loafers and such, begun to come in and buy tickets for the southbound. The agent said how he noticed there was some folks in the waitingroom when he come in after supper at half past seven, but that he never noticed particular until she come to the ticket window and asked what time the train left for Jefferson. He said he was busy at the time and that he just glanced up and says, 'Tomorrow,' without stopping what he was doing. Then he said that after a while something

· 340 ·

made him look up, and there was that round face watching him and that plume still in the window, and she says,

"'I want two tickets on it.'

"'That train is not due until two o'clock in the morning,' the agent says. He didn't recognise her either. 'If you want to get to Jefferson anytime soon, you'd better go to town and hire a car. Do you know which way town is?' But he said she just stood there, counting nickels and dimes out of that knotted rag, and he came and gave her the two tickets and then he looked past her through the window and saw Uncle Doc and he knew who she was. And he said how they sat there and the folks for the southbound come in and the train come and left and they still set there. He said how Uncle Doc still looked like he was asleep, or doped or something. And then the train went, but some of the folks didn't go back to town. They stayed there, looking in the window, and now and then they would come in and look at Uncle Doc and his wife setting on the bench, until the agent turned off the lights in the waitingroom.

"Some of the folks stayed, even after that. They could look in the window and see them setting there in the dark. Maybe they could see the plume, and the white of Uncle Doc's head. And then Uncle Doc begun to wake up. It wasn't like he was surprised to find where he was, nor that he was where he didn't want to be. He just roused up, like he had been coasting for a long time now, and now was the time to put on the power again. They could hear her saying 'Shhhhhh. Shhhhhhhh,' to him, and then his voice would break out. They were still setting there when the agent turned on the lights and told them that the two o'clock train was coming, with her saying 'Shhhhhh. Shhhhhhhhhh' like to a baby, and Uncle Doc hollering, 'Bitchery and abomination! Abomination and bitchery!'"

· 341 ·

.16.

WHEN his knock gets no response, Byron leaves the porch and goes around the house and enters the small, enclosed back yard. He sees the chair at once beneath the mulberry tree. It is a canvas deck chair, mended and faded and sagged so long to the shape of Hightower's body that even when empty it seems to hold still in ghostly embrace the owner's obese shapelessness; approaching, Byron thinks how the mute chair evocative of disuse and supineness and shabby remoteness from the world, is somehow the symbol and the being too of the man himself. 'That I am going to disturb again,' he thinks, with that faint lift of lip, thinking *Again? The disturbing I have done him, even he will see that that disturbing is nothing now. And on Sunday again. But then I reckon Sunday would want to take revenge on him too, being as Sunday was invented by folks*

He comes up behind the chair and looks down into it. Hightower is asleep. Upon the swell of his paunch, where the white shirt (it is a clean and fresh one now) balloons out of the worn black trousers, an open book lies face down. Upon the book Hightower's hands are folded, peaceful, benignant, almost pontifical. The shirt is made after an old fashion, with a pleated though carelessly ironed bosom, and he wears no collar. His mouth is open, the loose and flabby flesh sagging away from the round orifice in which the stained lower teeth show, and from the still fine nose which alone age, the defeat of sheer years, has not changed. Looking down at the unconscious face, it seems to Byron as though the whole man were fleeing away from the nose which holds invincibly to something yet of pride and courage above the sluttishness of vanquishment like a forgotten flag above a ruined fortress. Again light, the reflection of sky beyond the mulberry leaves, glints and glares upon the spectacle lenses, so that Byron cannot tell just when Hightower's eyes open. He sees only the mouth shut, and a movement of the folded hands as Hightower sits up. "Yes," he says; "yes? Who is— Oh, Byron."

Byron looks down at him, his face quite grave. But it is not compassionate now. It is not anything: it is just quite sober and quite determined. He says, without any inflection at all: "They caught him yesterday. I dont reckon you have heard that any more than you heard about the killing."

"Caught him?"

"Christmas. In Mottstown. He came to town, and near as I can learn, he stood around on the street until somebody recognised him."

"Caught him." Hightower is sitting up in the chair now. "And you have come to tell me that he is—that they have . . ."

"No. Aint anybody done anything to him yet. He aint dead yet. He's in the jail. He's all right."

"All right. You say that he is all right. Byron says that

· 343 ·

he is all right—Byron Bunch has helped the woman's paramour sell his friend for a thousand dollars, and Byron says that it is all right. Has kept the woman hidden from the father of her child, while that— Shall I say, other paramour, Byron? Shall I say that? Shall I refrain from the truth because Byron Bunch hides it?"

"If public talking makes truth, then I reckon that is truth. Especially when they find out that I have got both of them locked up in jail."

"Both of them?"

"Brown too. Though I reckon most folks have about decided that Brown wasn't anymore capable of doing that killing or helping in it than he was in catching the man that did do it or helping in that. But they can all say that Byron Bunch has now got him locked up safe in jail."

"Ah, yes." Hightower's voice shakes a little, high and thin. "Byron Bunch, the guardian of public weal and morality. The gainer, the inheritor of rewards, since it will now descend upon the morganatic wife of— Shall I say that too? Shall I read Byron there too?" Then he begins to cry, sitting huge and lax in the sagging chair. "I dont mean that. You know I dont. But it is not right to bother me, to worry me, when I have—when I have taught myself to stay —have been taught by them to stay— That this should come to me, taking me after I am old, and reconciled to what they deemed—" Once before Byron saw him sit while sweat ran down his face like tears; now he sees the tears themselves run down the flabby cheeks like sweat.

"I know. It's a poor thing. A poor thing to worry you. I didn't know. I didn't know, when I first got into it. Or I would have . . . But you are a man of God. You cant dodge that."

"I am not a man of God. And not through my own desire. Remember that. Not of my own choice that I am no longer a man of God. It was by the will, the more than behest, of them like you and like her and like him in the jail yonder and like them who put him there to do their will upon, as they did upon me, with insult and violence upon those who like them were created by the same God and were driven by them to do that which they now turn and rend them for having done it. It was not my choice. Remember that."

"I know that. Because a man aint given that many choices. You made your choice before that." Hightower looks at him. "You were given your choice before I was born, and you took it before I or her or him either was born. That was your choice. And I reckon them that are good must suffer for it the same as them that are bad. The same as her, and him, and me. And the same as them others, that other woman."

"That other woman? Another woman? Must my life after fifty years be violated and my peace destroyed by two lost women, Byron?"

"This other one aint lost now. She has been lost for thirty years. But she is found now. She's his grandmother."

"Whose grandmother?"

"Christmas'," Byron says.

Waiting, watching the street and the gate from the dark study window, Hightower hears the distant music when it first begins. He does not know that he expects it, that on each Wednesday and Sunday night, sitting in the dark window, he waits for it to begin. He knows almost to the second when he should begin to hear it, without recourse to watch or clock. He uses neither, has needed neither for twentyfive years now. He lives dissociated from mechanical time. Yet for that reason he has never lost it. It is as though out of his subconscious he produces without volition the few crystallizations of stated instances by which his dead life in the actual world had been governed and ordered once. Without recourse to clock he could know immediately upon the thought just where, in his old life, he would be and what doing between the two fixed moments which marked the beginning and the end of Sunday morning service and Sunday evening service and prayer service on Wednesday night; just when he would have been entering the church, just when he would have been bringing to a calculated close prayer or sermon. So before twilight has completely faded he is saying to himself *Now they are gathering, approaching along streets slowly and turning in, greeting one another: the groups, the couples, the single ones. There is a little informal talking in the church itself, lowtoned, the ladies constant and a little sibilant with fans, nodding to arriving friends as they pass in the aisle. Miss Carruthers* (she was his organist and she has been dead almost twenty years) *is among them; soon she will rise and enter the organloft* Sunday evening prayer meeting. It has seemed to him always that at that hour man approaches nearest of all to God, nearer than at any other hour of all the seven days. Then alone, of all church gatherings, is there something of that peace which is the promise and the end of the Church. The mind and the heart purged then, if it is ever to be; the week and its whatever disasters finished and summed and expiated by the stern and formal fury of the morning service; the next week and its whatever disasters not yet born, the heart quiet now for a little while beneath the cool soft blowing of faith and hope.

Sitting in the dark window he seems to see them *Now they are gathering, entering the door. They are nearly all there now* And then he begins to say, "Now. Now," leaning a little forward; and then, as though it had waited for his signal, the music begins. The organ strains come rich and resonant through the summer night, blended, sonorous, with that quality of abjectness and sublimation, as if the freed voices themselves were assuming the shapes and attitudes of crucifixions, ecstatic, solemn, and profound in gathering volume. Yet even then the music has still a quality stern and implacable, deliberate and without passion so much as immolation, pleading, asking, for not love, not life, forbidding it to others, demanding in sonorous tones death as though death were the boon, like all Protestant music. It was as though they who accepted it and raised voices to praise it within praise, having been made what they were by that which the music praised and symbolised, they took revenge upon that which made them so by means of the praise itself. Listening, he seems to hear within it the apotheosis of his own history, his own land, his own environed blood: that people from which he sprang and among whom he lives who can never take either pleasure or catastrophe or escape from either, without brawling over it. Pleasure, ecstasy, they cannot seem to bear: their escape from it is in violence, in drinking and fighting and praying; catastrophe too, the violence identical and apparently inescapable *And so why should not their religion drive them to crucifixion of themselves and one another?* he thinks. It seems to him that he can hear within the music the declaration and dedication of that which they know that on the morrow they will have to do. It seems to him that the past week has rushed like a torrent and that the week to come, which will begin tomorrow, is the abyss, and that now on the brink of cataract the stream has raised a single blended and sonorous and austere cry, not for justification but as a dying salute before its own plunge, and not to any god but to the doomed man in the barred cell within hearing of them and of the two other churches, and in whose crucifixion they too will raise a cross. 'And they will do it gladly,' he says, in the dark window. He feels his mouth and jaw muscles tauten with something premonitory, something more terrible than laughing even. 'Since to pity him would be to admit selfdoubt and to hope for and need pity themselves. They will do it gladly, gladly. That's why it is so terrible, terrible, terrible.' Then, leaning forward, he sees three people approach and turn into the gate, in silhouette now against the street lamp, among the shadows. He has already recognised Byron and he looks at the two who follow him. A woman and a man he knows them to be, yet save for the skirt which one of them wears they are almost interchangeable: of a height, and of a width which is twice that of ordinary man or woman, like two bears. He begins to laugh before he can prepare to stop it. 'If Byron just had a handkerchief about his head, and earrings,' he thinks, laughing and laughing, making no sound, trying to prepare to stop it in order to go to the door when Byron will knock.

Byron leads them into the study—a dumpy woman in a purple dress and a plume and carrying an umbrella, with a perfectly immobile face, and a man incredibly dirty and apparently incredibly old, with a tobaccostained goat's beard and mad eyes. They enter not with diffidence, but with something puppetlike about them, as if they were operated by clumsy springwork. The woman appears to be the more assured, or at least the more conscious, of the two of them. It is as though, for all her frozen and mechanically moved inertia, she had come for some definite purpose or at least with some vague hope. But he sees at once that the man is in something like coma, as though oblivious and utterly indifferent to his whereabouts, and yet withal a quality latent and explosive, paradoxically rapt and alert at the same time.

"This is her," Byron says quietly. "This is Mrs Hines."

They stand there, motionless: the woman as though she had reached the end of a long journey and now among strange faces and surroundings waits, quiet, glacierlike, like something made of stone and painted, and the calm, rapt yet latently furious and dirty old man. It is as though neither of them had so much as looked at him, with curiosity or without. He indicates chairs. Byron guides the woman, who lowers herself carefully, clutching the umbrella. The man sits at once. Hightower takes his chair beyond the desk. "What is it she wants to talk to me about?" he says.

The woman does not move. Apparently she has not heard. She is like someone who has performed an arduous journey on the strength of a promise and who now ceases completely and waits. "This is him," Byron says. "This is Reverend Hightower. Tell him. Tell him what you want him to know." She looks at Byron when he speaks, her face quite blank. If there is inarticulateness behind it, articulateness is nullified by the immobility of the face itself; if hope or yearning, neither hope nor yearning show.

"Tell him," Byron says. "Tell him why you came. What you came to Jefferson for."

"It was because—" she says. Her voice is sudden and deep, almost harsh, though not loud. It is as though she had not expected to make so much noise when she spoke; she ceases in a sort of astonishment as though at the sound of her own voice, looking from one to the other of the two faces.

"Tell me," Hightower says. "Try to tell me."

"It's because I . . ." Again the voice ceases, dies harshly though still not raised, as though of its own astonishment. It is as if the three words were some automatic impediment which her voice cannot pass; they can almost watch her marshalling herself to go around them. "I aint never seen him when he could walk," she says. "Not for thirty years I never saw him. Never once walking on his own feet and calling his own name—"

"Bitchery and abomination!" the man says suddenly. His voice is high, shrill, strong. "Bitchery and abomination!" Then he ceases. Out of his immediate and dreamlike state he shouts the three words with outrageous and prophetlike suddenness, and that is all. Hightower looks at him, and then at Byron. Byron says quietly:

"He is their daughter's child. He—" with a slight movement of the head he indicates the old man, who is now watching Hightower with his bright, mad glare—"he took it right after it was born and carried it away. She didn't know what he did with it. She never even knew if it was still alive or not until—"

The old man interrupts again, with that startling suddenness. But he does not shout this time: his voice now is as calm and logical as Byron's own. He talks clearly, just a little jerkily: "Yes. Old Doc Hines took him. God give old Doc Hines his chance and so old Doc Hines give God His chance too. So out of the mouths of little children God used His will. The little children hollering Nigger! Nigger! at him in the hearing of God and man both, showing God's will. And old Doc Hines said to God, 'But that aint enough. Them children call one another worse than nigger,' and God said, 'You wait and you watch, because I aint got the time to waste neither with this world's sluttishness and bitchery. I have put the mark on him and now I am going to put the knowledge. And I have set you there to watch and guard My will. It will be yours to tend to it and oversee.'" His voice ceases; his tone does not drop at all. His voice just stops, exactly like when the needle is lifted from a phonograph record by the hand of someone who is not listening to the record. Hightower looks from him to Byron, also almost glaring.

"What's this? What's this?" he says.

"I wanted to fix it so she could come and talk to you without him being along," Byron says. "But there wasn't anywhere to leave him. She says she has to watch him. He was trying down in Mottstown yesterday to get the folks worked up to lynch him, before he even knew what he had done."

"Lynch him?" Hightower says. "Lynch his own grandson?"

"That's what she says," Byron says levelly. "She says that's what he come up here for. And she had to come with him to keep him from doing it."

The woman speaks again. Perhaps she has been listening. But there is no more expression on her face now than when she entered; woodenfaced, she speaks again in her dead voice, with almost the suddenness of the man. "For fifty years he has been like that. For more than fifty years, but for fifty years I have suffered it. Even before we were married, he was always fighting. On the very night that Milly was born, he was locked up in jail for fighting. That's what I have bore and suffered. He said he had to fight because he is littler than most men and so folks would try to put on him. That was his vanity and his pride. But I told him it was because the devil was in him. And that some day the devil was going to come on him and him not know it until too late, and the devil was going to say, 'Eupheus Hines, I have come to collect my toll.' That's what I told him, the next day after Milly was born and me still too weak to raise my head, and him just out of jail again. I told him so: how right then God had given him a sign and a warning: that him being locked up in a jail on the very hour and minute of his daughter's birth was the Lord's own token that heaven never thought him fitten to raise a daughter. A sign from God above that town (he was a brakeman then, on the railroad) was not doing him anything but harm. And he took it so himself then, because it was a sign, and we moved away from the towns then and after a while he got to be foreman at the sawmill, doing well because he hadn't begun then to take God's name in vain and in pride to justify and excuse the devil that was in him. So when Lem Bush's wagon passed that night coming home from the circus and never stopped to let Milly out and Eupheus come back into the house and flung the things out of the drawer until he come to the postol, I said, 'Eupheus, it's the devil. It's not Milly's safety that's quicking you now,' and he said, 'Devil or no devil. Devil or no devil,' and he hit me with his hand and I laid across the bed and watched him—" She ceases. But hers is on a falling inflection, as if the machine had run down in midrecord. Again Hightower looks from her to Byron with that expression of glaring amazement.

"That's how I heard it too," Byron says. "It was hard for me to get it straight too, at first. They were living at a sawmill that he was foreman of, over in Arkansas. The gal was about eighteen then. One night a circus passed the mill, on the way to town. It was December and there had been a lot of rain, and one of the wagons broke through a bridge close to the mill and the men come to their house to wake him up and borrow some log tackle to get the wagon out—"

"It's God's abomination of womanflesh!" the old man cries suddenly. Then his voice drops, lowers; it is as though he were merely gaining attention. He talks again rapidly, his tone plausible, vague, fanatic, speaking of himself again in the third person. "He knowed. Old Doc Hines knowed. He had seen the womansign of God's abomination already on her, under her clothes. So when he went and put on his raincoat and lit the lantern and come back, she was already at the door, with a raincoat on too and he said, 'You get on back to bed,' and she said, 'I want to go too,' and he said, 'You get on back inside that room,' and she went back and he went down and got the big tackle from the mill and got the wagon out. Till nigh daybreak he worked, believing she had obeyed the command of the father the Lord had given her. But he ought to knowed. He ought to knowed God's abomination of womanflesh; he should have knowed the walking shape of bitchery and abomination already stinking in God's sight. Telling old Doc Hines, that knowed better, that he was a Mexican. When old Doc

Hines could see in his face the black curse of God Almighty. Telling him—"

"What?" Hightower says. He speaks loudly, as if he had anticipated having to drown the other's voice by sheer volume. "What is this?"

"It was a fellow with the circus," Byron says. "She told him that the man was a Mexican, the daughter told him when he caught her. Maybe that's what the fellow told the gal. But he"—again he indicates the old man—"knew somehow that the fellow had nigger blood. Maybe the circus folks told him. I dont know. He aint never said how he found out, like that never made any difference. And I reckon it didn't, after the next night."

"The next night?"

"I reckon she slipped out that night when the circus was stuck. He says she did. Anyway, he acted like it, and what he did could not have happened if he hadn't known and she hadn't slipped out. Because the next day she went in to the circus with some neighbors. He let her go, because he didn't know then that she had slipped out the night before. He didn't suspect anything even when she came out to get into the neighbor's wagon with her Sunday dress on. But he was waiting for the wagon when it came back that night, listening for it, when it came up the road and passed the house like it was not going to stop to let her out. And he ran out and called, and the neighbor stopped the wagon and the gal wasn't in it. The neighbor said that she had left them on the circus lot, to spend the night with another girl that lived about six miles away, and the neighbor wondered how Hines didn't know about it, because he said that the gal had her grip with her when she got into the wagon. Hines hadn't seen the grip. And she—" this time he indicates the stonefaced woman; she may or may not be listening to what he is saying—"she says it was the devil that guided him. She says he could not have known anymore than she did, where the gal was then, and yet he come into the house and got his pistol and knocked her down across the bed when she tried to stop him and saddled his horse and rode off. And she said he took the only short cut he could possibly have taken, choosing it in the dark, out of a half a dozen of them, that would ever have caught up with them. And yet it wasn't any possible way that he could have known which road they had taken. But he did. He found them like he had known all the time just where they would be, like him and the man that his gal told him was a Mexican had made a date to meet there. It was like he knew. It was pitch dark, and even when he caught up with a buggy, there wasn't any way he could have told it was the one he wanted. But he rode right up behind the buggy, the first buggy he had seen that night. He rode up on the right side of it and he leaned down, still in the pitch dark and without saying a word and without stopping his horse, and grabbed the man that might have been a stranger or a neighbor for all he could have known by sight or hearing. Grabbed him by one hand and held the pistol against him with the other and shot him dead and brought the gal back home behind him on the horse. He left the buggy and the man both there in the road. It was raining again, too."

He ceases. At once the woman begins to speak, as though she has been waiting with rigid impatience for Byron to cease. She speaks in the same dead, level tone: the two voices in monotonous strophe and antistrophe: two bodiless voices recounting dreamily something performed in a region without dimension by people without blood: "I laid across the bed and I heard him go out and then I heard the horse come up from the barn and pass the house, already galloping. And I laid there without undressing, watching the lamp. The oil was getting low and after a while I got up and took it back to the kitchen and filled it and cleaned the wick and then I undressed and laid down, with the lamp burning. It was still raining and it was cold too and after a while I heard the horse come back into the yard and stop at the porch and I got up and put on my shawl and I heard them come into the house. I could hear Eupheus' feet and then Milly's feet, and they come on down the hall to the door and Milly stood there with the rain on her face and her hair and her new dress all muddy and her eyes shut and then Eupheus hit her and she fell to the floor and laid there and she didn't look any different in the face than when she was standing up. And Eupheus standing in the door wet and muddy too and he said, 'You said I was at the devil's work. Well, I have brought you back the devil's laidby crop. Ask her what she is toting now inside her. Ask her.' And I was that tired, and it was cold, and I said, 'What happened?' and he said, 'Go back yonder and look down in the mud and you will see. He might have fooled her that he was a Mexican. But he never fooled me. And he never fooled her. He never had to. Because you said once that someday the devil would come down on me for his toll. Well, he has. My wife has bore me a whore. But at least he done what he could when the time come to collect. He showed me the right road and he held the pistol steady.'

"And so sometimes I would think how the devil had conquered God. Because we found out Milly was going to have a child and Eupheus started out to find a doctor that would

· 356 ·

fix it. I believed that he would find one, and sometimes I thought it would be better so, if human man and woman was to live in the world. And sometimes I hoped he would, me being that tired and all when the trial was over and the circus owner come back and said how the man really was a part nigger instead of Mexican, like Eupheus said all the time he was, like the devil had told Eupheus he was a nigger. And Eupheus would take the pistol again and say he would find a doctor or kill one, and he would go away and be gone a week at a time, and all the folks knowing it and me trying to get Eupheus to lets move away because it was just that circus man that said he was a nigger and maybe he never knew for certain, and besides he was gone too and we likely wouldn't ever see him again. But Eupheus wouldn't move, and Milly's time coming and Eupheus with that pistol, trying to find a doctor that would do it. And then I heard how he was in jail again; how he had been going to church and to prayer meeting at the different places where he would be trying to find a doctor, and how one night he got up during prayer meeting and went to the pulpit and begun to preach himself, yelling against niggers, for the white folks to turn out and kill them all, and the folks in the church made him quit and come down from the pulpit and he threatened them with the pistol, there in the church, until the law came and arrested him and him like a crazy man for a while. And they found out how he had beat up a doctor in another town and run away before they could catch him. So when he got out of jail and got back home Milly's time was about on her. And I thought then that he had give up, had seen God's will at last, because he was quiet about the house, and one day he found the clothes me and Milly had been getting ready and kept hid from him, and he never said nothing except to ask when it would be. Every day he would ask, and we thought that he had give up, that maybe going to them churches or being in jail again had reconciled him like it had on that night when Milly was born. And so the time come and one night Milly waked me and told me it had started and I dressed and told Eupheus to go for the doctor and he dressed and went out. And I got everything ready and we waited and the time when Eupheus and the doctor should have got back come and passed and Eupheus wasn't back neither and I waited until the doctor would have to get there pretty soon and then I went out to the front porch to look and I saw Eupheus setting on the top step with the shotgun across his lap and he said, 'Get back into that house, whore's dam,' and I said, 'Eupheus,' and he raised the shotgun and said, 'Get back into that house. Let the devil gather his own crop: he was the one that laid it by.' And I tried to get out the back way and he heard me and run around the house with the gun and he hit me with the barrel of it and I went back to Milly and he stood outside the hall door where he could see Milly until she died. And then he come in to the bed and looked at the baby and he picked it up and held it up, higher than the lamp, like he was waiting to see if the devil or the Lord would win. And I was that tired, setting by the bed, looking at his shadow on the wall and the shadow of his arms and the bundle high up on the wall. And then I thought that the Lord had won. But now I dont know. Because he laid the baby back on the bed by Milly and he went out. I heard him go out the front door and then I got up and built up the fire in the stove and heated some milk." She ceases; her harsh, droning voice dies. Across the desk Hightower watches her: the still, stonefaced woman in the purple dress, who has not moved since she entered the room. Then she begins to speak again, without moving, almost without lip movement, as if she were a puppet and the voice that of a ventriloquist in the next room.

"And Eupheus was gone. The man that owned the mill didn't know where he had gone to. And he got a new foreman, but he let me stay in the house a while longer because we didn't know where Eupheus was, and it coming winter and me with the baby to take care of. And I didn't know where Eupheus was any more than Mr Gillman did, until the letter came. It was from Memphis and it had a post-office moneypaper in it, and that was all. So I still didn't know. And then in November another moneypaper came, without any letter or anything. And I was that tired, and then two days before Christmas I was out in the back yard, chopping wood, and I come back into the house and the baby was gone. I hadn't been out of the house an hour, and it looked like I could have seen him when he come and went. But I didn't. I just found the letter where Eupheus had left it on the pillow that I would put between the baby and the edge of the bed so he couldn't roll off, and I was that tired. And I waited, and after Christmas Eupheus come home, and he wouldn't tell me. He just said that we were going to move, and I thought that he had already took the baby there and he had come back for me. And he wouldn't tell me where we were going to move to but it didn't take long and I was worried nigh crazy how the baby would get along until we got there and he still wouldn't tell me and it was like we wouldn't ever get there. Then we got there and the baby wasn't there and I said, 'You tell me what you have done with Joey. You got to tell me,' and he looked at me like he looked at Milly that night when she laid on the bed and died and he said, 'It's the Lord God's abomination, and I am the instrument of His will.' And he went away the next day and I didn't know where he had gone, and another moneypaper came, and the next month Eupheus come home and said he was working in Memphis. And I knew he had Joey hid somewhere in Memphis and I thought that that was something because he could be there to see to Joey even if I wasn't. And I knew that I would have to wait on Eupheus' will to know, and each time I would think that maybe next time he will take me with him to Memphis. And so I waited. I sewed and made clothes for Joey and I would have them all ready when Eupheus would come home and I would try to get him to tell me if the clothes fit Joey and if he was all right and Eupheus wouldn't tell me. He would sit and read out of the Bible, loud, without nobody there to hear it but me, reading and hollering loud out of the Bible like he believed I didn't believe what it said. But he would not tell me for five years and I never knew whether he took Joey the clothes I made or not. And I was afraid to ask, to worry at him, because it was something that he was there where Joey was, even if I wasn't. And then after five years he came home one day and he said, 'We are going to move,' and I thought that now it would be, I will see him again now; if it was a sin, I reckon we have all paid it out now, and I even forgave Eupheus. Because I thought that we were going to Memphis this time, at last. But it was not to Memphis. We come to Mottstown. We had to pass through Memphis, and I begged him. It was the first time I had ever begged him. But I did then, just for a minute, a second; not to touch him or talk to him or nothing. But

Eupheus wouldn't. We never even left the depot. We got off of one train and we waited seven hours without even leaving the depot, until the other train come, and we come to Mottstown. And Eupheus never went back to Memphis to work anymore, and after a while I said, 'Eupheus,' and he looked at me and I said, 'I done waited five years and I aint never bothered you. Cant you tell me just once if he is dead or not?' and he said, 'He is dead,' and I said, 'Dead to the living world, or just dead to me? If he is just dead to me, even. Tell me that much, because in five years I have not bothered you,' and he said, 'He is dead to you and to me and to God and to all God's world forever and ever more.'"

She ceases again. Beyond the desk Hightower watches her with that quiet and desperate amazement. Byron too is motionless, his head bent a little. The three of them are like three rocks above a beach, above ebbtide, save the old man. He has been listening now, almost attentively, with that ability of his to flux instantaneously between complete attention that does not seem to hear, and that comalike bemusement in which the stare of his apparently inverted eye is as uncomfortable as though he held them with his hand. He cackles, suddenly, bright, loud, mad; he speaks, incredibly old, incredibly dirty. "It was the Lord. *He* was there. Old Doc Hines give God His chance too. The Lord told old Doc Hines what to do and old Doc Hines done it. Then the Lord said to old Doc Hines, 'You watch, now. Watch My will a-working.' And old Doc Hines watched and heard the mouths of little children, of God's own fatherless and motherless, putting His words and knowledge into their mouths even when they couldn't know it since they were without sin yet, even the girl ones without sin and bitchery yet: Nigger! Nigger! in the innocent mouths of little children. 'What did I tell you?' God said to old Doc Hines. 'And now I've set My will to working and now I'm gone. There aint enough sin here to keep Me busy because what do I care for the fornications of a slut, since that is a part of My purpose too,' and old Doc Hines said, 'How is the fornications of a slut a part of Your purpose too?' and God said, 'You wait and see. Do you think it is just chanceso that I sent that young doctor to be the one that found My abomination laying wrapped in that blanket on that doorstep that Christmas night? Do you think it was just chanceso that the Madam should have been away that night and give them young sluts the chance and call to name him Christmas in sacrilege of My son? So I am gone now, because I have set My will a-working and I can leave you here to watch it.' So old Doc Hines he watched and he waited. From God's own boiler room he watched them children, and the devil's walking seed unbeknownst among them, polluting the earth with the working of that word on him. Because he didn't play with the other children no more now. He stayed by himself, standing still, and then old Doc Hines knew that he was listening to the hidden warning of God's doom, and old Doc Hines said to him, 'Why dont you play with them other children like you used to?' and he didn't say nothing and old Doc Hines said, 'Is it because they call you nigger?' and he didn't say nothing and old Doc Hines said, 'Do you think you are a nigger because God has marked your face?' and he said, 'Is God a nigger too?' and old Doc Hines said, 'He is the Lord God of wrathful hosts, His will be done. Not yours and not mine, because you and me are both a part of His purpose and His vengeance.' And he went away and old Doc Hines watched him hearing and listening to the vengeful will of the Lord, until old Doc Hines found out how he was watching the nigger working in the yard, following him around the yard while he worked, until at last the nigger said, 'What you watching me for, boy?' and he said, 'How come you are a nigger?' and the nigger said, 'Who told you I am a nigger, you little white trash bastard?' and he says, 'I aint a nigger,' and the nigger says, 'You are worse than that. You dont know what you are. And more than that, you wont never know. You'll live and you'll die and you wont never know,' and he says, 'God aint no nigger,' and the nigger says, 'I reckon you ought to know what God is, because dont nobody but God know what you is.' But God wasn't there to say, because He had set His will to working and left old Doc Hines to watch it. From that very first night, when He had chose His own Son's sacred anniversary to set it a-working on, He set old Doc Hines to watch it. It was cold that night, and old Doc Hines standing in the dark just behind the corner where he could see the doorstep and the accomplishment of the Lord's will, and he saw that young doctor coming in lechery and fornication stop and stoop down and raise the Lord's abomination and tote it into the house. And old Doc Hines he followed and he seen and heard. He watched them young sluts that was desecrating the Lord's sacred anniversary with eggnog and whiskey in the Madam's absence, open the blanket. And it was her, the Jezebel of the doctor, that was the Lord's instrument, that said, 'We'll name him Christmas,' and another one said, 'What Christmas. Christmas what,' and God said to old Doc Hines, 'Tell them,' and they all looked at old Doc Hines with the reek of pollution on them, hollering, 'Why, it's Uncle Doc. Look what Santa Claus

brought us and left on the doorstep, Uncle Doc,' and old
Doc Hines said, 'His name is Joseph,' and they quit laughing and they looked at old Doc Hines and the Jezebel said,
'How do you know?' and old Doc Hines said, 'The Lord
says so,' and then they laughed again, hollering, 'It is so in
the Book: Christmas, the son of Joe. Joe, the son of Joe.
Joe Christmas,' they said, 'To Joe Christmas,' and they tried
to make old Doc Hines drink too, to the Lord's abomination, but he struck the cup aside. And he just had to watch
and to wait, and he did and it was in the Lord's good time,
for evil to come from evil. And the doctor's Jezebel come
running from her lustful bed, still astink with sin and fear.
'He was hid behind the bed,' she says, and old Doc Hines
said, 'You used that perfumed soap that tempted your own
undoing, for the Lord's abomination and outrage. Suffer it,'
and she said, 'You can talk to him. I have seen you. You
could persuade him,' and old Doc Hines said, 'I care no
more for your fornications than God does,' and she said,
'He will tell and I will be fired. I will be disgraced.' Stinking with her lust and lechery she was then, standing before old Doc Hines with the working of God's will on her
that minute, who had outraged the house where God
housed His fatherless and motherless. 'You aint nothing,'
old Doc Hines said. 'You and all sluts. You are a instrument of God's wrathful purpose that nere a sparrow can fall
to earth. You are a instrument of God, the same as Joe
Christmas and old Doc Hines.' And she went away and
old Doc Hines he waited and he watched and it wasn't
long before she come back and her face was like the face
of a ravening beast of the desert. 'I fixed him,' she said, and
old Doc Hines said, 'How fixed him,' because it was not
anything that old Doc Hines didn't know because the Lord

did not keep His purpose hid from His chosen instrument, and old Doc Hines said, 'You have served the foreordained will of God. You can go now and abominate Him in peace until the Day,' and her face looked like the ravening beast of the desert, laughing out of her rotten colored dirt at God. And they come and took him away. Old Doc Hines saw him go away in the buggy and he went back to wait for God and God come and He said to old Doc Hines, 'You can go too now. You have done My work. There is no more evil here now but womanevil, not worthy for My chosen instrument to watch.' And old Doc Hines went when God told him to go. But he kept in touch with God and at night he said, 'That bastard, Lord,' and God said, 'He is still walking My earth,' and old Doc Hines kept in touch with God and at night he said, 'That bastard, Lord,' and God said, 'He is still walking My earth,' and old Doc Hines kept in touch with God and one night he wrestled and he strove and he cried aloud, 'That bastard, Lord! I feel! I feel the teeth and the fangs of evil!' and God said, 'It's that bastard. Your work is not done yet. He's a pollution and a abomination on My earth.'"

The sound of music from the distant church has long since ceased. Through the open window there comes now only the peaceful and myriad sounds of the summer night. Beyond the desk Hightower sits, looking more than ever like an awkward beast tricked and befooled of the need for flight, brought now to bay by those who tricked and fooled it. The other three sit facing him; almost like a jury. Two of them are also motionless, the woman with that stone-visaged patience of a waiting rock, the old man with a spent quality like a charred wick of a candle from which the flame has been violently blown away. Byron alone seems to possess life. His face is lowered. He seems to muse upon one hand which lies upon his lap, the thumb and forefinger of which rub slowly together with a kneading motion while he appears to watch with musing absorption. When Hightower speaks, Byron knows that he is not addressing him, not addressing anyone in the room at all. "What do they want me to do?" he says. "What do they think, hope, believe, that I can do?"

Then there is no sound; neither the man nor the woman have heard, apparently. Byron does not expect the man to hear. 'He dont need any help,' he thinks. 'Not him. It's hindrance he needs'; thinking remembering the comastate of dreamy yet maniacal suspension in which the old man had moved from place to place a little behind the woman since he had met them twelve hours ago. 'It's hindrance he needs. I reckon it's a good thing for more folks than her that he is wellnigh helpless.' He is watching the woman. He says quietly, almost gently: "Go on. Tell him what you want. He wants to know what you want him to do. Tell him."

"I thought maybe—" she says. She speaks without stirring. Her voice is not tentative so much as rusty, as if it were being forced to try to say something outside the province of being said aloud, of being anything save felt, known. "Mr Bunch said that maybe—"

"What?" Hightower says. He speaks sharply, impatiently, his voice a little high; he too has not moved, sitting back in the chair, his hands upon the armrests. "What? That what?"

"I thought . . ." The voice dies again. Beyond the window the steady insects whirr. Then the voice goes on, flat,

. 366 .

toneless, she sitting also with her head bent a little, as if she too listened to the voice with the same quiet intentness: "He is my grandson, my girl's little boy. I just thought that if I . . . if he . . ." Byron listens quietly, thinking *It's right funny. You'd think they had done got swapped somewhere. Like it was him that had a nigger grandson waiting to be hung* The voice goes on. "I know it aint right to bother a stranger. But you are lucky. A bachelor, a single man that could grow old without the despair of love. But I reckon you couldn't never see it even if I could tell it right. I just thought that maybe if it could be for one day like it hadn't happened. Like folks never knew him as a man that had killed . . ." The voice ceases again. She has not stirred. It is as though she listened to it cease as she listened to it begin, with the same interest, the same quiet unastonishment.

"Go on," Hightower says, in that high impatient voice; "go on."

"I never saw him when he could walk and talk. Not for thirty years I never saw him. I am not saying he never did what they say he did. Ought not to suffer for it like he made them that loved and lost suffer. But if folks could maybe just let him for one day. Like it hadn't happened yet. Like the world never had anything against him yet. Then it could be like he had just went on a trip and grew man grown and come back. If it could be like that for just one day. After that I would not interfere. If he done it, I would not be the one to come between him and what he must suffer. Just for one day, you see. Like he had been on a trip and come back, telling me about the trip, without any living earth against him yet."

"Oh," Hightower says, in his shrill, high voice. Though

he has not moved, though the knuckles of the hands which grip the chairarms are taut and white, there begins to emerge from beneath his clothing a slow and repressed quivering. "Ah, yes," he says. "That's all. That's simple. Simple. Simple." Apparently he cannot stop saying it. "Simple. Simple." He has been speaking in a low tone; now his voice rises. "What is it they want me to do? What must I do now? Byron! Byron? What is it? What are they asking of me now?" Byron has risen. He now stands beside the desk, his hands on the desk, facing Hightower. Still Hightower does not move save for that steadily increasing quivering of his flabby body. "Ah, yes. I should have known. It will be Byron who will ask it. I should have known. That will be reserved for Byron and for me. Come, come. Out with it. Why do you hesitate now?"

Byron looks down at the desk, at his hands upon the desk. "It's a poor thing. A poor thing."

"Ah. Commiseration? After this long time? Commiseration for me, or for Byron? Come; out with it. What do you want me to do? For it is you: I know that. I have known that all along. Ah, Byron, Byron. What a dramatist you would have made."

"Or maybe you mean a drummer, a agent, a salesman," Byron says. "It's a poor thing. I know that. You dont need to tell me."

"But I am not clairvoyant, like you. You seem to know already what I could tell you, yet you will not tell me what you intend for me to know. What is it you want me to do? Shall I go plead guilty to the murder? Is that it?"

Byron's face cracks with that grimace faint, fleeting, sardonic, weary, without mirth. "It's next to that, I reckon." Then his face sobers; it is quite grave. "It's a poor thing to ask. God knows I know that." He watches his slow hand where it moves, preoccupied and trivial, upon the desk top. "I mind how I said to you once that there is a price for being good the same as for being bad; a cost to pay. And it's the good men that cant deny the bill when it comes around. They cant deny it for the reason that there aint any way to make them pay it, like a honest man that gambles. The bad men can deny it; that's why dont anybody expect them to pay on sight or any other time. But the good cant. Maybe it takes longer to pay for being good than for being bad. And it wont be like you haven't done it before, haven't already paid a bill like it once before. It oughtn't to be so bad now as it was then."

"Go on. Go on. What is it I am to do?"

Byron watches his slow and ceaseless hand, musing. "He aint never admitted that he killed her. And all the evidence they got against him is Brown's word, which is next to none. You could say he was here with you that night. Every night when Brown said he watched him go up to the big house and go in it. Folks would believe you. They would believe that, anyway. They would rather believe that about you than to believe that he lived with her like a husband and then killed her. And you are old now. They wouldn't do anything to you about it that would hurt you now. And I reckon you are used to everything else they can do."

"Oh," Hightower says. "Ah. Yes. Yes. They would believe it. That would be very simple, very good. Good for all. Then he will be restored to them who have suffered because of him, and Brown without the reward could be scared into making her child legitimate and then into fleeing again and forever this time. And then it would be just her and Byron. Since I am just an old man who has been fortunate enough to grow old without having to learn the despair of love." He is shaking, steadily; he looks up now. In the lamplight his face looks slick, as if it had been oiled. Wrung and twisted, it gleams in the lamplight; the yellowed, oftwashed shirt which was fresh this morning is damp with sweat. "It's not because I cant, dont dare to," he says; "it's because I wont! I wont! do you hear?" He raises his hands from the chairarms. "It's because I wont do it!" Byron does not move. His hand on the desk top has ceased; he watches the other, thinking *It aint me he is shouting at. It's like he knows there is something nearer him than me to convince of that* Because now Hightower is shouting, "I wont do it! I wont!" with his hands raised and clenched, his face sweating, his lip lifted upon his clenched and rotting teeth from about which the long sagging of flabby and puttycolored flesh falls away. Suddenly his voice rises higher yet. "Get out!" he screams. "Get out of my house! Get out of my house!" Then he falls forward, onto the desk, his face between his extended arms and his clenched fists. As, the two old people moving ahead of him, Byron looks back from the door, he sees that Hightower has not moved, his bald head and his extended and clench-fisted arms lying full in the pool of light from the shaded lamp. Beyond the open window the sound of insects has not ceased, not faltered.

. 17 .

THAT was Sunday night. Lena's child was born the next morning. It was just dawn when Byron stopped his galloping mule before the house which he had quitted not six hours ago. He sprang to the ground already running, and ran up the narrow walk toward the dark porch. He seemed to stand aloof and watch himself, for all his haste, thinking with a kind of grim unsurprise: 'Byron Bunch borning a baby. If I could have seen myself now two weeks ago, I would not have believed my own eyes. I would have told them that they lied.'

The window was dark now beyond which six hours ago he had left the minister. Running, he thought of the bald head, the clenched hands, the prone flabby body sprawled across the desk. 'But I reckon he has not slept much,' he thought. 'Even if he aint playing—playing—' He could not think of the word midwife, which he knew that Hightower would use. 'I reckon I dont have to think of it,' he thought. 'Like a fellow running from or toward a gun aint got time to worry whether the word for what he is doing is courage or cowardice.'

The door was not locked. Apparently he knew that it would not be. He felt his way into the hall, not quiet, not attempting to be. He had never been deeper into the house than the room where he had last seen the owner of it sprawled across the desk in the full downglare of the lamp. Yet he went almost as straight to the right door as if he knew, or could see, or were being led. 'That's what he'd call it,' he thought, in the fumbling and hurried dark. 'And she would too.' He meant Lena, lying yonder in the cabin, already beginning to labor. 'Only they would both have a different name for whoever did the leading.' He could hear Hightower snoring now, before he entered the room. 'Like he aint so much upset, after all,' he thought. Then he thought immediately: 'No. That aint right. That aint just. Because I dont believe that. I know that the reason he is asleep and I aint asleep is that he is an old man and he cant stand as much as I can stand.'

He approached the bed. The still invisible occupant snored profoundly. There was a quality of profound and complete surrender in it. Not of exhaustion, but surrender, as though he had given over and relinquished completely that grip upon that blending of pride and hope and vanity and fear, that strength to cling to either defeat or victory, which is the I-Am, and the relinquishment of which is usually death. Standing beside the bed Byron thought again *A poor thing. A poor thing* It seemed to him now that to wake the man from that sleep would be the sorest injury which he had ever done him. 'But it aint me that's waiting,' he thought. 'God knows that. Because I reckon He has been watching me too lately, like the rest of them, to see what I will do next.'

He touched the sleeper, not roughly, but firmly. Hightower ceased in midsnore; beneath Byron's hand he surged hugely and suddenly up. "Yes?" he said. "What? Who is it? Who is there?"

"It's me," Byron said. "It's Byron again. Are you awake now?"

"Yes. What—"

"Yes," Byron said. "She says it's about due now. That the time has come."

"She?"

"Tell me where the light . . . Mrs Hines. She is out there. I am going on for the doctor. But it may take some time. So you can take my mule. I reckon you can ride that far. Have you still got your book?"

The bed creaked as Hightower moved. "Book? My book?"

"The book you used when that nigger baby came. I just wanted to remind you in case you would need to take it with you. In case I dont get back with the doctor in time. The mule is out at the gate. He knows the way. I will walk on to town and get the doctor. I'll get back out there as soon as I can." He turned and recrossed the room. He could hear, feel, the other sitting up in the bed. He paused in the middle of the floor long enough to find the suspended light and turn it on. When it came on he was already moving on toward the door. He did not look back. Behind him he heard Hightower's voice:

"Byron! Byron!" He didn't pause, didn't answer.

Dawn was increasing. He walked rapidly along the empty street, beneath the spaced and failing street lamps about which bugs still whirled and blundered. But day was growing; when he reached the square the façade of its eastern side was in sharp relief against the sky. He was thinking rapidly. He had made no arrangement with a doctor. Now as he walked he was cursing himself in all the mixed terror and rage of any actual young father for what he now believed to have been crass and criminal negligence. Yet it was not exactly the solicitude of an incipient father. There was something else behind it, which he was not to recognise until later. It was as though there lurked in his mind, still obscured by the need for haste, something which was about to spring full clawed upon him. But what he was thinking was, 'I got to decide quick. He delivered that nigger baby all right, they said. But this is different. I ought to done it last week, seen ahead about a doctor instead of waiting, having to explain now, at the last minute, hunt from house to house until I find one that will come, that will believe the lies that I will have to tell. I be dog if it dont look like a man that has done as much lying lately as I have could tell a lie now that anybody would believe, man or woman. But it dont look like I can. I reckon it just aint in me to tell a good lie and do it well.' He walked rapidly, his footsteps hollow and lonely in the empty street; already his decision was made, without his even being aware of it. To him there was nothing either of paradox or of comedy about it. It had entered his mind too quickly and was too firmly established there when he became aware of it; his feet were already obeying it. They were taking him to the home of the same doctor who had arrived too late at the delivery of the negro child at which Hightower had officiated with his razor and his book.

The doctor arrived too late this time, also. Byron had to wait for him to dress. He was an oldish man now, and fussy, and somewhat disgruntled at having been wakened at this hour. Then he had to hunt for the switch key to his car, which he kept in a small metal strong box, the key to which in turn he could not find at once. Neither would he allow Byron to break the lock. So when they reached the cabin at last the east was primrosecolor and there was already a hint of the swift sun of summer. And again the two men, both older now, met at the door of a one-room cabin, the professional having lost again to the amateur, for as he entered the door, the doctor heard the infant cry. The doctor blinked at the minister, fretfully. "Well, doctor," he said, "I wish Byron had told me he had already called you in. I'd still be in bed." He thrust past the minister, entering. "You seem to have had better luck this time than you did the last time we consulted. Only you look about like you need a doctor yourself. Or maybe it's a cup of coffee you need." Hightower said something, but the doctor had gone on, without stopping to listen. He entered the room, where a young woman whom he had never seen before lay wan and spent on a narrow army cot, and an old woman in a purple dress whom he had also never seen before, held the child upon her lap. There was an old man asleep on a second cot in the shadow. When the doctor noticed him, he said to himself that the man looked like he was dead, so profoundly and peacefully did he sleep. But the doctor did not notice the old man at once. He went to the old woman who held the child. "Well, well," he said. "Byron must have been excited. He never told me the whole family would be on hand, grandpa and grandma too." The woman looked up at him. He thought, 'She looks about as much alive as he does, for all she is sitting up. Dont look like she has got enough gumption to know she is even a parent, let alone a grandparent.'

"Yes," the woman said. She looked up at him, crouching

over the child. Then he saw that her face was not stupid, vacuous. He saw that at the same time it was both peaceful and terrible, as though the peace and the terror had both died long ago and come to live again at the same time. But he remarked mainly her attitude at once like a rock and like a crouching beast. She jerked her head at the man; for the first time the doctor looked full at him where he lay sleeping upon the other cot. She said in a whisper at once cunning and tense with fading terror: "I fooled him. I told him you would come in the back way this time. I fooled him. But now you are here. You can see to Milly now. I'll take care of Joey." Then this faded. While he watched, the life, the vividness, faded, fled suddenly from a face that looked too still, too dull to ever have harbored it; now the eyes questioned him with a gaze dumb, inarticulate, baffled as she crouched over the child as if he had offered to drag it from her. Her movement roused it perhaps; it cried once. Then the bafflement too flowed away. It fled as smoothly as a shadow; she looked down at the child, musing, wooden faced, ludicrous. "It's Joey," she said. "It's my Milly's little boy."

And Byron, outside the door where he had stopped as the doctor entered, heard that cry and something terrible happened to him. Mrs Hines had called him from his tent. There was something in her voice so that he put on his trousers as he ran almost, and he passed Mrs Hines, who had not undressed at all, in the cabin door and ran into the room. Then he saw her and it stopped him dead as a wall. Mrs Hines was at his elbow, talking to him; perhaps he answered, talked back. Anyway he had saddled the mule and was already galloping toward town while he still seemed to be looking at her, at her face as she lay raised on her propped arms on the cot, looking down at the shape of her body beneath the sheet with wailing and hopeless terror. He saw that all the time he was waking Hightower, all the time he was getting the doctor started, while somewhere in him the clawed thing lurked and waited and thought was going too fast to give him time to think. That was it. Thought too swift for thinking, until he and the doctor returned to the cabin. And then, just outside the cabin door where he had stopped, he heard the child cry once and something terrible happened to him.

He knew now what it was that seemed to lurk clawed and waiting while he crossed the empty square, seeking the doctor whom he had neglected to engage. He knew now why he neglected to engage a doctor beforehand. It is because he did not believe until Mrs Hines called him from his tent that he (she) would need one, would have the need. It was like for a week now his eyes had accepted her belly without his mind believing. 'Yet I did know, believe,' he thought. 'I must have knowed, to have done what I have done: the running and the lying and the worrying at folks.' But he saw now that he did not believe until he passed Mrs Hines and looked into the cabin. When Mrs Hines' voice first came into his sleeping, he knew what it was, what had happened; he rose and put on, like a pair of hurried overalls, the need for haste, knowing why, knowing that for five nights now he had been expecting it. Yet still he did not believe. He knew now that when he ran to the cabin and looked in, he expected to see her sitting up; perhaps to be met by her at the door, placid, unchanged, timeless. But even as he touched the door with his hand he heard something which he had never heard before. It was a moaning wail, loud, with a quality at once passionate and abject, that seemed to be speaking clearly to something in a tongue which he knew was not his tongue nor that of any man. Then he passed Mrs Hines in the door and he saw her lying on the cot. He had never seen her in bed before and he believed that when or if he ever did, she would be tense, alert, maybe smiling a little, and completely aware of him. But when he entered she did not even look at him. She did not even seem to be aware that the door had opened, that there was anyone or anything in the room save herself and whatever it was that she had spoken to with that wailing cry in a tongue unknown to man. She was covered to the chin, yet her upper body was raised upon her arms and her head was bent. Her hair was loose and her eyes looked like two holes and her mouth was as bloodless now as the pillow behind her, and as she seemed in that attitude of alarm and surprise to contemplate with a kind of outraged unbelief the shape of her body beneath the covers, she gave again that loud, abject, wailing cry. Mrs Hines was now bending over her. She turned her head, that wooden face, across her purple shoulder. "Get," she said. "Get for the doctor. It's come now."

He did not remember going to the stable at all. Yet there he was, catching his mule, dragging the saddle out and clapping it on. He was working fast, yet thinking went slow enough. He knew why now. He knew now that thinking went slow and smooth with calculation, as oil is spread slowly upon a surface above a brewing storm. 'If I had known then,' he thought. 'If I had known then. If it had got through then.' He thought this quietly, in aghast despair, regret. 'Yes. I would have turned my back and rode the other way. Beyond the knowing and memory of man forever and ever I reckon I would have rode.' But he did not. He passed the cabin at a gallop, with thinking going smooth and steady, he not yet knowing why. 'If I can just get past and out of hearing before she hollers again,' he thought. 'If I can just get past before I have to hear her again.' That carried him for a while, into the road, the hard-muscled small beast going fast now, thinking, the oil, spreading steady and smooth: 'I'll go to Hightower first. I'll leave the mule for him. I must remember to remind him about his doctor book. I mustn't forget that,' the oil said, getting him that far, to where he sprang from the still running mule ánd into Hightower's house. Then he had something else. 'Now that's done,' thinking *Even if I cant get a regular doctor* That got him to the square and then betrayed him; he could feel it, clawed with lurking, thinking *Even if I dont get a regular doctor. Because I have never believed that I would need one. I didn't believe* It was in his mind, galloping in yoked and headlong paradox with the need for haste while he helped the old doctor hunt for the key to the strongbox in order to get the switch key for the car. They found it at last, and for a time the need for haste went hand in hand with movement, speed, along the empty road beneath the empty dawn—that, or he had surrendered all reality, all dread and fear, to the doctor beside him, as. people do. Anyway it got him back to the cabin, where the two of them left the car and approached the cabin door, beyond which the lamp still burned: for that interval he ran in the final hiatus of peace before the blow fell and the clawed thing overtook him from behind. Then he heard the child cry. Then he knew. Dawn was making fast. He stood quietly in the chill peace, the waking quiet—small, nondescript, whom no man or woman had ever turned to look at twice anywhere. He knew now that

there had been something all the while which had protected him against believing, with the believing protected
him. With stern and austere astonishment he thought *It
was like it was not until Mrs Hines called me and I heard
her and saw her face and knew that Byron Bunch was
nothing in this world to her right then, that I found out
that she is not a virgin* And he thought that that was terrible, but that was not all. There was something else. His
head was not bowed. He stood quite still in the augmenting dawn, while thinking went quietly *And this too is
reserved for me, as Reverend Hightower says. I'll have to
tell him now. I'll have to tell Lucas Burch* It was not unsurprise now. It was something like the terrible and irremediable despair of adolescence *Why, I didn't even believe
until now that he was so. It was like me, and her, and all
the other folks that I had to get mixed up in it, were just
a lot of words that never even stood for anything, were not
even us, while all the time what was us was going on and
going on without even missing the lack of words. Yes. It
aint until now that I ever believed that he is Lucas Burch.
That there ever was a Lucas Burch*

'Luck,' Hightower says; 'luck. I dont know whether I
had it or not.' But the doctor has gone on into the cabin.
Looking back for another moment, Hightower watches the
group about the cot, hearing still the doctor's cheery voice.
The old woman now sits quietly, yet looking back at her
it seems but a moment ago that he was struggling with her
for the child, lest she drop it in her dumb and furious terror. But no less furious for being dumb it was as, the child
snatched almost from the mother's body, she held it high
aloft, her heavy, bearlike body crouching as she glared at

the old man asleep on the cot. He was sleeping so when Hightower arrived. He did not seem to breathe at all, and beside the cot the woman was crouching in a chair when he entered. She looked exactly like a rock poised to plunge over a precipice, and for an instant Hightower thought *She has already killed him. She has taken her precautions well beforehand this time* Then he was quite busy; the old woman was at his elbow without his being aware of it until she snatched the still unbreathing child and held it aloft, glaring at the old sleeping man on the other cot with the face of a tiger. Then the child breathed and cried, and the woman seemed to answer it, also in no known tongue, savage and triumphant. Her face was almost maniacal as he struggled with her and took the child from her before she dropped it. "See," he said. "Look! He's quiet. He's not going to take it away this time." Still she glared at him, dumb, beastlike, as though she did not understand English. But the fury, the triumph, had gone from her face: she made a hoarse, whimpering noise, trying to take the child from him. "Careful, now," he said. "Will you be careful?" She nodded, whimpering, pawing lightly at the child. But her hands were steady, and he let her have it. And she now sits with it upon her lap while the doctor who had arrived too late stands beside the cot, talking in his cheerful, testy voice while his hands are busy. Hightower turns and goes out, lowering himself carefully down the broken step, to the earth like an old man, as if there were something in his flabby paunch fatal and highly keyed, like dynamite. It is now more than dawn; it is morning: already the sun. He looks about, pausing; he calls: "Byron." There is no answer. Then he sees that the mule, which he had tethered to a fence post nearby, is also gone. He sighs. 'Well,' he thinks. 'So I have reached the point where the crowning in-dignity which I am to suffer at Byron's hands is a two-mile walk back home. That's not worthy of Byron, of hatred. But so often our deeds are not. Nor we of our deeds.'

He walks back to town slowly—a gaunt, paunched man in a soiled panama hat and the tail of a coarse cotton night-shirt thrust into his black trousers. 'Luckily I did take time to put on my shoes,' he thinks. 'I am tired,' he thinks, fret-fully. 'I am tired, and I shall not be able to sleep.' He is thinking it fretfully, wearily, keeping time to his feet when he turns into his gate. The sun is now high, the town has wakened; he smells the smoke here and there of cooking breakfasts. 'The least thing he could have done,' he thinks, 'since he would not leave me the mule, would have been to ride ahead and start a fire in my stove for me. Since he thinks it better for my appetite to take a two-mile stroll be-fore eating.'

He goes to the kitchen and builds a fire in the stove, slowly, clumsily; as clumsily after twentyfive years as on the first day he had ever attempted it, and puts coffee on. 'Then I'll go back to bed,' he thinks. 'But I know I shall not sleep.' But he notices that his thinking sounds queru-lous, like the peaceful whining of a querulous woman who is not even listening to herself; then he finds that he is pre-paring his usual hearty breakfast, and he stops quite still, clicking his tongue as though in displeasure. 'I ought to feel worse than I do,' he thinks. But he has to admit that he does not. And as he stands, tall, misshapen, lonely in his lonely and illkept kitchen, holding in his hand an iron skillet in which yesterday's old grease is bleakly caked, there goes through him a glow, a wave, a surge of something almost hot, almost triumphant. 'I showed them!' he thinks.

'Life comes to the old man yet, while they get there too late. They get there for his leavings, as Byron would say.' But this is vanity and empty pride. Yet the slow and fading glow disregards it, impervious to reprimand. He thinks, 'What if I do? What if I do feel it? triumph and pride? What if I do?' But the warmth, the glow, evidently does not regard or need buttressing either; neither is it quenched by the actuality of an orange and eggs and toast. And he looks down at the soiled and empty dishes on the table and he says, aloud now: "Bless my soul. I'm not even going to wash them now." Neither does he go to his bedroom to try to sleep. He goes to the door and looks in, with that glow of purpose and pride, thinking, 'If I were a woman, now. That's what a woman would do: go back to bed to rest.' He goes to the study. He moves like a man with a purpose now, who for twentyfive years has been doing nothing at all between the time to wake and the time to sleep again. Neither is the book which he now chooses the Tennyson: this time also he chooses food for a man. It is *Henry IV* and he goes out into the back yard and lies down in the sagging deck chair beneath the mulberry tree, plumping solidly and heavily into it. 'But I shant be able to sleep,' he thinks, 'because Byron will be in soon to wake me. But to learn just what else he can think of to want me to do, will be almost worth the waking.'

He goes to sleep soon, almost immediately, snoring. Anyone pausing to look down into the chair would have seen, beneath the twin glares of sky in the spectacles, a face innocent, peaceful, and assured. But no one comes, though when he wakes almost six hours later, he seems to believe that someone has called him. He sits up abruptly, the chair creaking beneath him. "Yes?" he says. "Yes? What is it?"

But there is no one there, though for a moment longer he looks about, seeming to listen and to wait, with that air forceful and assured. And the glow is not gone either. 'Though I had hoped to sleep it off,' he thinks, thinking at once, 'No. I dont mean *hoped*. What is in my thought is *feared*. And so I have surrendered too,' he thinks, quiet, still. He begins to rub his hands, gently at first, a little guiltily. 'I have surrendered too. And I will permit myself. Yes. Perhaps this too is reserved for me. And so I shall permit myself.' And then he says it, thinks it *That child that I delivered. I have no namesake. But I have known them before this to be named by a grateful mother for the doctor who officiated. But then, there is Byron. Byron of course will take the pas of me. She will have to have others, more* remembering the young strong body from out whose travail even there shone something tranquil and unafraid. *More of them. Many more. That will be her life, her destiny. The good stock peopling in tranquil obedience to it the good earth; from these hearty loins without hurry or haste descending mother and daughter. But by Byron engendered next. Poor boy. Even though he did let me walk back home*

He enters the house. He shaves and removes the nightshirt and puts on the shirt which he had worn yesterday, and a collar and the lawn tie and the panama hat. The walk out to the cabin does not take him as long as the walk home did, even though he goes now through the woods where the walking is harder. 'I must do this more often,' he thinks, feeling the intermittent sun, the heat, smelling the savage and fecund odor of the earth, the woods, the loud silence. 'I should never have lost this habit, too. But perhaps they will both come back to me, if this itself be not the same as prayer.'

He emerges from the woods at the far side of the pasture behind the cabin. Beyond the cabin he can see the clump of trees in which the house had stood and burned, though from here he cannot see the charred and mute embers of what were once planks and beams. 'Poor woman,' he thinks. 'Poor, barren woman. To have not lived only a week longer, until luck returned to this place. Until luck and life returned to these barren and ruined acres.' It seems to him that he can see, feel, about him the ghosts of rich fields, and of the rich fecund black life of the quarters, the mellow shouts, the presence of fecund women, the prolific naked children in the dust before the doors; and the big house again, noisy, loud with the treble shouts of the generations. He reaches the cabin. He does not knock; with his hand already opening the door he calls in a hearty voice that almost booms: "Can the doctor come in?"

The cabin is empty save for the mother and child. She is propped up on the cot, the child at breast. As Hightower enters, she is in the act of drawing the sheet up over her bared bosom, watching the door not with alarm at all, but with alertness, her face fixed in an expression serene and warm, as though she were about to smile. He sees this fade. "I thought—" she says.

"Who did you think?" he says, booms. He comes to the cot and looks down at her, at the tiny, weazened, terracotta face of the child which seems to hang suspended without body and still asleep from the breast. Again she draws the sheet closer, modest and tranquil, while above her the gaunt, paunched, bald man stands with an expression on his face gentle, beaming, and triumphant. She is looking down at the child.

"It looks like he just cant get caught up. I think he is asleep again and I lay him down and then he hollers and I have to put him back again."

"You ought not to be here alone," he says. He looks about the room. "Where—"

"She's gone, too. To town. She didn't say, but that's where she has gone. He slipped out, and when she woke up she asked me where he was and I told her he went out, and she followed him."

"To town? Slipped out?" Then he says "Oh" quietly. His face is grave now.

"She watched him all day. And he was watching her. I could tell it. He was making out like he was asleep. She thought that he was asleep. And so after dinner she gave out. She hadn't rested any last night, and after dinner she set in the chair and dozed. And he was watching her, and he got up from the other cot, careful, winking and squinching his face at me. He went to the door, still winking and squinting back at me over his shoulder, and tiptoed out. And I never tried to stop him nor wake her, neither." She looks at Hightower, her eyes grave, wide. "I was scared to. He talks funny. And the way he was looking at me. Like all the winking and squinching was not for me to not wake her up, but to tell me what would happen to me if I did. And I was scared to. And so I laid here with the baby and pretty soon she jerked awake. And then I knew she hadn't aimed to go to sleep. It was like she come awake already running to the cot where he had been, touching it like she couldn't believe he had done got away. Because she stood there at the cot, pawing at the blanket like maybe she thought he was mislaid inside the blanket somewhere. And then she looked at me, once. And she wasn't winking and squinting, but I nigh wished she was. And she asked me and I told her and she put on her hat and went out." She looks at Hightower. "I'm glad she's gone. I reckon I ought not to say it, after all she done for me. But . . ."

Hightower stands over the cot. He does not seem to see her. His face is very grave; it is almost as though it had grown ten years older while he stood there. Or like his face looks now as it should look and that when he entered the room, it had been a stranger to itself. "To town," he says. Then his eyes wake, seeing again. "Well. It cant be helped now," he says. "Besides, the men downtown, the sane . . . there will be a few of them. . . . Why are you glad they are gone?"

She looks down. Her hand moves about the baby's head, not touching it: a gesture instinctive, unneeded, apparently unconscious of itself. "She has been kind. More than kind. Holding the baby so I could rest. She wants to hold him all the time, setting there in that chair— You'll have to excuse me. I aint once invited you to set." She watches him as he draws the chair up to the cot and sits down. ". . . Setting there where she could watch him on the cot, making out that he was asleep." She looks at Hightower; her eyes are questioning, intent. "She keeps on calling him Joey. When his name aint Joey. And she keeps on . . ." She watches Hightower. Her eyes are puzzled now, questioning, doubtful. "She keeps on talking about— She is mixed up someway. And sometimes I get mixed up too, listening, having to . . ." Her eyes, her words, grope, fumble.

"Mixed up?"

"She keeps on talking about him like his pa was that . . .

the one in jail, that Mr Christmas. She keeps on, and then I get mixed up and it's like sometimes I cant—like I am mixed up too and I think that his pa is that Mr—Mr Christmas too—" She watches him; it is as though she makes a tremendous effort of some kind. "But I know that aint so. I know that's foolish. It's because she keeps on saying it and saying it, and maybe I aint strong good yet, and I get mixed up too. But I am afraid. . . ."

"Of what?"

"I dont like to get mixed up. And I am afraid she might get me mixed up, like they say how you might cross your eyes and then you cant uncross . . ." She stops looking at him. She does not move. She can feel him watching her.

"You say the baby's name is not Joe. What is his name?"

For a moment longer she does not look at Hightower. Then she looks up. She says, too immediately, too easily: "I aint named him yet."

And he knows why. It is as though he sees her for the first time since he entered. He notices for the first time that her hair has been recently combed and that she has freshened her face too, and he sees, half hidden by the sheet, as if she had thrust them hurriedly there when he entered, a comb and a shard of broken mirror. "When I came in, you were expecting someone. And it was not me. Who were you expecting?"

She does not look away. Her face is neither innocent nor dissimulating. Neither is it placid and serene. "Expecting?"

"Was it Byron Bunch you expected?" Still she does not look away. Hightower's face is sober, firm, gentle. Yet in it is that ruthlessness which she has seen in the faces of a few good people, men usually, whom she has known. He leans forward and lays his hand on hers where it supports the child's body. "Byron is a good man," he says.

"I reckon I know that, well as anybody. Better than most."

"And you are a good woman. Will be. I dont mean—" he says quickly. Then he ceases. "I didn't mean—"

"I reckon I know," she says.

"No. Not this. This does not matter. This is not anything yet. It all depends on what you do with it, afterward. With yourself. With others." He looks at her; she does not look away. "Let him go. Send him away from you." They look at one another. "Send him away, daughter. You are probably not much more than half his age. But you have already outlived him twice over. He will never overtake you, catch up with you, because he has wasted too much time. And that too, his nothing, is as irremediable as your all. He can no more ever cast back and do, than you can cast back and undo. You have a manchild that is not his, by a man that is not him. You will be forcing into his life two men and only the third part of a woman, who deserves at the least that the nothing with which he has lived for thirty-five years be violated, if violated it must be, without two witnesses. Send him away."

"That aint for me to do. He is free. Ask him. I have not tried once to hold him."

"That's it. You probably could not have held him, if you had tried to. That's it. If you had known how to try. But then, if you had known that, you would not be here in this cot, with this child at your breast. And you wont send him away? You wont say the word?"

"I can say no more than I have said. And I said No to him five days ago."

"No?"

"He said for me to marry him. To not wait. And I said No."

"Would you say No now?"

She looks at him steadily. "Yes. I would say it now."

He sighs, huge, shapeless; his face is again slack, weary. "I believe you. You will continue to say it until after you have seen . . ." He looks at her again; again his gaze is intent, hard. "Where is he? Byron?"

She looks at him. After a while she says quietly: "I dont know." She looks at him; suddenly her face is quite empty, as though something which gave it actual solidity and firmness were beginning to drain out of it. Now there is nothing of dissimulation nor alertness nor caution in it. "This morning about ten o'clock he came back. He didn't come in. He just came to the door and he stood there and he just looked at me. And I hadn't seen him since last night and he hadn't seen the baby and I said, 'Come and see him,' and he looked at me, standing there in the door, and he said, 'I come to find out when you want to see him,' and I said, 'See who?' and he said, 'They may have to send a deputy with him but I can persuade Kennedy to let him come,' and I said, 'Let who come?' and he said, 'Lucas Burch,' and I said, 'Yes,' and he said, 'This evening? Will that do?' and I said, 'Yes,' and he went away. He just stood there, and then he went away." While he watches her with that despair of all men in the presence of female tears, she begins to cry. She sits upright, the child at her breast, crying, not loud and not hard, but with a patient and hopeless abjectness, not hiding her face. "And you worry me about if I said No or not and I already said No and you worry me and worry me and now he is already gone. I will never see him again."

And he sits there, and she bows her head at last, and he rises and stands over her with his hand on her bowed head, thinking *Thank God, God help me. Thank God, God help me*

He found Christmas' old path through the woods to the mill. He did not know that it was there, but when he found in which direction it ran, it seemed like an omen to him in his exultation. He believes her, but he wants to corroborate the information for the sheer pleasure of hearing it again. It is just four o'clock when he reaches the mill. He inquires at the office.

"Bunch?" the bookkeeper says. "You wont find him here. He quit this morning."

"I know, I know," Hightower says.

"Been with the company for seven years, Saturday evenings too. Then this morning he walked in and said he was quitting. No reason. But that's the way these hillbillies do."

"Yes, yes," Hightower says. "They are fine people, though. Fine men and women." He leaves the office. The road to town passes the planer shed, where Byron worked. He knows Mooney, the foreman. "I hear Byron Bunch is not with you anymore," he says, pausing.

"Yes," Mooney says. "He quit this morning." But Hightower is not listening; the overalled men watch the shabby, queershaped, not-quite-familiar figure looking with a kind of exultant interest at the walls, the planks, the cryptic machinery whose very being and purpose he could not have understood or even learned. "If you want to see him," Mooney says, "I reckon you'll find him downtown at the courthouse."

"At the courthouse?"

"Yes, sir. Grand Jury meets today. Special call. To indict that murderer."

"Yes, yes," Hightower says. "So he is gone. Yes. A fine young man. Goodday, goodday, gentlemen. Goodday to you." He goes on, while the men in overalls look after him for a time. His hands are clasped behind him. He paces on, thinking quietly, peacefully, sadly: 'Poor man. Poor fellow. No man is, can be, justified in taking human life; least of all, a warranted officer, a sworn servant of his fellowman. When it is sanctioned publicly in the person of an elected officer who knows that he has not himself suffered at the hands of his victim, call that victim by what name you will, how can we expect an individual to refrain when he believes that he has suffered at the hands of *his* victim?' He walks on; he is now in his own street. Soon he can see his fence, the signboard; then the house beyond the rich foliage of August. 'So he departed without coming to tell me goodbye. After all he has done for me. Fetched to me. Ay; given, restored, to me. It would seem that this too was reserved for me. And this must be all.'

But it is not all. There is one thing more reserved for him.

.18.

WHEN Byron reached town he found that he could not see the sheriff until noon, since the sheriff would be engaged all morning with the special Grand Jury. "You'll have to wait," they told him.

"Yes," Byron said. "I know how."

"Know how what?" But he did not answer. He left the sheriff's office and stood beneath the portico which faced the south side of the square. From the shallow, flagged terrace the stone columns rose, arching, weathered, stained with generations of casual tobacco. Beneath them, steady and constant and with a grave purposelessness (and with here and there, standing motionless or talking to one another from the sides of their mouths, some youngish men, townsmen, some of whom Byron knew as clerks and young lawyers and even merchants, who had a generally identical authoritative air, like policemen in disguise and not especially caring if the disguise hid the policeman or not) countrymen in overalls moved, with almost the air of monks in a cloister, speaking quietly among themselves of money and crops, looking quietly now and then upward at the ceiling beyond which the Grand Jury was preparing behind locked doors to take the life of a man whom few of them had ever seen to know, for having taken the life of a woman whom even fewer of them had known to see. The wagons and the dusty cars in which they had come to town were ranked about the square, and along the streets and in and out of the stores the wives and daughters who had come to town with them moved in clumps, slowly and also aimlessly as cattle or clouds. Byron stood there for quite a while, motionless, not leaning against anything—a small man who had lived in the town seven years yet whom even fewer of the country people than knew either the murderer or the murdered, knew by name or habit.

Byron was not conscious of this. He did not care now, though a week ago it would have been different. Then he would not have stood here, where any man could look at him and perhaps recognise him: *Byron Bunch, that weeded another man's laidby crop, without any halvers. The fellow that took care of another man's whore while the other fellow was busy making a thousand dollars. And got nothing for it. Byron Bunch that protected her good name when the woman that owned the good name and the man she had given it to had both thrown it away, that got the other fellow's bastard born in peace and quiet and at Byron Bunch's expense, and heard a baby cry once for his pay. Got nothing for it except permission to fetch the other fellow back to her soon as he got done collecting the thousand dollars and Byron wasn't needed anymore. Byron Bunch* 'And now I can go away,' he thought. He began to breathe deep. He could feel himself breathing deep, as if each time his insides were afraid that next breath they would not be able to give far enough and that something

· 394 ·

terrible would happen, and that all the time he could look down at himself breathing, at his chest, and see no movement at all, like when dynamite first begins, gathers itself for the now Now NOW, the shape of the outside of the stick does not change; that the people who passed and looked at him could see no change: a small man you would not look at twice, that you would never believe he had done what he had done and felt what he had felt, who had believed that out there at the mill on a Saturday afternoon, alone, the chance to be hurt could not have found him.

He was walking among the people. 'I got to go somewhere,' he thought. He could walk in time to that: 'I got to go somewhere.' That would get him along. He was still saying it when he reached the boardinghouse. His room faced the street. Before he realised that he had begun to look toward it, he was looking away. 'I might see somebody reading or smoking in the window,' he thought. He entered the hall. After the bright morning, he could not see at once. He could smell wet linoleum, soap. 'It's still Monday,' he thought. 'I had forgot that. Maybe it's next Monday. That's what it seems like it ought to be.' He did not call. After a while he could see better. He could hear the mop in the back of the hall or maybe the kitchen. Then against the rectangle of light which was the rear door, also open, he saw Mrs Beard's head leaning out, then her body in full silhouette, advancing up the hall.

"Well," she said, "it's Mister Byron Bunch. Mister Byron Bunch."

"Yessum," he said, thinking, 'Only a fat lady that never had much more trouble than a mopping pail would hold ought not to try to be . . .' Again he could not think of the word that Hightower would know, would use without having to think of it. 'It's like I not only cant do anything without getting him mixed up in it, I cant even think without him to help me out.'—"Yessum," he said. And then he stood there, not even able to tell her that he had come to say goodbye. 'Maybe I aint,' he thought. 'I reckon when a fellow has lived in one room for seven years, he aint going to get moved in one day. Only I reckon that aint going to interfere with her renting out his room.' —"I reckon I owe you a little room rent," he said.

She looked at him: a hard, comfortable face, not unkind either. "Rent for what?" she said. "I thought you was settled. Decided to tent for the summer." She looked at him. Then she told him. She did it gently, delicately, considering. "I done already collected the rent for that room."

"Oh," he said. "Yes. I see. Yes." He looked quietly up the scoured, linoleumstripped stairway, scuffed bare by the aid of his own feet. When the new linoleum was put down three years ago, he had been the first of the boarders to mount upon it. "Oh," he said. "Well, I reckon I better . . ."

She answered that too, immediately, not unkind. "I tended to that. I put everything you left in your grip. It's back in my room. If you want to go up and look for yourself, though?"

"No. I reckon you got every . . . Well, I reckon I . . ."

She was watching him. "You men," she said. "It aint a wonder womenfolks get impatient with you. You cant even know your own limits for devilment. Which aint more than I can measure on a pin, at that. I reckon if it wasn't for getting some woman mixed up in it to help you, you'd ever one of you be drug hollering into heaven before you was ten years old."

"I reckon you aint got any call to say anything against her," he said.

"No more I aint. I dont need to. Dont no other woman need to that is going to. I aint saying that it aint been women that has done most of the talking. But if you had more than mansense you would know that women dont mean anything when they talk. It's menfolks that take talking serious. It aint any woman that believes hard against you and her. Because it aint any woman but knows that she aint had any reason to have to be bad with you, even discounting that baby. Or any other man right now. She never had to. Aint you and that preacher and ever other man that knows about her already done everything for her that she could think to want? What does she need to be bad for? Tell me that."

"Yes," Byron says. He was not looking at her now. "I just come . . ."

She answered that too, before it was spoken. "I reckon you'll be leaving us soon." She was watching him. "What have they done this morning at the courthouse?"

"I don't know. They aint finished yet."

"I bound that, too. They'll take as much time and trouble and county money as they can cleaning up what us women could have cleaned up in ten minutes Saturday night. For being such a fool. Not that Jefferson will miss him. Cant get along without him. But being fool enough to believe that killing a woman will do a man anymore good than killing a man would a woman. . . . I reckon they'll let the other one go, now."

"Yessum. I reckon so."

"And they believed for a while that he helped do it. And so they will give him that thousand dollars to show it aint any hard feelings. And then they can get married. That's about right, aint it?"

"Yessum." He could feel her watching him, not unkindly.

"And so I reckon you'll be leaving us. I reckon you kind of feel like you have wore out Jefferson, dont you?"

"Something like that. I reckon I'll move on."

"Well, Jefferson's a good town. But it aint so good but what a footloose man like you can find in another one enough devilment and trouble to keep him occupied too. . . . You can leave your grip here until you are ready for it, if you want."

He waited until noon and after. He waited until he believed that the sheriff had finished his dinner. Then he went to the sheriff's home. He would not come in. He waited at the door until the sheriff came out—the fat man, with little wise eyes like bits of mica embedded in his fat, still face. They went aside, into the shade of a tree in the yard. There was no seat there; neither did they squat on their heels, as by ordinary (they were both countrybred) they would have done. The sheriff listened quietly to the man, the quiet little man who for seven years had been a minor mystery to the town and who had been for seven days wellnigh a public outrage and affront.

"I see," the sheriff said. "You think the time has come to get them married."

"I dont know. That's his business and hers. I reckon he better go out and see her, though. I reckon now is the time for that. You can send a deputy with him. I told her he would come out there this evening. What they do then is her business and hisn. It aint mine."

"Sho," the sheriff said. "It aint yourn." He was looking at the other's profile. "What do you aim to do now, Byron?"

"I dont know." His foot moved slowly upon the earth; he was watching it. "I been thinking about going up to Memphis. Been thinking about it for a couple of years. I might do that. There aint nothing in these little towns."

"Sho. Memphis aint a bad town, for them that like city life. Of course, you aint got any family to have to drag around and hamper you. I reckon if I had been a single man ten years ago I'd have done that too. Been better off, maybe. You're figuring on leaving right away, I reckon."

"Soon, I reckon." He looked up, then down again. He said: "I quit out at the mill this morning."

"Sho," the sheriff said. "I figured you hadn't walked all the way in since twelve and aimed to get back out there by one o'clock. Well, it looks like—" He ceased. He knew that by night the Grand Jury would have indicted Christmas, and Brown—or Burch—would be a free agent save for his bond to appear as a witness at next month's court. But even his presence would not be absolutely essential, since Christmas had made no denial and the sheriff believed that he would plead guilty in order to save his neck. 'And it wont do no harm, anyway, to throw the scare of God into that durn fellow, once in his life,' he thought. He said: "I reckon that can be fixed. Of course, like you say, I will have to send a deputy with him. Even if he aint going to run so long as he has any hope of getting some of that reward money. And provided he dont know what he is going to meet when he gets there. He dont know that yet."

"No," Byron said. "He dont know that. He dont know that she is in Jefferson."

"So I reckon I'll just send him out there with a deputy. Not tell him why: just send him out there. Unless you want to take him yourself."

"No," Byron said. "No. No." But he did not move.

"I'll just do that. You'll be gone by that time, I reckon. I'll just send a deputy with him. Will four o'clock do?"

"It'll be fine. It'll be kind of you. It'll be a kindness."

"Sho. Lots of folks beside me has been good to her since she come to Jefferson. Well, I aint going to say goodbye. I reckon Jefferson will see you again someday. Never knowed a man yet to live here a while and then leave it for good. Except maybe that fellow in the jail yonder. But he'll plead guilty, I reckon. Save his neck. Take it out of Jefferson though, anyway. It's right hard on that old lady that thinks she is his grandmother. The old man was downtown when I come home, hollering and ranting, calling folks cowards because they wouldn't take him out of jail right then and there and lynch him." He began to chuckle, heavily. "He better be careful, or Percy Grimm'll get him with that army of his." He sobered. "It's right hard on her. On women." He looked at Byron's profile. "It's been right hard on a lot of us. Well, you come back some day soon. Maybe Jefferson will treat you better next time."

At four o'clock that afternoon, hidden, he sees the car come up and stop, and the deputy and the man whom he knew by the name of Brown get out and approach the cabin. Brown is not handcuffed now, and Byron watches them reach the cabin and sees the deputy push Brown forward and into the door. Then the door closes behind Brown, and the deputy sits on the step and takes a sack of tobacco from his pocket. Byron rises to his feet. 'I can go now,' he thinks. 'Now I can go.' His hiding place is a clump of shrubbery on the lawn where the house once stood. On the opposite side of the clump, hidden from the cabin and the road both, the mule is tethered. Lashed behind the worn saddle is a battered yellow suitcase which is not leather. He mounts the mule and turns it into the road. He does not look back.

The mild red road goes on beneath the slanting and peaceful afternoon, mounting a hill. 'Well, I can bear a hill,' he thinks. 'I can bear a hill, a man can.' It is peaceful and still, familiar with seven years. 'It seems like a man can just about bear anything. He can even bear what he never done. He can even bear the thinking how some things is just more than he can bear. He can even bear it that if he could just give down and cry, he wouldn't do it. He can even bear it to not look back, even when he knows that looking back or not looking back wont do him any good.'

The hill rises, cresting. He has never seen the sea, and so he thinks. 'It is like the edge of nothing. Like once I passed it I would just ride right off into nothing. Where trees would look like and be called by something else except trees, and men would look like and be called by something else except folks. And Byron Bunch he wouldn't even have to be or not be Byron Bunch. Byron Bunch and his mule not anything with falling fast, until they would take fire like the Reverend Hightower says about them rocks running so fast in space that they take fire and burn up and there aint even a cinder to have to hit the ground.'

But then from beyond the hill crest there begins to rise that which he knows is there: the trees which are trees, the terrific and tedious distance which, being moved by blood, he must compass forever and ever between two inescapable horizons of the implacable earth. Steadily they rise, not portentous, not threatful. That's it. They are oblivious of him. 'Dont know and dont care,' he thinks. 'Like they were saying *All right. You say you suffer. All right. But in the first place, all we got is your naked word for it. And in the second place, you just say that you are Byron Bunch. And in the third place, you are just the one that calls yourself Byron Bunch today, now, this minute. . . .* 'Well,' he thinks, 'if that's all it is, I reckon I might as well have the pleasure of not being able to bear looking back too.' He halts the mule and turns in the saddle.

He did not realise that he has come so far and that the crest is so high. Like a shallow bowl the once broad domain of what was seventy years ago a plantation house lies beneath him, between him and the opposite ridge upon which is Jefferson. But the plantation is broken now by random negro cabins and garden patches and dead fields erosion gutted and choked with blackjack and sassafras and persimmon and brier. But in the exact center the clump of oaks still stand as they stood when the house was built, though now there is no house among them. From here he cannot even see the scars of the fire; he could not even tell where it used to stand if it were not for the oaks and the position of the ruined stable and the cabin beyond, the cabin toward which he is looking. It stands full and quiet in the afternoon sun, almost toylike; like a toy the deputy sits on the step. Then, as Byron watches, a man appears as though by magic at the rear of it, already running, in the act of running out from the rear of the cabin while the unsuspecting deputy sits quiet and motionless on the front step. For a while longer Byron too sits motionless, half turned in the saddle, and watches the tiny figure flee on across the barren slope behind the cabin, toward the woods.

Then a cold, hard wind seems to blow through him. It is at once violent and peaceful, blowing hard away like chaff or trash or dead leaves all the desire and the despair and the hopelessness and the tragic and vain imagining too. With the very blast of it he seems to feel himself rush back and empty again, without anything in him now which had not been there two weeks ago, before he ever saw her. The desire of this moment is more than desire: it is conviction quiet and assured; before he is aware that his brain has telegraphed his hand he has turned the mule from the road and is galloping along the ridge which parallels the running man's course when he entered the woods. He has not even named the man's name to himself. He does not speculate at all upon where the man is going, and why. It does not once enter his head that Brown is fleeing again, as he himself had predicted. If he thought about it at all, he probably believed that Brown was engaged, after his own peculiar fashion, in some thoroughly legitimate business having to do with his and Lena's departure. But he was not thinking about that at all; he was not thinking about Lena at all; she was as completely out of his mind as if he had never seen her face nor heard her name. He is thinking: 'I took care of his woman for him and I borned his child for him. And now there is one more thing I can do for him. I cant marry them, because I aint a minister. And I may not can catch him, because he's got a start on me. And I may not can whip him if I do, because he is bigger than me. But I can try it. I can try to do it.'

When the deputy called for him at the jail, Brown asked at once where they were going. Visiting, the deputy told him. Brown held back, watching the deputy with his handsome, spuriously bold face. "I dont want to visit nobody here. I'm a stranger here."

"You'd be strange anywhere you was at," the deputy said. "Even at home. Come on."

"I'm a American citizen," Brown said. "I reckon I got my rights, even if I dont wear no tin star on my galluses."

"Sho," the deputy said. "That's what I am doing now: helping you get your rights."

Brown's face lighted: it was a flash. "Have they— Are they going to pay—"

"That reward? Sho. I'm going to take you to the place myself right now, where if you are going to get any reward, you'll get it."

Brown sobered. But he moved, though he still watched the deputy suspiciously. "This here is a funny way to go about it," he said. "Keeping me shut up in jail while them bastards tries to beat me out of it."

"I reckon the bastard aint been whelped yet that can beat you at anything," the deputy said. "Come on. They're waiting on us."

They emerged from the jail. In the sunlight Brown blinked, looking this way and that, then he jerked his head up, looking back over his shoulder with that horselike movement. The car was waiting at the curb. Brown looked at the car and then at the deputy, quite sober, quite wary. "Where are we going in a car?" he said. "It wasn't too far for me to walk to the courthouse this morning."

"Watt sent the car to help bring back the reward in," the deputy said. "Get in."

Brown grunted. "He's done got mighty particular about my comfort all of a sudden. A car to ride in, and no handcuffs. And just one durn fellow to keep me from running away."

"I aint keeping you from running," the deputy said. He

· 404 ·

paused in the act of starting the car. "You want to run now?"

Brown looked at him, glaring, sullen, outraged, suspicious. "I see," he said. "That's his trick. Trick me into running and then collect that thousand dollars himself. How much of it did he promise you?"

"Me? I'm going to get the same as you, to a cent."

For a moment longer Brown glared at the deputy. He cursed, pointless, in a weak, violent way. "Come on," he said. "Let's go if we are going."

They drove out to the scene of the fire and the murder. At steady, almost timed intervals Brown jerked his head up and back with that movement of a free mule running in front of a car in a narrow road. "What are we going out here for?"

"To get your reward," the deputy said.

"Where am I going to get it?"

"In that cabin yonder. It's waiting for you there."

Brown looked about, at the blackened embers which had once been a house, at the blank cabin in which he had lived for four months sitting weathered and quiet in the sunlight. His face was quite grave, quite alert. "There's something funny about this. If Kennedy thinks he can tromple on my rights, just because he wears a durn little tin star . . ."

"Get on," the deputy said. "If you dont like the reward, I'll be waiting to take you back to jail any time you want. Just any time you want." He pushed Brown on, opening the cabin door and pushing him into it and closing the door behind him and sitting on the step.

Brown heard the door close behind him. He was still moving forward. Then, in the midst of one of those quick, jerking, allembracing looks, as if his eyes could not wait to take in the room, he stopped dead still. Lena on the cot watched the white scar beside his mouth vanish completely, as if the ebb of blood behind it had snatched the scar in passing like a rag from a clothesline. She did not speak at all. She just lay there, propped on the pillows, watching him with her sober eyes in which there was nothing at all— joy, surprise, reproach, love—while over his face passed shock, astonishment, outrage, and then downright terror, each one mocking in turn at the telltale little white scar, while ceaselessly here and there about the empty room went his harried and desperate eyes. She watched him herd them by will, like two terrified beasts, and drive them up to meet her own. "Well, well," he said. "Well, well, well. It's Lena." She watched him, holding his eyes up to hers like two beasts about to break, as if he knew that when they broke this time he would never catch them, turn them again, and that he himself would be lost. She could almost watch his mind casting this way and that, ceaseless, harried, terrified, seeking words which his voice, his tongue, could speak. "If it aint Lena. Yes, sir. So you got my message. Soon as I got here I sent you a message last month as soon as I got settled down and I thought it had got lost— It was a fellow I didn't know what his name was but he said he would take— He didn't look reliable but I had to trust him but I thought when I gave him the ten dollars for you to travel on that he . . ." His voice died somewhere behind his desperate eyes. Yet still she could watch his mind darting and darting as without pity, without anything at all, she watched him with her grave, unwinking, unbearable gaze, watched him fumble and flee and tack until at last all that remained in him of pride, of what sorry pride the desire for justification was, fled from him and left him naked. Then for the first time she spoke. Her voice was quiet, unruffled, cool.

"Come over here," she said. "Come on. I aint going to let him bite you." When he moved he approached on tiptoe. She saw that, though she was now no longer watching him. She knew that just as she knew that he was now standing with a kind of clumsy and diffident awe above her and the sleeping child. But she knew that it was not at and because of the child. She knew that in that sense he had not even seen the child. She could still see, feel, his mind darting and darting. *He is going to make out like he was not afraid* she thought. *He will have no more shame than to lie about being afraid, just as he had no more shame than to be afraid because he lied*

"Well, well," he said. "So there it is, sho enough."

"Yes," she said. "Will you set down?" The chair which Hightower had drawn up was still beside the cot. He had already remarked it. *She had it all ready for me* he thought. Again he cursed, soundless, badgered, furious. *Them bastards. Them bastards* But his face was quite smooth when he sat down.

"Yes, sir. Here we are again. Same as I had planned it. I would have had it all fixed up ready for you, only I have been so busy lately. Which reminds me—" Again he made that abrupt, mulelike, backlooking movement of the head. She was not looking at him. She said:

"There is a preacher here. That has already come to see me."

"That's fine," he said. His voice was loud, hearty. Yet the heartiness, like the timbre, seemed to be as impermanent as the sound of the words, vanishing, leaving nothing, not even a definitely stated thought in the ear or the belief.

"That's just fine. Soon as I get caught up with all this business—" He jerked his arm in a gesture vague, embracing, looking at her. His face was smooth and blank. His eyes were bland, alert, secret, yet behind them there lurked still that quality harried and desperate. But she was not looking at him.

"What kind of work are you doing now? At the planing mill?"

He watched her. "No. I quit that." His eyes watched her. It was as though they were not his eyes, had no relation to the rest of him, what he did and what he said. "Slaving like a durn nigger ten hours a day. I got something on the string now that means money. Not no little piddling fifteen cents a hour. And when I get it, soon as I get a few little details cleared up, then you and me will . . ." Hard, intent, secret, the eyes watched her, her lowered face in profile. Again she heard that faint, abrupt sound as he jerked his head up and back. "And that reminds me—"

She had not moved. She said: "When will it be, Lucas?" Then she could hear, feel, utter stillness, utter silence.

"When will what be?"

"You know. Like you said. Back home. It was all right for just me. I never minded. But it's different now. I reckon I got a right to worry now."

"Oh, that," he said. "That. Dont you worry about that. Just let me get this here business cleaned up and get my hands on that money. It's mine by right. There cant nere a bastard one of them—" He stopped. His voice had begun to rise, as though he had forgot where he was and had been thinking aloud. He lowered it; he said: "You just leave it to me. Dont you worry none. I aint never give you no reason yet to worry, have I? Tell me that."

"No. I never worried. I knowed I could depend on you."

"Sho you knowed it. And these here bastards—these here—" He had risen from the chair. "Which reminds me—" She neither looked up nor spoke while he stood above her with those eyes harried, desperate, and importunate. It was as if she held him there and that she knew it. And that she released him by her own will, deliberately.

"I reckon you are right busy now, then."

"For a fact, I am. With all I got to bother me, and them bastards—" She was looking at him now. She watched him as he looked at the window in the rear wall. Then he looked back at the closed door behind him. Then he looked at her, at her grave face which had either nothing in it, or everything, all knowledge. He lowered his voice. "I got enemies here. Folks that dont want me to get what I done earned. So I am going to—" Again it was as though she held him, forcing him to, trying him with, that final lie at which even his sorry dregs of pride revolted; held him neither with rods nor cords but with something against which his lying blew trivial as leaves or trash. But she said nothing at all. She just watched him as he went on tiptoe to the window and opened it without a sound. Then he looked at her. Perhaps he thought that he was safe then, that he could get out the window before she could touch him with a physical hand. Or perhaps it was some sorry tagend of shame, as a while ago it had been pride. Because he looked at her, stripped naked for the instant of verbiage and deceit. His voice was not much louder than a whisper: "It's a man outside. In front, waiting for me." Then he was gone, through the window, without a sound, in a single motion almost like a long snake. From beyond the window she heard a single faint sound as he began to run. Then only did she move, and then but to sigh once, profoundly. "Now I got to get up again," she said, aloud.

When Brown emerges from the woods, onto the railroad right-of-way, he is panting. It is not with fatigue, though the distance which he has covered in the last twenty minutes is almost two miles and the going was not smooth. Rather, it is the snarling and malevolent breathing of a fleeing animal: while he stands looking both ways along the empty track his face, his expression, is that of an animal fleeing alone, desiring no fellowaid, clinging to its solitary dependence upon its own muscles alone and which, in the pause to renew breath, hates every tree and grassblade in sight as if it were a live enemy, hates the very earth it rests upon and the very air it needs to renew breathing.

He has struck the railroad within a few hundred yards of the point at which he aimed. This is the crest of a grade where the northbound freights slow to a terrific and crawling gait of almost less than that of a walking man. A short distance ahead of him the twin bright threads appear to have been cut short off as though with scissors.

For a while he stands just within the screen of woods beside the right-of-way, still hidden. He stands like a man in brooding and desperate calculation, as if he sought in his mind for some last desperate cast in a game already lost. After standing for a moment longer in an attitude of listening, he turns and runs again, through the woods and paralleling the track. He seems to know exactly where he is going; he comes presently upon a path and follows it, still running, and emerges into a clearing in which a negro cabin sits. He approaches the front, walking now. On the porch an old negro woman is sitting, smoking a pipe, her head wrapped in a white cloth. Brown is not running, but he is breathing fast, heavily. He quiets it to speak. "Hi, Aunty," he says, "who's here?"

The old negress removes the pipe. "Ise here. Who wanter know?"

"I got to send a message back to town. In a hurry." He holds his breathing down to talk. "I'll pay. Aint there somebody here that can take it?"

"If it's all that rush, you better tend to it yourself."

"I'll pay, I tell you!" he says. He speaks with a kind of raging patience, holding his voice, his breathing, down. "A dollar, if he just goes quick enough. Aint there somebody here that wants to make a dollar? Some of the boys?"

The old woman smokes, watching him. With an aged an inscrutable midnight face she seems to contemplate him with a detachment almost godlike but not at all benign. "A dollar cash?"

He makes a gesture indescribable, of hurry and leashed rage and something like despair. He is about to turn away when the negress speaks again. "Aint nobody here but me and the two little uns. I reckon they'd be too little for you."

Brown turns back. "How little? I just want somebody that can take a note to the sheriff in a hurry and—"

"The sheriff? Then you come to the wrong place. I aint ghy have none of mine monkeying around no sheriff. I done had one nigger that thought he knowed a sheriff well enough to go and visit with him. He aint never come back, neither. You look somewhere else."

But Brown is already moving away. He does not run at once. He has not yet thought about running again; for the moment he cannot think at all. His rage and impotence is now almost ecstatic. He seems to muse now upon a sort of timeless and beautiful infallibility in his unpredictable frustrations. As though somehow the very fact that he should be so consistently supplied with them elevates him somehow above the petty human hopes and desires which they abrogate and negative. Hence the negress has to shout twice at him before he hears and turns. She has said nothing, she has not moved: she merely shouted. She says, "Here one will take it for you."

Standing beside the porch now, materialised apparently from thin air, is a negro who may be either a grown imbecile or a hulking youth. His face is black, still, also quite inscrutable. They stand looking at one another. Or rather, Brown looks at the negro. He cannot tell if the negro is looking at him or not. And that too seems somehow right and fine and in keeping: that his final hope and resort should be a beast that does not appear to have enough ratiocinative power to find the town, let alone any given individual in it. Again Brown makes an indescribable gesture. He is almost running now, back toward the porch, pawing at his shirt pocket. "I want you to take a note to town and bring me back an answer," he says. "Can you do it?" But he does not listen for a reply. He has taken from his shirt a scrap of soiled paper and a chewed pencil stub, and bending over the edge of the porch, he writes, laborious and hurried, while the negress watches him:

Mr Wat Kenedy Dear sir please give barer My reward Money for captain Murder Xmas rapp it up in Paper 4 given it toe barer yrs truly

He does not sign it. He snatches it up, glaring at it, while the negress watches him. He glares at the dingy and innocent paper, at the labored and hurried pencilling in which he had succeeded for an instant in snaring his whole soul and life too. Then he claps it down and writes *not Sined but All rigt You no who* and folds it and gives it to the negro. "Take it to the sheriff. Not to nobody else. You reckon you can find him?"

"If the sheriff dont find him first," the old negress says. "Give it to him. He'll find him, if he is above ground. Git your dollar and go on, boy."

The negro had started away. He stops. He just stands there, saying nothing, looking at nothing. On the porch the negress sits, smoking, looking down at the white man's weak, wolflike face: a face handsome, plausible, but drawn now by a fatigue more than physical, into a spent and vulpine mask. "I thought you was in a hurry," she says.

"Yes," Brown says. He takes a coin from his pocket. "Here. And if you bring me back the answer to that inside of an hour, I'll give you five more like it."

"Git on, nigger," the woman says. "You aint got all day. You want the answer brought back here?"

For a moment longer Brown looks at her. Then again caution, shame, all flees from him. "No. Not here. Bring it to the top of the grade yonder. Walk up the track until I call to you. I'll be watching you all the time too. Dont you forget that. Do you hear?"

"You needn't to worry," the negress says. "He'll git there with it and git back with the answer, if dont nothing stop him. Git on, boy."

The negro goes on. But something does stop him, before he has gone a half mile. It is another white man, leading a mule.

"Where?" Byron says. "Where did you see him?"

"Just now. Up yon at de house." The white man goes on, leading the mule. The negro looks after him. He did not show the white man the note because the white man did not ask to see it. Perhaps the reason the white man did not ask to see the note was that the white man did not know that he had a note; perhaps the negro is thinking this, because for a while his face mirrors something terrific and subterranean. Then it clears. He shouts. The white man turns, halting. "He aint dar now," the negro shouts. "He say he gwine up ter de railroad grade to wait."

"Much obliged," the white man says. The negro goes on.

Brown returned to the track. He was not running now. He was saying to himself, 'He wont do it. He cant do it. I know he cant find him, cant get it, bring it back.' He called no names, thought no names. It seemed to him now that they were all just shapes like chessmen—the negro, the sheriff, the money, all—unpredictable and without reason moved here and there by an Opponent who could read his moves before he made them and who created spontaneous rules which he and not the Opponent, must follow. He was for the time being even beyond despair as he turned from the rails and entered the underbrush near the crest of the grade. He moved now without haste, gauging his distance as though there were nothing else in the world or in his life at least, save that. He chose his place and sat down, hidden from the track but where he himself could see it.

'Only I know he wont do it,' he thinks. 'I dont even expect it. If I was to see him coming back with the money in his hand, I would not believe it. It wouldn't be for me. I would know that. I would know that it was a mistake. I would say to him *You go on. You are looking for some-*

body else beside me. You aint looking for Lucas Burch. No,
sir, Lucas Burch dont deserve that money, that reward. He
never done nothing to get it. No, sir' He begins to laugh,
squatting, motionless, his spent face bent, laughing. 'Yes, sir.
All Lucas Burch wanted was justice. Just justice. Not that
he told them bastards the murderer's name and where to
find him only they wouldn't try. They never tried because
they would have had to give Lucas Burch the money.
Justice.' Then he says aloud, in a harsh, tearful voice:
"Justice. That was all. Just my rights. And them bastards
with their little tin stars, all sworn everyone of them on
oath, to protect a American citizen." He says it harshly,
almost crying with rage and despair and fatigue: "I be
dog if it aint enough to make a man turn downright bowl-
sheyvick." Thus he hears no sound at all until Byron speaks
directly behind him:

"Get up onto your feet."

It does not last long. Byron knew that it was not going
to. But he did not hesitate. He just crept up until he could
see the other, where he stopped, looking at the crouching
and unwarned figure. 'You're bigger than me,' Byron
thought. 'But I dont care. You've had every other advantage of me. And I dont care about that neither. You've
done throwed away twice inside of nine months what I
aint had in thirtyfive years. And now I'm going to get
the hell beat out of me and I dont care about that, neither.'

It does not last long. Brown, whirling, takes advantage
of his astonishment even. He did not believe that any man,
catching his enemy sitting, would give him a chance to get
on his feet, even if the enemy were not the larger of the
two. He would not have done it himself. And the fact
that the smaller man did do it when he would not have,

was worse than insult: it was ridicule. So he fought with even a more savage fury than he would have if Byron had sprung upon his back without warning: with the blind and desperate valor of a starved and cornered rat he fought.

It lasted less than two minutes. Then Byron was lying quietly among the broken and trampled undergrowth, bleeding quietly about the face, hearing the underbrush crashing on, ceasing, fading into silence. Then he is alone. He feels no particular pain now, but better than that, he feels no haste, no urgency, to do anything or go anywhere. He just lies bleeding and quiet, knowing that after a while will be time enough to reenter the world and time.

He does not even wonder where Brown has gone. He does not have to think about Brown now. Again his mind is filled with still shapes like discarded and fragmentary toys of childhood piled indiscriminate and gathering quiet dust in a forgotten closet—Brown. Lena Grove. Hightower. Byron Bunch—all like small objects which had never been alive, which he had played with in childhood and then broken and forgot. He is lying so when he hears the train whistle for a crossing a half mile away.

This rouses him; this is the world and time too. He sits up, slowly, tentatively. 'Anyway, I aint broke anything,' he thinks. 'I mean, he aint broke anything that belongs to me.' It is getting late: it is time now, with distance, moving, in it. 'Yes. I'll have to be moving. I'll have to get on so I can find me something else to meddle with.' The train is coming nearer. Already the stroke of the engine has shortened and become heavier as it begins to feel the grade; presently he can see the smoke. He seeks in his pocket for a handkerchief. He has none, so he tears the tail from his shirt and dabs at his face gingerly, listening to the short, blasting reports of the locomotive exhaust just over the grade. He moves to the edge of the undergrowth, where he can see the track. The engine is in sight now, almost head-on to him beneath the spaced, heavy blasts of black smoke. It has an effect of terrific nomotion. Yet it does move, creeping terrifically up and over the crest of the grade. Standing now in the fringe of bushes he watches the engine approach and pass him, laboring, crawling, with the rapt and boylike absorption (and perhaps yearning) of his country raising. It passes; his eye moves on, watching the cars as they in turn crawl up and over the crest, when for the second time that afternoon he sees a man materialise apparently out of air, in the act of running.

Even then he does not realise what Brown is about. He has progressed too far into peace and solitude to wonder. He just stands there and watches Brown run to the train, stooping, fleeing, and grasp the iron ladder at the end of a car and leap upward and vanish from sight as though sucked into a vacuum. The train is beginning to increase its speed; he watches the approach of the car where Brown vanished. It passes; clinging to the rear of it, between it and the next car, Brown stands, his face leaned out and watching the bushes. They see one another at the same moment: the two faces, the mild, nondescript, bloody one and the lean, harried, desperate one contorted now in a soundless shouting above the noise of the train, passing one another as though on opposite orbits and with an effect as of phantoms or apparitions. Still Byron is not thinking. "Great God in the mountain," he says, with childlike and almost ecstatic astonishment; "he sho knows how to jump a train. He's sho done that before." He is not thinking at all. It is as though the moving wall of dingy cars were a

· 417 ·

dyke beyond which the world, time, hope unbelievable and certainty incontrovertible, waited, giving him yet a little more of peace. Anyway, when the last car passes, moving fast now, the world rushes down on him like a flood, a tidal wave.

It is too huge and fast for distance and time; hence no path to be retraced, leading the mule for a good way before he remembers to get on it and ride. It is as though he has already and long since outstripped himself, already waiting at the cabin until he can catch up and enter. *And then I will stand there and I will* . . . He tries it again: *Then I will stand there and I will* . . . But he can get no further than that. He is in the road again now, approaching a wagon homeward bound from town. It is about six o'clock. He does not give up, however. *Even if I cant seem to get any further than that: when I will open the door and come in and stand there. And then I will. Look at her. Look at her. Look at her—* The voice speaks again:

"—excitement, I reckon."

"What?" Byron says. The wagon has halted. He is right beside it, the mule stopped too. On the wagon seat the man speaks again, in his flat, complaining voice:

"Durn the luck. Just when I had to get started for home. I'm already late."

"Excitement?" Byron says. "What excitement?"

The man is looking at him. "From your face, a man would say you had been in some excitement yourself."

"I fell down," Byron says. "What excitement in town this evening?"

"I thought maybe you hadn't heard. About an hour ago. That nigger, Christmas. They killed him."

. 19 .

ABOUT the suppertables on that Monday night, what the town wondered was not so much how Christmas had escaped but why when free, he had taken refuge in the place which he did, where he must have known he would be certainly run to earth, and why when that occurred he neither surrendered nor resisted. It was as though he had set out and made his plans to passively commit suicide.

There were many reasons, opinions, as to why he had fled to Hightower's house at the last. "Like to like," the easy, the immediate, ones said, remembering the old tales about the minister. Some believed it to have been sheer chance; others said that the man had shown wisdom, since he would not have been suspected of being in the minister's house at all if someone had not seen him run across the back yard and run into the kitchen.

Gavin Stevens though had a different theory. He is the District Attorney, a Harvard graduate, a Phi Beta Kappa: a tall, loosejointed man with a constant cob pipe, with an untidy mop of irongray hair, wearing always loose and unpressed dark gray clothes. His family is old in Jefferson; his ancestors owned slaves there and his grandfather knew (and also hated, and publicly congratulated Colonel Sartoris when they died) Miss Burden's grandfather and brother. He has an easy quiet way with country people, with the voters and the juries; he can be seen now and then squatting among the overalls on the porches of country stores for a whole summer afternoon, talking to them in their own idiom about nothing at all.

On this Monday night there descended from the nine o'clock southbound train a college professor from the neighboring State University, a schoolmate of Stevens' at Harvard, come to spend a few days of the vacation with his friend. When he descended from the train he saw his friend at once. He believed that Stevens had come down to meet him until he saw that Stevens was engaged with a queer-looking old couple whom he was putting on the train. Looking at them, the professor saw a little, dirty old man with a short goat's beard who seemed to be in a state like catalepsy, and an old woman who must have been his wife —a dumpy creature with a face like dough beneath a nodding and soiled white plume, shapeless in a silk dress of an outmoded shape and in color regal and moribund. For an instant the professor paused in a sort of astonished interest, watching Stevens putting into the woman's hand, as into the hand of a child, two railroad tickets; moving again and approaching and still unseen by his friend, he overheard Stevens' final words as the flagman helped the old people into the vestibule: "Yes, yes," Stevens was saying, in a tone soothing and recapitulant; "he'll be on the train tomorrow morning. I'll see to it. All you'll have to do is to arrange for the funeral, the cemetery. You take Granddad on home and put him to bed. I'll see that the boy is on the train in the morning."

Then the train began to move and Stevens turned and saw the professor. He began the story as they rode to town and finished it as they sat on the veranda of Stevens' home, and there recapitulated. "I think I know why it was, why he ran into Hightower's house for refuge at the last. I think it was his grandmother. She had just been with him in his cell when they took him back to the courthouse again; she and the grandfather—that little crazed old man who wanted to lynch him, who came up here from Mottstown for that purpose. I dont think that the old lady had any hope of saving him when she came, any actual hope. I believe that all she wanted was that he die 'decent,' as she put it. Decently hung by a Force, a principle; not burned or hacked or dragged dead by a Thing. I think she came here just to watch that old man, lest he be the straw that started the hurricane, because she did not dare let him out of her sight. Not that she doubted that Christmas was her grandchild, you understand. She just didn't hope. Didn't know how to begin to hope. I imagine that after thirty years the machinery for hoping requires more than twentyfour hours to get started, to get into motion again.

"But I believe that, having got started physically by the tide of the old man's insanity and conviction, before she knew it she had been swept away too. So they came here. They got here on the early train, about three o'clock Sunday morning. She made no attempt to see Christmas. Perhaps she was watching the old man. But I dont think so. I dont think that the hoping machine had got started then, either. I dont think that it ever did start until that baby was born out there this morning, born right in her face, you might say; a boy too. And she had never seen the mother before, and the father at all, and that grandson whom she had never seen as a man; so to her those thirty years just were not. Obliterated when that child cried. No longer existed.

"It was all coming down on her too fast. There was too much reality that her hands and eyes could not deny, and too much that must be taken for granted that her hands and eyes could not prove; too much of the inexplicable that hands and eyes were asked too suddenly to accept and believe without proof. After the thirty years it must have been like a person in solitary blundering suddenly into a room full of strange people all talking at once and she casting desperately about for anything that would hold sanity together by choosing some logical course of action which would be within her limitations, which she could have some assurance of being able to perform. Until that baby was born and she found some means by which she could stand alone, as it were, she had been like an effigy with a mechanical voice being hauled about on a cart by that fellow Bunch and made to speak when he gave the signal, as when he took her last night to tell her story to Doctor Hightower.

"And she was still groping, you see. She was still trying to find something which that mind which had apparently not run very much in thirty years, could believe in, admit to be actual, real. And I think that she found it there, at Hightower's, for the first time: someone to whom she could tell it, who would listen to her. Very likely that was the first time she had ever told it. And very likely she learned it herself then for the first time, actually saw it whole and real at the same time with Hightower. So I dont think it is so strange that for the time she got not only the child but his parentage as well mixed up, since in that cabin those thirty years did not exist—the child and its father whom she had never seen, and her grandson whom she had not seen since he was a baby like the other, and whose father likewise to her had never existed, all confused. And that, when hope did begin to move in her, she should have turned at once, with that sublime and boundless faith of her kind in those who are the voluntary slaves and the sworn bondsmen of prayer, to the minister.

"That's what she was telling Christmas in the jail today, when the old man, watching his chance, had slipped away from her and she followed him to town and found him on the street corner again, mad as a hatter and completely hoarse, preaching lynching, telling the people how he had grandfathered the devil's spawn and had kept it in trust for this day. Or perhaps she was on her way to see him in the jail when she left the cabin. Anyway she left the old man alone as soon as she saw that his audience was more interested than moved, and went on to the sheriff. He had just got back from dinner and for a while he could not understand what she wanted. She must have sounded quite crazy to him, with that story of hers, in that hopelessly respectable Sunday dress, planning a jailbreak. But he let her go to the jail, with a deputy. And there, in the cell with him, I believe she told him about Hightower, that Hightower could save him, was going to save him.

"But of course I dont know what she told him. I dont believe that any man could reconstruct that scene. I dont think that she knew herself, planned at all what she would say, because it had already been written and worded for her on the night when she bore his mother, and that was now so long ago that she had learned it beyond all forgetting and then forgot the words. Perhaps that's why he believed her at once, without question. I mean, because she did not worry about what to say, about plausibility or the possibility of incredulity on his part: that somewhere, somehow, in the shape or presence or whatever of that old outcast minister was a sanctuary which would be inviolable not only to officers and mobs, but to the very irrevocable past; to whatever crimes had molded and shaped him and left him at last high and dry in a barred cell with the shape of an incipient executioner everywhere he looked.

"And he believed her. I think that is what gave him not the courage so much as the passive patience to endure and recognise and accept the one opportunity which he had to break in the middle of that crowded square, manacled, and run. But there was too much running with him, stride for stride with him. Not pursuers: but himself: years, acts, deeds omitted and committed, keeping pace with him, stride for stride, breath for breath, thud for thud of the heart, using a single heart. It was not alone all those thirty years which she did not know, but all those successions of thirty years before that which had put that stain either on his white blood or his black blood, whichever you will, and which killed him. But he must have run with believing for a while; anyway, with hope. But his blood would not be quiet, let him save it. It would not be either one or the other and let his body save itself. Because the black blood drove him first to the negro cabin. And then the white blood drove him out of there, as it was the black blood which snatched up the pistol and the white blood which would not let him fire it. And it was the white blood which sent him to the minister, which rising in him for the last

· 424 ·

and final time, sent him against all reason and all reality, into the embrace of a chimera, a blind faith in something read in a printed Book. Then I believe that the white blood deserted him for the moment. Just a second, a flicker, allowing the black to rise in its final moment and make him turn upon that on which he had postulated his hope of salvation. It was the black blood which swept him by his own desire beyond the aid of any man, swept him up into that ecstasy out of a black jungle where life has already ceased before the heart stops and death is desire and fulfillment. And then the black blood failed him again, as it must have in crises all his life. He did not kill the minister. He merely struck him with the pistol and ran on and crouched behind that table and defied the black blood for the last time, as he had been defying it for thirty years. He crouched behind that overturned table and let them shoot him to death, with that loaded and unfired pistol in his hand."

In the town on that day lived a young man named Percy Grimm. He was about twentyfive and a captain in the State national guard. He had been born in the town and had lived there all his life save for the periods of the summer encampments. He was too young to have been in the European War, though it was not until 1921 or '22 that he realised that he would never forgive his parents for that fact. His father, a hardware merchant, did not understand this. He thought that the boy was just lazy and in a fair way to become perfectly worthless, when in reality the boy was suffering the terrible tragedy of having been born not alone too late but not late enough to have escaped first hand knowledge of the lost time when he should have been a man instead of a child. And now, with the hysteria passed away and the ones who had been loudest in the hysteria and even the ones, the heroes who had suffered and served, beginning to look at one another a little askance, he had no one to tell it, to open his heart to. In fact, his first serious fight was with an exsoldier who made some remark to the effect that if he had to do it again, he would fight this time on the German side and against France. At once Grimm took him up. "Against America too?" he said.

"If America's fool enough to help France out again," the soldier said. Grimm struck him at once; he was smaller than the soldier, still in his teens. The result was foregone; even Grimm doubtless knew that. But he took his punishment until even the soldier begged the bystanders to hold the boy back. And he wore the scars of that battle as proudly as he was later to wear the uniform itself for which he had blindly fought.

It was the new civilian-military act which saved him. He was like a man who had been for a long time in a swamp, in the dark. It was as though he not only could see no path ahead of him, he knew that there was none. Then suddenly his life opened definite and clear. The wasted years in which he had shown no ability in school, in which he had been known as lazy, recalcitrant, without ambition, were behind him, forgotten. He could now see his life opening before him, uncomplex and inescapable as a barren corridor, completely freed now of ever again having to think or decide, the burden which he now assumed and carried as bright and weightless and martial as his insignatory brass: a sublime and implicit faith in physical courage and blind obedience, and a belief that the white race is superior to any and all other races and that the American is superior to all other white races and that the

American uniform is superior to all men, and that all that would ever be required of him in payment for this belief, this privilege, would be his own life. On each national holiday that had any martial flavor whatever he dressed in his captain's uniform and came down town. And those who saw him remembered him again on the day of the fight with the exsoldier as, glittering, with his marksman's badge (he was a fine shot) and his bars, grave, erect, he walked among the civilians with about him an air half belligerent and half the selfconscious pride of a boy.

He was not a member of the American Legion, but that was his parents' fault and not his. But when Christmas was fetched back from Mottstown on that Saturday afternoon, he had already been to the commander of the local Post. His idea, his words, were quite simple and direct. "We got to preserve order," he said. "We must let the law take its course. The law, the nation. It is the right of no civilian to sentence a man to death. And we, the soldiers in Jefferson, are the ones to see to that."

"How do you know that anybody is planning anything different?" the legion commander said. "Have you heard any talk?"

"I dont know. I haven't listened." He didn't lie. It was as though he did not attach enough importance to what might or might not have been said by the civilian citizens to lie about it. "That's not the question. It's whether or not we, as soldiers, that have worn the uniform, are going to be the first to state where we stand. To show these people right off just where the government of the country stands on such things. That there wont be any need for them even to talk." His plan was quite simple. It was to form the legion Post into a platoon, with himself in command vide his active commission. "But if they dont want me to command, that's all right too. I'll be second, if they say. Or a sergeant or a corporal." And he meant it. It was not vain glory that he wanted. He was too sincere. So sincere, so humorless, that the legion commander withheld the flippant refusal he was about to make.

"I still dont think that there is any need of it. And if there was, we would all have to act as civilians. I couldn't use the Post like that. After all, we are not soldiers now. I dont think I would, if I could."

Grimm looked at him, without anger, but rather as if he were some kind of bug. "Yet you wore the uniform once," he said, with a kind of patience. He said: "I suppose you went use your authority to keep me from talking to them, will you? As individuals?"

"No. I haven't any authority to do that, anyway. But just as individuals, mind. You mustn't use my name at all."

Then Grimm gave him a shot on his own account. "I am not likely to do that," he said. Then he was gone. That was Saturday, about four o'clock. For the rest of that afternoon he circulated about the stores and offices where the legion members worked, so that by nightfall he had enough of them also worked up to his own pitch to compose a fair platoon. He was indefatigable, restrained yet forceful; there was something about him irresistible and prophetlike. Yet the recruits were with the commander in one thing: the official designation of the legion must be kept out of it—whereupon and without deliberate intent, he had gained his original end: he was now in command. He got them all together just before suppertime and divided them into squads and appointed officers and a staff; the younger ones, the ones who had not gone to France, taking proper fire by now. He addressed them, briefly, coldly: ". . . order . . . course of justice . . . let the people see that we have worn the uniform of the United States . . . And one thing more." For the moment now he had descended to familiarity: the regimental commander who knows his men by their first names. "I'll leave this to you fellows. I'll do what you say. I thought it might be a good thing if I wear my uniform until this business is settled. So they can see that Uncle Sam is present in more than spirit."

"But he's not," one said quickly, immediately; he was of the same cut as the commander, who by the way was not present. "This is not government trouble yet. Kennedy might not like it. This is Jefferson's trouble, not Washington's."

"Make him like it," Grimm said. "What does your legion stand for, if not for the protection of America and Americans?"

"No," the other said. "I reckon we better not make a parade out of this. We can do what we want without that. Better. Aint that right, boys?"

"All right," Grimm said. "I'll do as you say. But every man will want a pistol. We'll have a small arms' inspection here in one hour. Every man will report here."

"What's Kennedy going to say about pistols?" one said.

"I'll see to that," Grimm said. "Report here in one hour exactly, with side arms." He dismissed them. He crossed the quiet square to the sheriff's office. The sheriff was at home, they told him. "At home?" he repeated. "Now? What's he doing at home now?"

"Eating, I reckon. A man as big as him has got to eat several times a day."

"At home," Grimm repeated. He did not glare; it was

· 429 ·

again that cold and detached expression with which he had looked at the legion commander. "Eating," he said. He went out, already walking fast. He recrossed the empty square, the quiet square empty of people peacefully at suppertables about that peaceful town and that peaceful country. He went to the sheriff's home. The sheriff said No at once.

"Fifteen or twenty folks milling around the square with pistols in their pants? No, no. That wont do. I cant have that. That wont do. You let me run this."

For a moment longer Grimm looked at the sheriff. Then he turned, already walking fast again. "All right," he said. "If that's the way you want it. I dont interfere with you and you dont interfere with me, then." It didn't sound like a threat. It was too flat, too final, too without heat. He went on, rapidly. The sheriff watched him; then he called. Grimm turned.

"You leave yours at home, too," the sheriff said. "You hear me?" Grimm didn't answer. He went on. The sheriff watched him out of sight, frowning.

That evening after supper the sheriff went back downtown—something he had not done for years save when urgent and inescapable business called. He found a picket of Grimm's men at the jail, and another in the courthouse, and a third patrolling the square and the adjacent streets. The others, the relief, they told the sheriff, were in the cotton office where Grimm was employed, which they were using for an orderly room, a P.C. The sheriff met Grimm on the street, making a round of inspection. "Come here, boy," the sheriff said. Grimm halted. He did not approach; the sheriff went to him. He patted Grimm's hip with a fat hand. "I told you to leave that at home," he said. Grimm said nothing. He watched the sheriff levelly. The sheriff sighed. "Well, if you wont, I reckon I'll have to make you a special deputy. But you aint to even show that gun unless I tell you to. You hear me?"

"Certainly not," Grimm said. "You certainly wouldn't want me to draw it if I didn't see any need to."

"I mean, not till I tell you to."

"Certainly," Grimm said, without heat, patiently, immediately. "That's what we both said. Dont you worry. I'll be there."

Later, as the town quieted for the night, as the picture show emptied and the drug stores closed one by one, Grimm's platoon began to drop off too. He did not protest, watching them coldly; they became a little sheepish, defensive. Again without knowing it he had played a trump card. Because of the fact that they felt sheepish, feeling that somehow they had fallen short of his own cold ardor, they would return tomorrow if just to show him. A few remained; it was Saturday night anyhow, and someone got more chairs from somewhere and they started a poker game. It ran all night, though from time to time Grimm (he was not in the game; neither would he permit his second in command, the only other there who held the equivalent of commissioned rank, to engage) sent a squad out to make a patrol of the square. By this time the night marshal was one of them, though he too did not take a hand in the game.

Sunday was quiet. The poker game ran quietly through that day, broken by the periodical patrols, while the quiet church bells rang and the congregations gathered in decorous clumps of summer colors. About the square it was already known that the special Grand Jury would meet tomorrow. Somehow the very sound of the two words with their evocation secret and irrevocable and something of a hidden and unsleeping and omnipotent eye watching the doings of men, began to reassure Grimm's men in their own makebelieve. So quickly is man unwittingly and unpredictably moved that without knowing that they were thinking it, the town had suddenly accepted Grimm with respect and perhaps a little awe and a deal of actual faith and confidence, as though somehow his vision and patriotism and pride in the town, the occasion, had been quicker and truer than theirs. His men anyway assumed and accepted this; after the sleepless night, the tenseness, the holiday, the suttee of volition's surrender, they were almost at the pitch where they might die for him, if occasion rose. They now moved in a grave and slightly aweinspiring reflected light which was almost as palpable as the khaki would have been which Grimm wished them to wear, wished that they wore, as though each time they returned to the orderly room they dressed themselves anew in suave and austerely splendid scraps of his dream.

This lasted through Sunday night. The poker game ran. The caution, the surreptitiousness, which had clothed it was now gone. There was something about it too assured and serenely confident to the braggadocio; tonight when they heard the marshal's feet on the stairs, one said, "Ware M.P.'s," and for an instant they glanced at one another with hard, bright, daredevil eyes; then one said, quite loud: "Throw the son of a bitch out," and another through pursed lips made the immemorial sound. And so the next morning, Monday, when the first country cars and wagons began to gather, the platoon was again intact. And they now wore uniforms. It was their faces. Most of them were of an age, a generation, an experience. But it was more than that. They now had a profound and bleak gravity as they stood where crowds milled, grave, austere, detached, looking with blank, bleak eyes at the slow throngs who, feeling, sensing without knowing, drifted before them, slowing, staring, so that they would be ringed with faces rapt and empty and immobile as the faces of cows, approaching and drifting on, to be replaced. And all morning the voices came and went, in quiet question and answer: "There he goes. That young fellow with the automatic pistol. He's the captain of them. Special officer sent by the governor. He's the head of the whole thing. Sheriff aint got no say in it today."

Later, when it was too late, Grimm told the sheriff: "If you had just listened to me. Let me bring him out of that cell in a squad of men, instead of sending him across the square with one deputy and not even handcuffed to him, in all that crowd where that damned Buford didn't dare shoot, even if he could hit a barn door."

"How did I know he aimed to break, would think of trying it right then and there?" the sheriff said. "When Stevens had done told me he would plead guilty and take a life sentence."

But it was too late then. It was all over then. It happened in the middle of the square, halfway between the sidewalk and the courthouse, in the midst of a throng of people thick as on Fair Day, though the first that Grimm knew of it was when he heard the deputy's pistol twice, fired into the air. He knew at once what had happened, though he was at the time inside the courthouse. His reaction was definite and immediate. He was already running toward the shots when he shouted back over his shoulder at the man who had tagged him now for almost fortyeight hours as half aide and half orderly: "Turn in the fire alarm!"

"The fire alarm?" the aide said. "What—"

"Turn in the fire alarm!" Grimm shouted back. "It dont matter what folks think, just so they know that something . . ." He did not finish; he was gone.

He ran among running people, overtaking and passing them, since he had an objective and they did not; they were just running, the black, blunt, huge automatic opening a way for him like a plow. They looked at his tense, hard, young face with faces blanched and gaped, with round, toothed orifices; they made one long sound like a murmuring sigh: "There . . . went that way . . ." But already Grimm had seen the deputy, running, his pistol aloft in his hand. Grimm glanced once about and sprang forward again; in the throng which had evidently been pacing the deputy and the prisoner across the square was the inevitable hulking youth in the uniform of the Western Union, leading his bicycle by the horns like a docile cow. Grimm rammed the pistol back into the holster and flung the boy aside and sprang onto the bicycle, with never a break in motion.

The bicycle possessed neither horn nor bell. Yet they sensed him somehow and made way; in this too he seemed to be served by certitude, the blind and untroubled faith in the rightness and infallibility of his actions. When he overtook the running deputy he slowed the bicycle. The deputy turned upon him a face sweating, gaped with shouting and running. "He turned," the deputy screamed. "Into that alley by—"

"I know," Grimm said. "Was he handcuffed?"

"Yes!" the deputy said. The bicycle leaped on.

'Then he cant run very fast,' Grimm thought. 'He'll have to hole up soon. Get out of the open, anyway.' He turned into the alley, fast. It ran back between two houses, with a board fence on one side. At that moment the fire siren sounded for the first time, beginning and mounting to a slow and sustained scream that seemed at last to pass beyond the realm of hearing, into that of sense, like soundless vibration. Grimm wheeled on, thinking swiftly, logically, with a kind of fierce and constrained joy. 'The first thing he will want is to get out of sight,' he thought, looking about. On one hand the lane was open, on the other stood the board fence six feet high. At the end it was cut short off by a wooden gate, beyond which was a pasture and then a deep ditch which was a town landmark. The tops of tall trees which grew in it just showed above the rim; a regiment could hide and deploy in it. "Ah," he said, aloud. Without stopping or slowing he swept the bicycle around and pedalled back down the lane toward the street which he had just quitted. The wail of the siren was dying now, descending back into hearing again, and as he slewed the bicycle into the street he saw briefly the running people and a car bearing down upon him. For all his pedalling the car overtook him; its occupants leaned shouting toward his set, forwardlooking face. "Get in here!" they shouted. "In here!" He did not answer. He did not look at them. The car had overshot him, slowing; now he passed it at his swift, silent, steady pace; again the car speeded up and passed him, the men leaning out and looking ahead. He was going fast too, silent, with the delicate swiftness of an apparition, the implacable undeviation of Juggernaut or Fate. Behind him the siren began again its rising wail.

When next the men in the car looked back for him, he had vanished completely.

He had turned full speed into another lane. His face was rocklike, calm, still bright with that expression of fulfillment, of grave and reckless joy. This lane was more rutted than the other, and deeper. It came out at last upon a barren knoll where, springing to earth while the bicycle shot on, falling, he could see the full span of the ravine along the edge of town, his view of it broken by two or three negro cabins which lined the edge of it. He was quite motionless, still, alone, fateful, like a landmark almost. Again from the town behind him the scream of the siren began to fall.

Then he saw Christmas. He saw the man, small with distance, appear up out of the ditch, his hands close together. As Grimm watched he saw the fugitive's hands glint once like the flash of a heliograph as the sun struck the handcuffs, and it seemed to him that even from here he could hear the panting and desperate breath of the man who even now was not free. Then the tiny figure ran again and vanished beyond the nearest negro cabin.

Grimm ran too now. He ran swiftly, yet there was no haste about him, no effort. There was nothing vengeful about him either, no fury, no outrage. Christmas saw that, himself. Because for an instant they looked at one another almost face to face. That was when Grimm, running, was in the act of passing beyond the corner of the cabin. At that instant Christmas leaped from the rear window of it, with an effect as of magic, his manacled hands high and now glinting as if they were on fire. For an instant they glared at one another, the one stopped in the act of crouching from the leap, the other in midstride of running, before Grimm's

· 436 ·

momentum carried him past the corner. In that instant he saw that Christmas now carried a heavy nickelplated pistol. Grimm whirled and turned and sprang back past the corner, drawing the automatic.

He was thinking swiftly, calmly, with that quiet joy: 'He can do two things. He can try for the ditch again, or he can dodge around the house until one of us gets a shot. And the ditch is on his side of the house.' He reacted immediately. He ran at full speed around the corner which he had just turned. He did it as though under the protection of a magic or a providence, or as if he knew that Christmas would not be waiting there with the pistol. He ran on past the next corner without pausing.

He was beside the ditch now. He stopped, motionless in midstride. Above the blunt, cold rake of the automatic his face had that serene, unearthly luminousness of angels in church windows. He was moving again almost before he had stopped, with that lean, swift, blind obedience to whatever Player moved him on the Board. He ran to the ditch. But in the beginning of his plunge downward into the brush that choked the steep descent he turned, clawing. He saw now that the cabin sat some two feet above the earth. He had not noticed it before, in his haste. He knew now that he had lost a point. That Christmas had been watching his legs all the time beneath the house. He said, "Good man."

His plunge carried him some distance before he could stop himself and climb back out. He seemed indefatigable, not flesh and blood, as if the Player who moved him for pawn likewise found him breath. Without a pause, in the same surge that carried him up out of the ditch again, he was running again. He ran around the cabin in time to see

Christmas fling himself over a fence three hundred yards away. He did not fire, because Christmas was now running through a small garden and straight toward a house. Running, he saw Christmas leap up the back steps and enter the house. "Hah," Grimm said. "The preacher's house. Hightower's house."

He did not slow, though he swerved and ran around the house and to the street. The car which had passed him and lost him and then returned was just where it should have been, just where the Player had desired it to be. It stopped without signal from him and three men got out. Without a word Grimm turned and ran across the yard and into the house where the old disgraced minister lived alone, and the three men followed, rushing into the hall, pausing, bringing with them into its stale and cloistral dimness something of the savage summer sunlight which they had just left.

It was upon them, of them: its shameless savageness. Out of it their faces seemed to glare with bodiless suspension as though from haloes as they stooped and raised Hightower, his face bleeding, from the floor where Christmas, running up the hall, his raised and armed and manacled hands full of glare and glitter like lightning bolts, so that he resembled a vengeful and furious god pronouncing a doom, had struck him down. They held the old man on his feet.

"Which room?" Grimm said, shaking him. "Which room, old man?"

"Gentlemen!" Hightower said. Then he said: "Men! Men!"

"Which room, old man?" Grimm shouted.

They held Hightower on his feet; in the gloomy hall, after the sunlight, he too with his bald head and his big pale face streaked with blood, was terrible. "Men!" he cried. "Listen to me. He was here that night. He was with me the night of the murder. I swear to God—"

"Jesus Christ!" Grimm cried, his young voice clear and outraged like that of a young priest. "Has every preacher and old maid in Jefferson taken their pants down to the yellowbellied son of a bitch?" He flung the old man aside and ran on.

It was as though he had been merely waiting for the Player to move him again, because with that unfailing certitude he ran straight to the kitchen and into the doorway, already firing, almost before he could have seen the table overturned and standing on its edge across the corner of the room, and the bright and glittering hands of the man who crouched behind it, resting upon the upper edge. Grimm emptied the automatic's magazine into the table; later someone covered all five shots with a folded handkerchief.

But the Player was not done yet. When the others reached the kitchen they saw the table flung aside now and Grimm stooping over the body. When they approached to see what he was about, they saw that the man was not dead yet, and when they saw what Grimm was doing one of the men gave a choked cry and stumbled back into the wall and began to vomit. Then Grimm too sprang back, flinging behind him the bloody butcher knife. "Now you'll let white women alone, even in hell," he said. But the man on the floor had not moved. He just lay there, with his eyes open and empty of everything save consciousness, and with something, a shadow, about his mouth. For a long moment he looked up at them with peaceful and unfathomable and unbearable eyes. Then his face, body, all, seemed to collapse.

to fall in upon itself, and from out the slashed garments about his hips and loins the pent black blood seemed to rush like a released breath. It seemed to rush out of his pale body like the rush of sparks from a rising rocket; upon that black blast the man seemed to rise soaring into their memories forever and ever. They are not to lose it, in whatever peaceful valleys, beside whatever placid and reassuring streams of old age, in the mirroring faces of whatever children they will contemplate old disasters and newer hopes. It will be there, musing, quiet, steadfast, not fading and not particularly threatful, but of itself alone serene, of itself alone triumphant. Again from the town, deadened a little by the walls, the scream of the siren mounted toward its unbelievable crescendo, passing out of the realm of hearing.

NOW the final copper light of afternoon fades; now the street beyond the low maples and the low signboard is prepared and empty, framed by the study window like a stage.

He can remember how when he was young, after he first came to Jefferson from the seminary, how that fading copper light would seem almost audible, like a dying yellow fall of trumpets dying into an interval of silence and waiting, out of which they would presently come. Already, even before the falling horns had ceased, it would seem to him that he could hear the beginning thunder not yet louder than a whisper, a rumor, in the air.

But he had never told anyone that. Not even her. Not even her in the days when they were still the night's lovers, and shame and division had not come and she knew and had not forgot with division and regret and then despair, why he would sit here at this window and wait for nightfall, for the instant of night. Not even to her, to woman. *The* woman. Woman (not the seminary, as he had once believed): the Passive and Anonymous whom God had created to be not alone the recipient and receptacle of the seed of his body but of his spirit too, which is truth or as near truth as he dare approach.

He was an only child. When he was born his father was fifty years old, and his mother had been an invalid for almost twenty years. He grew up to believe that this was the result of the food which she had had to subsist on during the last year of the Civil War. Perhaps this was the reason. His father had owned no slaves, though he was the son of a man who did own slaves at the time. He could have owned them. But though born and bred and dwelling in an age and land where to own slaves was less expensive than not to own them, he would neither eat food grown and cooked by, nor sleep in a bed prepared by, a negro slave. Hence during the war and while he was absent from home, his wife had no garden save what she could make herself or with the infrequent aid of neighbors. And this aid the husband would not allow her to accept for the reason that it could not be repaid in kind. "God will provide," he said.

"Provide what? Dandelions and ditch weeds?"

"Then He will give us the bowels to digest them."

He was a minister. For a year he had been leaving home early each Sunday morning before his father (this was before the son's marriage) who though a member in good standing of the Episcopal church had not entered any church since the son could remember, discovered where he went. He found that the son, then just turned twentyone, was riding sixteen miles each Sunday to preach in a small Presbyterian chapel back in the hills. The father laughed. The son listened to the laughter as he would if it had been shouts or curses: with a cold and respectful detachment, saying nothing. The next Sunday he went back to his congregation.

When the war began, the son was not among the first to go. Neither was he among the last. And he stayed with the troops for four years, though he fired no musket and wore instead of uniform the somber frock coat which he had purchased to be married in and which he had used to preach in. When he returned home in '65 he still wore it, though he never put it on again after that day when the wagon stopped at the front steps and two men lifted him down and carried him into the house and laid him on the bed. His wife removed the coat and put it away in a trunk in the attic. It stayed there for twentyfive years, until one day his son opened the trunk and took it out and spread out the carefold folds in which it had been arranged by hands that were now dead.

He remembers it now, sitting in the dark window in the quiet study, waiting for twilight to cease, for night and the galloping hooves. The copper light has completely gone now; the world hangs in a green suspension in color and texture like light through colored glass. Soon it will be time to begin to say *Soon now. Now soon* 'I was eight then,' he thinks. 'It was raining.' It seems to him that he can still smell the rain, the moist grieving of the October earth, and the musty yawn as the lid of the trunk went back. Then the garment, the neat folds. He did not know what it was, because at first he was almost overpowered by the evocation of his dead mother's hands which lingered among the folds. Then it opened, tumbling slowly. To him, the child, it seemed unbelievably huge, as though made for a giant; as though merely from having been worn by one of them, the cloth itself had assumed the properties of those phantoms who loomed heroic and tremendous against a background of thunder and smoke and torn flags which now filled his waking and sleeping life.

The garment was almost unrecognisable with patches. Patches of leather, mansewn and crude, patches of Confederate grey weathered leafbrown now, and one that stopped his very heart: it was blue, dark blue; the blue of the United States. Looking at this patch, at the mute and anonymous cloth, the boy, the child born into the autumn of his mother's and father's lives, whose organs already required the unflagging care of a Swiss watch, would experience a kind of hushed and triumphant terror which left him a little sick.

That evening at supper he would be unable to eat. Looking up, the father, now a man nearing sixty, would find the child staring at him with terror and awe and with something else. Then the man would say, "What have you been into now?" and the child could not answer, could not speak, staring at his father with on his child's face an expression as of the Pit itself. That night in bed he would not be able to sleep. He would lie rigid, not even trembling, in his dark bed while the man who was his father and his only remaining relative, and between whom and himself there was so much of distance in time that not even the decades of years could measure, that there was not even any physical resemblance, slept walls and floors away. And the next day the child would suffer one of his intestinal fits. But he would not tell what it was, not even to the negro woman who ran the household and who was his mother too and nurse. Gradually his strength would return. And then one day he would steal again to the attic and open the trunk and take out the coat and touch the blue patch with that horrified triumph and sick joy and wonder if his father had killed the man from whose blue coat the patch came, wondering with still more horror yet at the depth and strength of his desire and dread to know. Yet on the very next day, when he knew that his father had gone to call upon one of his country patients and would not possibly return before dark, he would go to the kitchen and say to the negro woman: "Tell again about grandpa. How many Yankees did he kill?" And when he listened now it was without terror. It was not even triumph: it was pride.

This grandfather was the single thorn in his son's side. The son would no more have said that than he would have thought it, anymore than it would ever have occurred to either of them to wish mutually that he had been given a different son or a different father. Their relations were peaceable enough, being on the son's part a cold, humorless, automatically respectful reserve, and on the father's a bluff, direct, coarsely vivid humor which lacked less of purport than wit. They lived amicably enough in the two-storey house in town, though for some time now the son had refused, quiet and firm, to eat any food prepared by the slave woman who had raised him from babyhood. He cooked his own food in the kitchen, to the negress' outraged indignation, and put it on the table himself and ate it face to face with his father, who saluted him punctiliously and unfailingly with a glass of Bourbon whiskey: this too the son did not touch and had never tasted.

On the son's wedding day the father surrendered the house. He was waiting on the porch, with the key to the house in his hand, when the bride and groom arrived. He wore his hat and cloak. About him was piled his personal luggage and behind him stood the two slaves which he owned: the negro woman who cooked, and his 'boy,' a man older than himself and who did not have one remaining hair, who was the cook's husband. He was not a planter; he was a lawyer, who had learned law somewhat as his son was to learn medicine, "by main strength and the devil's grace and luck" as he put it. He had already bought for himself a small house two miles in the country, and his surrey and his matched team stood before the porch waiting while he too stood, his hat tilted back and his legs apart —a hale, bluff, rednosed man with the moustache of a brigand chief—while the son, and the daughter-in-law whom he had never seen before, came up the path from the gate. When he stooped and saluted her, she smelled whiskey and cigars. "I reckon you'll do," he said. His eyes were bluff and bold, but kind. "All the sanctimonious cuss wants anyway is somebody that can sing alto out of a Presbyterian hymnbook, where even the good Lord Himself couldn't squeeze in any music."

He drove away in the tasselled surrey, with his personal belongings about him—his clothes, his demijohn, his slaves. The slave cook did not even remain to prepare the first meal. She was not offered, and so not refused. The father never entered the house again alive. He would have been welcome. He and the son both knew this, without it ever being said. And the wife—she was one of many children of a genteel couple who had never got ahead and who seemed to find in the church some substitute for that which lacked upon the dinnertable—liked him, admired him in a hushed, alarmed, secret way: his swagger, his bluff and simple adherence to a simple code. They would hear of his doings though, of how in the next summer after he removed to the country he invaded a protracted al fresco church revival being held in a nearby grove and turned it into a week of amateur horse racing while to a dwindling congregation gaunt, fanaticfaced country preachers thundered anathema from the rustic pulpit at his oblivious and unregenerate head. His reason for not visiting his son and his daughter-in-law was apparently frank: "You'd find me dull and I'd find you dull. And who knows? the cuss might corrupt me. Might corrupt me in my old age into heaven." But that was not the reason. The son knew that it was not, who would have been first to fight the aspersion were it to come from another: that there was delicacy of behavior and thought in the old man.

The son was an abolitionist almost before the sentiment had become a word to percolate down from the North. Though when he learned that the Republicans did have a name for it, he completely changed the name of his conviction without abating his principles or behavior one jot. Even then, not yet thirty, he was a man of Spartan sobriety beyond his years, as the offspring of a not overly particular servant of Chance and the bottle often is. Perhaps that accounted for the fact that he had no child until after the war, from which he returned a changed man, 'deodorised,' as his dead father would have put it, of sanctity somewhat. Although during those four years he had never fired a gun, his service was not alone that of praying and preaching to troops on Sunday mornings. When he returned home with his wound and recovered and established himself as a doctor, he was only practising the surgery and the pharmacy which he had practised and learned on the bodies of friend and foe alike while helping the doctors at the front. This probably of all the son's doings the father would have enjoyed the most: that the son had taught himself a profession on the invader and devastator of his country.

'But sanctity is not the word for him,' the son's son in turn thinks, sitting at the dark window while outside the world hangs in that green suspension beyond the faded trumpets. 'Grandfather himself would have been the first to confront any man that employed that term.' It was some throwback to the austere and not dim times not so long passed, when a man in that country had little of himself to waste and little time to do it in, and had to guard and protect that little not only from nature but from man too, by means of a sheer foritude that did not offer, in his life-time anyway, physical ease for reward. That was where his disapproval of slavery lay, and of his lusty and sacri-legious father. The very fact that he could and did see no paradox in the fact that he took an active part in a partisan war and on the very side whose principles opposed his own, was proof enough that he was two separate and complete people, one of whom dwelled by serene rules in a world where reality did not exist.

But the other part of him, which lived in the actual world, did as well as any and better than most. He lived by his principles in peace, and when war came he carried them into war and lived by them there; when there was preaching on peaceful Sundays in quiet groves to be done, he had done it, without any particular equipment for it other than his will and his convictions and what he could pick up as he went along; when there was the saving of wounded men under fire and the curing of them without proper tools, he did that too, again without other equip-ment save his strength and courage and what he could pick up as he went along. And when the war was lost and the other men returned home with their eyes stubbornly reverted toward what they refused to believe was dead, he looked forward and made what he could of defeat by making practical use of that which he had learned in it. He turned doctor. One of his first patients was his wife. Possibly he kept her alive. At least, he enabled her to produce life, though he was fifty and she past forty when the son was born. That son grew to manhood among phantoms, and side by side with a ghost.

The phantoms were his father, his mother, and an old negro woman. The father who had been a minister without a church and a soldier without an enemy, and who in defeat had combined the two and become a doctor, a surgeon. It was as though the very cold and uncompromising conviction which propped him upright, as it were, between puritan and cavalier, had become not defeated and not discouraged, but wiser. As though it had seen in the smoke of cannon as in a vision that the layingon of hands meant literally that. As if he came suddenly to believe that Christ had meant that him whose spirit alone required healing, was not worth the having, the saving. That was one phantom. The second was the mother whom he remembers first and last as a thin face and tremendous eyes and a spread of dark hair on a pillow, with blue, still, almost skeleton hands. If on the day of her death he had been told that he had ever seen her otherwise than in bed, he would not have believed it. Later he remembered differently: he did remember her moving about the house, attending to household affairs. But at eight and nine and ten he thought of her as without legs, feet; as being only that thin face and the two eyes which seemed daily to grow bigger and bigger, as though about to embrace all seeing, all life, with one last terrible glare of frustration and suffering and fore-knowledge, and that when that finally happened, he would hear it: it would be a sound, like a cry. Already, before she died, he could feel them through all walls. They were the house: he dwelled within them, within their dark and all-embracing and patient aftermath of physical betrayal. He and she both lived in them like two small, weak beasts in a den, a cavern, into which now and then the father entered —that man who was a stranger to them both, a foreigner, almost a threat: so quickly does the body's wellbeing alter and change the spirit. He was more than a stranger: he was an enemy. He smelled differently from them. He spoke with a different voice, almost in different words, as though he dwelled by ordinary among different surroundings and in a different world; crouching beside the bed the child could feel the man fill the room with rude health and unconscious contempt, he too as helpless and frustrated as they.

The third phantom was the negro woman, the slave, who had ridden away in the surrey that morning when the son and his bride came home. She rode away a slave; she returned in '66 still a slave, on foot now—a huge woman, with a face both irascible and calm: the mask of a black tragedy between scenes. After her master's death and until she was convinced at last that she would never more see either him or her husband—the 'boy,' who had followed the master to the war and who also did not return—she refused to leave the house in the country to which her master had moved and of which he had left in her charge when he rode away. After the father's death the son went out, to close the house and remove his father's private possessions, and he offered to make provision for her. She refused. She also refused to leave. She made her own small kitchen garden and she lived there, alone, waiting for her husband to return, the rumor of whose death she refused to believe. It was just rumor, vague: how, following his master's death in Van Dorn's cavalry raid to destroy Grant's stores in Jefferson, the negro had been inconsolable. One night he disappeared from the bivouac. Presently there began to come back tales of a crazy negro who had been halted by Confederate pickets close to the enemy's front, who told the same garbled story about a missing master who was being held for ransom by the Yankees. They could not make him even entertain for a moment the idea that the master might be dead. "No, suh," he would say. "Not Marse Gail. Not him. Dey wouldn't *dare* to kill a Hightower. Dey wouldn't *dare*. Dey got 'im hid somewhar, tryin' to sweat outen him whar me and him hid Mistis' coffee pot and de gole waiter. Dat's all dey wants." Each time he would escape. Then one day word came back from the Federal lines of a negro who had attacked a Yankee officer with a shovel, forcing the officer to shoot him to protect his own life.

The woman would not believe this for a long time. "Not dat he aint fool enough to done it," she said. "He jest aint got ernough sense to know a Yankee to hit at wid a shovel if he wuz to see um." She said that for over a year. Then one day she appeared at the son's home, the house which she had quitted ten years ago and had not entered since, carrying her possessions in a handkerchief. She walked into the house and said: "Here I is. You got ernough wood in de box ter cook supper wid?"

"You're free, now," the son told her.

"Free?" she said. She spoke with still and brooding scorn.

"Free? Whut's freedom done except git Marse Gail killed and made a bigger fool outen Pawmp den even de Lawd Hisself could do? Free? Dont talk ter me erbout freedom."

This was the third phantom. With this phantom the child ('and he little better than a phantom too, then,' that same child now thinks beside the fading window) talked about the ghost. They never tired: the child with rapt, wide, half dread and half delight, and the old woman with musing and savage sorrow and pride. But this to the child was just peaceful shuddering of delight. He found no terror in the knowledge that his grandfather on the contrary had killed men 'by the hundreds' as he was told and believed, or in the fact that the negro Pomp had been trying to kill a man when he died. No horror here because they were just ghosts, never seen in the flesh, heroic, simple, warm; while the father which he knew and feared was a phantom which would never die. 'So it's no wonder,' he thinks, 'that I skipped a generation. It's no wonder that I had no father and that I had already died one night twenty years before I saw light. And that my only salvation must be to return to the place to die where my life had already ceased before it began.'

While at the seminary, after he first came there, he often thought how he would tell them, the elders, the high and sanctified men who were the destiny of the church to which he had willingly surrendered. How he would go to them and say, "Listen. God must call me to Jefferson because my life died there, was shot from the saddle of a galloping horse in a Jefferson street one night twenty years before it was ever born." He thought that he could say that, at first. He believed that they would comprehend. He went there, chose that as his vocation, with that as his purpose. But he believed in more than that. He had believed in the church too, in all that it ramified and evoked. He believed with a calm joy that if ever there was shelter, it would be the Church; that if ever truth could walk naked and without shame or fear, it would be in the seminary. When he believed that he had heard the call it seemed to him that he could see his future, his life, intact and on all sides complete and inviolable, like a classic and serene vase, where the spirit could be born anew sheltered from the harsh gale of living and die so, peacefully, with only the far sound of the circumvented wind, with scarce even a handful of rotting dust to be disposed of. That was what the word seminary meant: quiet and safe walls within which the hampered and garmentworried spirit could learn anew serenity to contemplate without horror or alarm its own nakedness.

'But there are more things in heaven and earth too than truth,' he thinks, paraphrases, quietly, not quizzical, not humorous; not unquizzical and not humorless too. Sitting in the failing dusk, his head in its white bandage looming bigger and more ghostly than ever, he thinks, 'More things indeed,' thinking how ingenuity was apparently given man in order that he may supply himself in crises with shapes and sounds with which to guard himself from truth. He had at least one thing to not repent: that he had not made the mistake of telling the elders what he had planned to say. He had not needed to live in the seminary a year before he learned better than that. And more, worse: that with the learning of it, instead of losing something he had gained, had escaped from something. And that that gain had colored the very face and shape of love.

She was the daughter of one of the ministers, the teachers, in the college. Like himself, she was an only child. He believed at once that she was beautiful, because he had heard of her before he ever saw her and when he did see her he did not see her at all because of the face which he had already created in his mind. He did not believe that she could have lived there all her life and not be beautiful. He did not see the face itself for three years. By that time there had already been for two years a hollow tree in which they left notes for one another. If he believed about that at all, he believed that the idea had sprung spontaneously between them, regardless of whichever one thought of it, said it, first. But in reality he had got the idea not from her or from himself, but from a book. But he did not see her face at all. He did not see a small oval narrowing too sharply to chin and passionate with discontent (she was a year or two or three older than he was, and he did not know it, was never to know it). He did not see that for three years her eyes had watched him with almost desperate calculation, like those of a harassed gambler.

Then one night he saw her, looked at her. She spoke suddenly and savagely of marriage. It was without preamble or warning. It had never been mentioned between them. He had not even ever thought of it, thought the word. He had accepted it because most of the faculty were married. But to him it was not men and women in sanctified and living physical intimacy, but a dead state carried over into and existing still among the living like two shadows chained together with the shadow of a chain. He was used to that; he had grown up with a ghost. Then one evening she talked suddenly, savagely. When he found out at last what she meant by escape from her present life, he felt no surprise. He was too innocent. "Escape?" he said. "Escape from what?"

"This!" she said. He saw her face for the first time as a living face, as a mask before desire and hatred: wrung, blind, headlong with passion. Not stupid: just blind, reckless, desperate. "All of it! All! All!"

He was not surprised. He believed at once that she was right, and that he just had not known better. He believed at once that his own belief about the seminary had been wrong all the while. Not seriously wrong, but false, incorrect. Perhaps he had already begun to doubt himself, without knowing it until now. Perhaps that was why he had not yet told them why he must go to Jefferson. He had told her, a year ago, why he wanted to, must, go there, and that he intended to tell them the reason, she watching him with those eyes which he had not yet seen. "You mean," he said, "that they would not send me? arrange for me to go? That that would not be reason enough?"

"Certainly it wouldn't," she said.

"But why? That's the truth. Foolish, maybe. But true. And what is the church for, if not to help those who are foolish but who want truth? Why wouldn't they let me go?"

"Why, I wouldn't let you go myself, if I were them and you gave me that as your reason."

"Oh," he said. "I see." But he did not see, exactly, though he believed that he could have been wrong and that she was right. And so when a year later she talked to him suddenly of marriage and escape in the same words, he was not surprised, not hurt. He just thought quietly, 'So this is love. I see. I was wrong about it too,' thinking as he had thought before and would think again and as every other man has thought: how false the most profound book turns out to be when applied to life.

He changed completely. They planned to be married. He knew now that he had seen all the while that desperate calculation in her eyes. 'Perhaps they were right in putting love into books,' he thought quietly. 'Perhaps it could not live anywhere else.' The desperation was still in them, but now that there were definite plans, a day set, it was quieter, mostly calculation. They talked now of his ordination, of how he could get Jefferson as his call. "We'd better go to work right away," she said. He told her that he had been working for that since he was four years old; perhaps he was being humorous, whimsical. She brushed it aside with that passionate and leashed humorlessness, almost inattention, talking as though to herself of men, names, to see, to grovel to or threaten, outlining to him a campaign of abasement and plotting. He listened. Even the faint smile, whimsical, quizzical, perhaps of despair, did not leave his face. He said, "Yes. Yes. I see. I understand," as she talked. It was as if he were saying *Yes. I see. I see now. That's how they do such, gain such. That's the rule. I see now*

At first, when the demagoguery, the abasement, the small lying had its reverberation in other small lies and ultimate threats in the form of requests and suggestions among the hierarchate of the Church and he received the call to Jefferson, he forgot how he had got it for the time. He did not remember until after he was settled in Jefferson; certainly not while the train of the journey's last stage fled toward the consummation of his life across a land similar to that where he had been born. But it looked different, though he knew that the difference lay not outside but inside the car window against which his face was almost pressed like that of a child, while his wife beside him had also now something of eagerness in her face, beside hunger and desperation.

They had been married now not quite six months. They had married directly after his graduation. Not once since then had he seen the desperation naked in her face. But neither had he seen passion again. And again he thought quietly, without much surprise and perhaps without hurt: *I see. That's the way it is. Marriage. Yes. I see now*

The train rushed on. Leaning to the window, watching the fleeing countryside, he talked in the bright, happy voice of a child: "I could have come to Jefferson before, at almost any time. But I didn't. I could have come at any time. There is a difference, you know, between civilian and military casualness. Military casualness? Ah, it was the casualness of desperation. A handful of men (he was not an officer: I think that was the only point on which father and old Cinthy were ever in accord: that grandfather wore no sword, galloped with no sword waving in front of the rest of them) performing with the grim levity of schoolboys a prank so foolhardy that the troops who had opposed them for four years did not believe that even they would have attempted it. Riding for a hundred miles through a country where every grove and hamlet had its Yankee bivouac, and into a garrisoned town—I know the very street that they rode into town upon and then out again. I have never seen it, but I know exactly how it will look. I know exactly how the house that we will someday own and live in upon the street will look. It wont be at first, for a while. We will have to live in the parsonage at first. But soon, as soon as we can, where we can look out the window and see the street, maybe even the hoofmarks or their shapes in the air, because the same air will be there even if the dust, the mud, is gone— Hungry, gaunt, yelling, setting fire to the store depots of a whole carefully planned campaign and riding out again. No looting at all: no stopping for even shoes, tobacco. I tell you, they were not men after spoils and glory; they were boys riding the sheer tremendous tidal wave of desperate living. Boys. Because this. This is beautiful. Listen. Try to see it. Here is that fine shape of eternal youth and virginal desire which makes heroes. That makes the doings of heroes border so close upon the unbelievable that it is no wonder that their doings must emerge now and then like gunflashes in the smoke, and that their very physical passing becomes rumor with a thousand faces before breath is out of them, lest paradoxical truth outrage itself. Now this is what Cinthy told me. And I believe. I know. It's too fine to doubt. It's too fine, too simple, ever to have been invented by white thinking. A negro might have invented it. And if Cinthy did, I still believe. Because even fact cannot stand with it. I dont know whether grandfather's squadron were lost or not. I dont think so. I think that they did it deliberately, as boys who had set fire to an enemy's barn, without taking so much as a shingle or a door hasp, might pause in flight to steal a few apples from a neighbor, a friend. Mind you, they were hungry. They had been hungry for three years. Perhaps they were used to that. Anyway, they had just set fire to tons of food and clothing and tobacco and liquors, taking nothing though there had not been issued any order against looting, and they turn now, with all that for background, backdrop: the consternation, the conflagration; the sky itself must have been on fire. You can see it, hear it: the shouts, the shots, the shouting of triumph and terror, the drumming hooves, the trees uprearing against that red glare as though fixed too in terror, the sharp gables of houses like the jagged edge of the exploding and ultimate earth. Now it is a close place:

you can feel, hear in the darkness horses pulled short up, plunging; clashes of arms; whispers overloud, hard breathing, the voices still triumphant; behind them the rest of the troops galloping past toward the rallying bugles. That you must hear, feel: then you see. You see before the crash, in the abrupt red glare the horses with wide eyes and nostrils in tossing heads, sweatstained; the gleam of metal, the white gaunt faces of living scarecrows who have not eaten all they wanted at one time since they could remember; perhaps some of them had already dismounted, perhaps one or two had already entered the henhouse. All this you see before the crash of the shotgun comes: then blackness again. It was just the one shot. 'And of course he would be right in de way of hit,' Cinthy said. 'Stealin' chickens. A man growed, wid a married son, gone to a war whar his business was killin' Yankees, killed in somebody else's henhouse wid a han'ful of feathers.' Stealing chickens." His voice was high, childlike, exalted. Already his wife was clutching his arm: *Shhhhhhh! Shhhhhhhhh! People are looking at you!* But he did not seem to hear her at all. His thin, sick face, his eyes, seemed to exude a kind of glow. "That was it. They didn't know who fired the shot. They never did know. They didn't try to find out. It may have been a woman, likely enough the wife of a Confederate soldier. I like to think so. It's fine so. Any soldier can be killed by the enemy in the heat of battle, by a weapon approved by the arbiters and rulemakers of warfare. Or by a woman in a bedroom. But not with a shotgun, a fowling piece, in a henhouse. And so is it any wonder that this world is peopled principally by the dead? Surely, when God looks about at their successors, He cannot be loath to share His own with us."

· 459 ·

"Hush! Shhhhhhhhh! They are looking at us!"

Then the train was slowing into the town; the dingy purlieus slid vanishing past the window. He still looked out—a thin, vaguely untidy man with still upon him something yet of the undimmed glow of his calling, his vocation —quietly surrounding and enclosing and guarding his urgent heart, thinking quietly how surely heaven must have something of the color and shape of whatever village or hill or cottage of which the believer says, This is my own. The train stopped: the slow aisle, still interrupted with outlooking, then the descent among faces grave, decorous, and judicial: the voices, the murmurs, the broken phrases kindly yet still reserved of judgment, not yet giving and (let us say it) prejudicial. 'I admitted that ' he thinks. 'I believe that I accepted it. But perhaps that was all I did do, God forgive me.' The earth has almost faded from sight. It is almost night now. His bandagedistorted head has no depth, no solidity; immobile, it seems to hang suspended above the twin pale blobs which are his hands lying upon the ledge of the open window. He leans forward. Already he can feel the two instants about to touch: the one which is the sum of his life, which renews itself between each dark and dusk, and the suspended instant out of which the *soon* will presently begin. When he was younger, when his net was still too fine for waiting, at this moment he would sometimes trick himself and believe that he heard them before he knew that it was time.

'Perhaps that is all I ever did, have ever done,' he thinks, thinking of the faces: the faces of old men naturally dubious of his youth and jealous of the church which they were putting into his hands almost as a father surrenders a bride: the faces of old men lined by that sheer accumulation of frustration and doubt which is so often the other side of the picture of hale and respected full years—the side, by the way, which the subject and proprietor of the picture has to look at, cannot escape looking at. 'They did their part; they played by the rules,' he thinks. 'I was the one who failed, who infringed. Perhaps that is the greatest social sin of all; ay, perhaps moral sin.' Thinking goes quietly, tranquilly, flowing on, falling into shapes quiet, not assertive, not reproachful, not particularly regretful. He sees himself a shadowy figure among shadows, paradoxical, with a kind of false optimism and egoism believing that he would find in that part of the Church which most blunders, dream-recovering, among the blind passions and the lifted hands and voices of men, that which he had failed to find in the Church's cloistered apotheosis upon earth. It seems to him that he has seen it all the while: that that which is destroying the Church is not the outward groping of those within it nor the inward groping of those without, but the professionals who control it and who have removed the bells from its steeples. He seems to see them, endless, without order, empty, symbolical, bleak, skypointed not with ecstasy or passion but in adjuration, threat, and doom. He seems to see the churches of the world like a rampart, like one of those barricades of the middleages planted with dead and sharpened stakes, against truth and against that peace in which to sin and be forgiven which is the life of man.

'And I accepted that,' he thinks. 'I acquiesced. Nay, I did worse: I served it. I served it by using it to forward my own desire. I came here where faces full of bafflement and hunger and eagerness waited for me, waiting to believe; I did not see them. Where hands were raised for what they believed that I would bring them; I did not see them. I brought with me one trust, perhaps the first trust of man, which I had accepted of my own will before God; I considered that promise and trust of so little worth that I did not know that I had even accepted it. And if that was all I did for her, what could I have expected? what could I have expected save disgrace and despair and the face of God turned away in very shame? Perhaps in the moment when I revealed to her not only the depth of my hunger but the fact that never and never would she have any part in the assuaging of it; perhaps at that moment I became her seducer and her murderer, author and instrument of her shame and death. After all, there must be some things for which God cannot be accused by man and held responsible. There must be.' Thinking begins to slow now. It slows like a wheel beginning to run in sand, the axle, the vehicle, the power which propels it not yet aware.

He seems to watch himself among faces, always among, enclosed and surrounded by, faces, as though he watched himself in his own pulpit, from the rear of the church, or as though he were a fish in a bowl. And more than that: the faces seem to be mirrors in which he watches himself. He knows them all; he can read his doings in them. He seems to see reflected in them a figure antic as a showman, a little wild: a charlatan preaching worse than heresy, in utter disregard of that whose very stage he preempted, offering instead of the crucified shape of pity and love, a swaggering and unchastened bravo killed with a shotgun in a peaceful henhouse, in a temporary hiatus of his own avocation of killing. The wheel of thinking slows; the axle knows it now but the vehicle itself is still unaware.

He sees the faces which surround him mirror astonishment, puzzlement, then outrage, then fear, as if they looked beyond his wild antics and saw behind him and looking down upon him, in his turn unaware, the final and supreme Face Itself, cold, terrible because of Its omniscient detachment. He knows that they see more than that: that they see the trust of which he proved himself unworthy, being used now for his chastisement; it seems to him now that he talks to the Face: "Perhaps I accepted more than I could perform. But is that criminal? Shall I be punished for that? Shall I be held responsible for that which was beyond my power?" And the Face: "It was not to accomplish that that you accepted her. You took her as a means toward your own selfishness. As an instrument to be called to Jefferson; not for My ends, but for your own."

'Is that true?' he thinks. 'Could that have been true?' He sees himself again as when the shame came. He remembers that which he had sensed before it was born, hiding it from his own thinking. He sees himself offer as a sop fortitude and forbearance and dignity, making it appear that he resigned his pulpit for a martyr's reasons, when at the very instant there was within him a leaping and triumphant surge of denial behind a face which had betrayed him, believing itself safe behind the lifted hymnbook, when the photographer pressed his bulb.

He seems to watch himself, alert, patient, skillful, playing his cards well, making it appear that he was being driven, uncomplaining, into that which he did not even then admit had been his desire since before he entered the seminary. And still casting his sops as though he were flinging rotten fruit before a drove of hogs: the meagre income from his father which he continued to divide with the Memphis institution; allowing himself to be persecuted, to be dragged from his bed at night and carried into the woods and beaten with sticks, he all the while bearing in the town's sight and hearing, without shame, with that patient and voluptuous ego of the martyr, the air, the behavior, the *How long, O Lord* until, inside his house again and the door locked, he lifted the mask with voluptuous and triumphant glee: *Ah. That's done now. That's past now. That's bought and paid for now*

'But I was young then,' he thinks. 'I too had to do, not what I could, but what I knew.' Thinking is running too heavily now; he should know it, sense it. Still the vehicle is unaware of what it is approaching. 'And after all, I have paid. I have bought my ghost, even though I did pay for it with my life. And who can forbid me doing that? It is any man's privilege to destroy himself, so long as he does not injure anyone else, so long as he lives to and of himself—" He stops suddenly. Motionless, unbreathing, there comes upon him a consternation which is about to be actual horror. He is aware of the sand now; with the realization of it he feels within himself a gathering as though for some tremendous effort. Progress now is still progress, yet it is now indistinguishable from the recent past like the already traversed inches of sand which cling to the turning wheel, raining back with a dry hiss that before this should have warned him: '. . . revealed to my wife my hunger, my ego . . . instrument of her despair and shame . . .' and without his having thought it at all, a sentence seems to stand fullsprung across his skull, behind his eyes: *I dont want to think this. I must not think this. I dare not think this* As he sits in the window, leaning forward above his motionless hands, sweat begins to pour from him, springing out like blood, and pouring. Out of the instant the sand-clutched wheel of thinking turns on with the slow implacability of a mediæval torture instrument, beneath the wrenched and broken sockets of his spirit, his life: 'Then, if this is so, if I am the instrument of her despair and death, then I am in turn instrument of someone outside myself. And I know that for fifty years I have not even been clay: I have been a single instant of darkness in which a horse galloped and a gun crashed. And if I am my dead grandfather on the instant of his death, then my wife, his grandson's wife . . . the debaucher and murderer of my grandson's wife, since I could neither let my grandson live or die . . ."

The wheel, released, seems to rush on with a long sighing sound. He sits motionless in its aftermath, in his cooling sweat, while the sweat pours and pours. The wheel whirls on. It is going fast and smooth now, because it is freed now of burden, of vehicle, axle, all. In the lambent suspension of August into which night is about to fully come, it seems to engender and surround itself with a faint glow like a halo. The halo is full of faces. The faces are not shaped with suffering, not shaped with anything: not horror, pain, not even reproach. They are peaceful, as though they have escaped into an apotheosis; his own is among them. In fact, they all look a little alike, composite of all the faces which he has ever seen. But he can distinguish them one from another: his wife's; townspeople, members of that congregation which denied him, which had met him at the station that day with eagerness and hunger; Byron Bunch's; the woman with the child; and that of the man called Christmas. This face alone is not clear. It is confused more than any other, as though in the now peaceful throes of a more recent, a more inextricable, compositeness. Then he can see that it is two faces which seem to strive (but not of themselves striving or desiring it: he knows that, but because of the motion and desire of the wheel itself) in turn to free themselves one from the other, then fade and blend again. But he has seen now, the other face, the one that is not Christmas. 'Why, it's . . .' he thinks. 'I have seen it, recently . . . Why, it's that . . . boy. With that black pistol, automatic they call them. The one who . . into the kitchen where . . killed, who fired the . . .' Then it seems to him that some ultimate dammed flood within him breaks and rushes away. He seems to watch it, feeling himself losing contact with earth, lighter and lighter, emptying, floating. 'I am dying,' he thinks. 'I should pray. I should try to pray.' But he does not. He does not try. 'With all air, all heaven, filled with the lost and unheeded crying of all the living who ever lived, wailing still like lost children among the cold and terrible stars. . . . I wanted so little. I asked so little. It would seem . . .' The wheel turns on. It spins now, fading, without progress, as though turned by that final flood which had rushed out of him, leaving his body empty and lighter than a forgotten leaf and even more trivial than flotsam lying spent and still upon the window ledge which has no solidity beneath hands that have no weight; so that it can be now Now

It is as though they had merely waited until he could find something to pant with, to be reaffirmed in triumph and desire with, with this last left of honor and pride and life. He hears above his heart the thunder increase, myriad and drumming. Like a long sighing of wind in trees it begins, then they sweep into sight, borne now upon a cloud of phantom dust. They rush past, forwardleaning in the saddles, with brandished arms, beneath whipping ribbons from slanted and eager lances; with tumult and soundless yelling they sweep past like a tide whose crest is jagged with the wild heads of horses and the brandished arms of men like the crater of the world in explosion. They rush past, are gone; the dust swirls skyward sucking, fades away into the night which has fully come. Yet, leaning forward in the window, his bandaged head huge and without depth upon the twin blobs of his hands upon the ledge, it seems to him that he still hears them: the wild bugles and the clashing sabres and the dying thunder of hooves.

.21.

THERE lives in the eastern part of the state a furniture repairer and dealer who recently made a trip into Tennessee to get some old pieces of furniture which he had bought by correspondence. He made the journey in his truck, carrying with him, since the truck (it had a housed-in body with a door at the rear) was new and he did not intend to drive it faster than fifteen miles an hour, camping equipment to save hotels. On his return home he told his wife of an experience which he had had on the road, which interested him at the time and which he considered amusing enough to repeat. Perhaps the reason why he found it interesting and that he felt that he could make it interesting in the retelling is that he and his wife are not old either, besides his having been away from home (due to the very moderate speed which he felt it wise to restrict himself to) for more than a week. The story has to do with two people, passengers whom he picked up; he names the town, in Mississippi, before he entered Tennessee:

"I had done decided to get some gas and I was already slowing into the station when I saw this kind of young, pleasantfaced gal standing on the corner, like she was waiting for somebody to come along and offer her a ride. She was holding something in her arms. I didn't see what it was at first, and I didn't see the fellow that was with her at all until he come up and spoke to me. I thought at first that I didn't see him before was because he wasn't standing where she was. Then I saw that he was the kind of fellow you wouldn't see the first glance if he was alone by himself in the bottom of a empty concrete swimming pool.

"So he come up and I said, quick like: 'I aint going to Memphis, if that's what you want. I am going up past Jackson, Tennessee.' And he says,

" 'That'll be fine. That would just suit us. It would be a accommodation.' And I says,

" 'Where do you all want to go to?' And he looked at me, like a fellow that aint used to lying will try to think up one quick when he already knows that he likely aint going to be believed. 'You're just looking around, are you?' I says.

" 'Yes,' he says. 'That's it. We're just travelling. Wherever you could take us, it would be a big accommodation.'

"So I told him to get in. 'I reckon you aint going to rob and murder me.' He went and got her and come back. Then I saw that what she was carrying was a baby, a critter not yearling size. He made to help her into the back of the truck and I says, 'Whyn't one of you ride up here on the seat?' and they talked some and then she come and got on the seat and he went back into the filling station and got one of these leatherlooking paper suit cases and put it into the bed and got in too. And here we went, with her on the seat, holding the baby and looking back now and then to see if he hadn't maybe fell out or something.

"I thought they was husband and wife at first. I just

never thought anything about it, except to wonder how a young, strapping gal like her ever come to take up with him. It wasn't anything wrong with him. He looked like a good fellow, the kind that would hold a job steady and work at the same job a long time, without bothering anybody about a raise neither, long as they let him keep on working. That was what he looked like. He looked like except when he was at work, he would just be something around. I just couldn't imagine anybody, any woman, knowing that they had ever slept with him, let alone having anything to show folks to prove it."

Aint you shamed? his wife says. *Talking that way before a lady* They are talking in the dark.

Anyway, I cant see you blushing any he says. He continues: "I never thought anything about it until that night when we camped. She was sitting up on the seat by me, and I was talking to her, like a fellow would, and after a while it begun to come out how they had come from Alabama. She kept on saying, 'We come,' and so I thought she meant her and the fellow in the back. About how they had been on the road nigh eight weeks now. 'You aint had that chap no eight weeks,' I says. 'Not if I know color,' and she said it was just born three weeks ago, down at Jefferson, and I said, "Oh. Where they lynched that nigger. You must have been there then,' and she clammed up. Like he had done told her not to talk about it. I knowed that's what it was. So we rode on and then it was coming toward night and I said, 'We'll be in a town soon. I aint going to sleep in town. But if you all want to go on with me tomorrow, I'll come back to the hotel for you in the morning about six o'clock,' and she sat right still, like she was waiting for him to say, and after a while he says,

· 470 ·

"'I reckon with this here truck house you dont need to worry about hotels,' and I never said anything and we was coming into the town and he said, 'Is this here any size town?'

"'I dont know,' I says. 'I reckon they'll have a boarding house or something here though.' And he says,

"'I was wondering if they would have a tourist camp.' And I never said anything and he said, 'With tents for hire. These here hotels are high, and with folks that have a long piece to go.' They hadn't never yet said where they was going. It was like they didn't even know themselves, like they was just waiting to see where they could get to. But I didn't know that, then. But I knowed what he wanted me to say, and that he wasn't going to come right out and ask me himself. Like if the Lord aimed for me to say it, I would say it, and if the Lord aimed for him to go to a hotel and pay maybe three dollars for a room, he would do that too. So I says,

"'Well, it's a warm night. And if you folks dont mind a few mosquitoes and sleeping on them bare boards in the truck.' And he says,

"'Sho. It will be fine. It'll be mighty fine for you to let her.' I noticed then how he said *her*. And I begun to notice how there was something funny and kind of strained about him. Like when a man is determined to work himself up to where he will do something he wants to do and that he is scared to do. I dont mean it was like he was scared of what might happen to him, but like it was something that he would die before he would even think about doing it if he hadn't just tried everything else until he was desperate. That was before I knew. I just couldn't understand what in the world it could be then. And if it hadn't been for that

· 471 ·

night and what happened, I reckon I would not have known at all when they left me at Jackson."

What was it he aimed to do? the wife says.

You wait till I come to that part. Maybe I'll show you, too He continues: "So we stopped in front of the store. He was already jumping out before the truck had stopped. Like he was afraid I would beat him to it, with his face all shined up like a kid trying to do something for you before you change your mind about something you promised to do for him. He went into the store on a trot and came back with so many bags and sacks he couldn't see over them, so that I says to myself, 'Look a here, fellow. If you are aiming to settle down permanent in this truck and set up housekeeping.' Then we drove on and came pretty soon to a likely place where I could drive the truck off the road, into some trees, and he jumps down and runs up and helps her down like she and the kid were made out of glass or eggs. And he still had that look on his face like he pretty near had his mind made up to do whatever it was he was desperated up to do, if only nothing I did or she did beforehand would prevent it, and if she only didn't notice in his face that he was desperated up to something. But even then I didn't know what it was."

What was it? the wife says

I just showed you once. You aint ready to be showed again, are you?

I reckon I dont mind if you dont. But I still dont see anything funny in that. How come it took him all that time and trouble, anyway?

It was because they were not married the husband says. *It wasn't even his child. I didn't know it then, though. I didn't find that out until I heard them talking that night by the fire, when they didn't know I heard, I reckon. Before he had done got himself desperated up all the way. But I reckon he was desperate enough, all right. I reckon he was just giving her one more chance* He continues: "So there he was skirmishing around, getting camp ready, until he got me right nervous: him trying to do everything and not knowing just where to begin or something. So I told him to go rustle up some firewood, and I took my blankets and spread them out in the truck. I was a little mad, then, at myself about how I had got into it now and I would have to sleep on the ground with my feet to the fire and nothing under me. So I reckon I was short and grumpy maybe, moving around, getting things fixed, and her sitting with her back to a tree, giving the kid his supper under a shawl and saying ever so often how she was ashamed to inconvenience me and that she aimed to sit up by the fire because she wasn't tired noway, just riding all day long and not doing anything. Then he came back, with enough wood to barbecue a steer, and she began to tell him and he went to the truck and taken out that suitcase and opened it and taken out a blanket. Then we had it, sho enough. It was like those two fellows that used to be in the funny papers, those two Frenchmen that were always bowing and scraping at the other one to go first, making out like we had all come away from home just for the privilege of sleeping on the ground, each one trying to lie faster and bigger than the next. For a while I was a mind to say, 'All right. If you want to sleep on the ground, do it. Because be durned if I want to.' But I reckon you might say that I won. Or that me and him won. Because it wound up by him fixing their blanket in the truck, like we all might have known all the time it would be, and me and him spreading mine out before the fire. I reckon he knew that would be the way of it, anyhow. If they had come all the way from south Alabama like she claimed. I reckon that was why he brought in all that firewood just to make a pot of coffee with and heat up some tin cans. Then we ate, and then I found out."

Found out what? What it was he wanted to do?

Not right then. I reckon she had a little more patience than you He continues: "So we had eaten and I was lying down on the blanket. I was tired, and getting stretched out felt good. I wasn't aiming to listen, anymore than I was aiming to look like I was asleep when I wasn't. But they had asked me to give them a ride; it wasn't me that insisted on them getting in my truck. And if they seen fit to go on and talk without making sho nobody could hear them, it wasn't any of my business. And that's how I found out that they were hunting for somebody, following him, or trying to. Or she was, that is. And so all of a sudden I says to myself, 'Ah-ah. Here's another gal that thought she could learn on Saturday night what her mammy waited until Sunday to ask the minister.' They never called his name. And they didn't know just which way he had run. And I knew that if they had known where he went, it wouldn't be by any fault of the fellow that was doing the running. I learned that quick. And so I heard him talking to her, about how they might travel on like this from one truck to another and one state to another for the rest of their lives and not find any trace of him, and her sitting there on the log, holding the chap and listening quiet as a stone and pleasant as a stone and just about as nigh to being moved or persuaded. And I says to myself, 'Well, old fellow, I reckon it aint only since she has been riding on the seat of my truck while you rode with your feet hanging out the back end of it that she has travelled out in front on this trip.' But I never said anything. I just lay there and them talking, or him talking, not loud. He hadn't even mentioned marriage, neither. But that's what he was talking about, and her listening placid and calm, like she had heard it before and she knew that she never even had to bother to say either yes or no to him. Smiling a little she was. But he couldn't see that.

"Then he give up. He got up from the log and walked away. But I saw his face when he turned and I knew that he hadn't give up. He knew that he had just give her one more chance and that now he had got himself desperated up to risking all. I could have told him that he was just deciding now to do what he should have done in the first place. But I reckon he had his own reasons. Anyway he walked off into the dark and left her sitting there, with her face kind of bent down a little and that smile still on it. She never looked after him, neither. Maybe she knew he had just gone off by himself to get himself worked up good to what she might have been advising him to do all the time, herself, without saying it in out and out words, which a lady naturally couldn't do; not even a lady with a Saturday night family.

"Only I dont reckon that was it either. Or maybe the time and place didn't suit her, let alone a audience. After a while she got up and looked at me, but I never moved, and then she went and climbed into the truck and after a while I heard her quit moving around and I knew that she had done got fixed to sleep. And I lay there—I had done got kind of waked up myself, now—and it was a right smart while. But I knew that he was somewhere close, waiting maybe for the fire to die down or for me to get good to sleep. Because, sho enough, just about the time the fire had died down good, I heard him come up, quiet as a cat, and stand over me, looking down at me, listening. I never made a sound; I dont know but I might have fetched a snore or two for him. Anyway, he goes on toward the truck, walking like he had eggs under his feet, and I lay there and watched him and I says to myself, 'Old boy, if you'd a just done this last night, you'd a been sixty miles further south than you are now, to my knowledge. And if you'd a done it two nights ago, I reckon I wouldn't ever have laid eyes on either one of you.' Then I got a little worried. I wasn't worried about him doing her any harm she didn't want done to her. In fact, I was pulling for the little cuss. That was it. I couldn't decide what I had better do when she would begin to holler. I knew that she would holler, and if I jumped up and run to the truck, it would scare him off, and if I didn't come running, he would know that I was awake and watching him all the time, and he'd be scared off faster than ever. But I ought not to worried. I ought to have known that from the first look I'd taken at her and at him."

I reckon the reason you knew you never had to worry was that you had already found out just what she would do in a case like that the wife says.

Sho the husband says. *I didn't aim for you to find that out. Yes, sir. I thought I had covered my tracks this time*

Well, go on. What happened?

What do you reckon happened, with a big strong gal like that, without any warning that it was just him, and a durn little cuss that already looked like he had reached the point where he could bust out crying like another baby? He continues: "There wasn't any hollering or anything. I just watched him climb slow and easy into the truck and disappear and then didn't anything happen for about while you could count maybe fifteen slow, and then I heard one kind of astonished sound she made when she woke up, like she was just surprised and then a little put out without being scared at all, and she says, not loud neither: 'Why, Mr Bunch. Aint you ashamed. You might have woke the baby, too.' Then he come out the back door of the truck. Not fast, and not climbing down on his own legs at all. I be dog if I dont believe she picked him up and set him back outside on the ground like she would that baby if it had been about six years old, say, and she says, 'You go and lay down now, and get some sleep. We got another fur piece to go tomorrow.'

"Well, I was downright ashamed to look at him, to let him know that any human man had seen and heard what happened. I be dog if I didn't want to find the hole and crawl into it with him. I did for a fact. And him standing there where she had set him down. The fire had burned down good now and I couldn't hardly see him at all. But I knew about how I would have been standing and feeling if I was him. And that would have been with my head bowed, waiting for the Judge to say, 'Take him out of here and hang him quick.' And I didn't make a sound, and after a while I heard him go on off. I could hear the bushes popping, like he had just struck off blind through the woods. And when daylight came he hadn't got back.

"Well, I didn't say anything. I didn't know what to say. I kept on believing that he would show up, would come walking up out of the bushes, face or no face. So I built up the fire and got breakfast started, and after a while I heard her climbing out of the truck. I never looked around. But

I could hear her standing there like she was looking around, like maybe she was trying to tell by the way the fire or my blanket looked if he was there or not. But I never said anything and she never said anything. I wanted to pack up and get started. And I knew I couldn't leave her in the middle of the road. And that if my wife was to hear about me travelling the country with a goodlooking country gal and a three weeks' old baby, even if she did claim she was hunting for her husband. Or both husbands now. So we ate and then I said, 'Well, I got a long road and I reckon I better get started.' And she never said nothing at all. And when I looked at her I saw that her face was just as quiet and calm as it had ever been. I be dog if she was even surprised or anything. And there I was, not knowing what to do with her, and she done already packed up her things and even swept the truck out with a gum branch before she put in that paper suitcase and made a kind of cushion with the folded blanket at the back end of the truck; and I says to myself, 'It aint any wonder you get along. When they up and run away on you, you just pick up whatever they left and go on.'——, 'I reckon I'll ride back here,' she says.

" 'It'll be kind of rough on the baby,' I says.

" 'I reckon I can hold him up,' she says.

" 'Suit yourself,' I says. And we drove off, with me hanging out the seat to look back, hoping that he would show up before we got around the curve. But he never. Talk about a fellow being caught in the depot with a strange baby on his hands. Here I was with a strange woman and a baby too, expecting every car that come up from behind and passed us to be full of husbands and wives too, let alone sheriffs. We were getting close to the Tennessee line then and I had my mind all fixed how I would either burn that new truck up or get to a town big enough to have one of these ladies' welfare societies in it that I could turn her over to. And now and then I would look back, hoping that maybe he had struck out afoot after us, and I would see her sitting there with her face as calm as church, holding that baby up so it could eat and ride the bumps at the same time. You cant beat them." He lies in the bed, laughing. "Yes, sir. I be dog if you can beat them."

Then what? What did she do then?

Nothing. Just sitting there, riding, looking out like she hadn't ever seen country—roads and trees and fields and telephone poles—before in her life. She never saw him at all until he come around to the back door of the truck. She never had to. All she needed to do was wait. And she knew that

Him?

Sho. He was standing at the side of the road when we come around the curve. Standing there, face and no face, hangdog and determined and calm too, like he had done desperated himself up for the last time, to take the last chance, and that now he knew he wouldn't ever have to desperate himself again He continues: "He never looked at me at all. I just stopped the truck and him already running back to go around to the door where she was sitting. And he come around the back of it and he stood there, and her not even surprised. 'I done come too far now,' he says. 'I be dog if I'm going to quit now.' And her looking at him like she had known all the time what he was going to do before he even knew himself that he was going to, and that whatever he done, he wasn't going to mean it.

"'Aint nobody never said for you to quit,' she says." He laughs, lying in the bed, laughing. "Yes, sir. You cant beat a woman. Because do you know what I think? I think she was just travelling. I dont think she had any idea of finding whoever it was she was following. I dont think she had ever aimed to, only she hadn't told him yet. I reckon this was the first time she had ever been further away from home than she could walk back before sun-down in her life. And that she had got along all right this far, with folks taking good care of her. And so I think she had just made up her mind to travel a little further and see as much as she could, since I reckon she knew that when she settled down this time, it would likely be for the rest of her life. That's what I think. Sitting back there in that truck, with him by her now and the baby that hadn't never stopped eating, that had been eating breakfast now for about ten miles, like one of these dining cars on the train, and her looking out and watching the telephone poles and the fences passing like it was a circus parade. Be-cause after a while I says, 'Here comes Saulsbury,' and she says,

" 'What?' and I says,

" 'Saulsbury, Tennessee,' and I looked back and saw her face. And it was like it was already fixed and waiting to be surprised, and that she knew that when the surprise come, she was going to enjoy it. And it did come and it did suit her. Because she said,

" 'My, my. A body does get around. Here we aint been coming from Alabama but two months, and now it's already Tennessee.' "

MODERN LIBRARY COLLEGE EDITIONS